# Dig Two Graves

# Dig Two Graves

Gigi Johnston

Copyright © 2024 Gigi Johnston

The moral right of the author has been asserted.

Apart from any fair dealing for the purposes of research or private study, or criticism or review, as permitted under the Copyright, Designs and Patents Act 1988, this publication may only be reproduced, stored or transmitted, in any form or by any means, with the prior permission in writing of the publishers, or in the case of reprographic reproduction in accordance with the terms of licences issued by the Copyright Licensing Agency. Enquiries concerning reproduction outside those terms should be sent to the publishers.

This is a work of fiction. Names, characters, businesses, places, events and incidents are either the products of the author's imagination or used in a fictitious manner. Any resemblance to actual persons, living or dead, or actual events is purely coincidental.

Troubador Publishing Ltd
Unit E2 Airfield Business Park,
Harrison Road, Market Harborough,
Leicestershire LE16 7UL
Tel: 0116 279 2299
Email: books@troubador.co.uk
Web: www.troubador.co.uk

ISBN 978 1 80514 512 7

British Library Cataloguing in Publication Data.
A catalogue record for this book is available from the British Library.

Printed and bound by CPI Group (UK) Ltd, Croydon, CR0 4YY
Typeset in 11pt Minion Pro by Troubador Publishing Ltd, Leicester, UK

# CONTENTS

**PROLOGUE** ix

**PART 1** ACE 1
**PART 2** PAIRS 27
**PART 3** CLUBS 58
**PART 4** HEARTS 141
**PART 5** THE HAND IS REVEALED 236

**EPILOGUE** 341

"Before you embark on a journey of revenge, dig two graves"

> CONFUCIUS
> (Chinese philosopher, born 6th century BCE)

# PROLOGUE

*The killer pauses in the shadows. His target is home and alone. His heartbeat increases then slows as his fingers glide over the weapon. The weapon is familiar, and the familiarity boosts his confidence. The killer waits a few moments for the clouds to obscure the moon before he creeps towards the house. Tonight, the time has come. Tonight, retribution begins.*

\*

*Several miles away, a girl lies on a dirty bed in a basement room, staring into the encroaching darkness. She has no control over the light: her right wrist is tightly encased in a metal cuff, which, in turn, is linked to a chain anchored in the wall. The only time she is released from bondage is when her captors want sex. But the darkness no longer fazes her. She is used to it. It has been this way for fourteen years.*

# PART 1

# ACE

"I'm doomed!"

Jenna Jones kicked off her heels, tossed her short blonde hair out of her face and slumped back into the tatty faux-leather sofa in the lounge of her rented flat. "Enough!" she groaned to her two flatmates. "I've had it with dating agencies."

"I take it today's lunchtime date didn't go too well?" said Helen Atherton, an old school friend of Jenna's and now colleague in the Metropolitan Police.

Jenna looked at her two friends, who were also slumped in each of the two faux-leather armchairs, which complemented the sofa. You couldn't sit on any of the three seats without slouching, but canvassing the landlord for new furniture might mean an unwelcome hike in the rent, so the girls put up with it. Jenna shook her head and scowled.

"Why do they keep sending me these prize idiots? Honestly, if they gave out awards for the best mismatch in dating agency history, then today's meeting between Harvey Pryce and me would win hands down. I had to endure a two-hour lecture on farming methods, for goodness' sake. What's that all about?" She shrugged her shoulders, exasperated.

"At least Nick Bailey didn't lecture you on farming," said Lucy Macleod, Jenna's other flatmate. "Though he wasn't averse to a roll in the hay, so to speak!"

"Nick Bailey was a serial philanderer," Jenna said. "End of story. And I need a drink." She got up from the sofa and headed for the kitchen. "Anyone else?"

"Not me, thanks," said Lucy. "I'm on duty tonight. A&E. I'll need my wits about me."

"Well, I can't have you drink all alone." Helen raised her voice to reach Jenna, who was already in the kitchen. "There's an open bottle in the fridge, and we're not on duty till seven tomorrow morning."

Helen lowered her voice again and looked at Lucy with a wry smile. "'*Doomed*'? I ask you!" They both gave their heads a slight shake. "But she's right in a way," said Helen. "She never seems to get lucky with guys, does she? And how does someone that good in the looks department end up needing a dating agency, for heaven's sake?"

Lucy lowered her voice. "We both know she doesn't *need* a dating agency," said Lucy. "Thing is, she doesn't believe in herself, does she? I guess when you've lost your mum so young...You know... A boyfriend is a confidence booster, a 'must-have'!" Lucy stopped to think. She continued, "As for luck, she's certainly not unlucky to be rid of Nick Bailey. And as for Tom, 'whatever-his-name-was' no sooner did he find out what she did for a living than he scarpered. Can't be too unlucky being rid of a shady character like that, can it?" Lucy paused for a moment. "I take it someone looked into the guy in case he had something to hide?"

"First thing we did," said Helen. "Left it with Andy at the nick. Anyway, I'd better give Jen a hand in the kitchen. Have a chat. Maybe she needs to get things off her chest."

Jenna had already started on the salad. It was a good staple to go with whatever else they were going to have, whether it was to be a take-away or otherwise, and it gave her time to think. She took up her favourite long-bladed sharp knife and a chopping board, halved several cherry tomatoes, scattered them over baby-leaf salad and then took a sip of the chilled wine. Maybe it was time to back off dating for a while. Give herself time to get over the Bailey betrayal. Join a club? Look up old friends? "And why am I trying so hard anyway?" she muttered under her breath. "I'm not even thirty!" It wouldn't hurt to be celibate for a while, she thought. She sliced cucumber thinly and arranged the pieces over the green leaves. Therapeutic.

Helen came into the kitchen, took hold of a small knife and began to skin an avocado. No words were needed. Between them, they had the salad thing down to a fine art. Jenna took a bowl, poured in a slug of virgin olive oil and added a drop of balsamic. Then she grabbed a cut lemon and squeezed it hard over the bowl, reminding her of what she'd really like to do to Nick Bailey, and began to whisk the contents together.

"Actually, I really am going to call it a day with dating agencies," she announced. "Go without for a while. Who knows, if I like it enough, I might even join a nunnery!"

Helen finished arranging the avocado pieces around the tomato and cucumber, snatched some basil leaves from a pot on the kitchen shelf to scatter and stood back to let Jenna pour the dressing.

"You could always try batting on my side!" said Helen

with a laugh. Lucy popped her head around the door. "Good news, Luce. Jenna's giving up men for a while," Helen joked. "I may get lucky yet!" Pouring herself a glass of wine, she followed Lucy's gaze. " Anyway, the salad's ready…"

Lucy flipped open her mobile. "Usual pizza toppings, everyone?"

\*

Detective Inspector Dominic Brady sat down at his desk and logged on. He always arrived early on a Monday morning to check emails for updates on pending cases. He had completed a case four days previously when, after a lot of hard graft, he and his team had finally secured a guilty verdict from the jury at the Old Bailey. Brady allowed himself a moment to feel deeply satisfied. The guy had killed his girlfriend, had tried to plead not guilty, then had entered a plea of manslaughter. But, in the end, the evidence gathered by Brady and his Murder Investigation Team (MIT) was just too persuasive, and the guilty verdict became gloriously inevitable.

Brady trawled through the emails, deleted several of the reminder variety and considered how impressed he'd been by the newest member of the MIT. Acting Detective Sergeant Jenna Jones had an eye for detail that he hadn't witnessed in a long while, and her observations, both seen and heard, clearly helped to move the case towards its welcome conclusion. Unusual for one so young, but she was a quick learner with a lot of natural talent. No wonder she'd been appointed acting sergeant. Also fairly new to the team, DC Helen Atherton was a good copper, too; a bit of a lateral thinker at times, which was useful, but her number-one ability was to spot the seemingly invisible in amongst reams of paper documents or CCTV footage. She was unbelievably patient and could trawl for hours, as fresh at the end of it as she had been at the start. Yes, the two women were both very good at their jobs. Brady had noted their skills just as he had when Andy Cartwright and Jamie Grant had first been assigned to his team more than two years previously, and he'd played them all according to their strengths with excellent results. But he'd been in the job long enough to know that cases didn't always end like that, even with the perfect team of investigators, and so the glow began to diminish almost as quickly as it had blossomed. Add to that the fact that he was now facing any potential new cases without his usual experienced sergeant, Beth Harrison, away on maternity leave, and he knew for sure that the coming months could be tough. He drew in a deep breath: back to reality.

Five emails left: pending cases. Brady was just beginning to consider whether to ask Atherton to review some newly arrived CCTV footage relating to one when the phone rang.

"Yeah, Dom." It was Brady's superior, Detective Chief Inspector Carlton Delgado, who headed the MIT. "Congratulations on the Curtis case last week."

"Thanks, sir," said Brady.

"'Fraid I've got a new one for you. The Kingston branch took a call just before midnight from a woman who got home to find her husband dead. Not a pleasant sight, apparently, so clearly not a natural death. The locals are already there and asking for our opinion. Scene of crime officers are heading there as we speak. I want you to be the senior investigating officer. I'll meet up with you later at Kingston nick."

Definitely back to reality, thought Brady. He looked at his watch. It was just before 7.00 a.m. Picking up his mobile, he called several coded numbers to assemble the troops.

\*

DI Brady and Acting Sergeant Jenna Jones arrived at the palatial house in Kingston's select Coombe area and cruised slowly up a sweeping driveway towards a grand porch. Brady parked the car. The front door was already open, and a scene of crime officer (SOCO) showed them into the lounge where two of his colleagues, kitted out in protective suits, were at work. One was busy dusting for prints. The other, a female officer, was using tweezers to place something minute in an evidence bag. The third person already in the room was the forensic pathologist hovering over the covered body. Brady made his way towards the familiar face.

"What have we got, Keith?"

"Male, white, Caucasian, probably early fifties." Dr Keith Wilson looked at Brady, expressionless. "Garroted," he added. A light-hearted character when off duty, Wilson was sombre and to the point in his line of work. "No spilt blood. What you might call a nice clean op." He frowned slightly. "But there's something else here you two ought to see." He drew back the cover from the top of the head, revealing a shock of silver hair crowning a tanned face, which, despite its maturity, was fit and well-chiselled.

Brady squatted down to scrutinise the throat area, which was not immediately obvious as the victim lay on his front, with his face turned to one side. The face was swollen and purplish, and a huge bluish tongue protruded from the side of the mouth. Brady heard Jenna catch her breath slightly as she moved closer in to observe the wounds. Her first strangulation, he thought.

"See the marks of the ligature, here and here." Dr Wilson indicated dark bruising on the upturned right side of the Adam's apple and a little further away towards the right earlobe. Then he drew the cover further down towards the mid-leg area. "There. How incongruous is that?" he said, indicating the rectal area.

Brady, now on his knees, shuffled to his left while Jenna walked around the body and took up a squatting stance opposite Brady, whose gaze fell on the victim's buttocks. There, jutting out from the dead man's rectum, was a single, wilting red rose. And scrawled in black felt-tip on his left buttock was the letter V. Brady looked at Dr Wilson, then at Jenna, and raised his eyebrows.

"Well, I never," said Jenna. "Interesting message." She recalled the information, which had reached them in the squad car via Bluetooth. "Nathaniel Compton. Big cheese in a big company." She looked at Brady, then glanced back at the body. "Someone called 'V' didn't like you…"

"Is that an initial 'V' or the Roman numeral five?" Brady said. "It's encased in parallel lines."

"Maybe it's both," Jenna suggested.

"I've scanned with the UV. No semen, no significant trace evidence," Wilson said. "Anyway, now you've seen this little work of art, I can move the body back to the lab." He looked at his watch. "I can do a further prelim this afternoon and let you have any findings before close of play if you like."

"That would be good, Keith," said Brady. "Does the floral tribute go, too?"

Dr Wilson replaced the cover over the body. "Its removal may reveal minute details of forensic interest, so yes, the flower goes in situ." Unusually, Dr Wilson uttered the faintest of sighs as if anticipating the gravity of the coming afternoon's workload. "I'll ring you later."

\*

Brady and Jones sat in the kitchen with Mrs Compton, who, considering the circumstances, seemed remarkably calm. Shock can emerge in many different guises, Brady knew. He had seen lots of strange reactions to bad news in his time, including laughter. There was no doubt that Mrs Compton was pale. But there were no tears. He nodded at Jenna to proceed.

"Mrs Compton," Jenna began, "I'm very sorry to have to ask you a few questions at this difficult time, but I'm sure you'll appreciate that the more information we have and the sooner we have it, the better our chances are of tracking down your husband's…" she hesitated momentarily. Still, there was no way around it, "… killer."

"Yes, I know," said Mrs Compton, quietly and precisely. She sipped tea from her mug.

"Your husband was chief executive officer at Ace Haulage, is that right?" asked Jenna. The widow nodded. "Can you think – did he say – if he was involved in any big deals lately, which might have gone wrong or made someone angry? Or do you have friends, acquaintances, or neighbours even who might have fallen out with your husband?"

"Not as far as I know," Mrs Compton replied. "My husband was a clever man and a competent professional.

His colleagues actually called him 'The Ace', you know. He seemed to be well-liked and respected, too." She sighed. "And he was a good father to our three boys." There was a moment of hesitation, and then she went on. "However," she said, and for the first time, she looked Jenna straight in the eyes. "We did have an… er… open marriage – you know, no questions asked… So I suppose there might be a significant part of his life which is unknown to me."

Jenna looked at Brady, who remained poker-faced. He nodded at her again to proceed.

"How often would he… er… take advantage of your open marriage arrangement?"

"About once a week, give or take," Mrs Compton replied. "The same as me."

"And you have no idea where he went or with whom?" Jenna kept her voice as non-judgemental as she could.

"None whatsoever. I suppose my husband may have said something to his colleagues; after all, men have got to brag about their conquests to somebody, haven't they?" Mrs Compton shot a glance at Brady, who refused to take the bait and remained very still.

"Well, we shall be talking to your husband's staff next," said Jenna. "May we take a look at his belongings now? We'll try not to make too much mess."

Mrs Compton nodded and got up to take them through a maze of wide passageways, which led to her husband's suite of rooms. On the way, Brady asked if the property had CCTV; he was sure he'd seen a camera as they'd approached the house. "Yes, there are cameras," she said, "but we only activate them when we go out."

"So, was there no forced entry?"

"No broken windows, if that's what you mean," Mrs Compton replied.

So the victim probably knew his killer and let him in, Brady reflected. He'd already dispatched two of his MIT officers to make house-to-house enquiries in the neighbourhood, but he wasn't expecting miracles. The houses in this area seemed to sit on their own private estates, making it difficult for a neighbourhood watch to be truly effective.

The house was vast, but they finally arrived in front of a large door flanked by a mahogany table supporting a large sculpture of a male nude in bronze. Mrs Compton stopped. "Well, as you can probably see, this is the 'male wing' of the house! I'll leave you to look around."

As she turned to leave them, Jenna suddenly remembered the rose, which Mrs Compton would have seen when she discovered her husband's body.

"Mrs Compton, do you mind if I ask you one more question?" she said. The widow opened her hands, palms up as if to say, 'Go ahead'. "I'm sorry to ask, but is it possible that your husband was..." she couldn't help glancing at the bronze sculpture "... having a homosexual affair?"

Mrs Compton uttered a harsh laugh and shook her head. "Highly unlikely," she replied, "given the verbal digs I've had to take from him." She waited for the penny to drop. "*I'm* the homosexual."

\*

Dominic Brady sat at the traffic lights and waited for green. Wilson had phoned him much later than he'd expected with the preliminary findings ahead of the post-mortem, and so Brady had finally left the station a little after 8.20 p.m., meaning that his shift had been nearly fourteen hours long. He pushed his thumb and forefinger into his closed eyes and massaged the lids. Not much of an evening left, he thought. A sharp toot behind him made him jump, and he realised that the lights had changed and that he was holding up a queue of traffic. He sped away.

It was nine when he reached home. Just enough time to eat, rest a little and consider what Wilson had said, which really wasn't very much more than what had already been said earlier in the day. A light rain had begun to fall, and on his journey, the wipers had struck up their rhythmical cadence, back and forth, back and forth. They would have sent him to sleep had he driven any longer. He switched them off, along with the lights, killed the engine and got out of the car, drawing in a deep breath as he did so. Night air. He savoured it. So it was London air. So it was probably polluted. But he drew it in as if his life depended on it. He found it revived him sufficiently to face going into the house. He hesitated. He imagined Kathleen sobbing as she asked him why he never seemed to be there for her these days. It was a scene he'd witnessed all too regularly lately, and he didn't seem to have a convincing answer for her.

He drew in another deep breath, conscious now of the rain stinging his face and beginning to seep beneath his black trench coat. He locked the car and, bracing himself for another angry tirade from his wife, he approached the front door. As he put his key in the lock, his heart suddenly lurched: a shrill scream shattered the hush of the night. He tore through the door, slung his briefcase to the floor and took the stairs three at a time to get to the master bedroom, where the noise had come from.

As he flung the door open, he made out a shape slumped on the floor. He hit the light switch. Kathleen lay in front of him, a kitchen knife in her hand. She was bleeding heavily.

"No!" he yelled, throwing himself onto the floor and grabbing her wounded wrist. She groaned. With his free hand, he yanked a handkerchief from his trouser pocket and wrapped it as tightly around the wrist as he could, using both hands to make a tourniquet to stem the bleeding, which he saw with some relief was pulsing rather than spurting. Nevertheless, he maintained pressure on the wound with one hand while whipping his phone out with the other.

Kathleen groaned again and then whimpered.

"It's all right," Brady whispered. "We'll have help here very soon."

\*

The thumb and forefinger were back on the closed eyelids again, pressing, rubbing, even prodding. Sleep seemed to be a luxury these days that would have to wait. For now, Brady just wanted to stay awake and think through the evening's events. Kathleen had not lost too much blood, thankfully, but the registrar had said that he would keep her in for observation and have his team assess her mental stability.

Brady bit on a fingernail with such force that he managed to draw blood. When he thought about it, he realised her illness was so bad it all too frequently seemed to pitch her into the darkest depths. He felt guilty, so much so that he found himself trying to recall when he *had* been there for her. He knew she got depressed from time to time. Really down. But had he done all he could to help? He wasn't sure.

On occasions, he would come home from work and find her in the same position as he'd left her that morning – on the bed, staring at the ceiling.

She'd once told him that her depression was like a black veil draping itself over her mind. "… hanging behind my eyes," she'd said. "Some mornings, I can wake and draw the veil right back and let the sun shine in. Other days I can move it a little and let in a small chink of light. But then there are days when the veil is too heavy to move. Those days, all I see is black." He'd seen tears welling up in her eyes and had pulled her towards him to comfort her, but she hadn't finished speaking and had pushed away from him. "Listen, Dom," she'd continued, "I live in fear of the day the veil finally refuses to lift." This description had sent a shiver down his spine. He sat and wondered now if this was that day.

The cover story for the kids was always the same: "Mum's not feeling very well." Fortunately, they were old enough to let themselves in and out of the house and order a take-away if necessary. But then, he thought, didn't everybody get depressed at times? And she'd had help from her mental health team during the year. So it wasn't as if people hadn't been trying to help her. And he had helped arrange for Cognitive Behaviour Therapy for her, though she hadn't thought much of the classes. She'd always seemed to come out in a worse state of mind than when she went in. Strangely, though, at other times, she'd be high as a kite, on top of the world, chattering away twenty to the dozen and flitting excitedly about the house. Up and down she went. He would have to tell all of this, including the description of the black veil, to whoever was in charge of her mental health assessment at the hospital.

He'd been invited to stay the night in hospital by the registrar, and having travelled in the ambulance with his wife and therefore being now without his car, he decided that it was probably the best idea. He'd call for a squad car to pick him up at six, which gave him maybe five hours to rest. Jesus. He hadn't even eaten. And what should he say to the kids? Luckily, it was half-term (Luckily? Or had she planned it that way?), and they were staying at Kathleen's mother's for three nights. But he would have to tell them their mother was in hospital. Though he could be economical with the truth, he supposed. Say she'd had an accident while chopping food in the kitchen. Kieran might buy that. He raided the fridge often enough, but as far as food preparation went, that was definitely not his area of expertise. Shona, however, at fourteen, was old enough and bright enough to see through any web of lies. God! Better clean up the bedroom carpet before she saw the bloodstains. The thought sent a sudden wave of panic through him.

He breathed deeply, stood up and made his way to the small anteroom where he was to stay the night. He knew he didn't have all the answers. Actually, he thought, I don't think I have any of the answers. Despair began to invade his senses. As he lay down on the narrow hospital bed, closing his heavy lids at last, he anticipated a long period of wakefulness ahead while he struggled with all the crap flooding his mind. In fact, he was so tired he slept immediately.

\*

But someone else lay wide awake as the dawn broke. Sleep eluded this ex-soldier. He threw the covers off, sat up, and ran his hands through his hair. His thoughts tracked back to his childhood and his arrival at the children's home.

It should have been a brilliant place to live out a childhood: a beautiful ivy-clad manor house set in huge grounds with countless hidden nooks to explore and ancient oaks to climb and so close to the Thames you could smell the water and hear the cry of the waterfowl. Seven years he was there and, despite his orphaned status, it could have been a time of innocence and laughter. Instead, what he thought was a safe haven became a living hell, and the words 'I love you' became the sickening prologue to an endless nightmare. And finally, after his elders had committed the most heinous act of all, he'd run. Straight on to the streets of London. Straight into the arms of the pimps and the pushers like Danny-Boy and Jojo. He'd hustled to get money for food. He'd known hunger, pain and cold. He'd ground out an existence in the shadows of the city's dark underbelly.

And then, a blessing in disguise: he was caught, running an errand for Jojo, in possession of a pouch of heroin destined for an address in Bow. He hadn't grassed either. His time at Feltham could have been shorter if he'd given the police the information they wanted, but he'd observed enough of life, even at eighteen, to know that the bad guys weren't all bad and the good guys weren't all good, so his loyalty to Jojo had held fast.

He lay back down on his bed, feeling his heartbeat slowing.

His probation officer had taken him straight to the Army Recruitment Office. It was probably the best thing that had ever happened to him. He did four and a half years in the military. He got fit; he grew confident and learnt to laugh again, something that he'd not done in years. He'd found his niche. And yes, he learnt to kill. Even better than that, he was taught by his sergeant how to kill without shedding blood. No mess. No trace evidence.

So, no regrets. I've taken out the enemy, he thought. That's all it amounts to.

And how easy he was to snare! Having listened to a few of his new colleagues at the pub talking about how one of the trolley girls had stumbled upon the boss staring at obscene images of children on his computer screen, he'd made up his mind there and then to go back to work and look up the photograph of the CEO on the company website. He'd logged on, located the appropriate link… and there he was!

The same man who had visited the children's home.

The same monster who had raped him when he was ten.

On his next night duty, he'd 'accidentally on purpose' entered his office when doing a security round. ("Sorry, sir, I didn't realise you were still here working.") He'd seen the images on the screen and had seized the moment, telling him that he, too, was 'into children', and it was that comment that had led to his invitation to Compton's home, under cover of darkness, to plan a few 'mutually pleasing activities' involving minors. It had all been so simple, though the sight of the photograph of Compton's own children displayed on his desk next to the computer had momentarily surprised and sickened him in equal measure. He had been trying hard, ever since the night of the execution, not to think of Compton as a father. Best to remember him as the vile serpent he was.

Who knows, perhaps he'd even saved Compton's sons from a fate worse than death.

But he had made one big mistake: he shouldn't have bought the flower from a shop. Supposing he was now on CCTV? Of course, on its own, his appearance in a florist's, buying a single rose, would not necessarily be suspicious. But he'd acted on impulse, not good coming from a soldier whose training had stressed the need to calculate risk before action, and it did mean he'd left his footprint behind, and he would much rather there was no evidence of his presence at all. He made up his mind to collect all future floral decorations at random, perhaps from suburban gardens, under cover of dusk.

At last, his restlessness ceased, and he began to feel drowsy. I've taken out the enemy, he reassured himself for the final time before he lost consciousness. He tapped into his inner steel, and within seconds, he was asleep.

\*

Jenna sat in Brady's office and watched him in silence as he ran his hands through his silvered dark hair, leant on his elbows and rubbed his eyes. He was a fit man, fit in every sense, she mused and was momentarily surprised at her thoughts, but lately, he had begun to look tired, and today, well, he was just plain haggard. The remains of a take-away breakfast scattered about his desk had also caught her eye.

"Are you okay?" she asked gently.

Brady opened his eyes. They were clearly sore and peered out at her from dark sockets.

"I spent the night in hospital. No, no, don't worry. Kathleen. She was... unwell."

"Nothing serious, I hope," said Jenna.

Brady closed his eyes again and saw the kitchen knife covered in his wife's blood. If that knife had gone a little deeper into the wrist... *Yeah... about as serious as it gets.*

"She's doing better this morning, thanks," replied Brady. "She'll be in for a few days, I think."

Jenna's intuition told her that there was a lot more to this story than she was being told, but if her boss wanted to say more, he would do so in his own time.

"So, did Dr Wilson discover anything of interest at the prelim?" she asked, not only to move the case along but also to distract Brady from what was clearly a personal dilemma.

Brady breathed deeply and summoned the energy to focus on the case again.

"To be honest," he said, "he didn't really add too much to what we learnt yesterday. I mean, you and I saw for ourselves some of the things he again mentioned over the phone: the ligature marks, the swollen tongue..." He began to reel off the signs of strangulation, without emotion, because he'd seen similar before, but, seeing her face losing some of its colour, he stopped. She was still new to such horrors. "Sorry," he said.

"Suppose I've got to get used to it," she said. "What about the rectal area? Any leads there?"

"Besides the flower and the felt-tip mark, nothing of interest except to confirm what his widow suggested: that he wasn't a practising homosexual."

"That felt-tip mark: do you think V is an initial? Or the number five?"

"We don't know enough yet to be able to tell." Brady shrugged his shoulders tiredly.

"So why would someone leave a flower, a rose, in someone else's butt?"

"Go on, think about it," said Brady. "Why do you suppose someone would leave a rose there?" He was glad it came out sounding like a tutor trying to train his student to think logically because, in reality, he was so weary he couldn't think at all.

However, Jenna had spent a good part of the previous evening turning this one over in her mind. "Roses are given to people you love, aren't they?" she said. "You know, birthdays, anniversaries, Valentine's Day, that sort of thing. But to accompany an act of hatred – a killing…" She sought for the right words. "The rose must be, well, a statement of irony." Brady raised his eyebrows, inviting her to expand on her thoughts. "'There, that's what I think of your love sort of message.' But I don't think that would come from his wife. They seemed to have had an arrangement that suited them pretty well, don't you think?" Brady nodded. "So, we ought to check out his lover or lovers. Perhaps one of them became disgruntled. In spite of the fact he was straight, perhaps he liked to," Jenna adopted a 'mockney' accent and whispered, "*give it up the arse!*"

Brady broke into a half-smile and then immediately checked himself and grew serious again. "Yeah, you might be right," he said, realising that he felt somewhat re-energised. "Now listen," he said. "DCs Cartwright and Grant are checking out Compton's sleeping partners. They've already set out with those addresses we came across yesterday, amongst Compton's personal effects. I want you to contact either Andy or Jamie and tell them your disgruntled lover theory so that they can add unwelcome or deviant sexual practices to their line of questioning. 'That's what I think of your love' sounds about right. I also agree with you about the wife. Their arrangement did seem to suit them well, and, besides, it seems to have been going on for years, so why would she want to do away with him now?"

Brady glanced at his notepad. "Yeah, two more things to give you food for thought: one, the IT boys are looking at Compton's phone and hard drive as we speak. Find out if they've discovered anything of interest. Liaise with Helen. She's good at computer detail." He picked up his pen and made another note on his pad. "We must get hold of his office computer, too, and get that over to Dinesh and his team." He paused. "And two, Wilson did say something else last night, come to think of it, that we didn't hear yesterday. He said it looked like the killer had strangled with precision: neat, tight, flawless. He said that normally, there is more extensive bruising as people struggle, shift or tussle with each other, especially as the perpetrator is usually nervous when committing such an act. But he said this strangulation looked like it had been delivered by someone trained to do it. He said it looked like a professional job."

"I guess Andy and Jamie need to know that, too," said Jenna, rising from her chair.

\*

Detective Constables Andy Cartwright and Jamie Grant sat in the squad car and munched on their chicken and mayo sandwiches. It had been a long morning, and both were famished. They'd only conducted three interviews, each of the three sessions having proceeded slowly as the interviewees were very upset and had needed many short breaks to compose themselves. These were three married women, two of them in very well-paid jobs, who'd been having casual sex with Nate Compton and were clearly very fond of him. Sometimes, it would seem, the fun took place all together.

"So," said Cartwright, "a guy gets strangled and has a rose shoved up his arse." He licked a blob of mayo off his finger. "Do we think that these ladies had anything to do with it? That's what the boss will want to know."

Grant swallowed the last of his sandwich, rubbed his hands together to shake off the crumbs and reached into his pocket for his notebook. "Not your everyday scenario, is it?" he said, flipping through the book to the notes he'd made during the morning. "Four-in-a-bed?" He chuckled. "I've heard of three, but four! Horny bugger."

"Lucky horny bugger, I think you'll find," Andy Cartwright responded. He reflected on the three women they'd interviewed. "They might have been in their midforties, but wow! I wouldn't say no!"

An ambulance shot by, lights full on, siren blaring, a reminder of the real world. Jamie consulted his notes. "They didn't always perform together, though, did they? Sometimes it was an individual… what did they call it?"

"Liaison," said Andy.

"Liaison?" replied Jamie, amused. "God – not only hot totty but posh hot totty! And NSA."

"NSA? That's a new one on me," Andy said.

"No strings attached. How lucky can you get?"

"Not so lucky in the end, though, was he?" Andy said, serious now. "Someone obviously took a dislike to him."

"If they had individual sessions as well as group sessions," Jamie mused, "then perhaps one of them was emerging as the favourite. And maybe one of the others, or even both of the others, didn't like that favouritism."

"Do you buy that?" asked Andy.

"Not really," said Jamie. "Besides, according to the pathologist, the killing appeared professional."

"Hired killer?" Andy didn't believe it for a moment, but it was important to cover every angle.

"But why would they? They seemed to be having such fun."

Andy grabbed his take-away coffee and took a swig, reflecting on the improbability of a killer hired by any or all of the morning's three interviewees.

"Have we got anything of interest for Brady, then?" he asked. "Or do we eliminate the curvy Colette, the irresistible Isabel and the... er..."

"... voluptuous Vanessa?" Jamie finished.

"And the voluptuous Vanessa, from our enquiries?"

Jamie looked again at his notes. "Yeah, I don't get the feeling they're prime suspects, do you?" He shook his head. "No, not even with Vanessa having that interesting initial 'V'," he said.

Andy sighed. "Back to base?"

Jamie turned the page of his notebook. "Hang on," he said.

"What is it?"

"Here's something..." He flipped a few more pages, turning between interviews. "Yeah, the two who worked for the bank each said that he sometimes liked them to dress up."

"I don't remember that," said Andy. "Did I go out of the room? Twice?"

Jamie looked at his colleague. "Mate, you're a coffeeholic. Of course, you went out of the room. More than twice."

Andy raised his eyebrows. "Dress up how?"

"As schoolgirls," said Jamie.

The eyebrows remained raised. "So, we do have something to tell Brady," said Andy, putting the key into the ignition.

\*

Jenna sat in the foyer at Ace Haulage the next day and took in her surroundings as she waited to talk to Harold Jenkins, the firm's acting CEO. This was obviously a company doing well. She noticed the smoky glass and stainless steel fittings, the plush carpeting and leather seats. A bronze sculpture of a nymph in flight – the Ace Haulage emblem – was suspended from a high ceiling, looking remarkably like the Rolls-Royce Spirit of Ecstasy but with just enough variation to avoid a lawsuit, probably. She'd noticed the emblem displayed along the sides of the many company trucks and lorries parked outside as she'd made her way in. The quality of the environment here was enhanced by the smart uniforms and air of efficiency of the company employees, several of whom had passed her by while she waited and all of whom had politely checked with her that she was 'being dealt with'. Impressive. Whatever else Nate Compton had been up to, she thought, he certainly knew how to run a successful company.

A security guard, who'd already passed her by once, was passing her by again from the opposite direction when he stopped in front of her and smiled: a warm smile which lit up his eyes.

"There's a drinks machine at the far end if you're interested," he said.

"And what's there to interest me?" Jenna replied teasingly, tilting her head to one side.

"Oh, the usual," said the guard. He hadn't lost his smile. "Tea, coffee, coke, but no G and T, I'm afraid!" His laughing eyes really were something.

Jenna played along. "So where does a girl have to go round here to get a G and T?" She smiled her best smile at him.

"Well," said the guard. "Not here. That's for sure. But back in town, near the station, there's The Oasis. Good on Friday nights – live music and dance. Great atmosphere."

A buzzer went off on his belt. He paused a moment, looking Jenna directly in the eyes. She was suddenly aware that this young man might just have asked her out on a date. Then he said, "Excuse me. I'm on call."

"I know the feeling," said Jenna, but he'd already turned to go. She watched him as he walked across the foyer and out of sight. Fit and friendly. "The Oasis," she whispered to herself.

"Detective Sergeant Jones?" A woman in her fifties was approaching her. "Mr Jenkins can see you now. Sorry to have kept you."

"Not a problem," replied Jenna. Her mind did a little flip. "Your staff have been... *very* pleasant."

\*

On the other side of the same industrial estate where Ace Haulage was sited, there was a small florist's shop where

Denise Ambrose was an employee. Denise Ambrose loved working with flowers. She couldn't help thinking that she'd landed a peach of a job, even though she was simply assisting while learning the trade in a small retail florist's in a large business park on the outskirts of Kingston. She had dreams of running her own florist business in the future, but for now, she was quite happy in her position as an apprentice, assembling the posies, the sprays and the bouquets. Sometimes, there was a really big order to work on. Only two weeks ago, they'd had to prepare a large deck for a coffin consisting of a dense variety of late summer fruits and flowers. It had been her job to select colours and shapes to reflect the 'summer bounty' theme requested by the family. She had also been shown by her employer how to weave them all together for maximum impact on the eye, and she had been so proud of the result that she had snapped it on her mobile to show her mother. However, job satisfaction could also be found in preparing the smallest of sprays for an old lady, a flower girl, or a loved one. She had even enjoyed selecting a single red rose for that nice-looking customer who had come in last week. The young man had told her that the rose was intended for an intimate moment. To see the smile spread warmly over his face had made her day.

Yes, Denise Ambrose did indeed love working with flowers, especially roses: a preference that had emerged in her childhood when she would stand and gaze in awe at the glorious display in the gardens of the local children's home, which stood just around the corner from her own home. Even as a child, she'd thought that the orphans there were privileged to be surrounded by such beauty. The sale of the red rose had actually taken her back in time to those moments of childhood rapture. When she had arrived home after work on the day of that particular sale, she had decided to walk a further quarter of a mile or so to behold once again the magnificent rose gardens of the children's home. And there they were: perfect, like the flowers in an old Dutch painting, unruffled by September rain.

Denise stood at length, drinking in the spectacle. Then she snapped the scene on her mobile before turning to head back home, wrapped in a warm glow.

She never would have believed that such a splendid setting masked some of the worst horrors known to mankind.

# PART 2

# PAIRS

The boy at the piano looked like an angel: white-blond hair, blue eyes framed by sweeping lashes and small red lips in a perfect Cupid's bow. He concentrated hard as he ran his fingers over the keys. A sudden discordant note made him stop and look up at his teacher for guidance.

"No, that's an F sharp," said Mr Dewar, sitting on the boy's right. "Can you hear the difference between the natural…" he depressed the white key "… and the sharp?" His finger moved up to the black key. "Don't forget, Samuel, to check the key you're in before you start to play. Do you see the sharp sign at the beginning? Remember that means that all Fs must be sharp unless otherwise shown."

The boy played the same four bars again and, this time, got it right. He turned his face to his teacher, seeking approval. Colin Dewar almost caught his breath, not at the music, which, in all honesty, was distinctly average but at the sheer beauty of the child himself. He ran his hand over the back of the boy's head, let his fingers linger on his neck… and felt a familiar stirring in his groin.

"That was lovely, Samuel," he whispered. "Lovely!"

The boy half smiled and then shifted his gaze to the wall beyond his teacher's face to avoid looking into his eyes any longer. Something in that look was making him feel slightly uncomfortable. He coughed, a pretend cough, which at least had the desired effect of removing his teacher's hand from his neck. He shuffled forward on the piano stool, looking back at the score and pretended to study it further. He placed his hands back on the keys to reinforce the impression.

"Samuel, we're having a little party at the Big House tonight. Will you play this piece for me there? Let everyone hear what a wonderful musician you are?"

At only eight years old, Samuel was not in a position to decline such an invitation. He'd been in the home for only two months, but he'd learnt quickly that you never said 'no' to any of the adults or there would be 'consequences'. He didn't know what 'consequences' were: the other children wouldn't talk about them. But he knew they were bad. He knew you could get locked up, for example. And his friend, Alfie, had told him there was a wailing ghost in the cellar. Samuel really didn't want to be locked up there. So he nodded and then closed his eyes as Mr Dewar's head moved closer to his. He felt the wetness of his teacher's pudgy lips on his forehead and the scratch of his coarse grey whiskers on his skin. He smelt the ever-so-slightly rotten pungency of his hot breath as the lips peeled away from his face, and he shuddered a little.

"Thank you, Samuel," said Mr Dewar. "You will enjoy our little party. I don't believe you've been to one of our little parties before, have you, Samuel?"

"No," said Samuel. What he had noticed was how tired

the other children were after a 'little party'… and how quiet they were. Nobody seemed to want to speak the day after a 'little party'.

"I'll make sure you have a nice time," said Mr Dewar.

\*

Colin Dewar played Beethoven. The expansive minor chords throbbed through his body as he kept the damper pedal down longer than indicated. He felt deep satisfaction. The previous night, he'd wooed the boy, sweet-talked him, caressed him and kissed him until he could no longer bear the tension. Then he'd taken him downstairs for a surprise. He ran his tongue over his lips, pausing from his piano playing. The ecstasy of what followed had been almost too much. A gourmet meal? A premier cru? A glimpse of paradise? He struggled to find a suitable metaphor to encapsulate the utter delight of the experience. The boy hadn't made much noise. He'd tensed at the point of entry and had sobbed into the pillow afterwards: all fairly normal for a first occasion. He loved his angelic looks and his innocent expression. He loved his soft skin. He loved him, and he'd told him so. He couldn't wait to see him again.

\*

Dewar sat at his computer and tweeted. He enjoyed tweeting. He thought that what he had to say was really worth reading, so he tweeted regularly. His penchant for little boys had to remain a secret, of course. People wouldn't understand. Instead, he tweeted about the other three loves of his life:

fine wine, Beethoven and watercolour. 'There's that amazing view of the river bend from Richmond Hill,' he tweeted three days after the party. 'I often go up there on a Sunday to have a sandwich and dabble with my paintbrush. On a nice day, you get to see the sun setting behind the bend in the river. It's glorious. Feel free to join me.' Dewar hoped to attract the attention of young artists, preferably male, who could share his love of landscape and possibly more.

One young male who saw Dewar's tweet had been directed there by his website, 'COLIN DEWAR FRCM', which was easily found on Google. People were so blinded by their own egos. They made themselves sitting targets. "Well," said the young man quietly to the screen. "Maybe I will join you. Maybe we'll take in the sunset. Then, maybe I'll suggest we take a little stroll someplace else – a different view of the river, which I think you'll appreciate. Just so happens it's somewhere secluded." The problem was the risk of being recognised. Colin Dewar had taught this young man music at the children's home for nearly five years, and, unlike the others in the ring, who'd come to him infrequently and usually in the hours of darkness, Dewar had taught him regularly and by daylight, so knew his face well. Even though it had become the face of an adult, Dewar may still see something familiar there. Time for a disguise.

\*

Distant thunder rumbled in a bruised-black sky. Heavy autumn rain thrashed the trees along the Thames towpath and swelled the river, which was threatening to burst its banks. Few walkers brave such conditions. But Clare Thomas pressed on, stopping every so often to catch her breath in the violent squall, always keeping an eye on Toby, who had trotted on ahead, sniffing here, marking there, oblivious to the driving rain and the ever deepening mud beneath his paws. Clare stopped and looked at the river, which had become wild. It was a serpentine giant, slithering at speed, stirring up mud and debris as it went, and the roaring wind whipped up its surface and created whirlpools, which sucked and spewed out alternately. Fascinated by this end-of-the-world scenario, Clare had forgotten to watch Toby, who, by now, had disappeared into the undergrowth.

"Tobes," she called into the wind. "Tobes!" She raised her voice in an attempt to match the din of the storm. She paced on ahead, along the muddy towpath, which was so sodden that Toby's tracks were lost in the mire. "Tobes!" She pulled wet hair out of her face, tucked it behind her ear and listened. A faint rustle in the undergrowth emerged between one gust of wind and the next, and she turned off the towpath and hurried into a wooded area towards the source of the rustling. "Tobes! Will you come here?"

Then she glimpsed his jet-black coat up ahead amongst dense bracken. He'd made a discovery and was excitedly pawing at it and whining. Clare moved towards her dog, then stopped and gaped. Half-hidden in the ferns was a body. It lay face down, motionless. Clare's heart rate rose as she moved nearer. She already knew what this was: the sort of thing she'd seen in television murder mysteries a hundred times before, only this time the corpse was real. She moved in closer. Judging by the size and shape, she could tell this was the body of a man, though his face was buried in mud. She moved closer still and lifted some fern fronds, which the rain had beaten into submission over the back and legs and what she saw made her pulse race even quicker. Clare dug deep into an inner pocket and retrieved her mobile, but there was no signal. She yanked Toby away from the body, put him on his leash and strode urgently back to the riverside with a reluctant Toby in tow. She tried the emergency services again and, this time, got through.

"Yes, there's a dead man in the undergrowth near the river at Ham," she told the switchboard breathlessly. "Yes, face down, and his trousers are down... Oh, and someone's written something on his bottom and left a flower..."

\*

Ironically, even as he constricted his throat, he felt grateful to Colin Dewar for teaching him to play the piano. He couldn't afford an upright and didn't have room for one anyway, so he was glad to have befriended the old lady next door. One morning, while they were both putting out the rubbish, she asked him if he would mind moving a little furniture around for her, including her piano. He told her he would come round that weekend and asked her if she still managed to play. She said she didn't and that it was really sad that such a beautiful instrument now only served to stand and gather dust. He watched her eyes twinkle as she recalled her playing days, and then she asked him if he played. He replied that he'd reached Grade Seven in his early teens, so she invited him to play her instrument, assuring him that she would be delighted if he were to bring a little music back into her life. And from then on, whenever he had a spare hour or two, he would go and sit in her house and drift into his own classical world of Bach and Brahms while she sat in an adjacent room, appreciating his astounding musicality.

During his escapes to the basement, he also noticed that every wall was lined from floor to ceiling with books. He'd always been drawn to libraries with their smell of musty old tomes, their never-ending aisles of characters, and the silence within which, far from threatening, offered warmth and security. To him, literature always promised a world of unknown adventure. He loved the fact that you could be transported to any dimension but were guaranteed, by the turn of the last page, to be returned, once more, to safety. So he asked to borrow the old lady's books as well.

But music was his main escape route. And in a childhood full of darkness and oppression, music had offered him light where there was shade. It had filled the void with enchantment, creating a new and beautiful world parallel to his dark existence. Here was a world where notes danced and musical phrases were bridged by uplifting crescendos or calming diminuendos.

Now, when he sat at her black Steinway, not dissimilar to the one he'd learnt on, he always returned to one piece: the "Moonlight Sonata". He supposed Beethoven's masterpiece reminded him of his life: the setting in C sharp minor recreating the desolate backdrop of his lonely childhood years; the notes imprisoned by slur lines, pitching and tossing on their emotional voyage and, finally, the calm equilibrium of the resolution, representing where he was now: balancing the scales of justice.

Two down and three to go…

\*

Detective Chief Inspector Carlton Delgado sat in the office he'd been allocated, staring out of the window at the rooftops and spires of the town outside. Kingston-on-Thames, the coronation seat of ancient kings, with its inhabitants and visitors still shopping, studying and trading as their predecessors had done for more than a thousand years. Somewhere out there, thought Delgado... He turned away from the window, picked up a photograph of his son, which he'd perched on the desk and studied it carefully. He'd actually managed to get time off to attend Courtney's graduation the previous summer and, for a moment, relived the pride he'd felt on that occasion. Courtney had since taken up a post-graduate course in forensic science, so it looked like he was to follow in his father's footsteps and join the force.

So, here's one to test you, he thought as he gazed at his son's image. No prints, bodily fluids or other trace evidence. No CCTV. Awaiting the results of the computer analysis, but nothing useful yet. No significant response to the victim's photograph out in the public domain. And now a second victim. So we may have a potential serial killer in our midst. What's our next move, son?

He'd just taken a call from his counterpart at Richmond, a much younger man named Mark Soderbergh, whom Delgado had never particularly warmed to and was thankful that their paths didn't cross that often. Too full of himself, thought Delgado. But their paths had to cross now: the Richmond outfit was obliged to network its find at Ham with a similar modus operandi nationwide. Of course, Delgado knew perfectly well what the next move was. He carefully put back his son's graduation photograph and checked his watch. After Soderbergh had rung an hour earlier, Delgado had called for an immediate case review, which he'd set for 14.30. His watch showed 2.25 p.m. He shut his eyes for a moment to clarify for himself the purpose of the meeting: review findings to date and set new targets, especially in light of the second victim. Delgado blinked his eyes open, then stood up and straightened his tie. He made his way to Room D32, the incident room. Inside, the Murder Investigation Team, comprising some twenty officers, had gathered. At the front was a rectangular oak table. Already seated behind it were DI Dominic Brady, Dr Keith Wilson, the forensic pathologist, and his assistant in the laboratory, Dr Sally Pritchard. There was an empty chair between Brady and Wilson. Delgado walked towards the gap, nodding to the audience as he did.

"Thank you, ladies and gents, for your prompt attendance," he began. "You'll all know by now that a second body was discovered yesterday, showing an identical MO to the case of the late Mr Compton." Delgado nodded at Brady and sat down. "Go ahead, Dom."

"Okay," said Brady. "We're here to review any significant material we've uncovered so far and work out next steps. Keith, I'm going to start with you. You've carried out a full post-mortem on the first victim, and if I'm right, you and Dr Pritchard were called to the riverside yesterday to take a look at victim number two. Could you tell everyone what you found?"

Wilson nodded. "Yes," he said. "Identical MO, including the floral calling card and the V-shaped signature on the buttocks, which was clear despite the recent rain. The full PM will be done Thursday, but the preliminary results strongly suggest that the pair are the work of the same killer."

Jenna Jones immediately visualised a swollen, purple face and an enigmatic double signature beneath the waist.

Brady turned to Wilson. "Have we got ID on the second victim yet?"

"His name's Colin Dewar," replied Wilson. "A fifty-six-year-old music teacher. That's all we know at the moment."

Brady's eyes moved to the IT whizz-kid, Dinesh Patel. "Dinesh, anything from Compton's computers or phone?"

"His phone is full of texts to the three ladies, but there's nothing significant there," Dinesh replied. "Nor was there anything of use on his home computer. But he may have been very careful about what he accessed at home."

"Meaning?" Brady asked.

"Well, at face value, his office computer looked like it had nothing to reveal, but yesterday, I finally got into the deleted memory and stumbled on something." Dinesh waited a moment to let his words sink in.

"Go on," said Brady.

"Child porn… to Level 4," said Dinesh.

There was more than one grimace around the table. Delgado shifted uncomfortably in his seat and looked back at Brady, whose eyes had turned to Cartwright and Grant.

"Andy, Jamie, didn't you report to me something about a liking for schoolgirls?"

"Adult women *dressed as* schoolgirls," Jamie reminded his boss.

"There could still be a connection, though, couldn't there?" Helen Atherton suggested. "The 'dressed as' could be an outlet for deviant desires and behaviours carried out in secret."

Brady nodded. "Unfortunately, that is always a

possibility. Helen, while we're with you, have you uncovered anything significant amongst Compton's documents?"

Helen shook her head. "All legal and above, I'm afraid. Not a hair out of place."

Brady turned once more to Jenna, sitting to Delgado's right. "Jenna, any luck with Compton's colleagues?"

"To use Helen's words," she said, "all legal and above. Of course, I only spoke to a few of his colleagues, and you may want me to go back and interview more of them to get a better picture." Jenna had a fleeting vision of the security guard, who'd smiled so playfully and spoken so charmingly to her and had to banish the thought from her head, although she was pleased she'd inadvertently given herself an excuse to return to Ace Haulage. However, Brady didn't take the bait; he replied with a simple 'maybe'. Another moment of quiet followed as everyone expected Brady to launch into a plan of action. But he didn't. Instead, to allow for a bit of creative thinking, he asked if anyone had any further thoughts or views about the case so far.

Jenna was quick to reply. "Firstly, where's the killer getting the roses from? If he's buying them singly, which is unusual, that might stick in some florist's mind. Unless, of course, he's just helping himself to outdoor blooms." Brady immediately made a note to have the local florist shops visited. "Secondly, the head of a haulage firm and a music teacher must have had something in common – something that somebody disliked so badly that he or she felt they both had to die…" She tailed off as all eyes turned towards her.

"Go on," said Brady, in his usual way.

"Well, if Compton was into child porn," said Jenna "and had a schoolgirl fetish and Dewar – is that the right name?

– taught music to children, I'm presuming he did, then the common denominator is children. I know I'm probably stating the obvious here, but perhaps they both took an unhealthy interest in the same child."

"Two strangulations of grown men are hardly the work of a child," Andy chipped in thoughtlessly. He was eager to say something to impress his superiors and always seemed ready to provoke Jenna just a little. She noticed he was smirking and held his gaze, her face expressionless. Then she turned her eyes back to Brady and Delgado.

"But children become adults. And abused children could become adults with a vengeance. Of course, this is the work of an adult…" She shot a glance at Andy and gave him a sarcastic half-smile. "An adult who, if I remember correctly, did a 'professional' killing job. But the question is, where was this person, let's say, between ten and twenty years ago? If this turns out to be a case of historic child abuse, then the question is: *who was that child?*"

\*

"She's good, isn't she?" Delgado said to Brady when the meeting was over, and all parties had been briefed with their own to-dos.

Brady didn't need to ask to whom his boss was referring. He'd already made a note to himself to get one of his team to look up old paedophile networks in case Jenna's theory was right.

"Actually, to be fair, they're all good, but she," Brady reflected, "doesn't miss a trick. She even mentioned that both killings had taken place on a Sunday night, two weeks apart; Sundays could have some significance. She's a quick thinker."

"Obviously. And keeps all options open," said Delgado. "I like it. Good detective work. You know, she won't be acting sergeant for long. Even when Harrison returns, this young woman will soon be sergeant proper and will probably zip through the ranks after that!"

"I've no doubt she has great potential." Brady paused. "She's one of the best I've ever worked with."

\*

Later that afternoon, Brady sat at his computer. He was pretty sure he'd covered all bases in the follow-up to this latest incident. The priority was to try and get a lead in this case via the second victim, and he hoped to secure this lead by sending out Jones and Atherton to interview Dewar's pupils. He had thought of sending out one male and one female detective. The Mars/Venus combination usually worked very effectively to produce a variety of questions from different perspectives. But, this time, he thought that two female police officers might make younger interviewees feel more at ease. Cartwright and Grant were therefore briefed to search Dewar's flat and, of course, retrieve any technology for Dinesh and his team. So Brady was sufficiently satisfied to allow himself to return to an earlier case in which, frustratingly, all leads had gone cold.

There was a knock at the door. Without taking his eyes off the screen, Brady called to whoever it was to come in. Jenna's face peeped around the door. "Sir, is it convenient?" she asked.

"Of course," said Brady. He observed her as she closed the door and walked towards the empty chair, which he'd indicated. "What can I do for you?" he said.

"I hope I didn't ramble on too much today," said Jenna. "I'm conscious I might have stopped others from having their say."

"If they'd had something worthwhile to say," Brady assured her, "they would have said it. So don't worry about it. Besides, in serious cases like this, maybe we shouldn't be worried about social niceties. Just say it, that's my opinion! Actually, what you said today made a lot of sense and guess what?" Brady pulled a face and exaggerated the word length. "Delgado was im…pressed!"

They both laughed together. Delgado rarely seemed impressed, and the laughter was a way of sharing a small dig at the superior, who was renowned for being sparing in his praise. "Thanks," said Jenna. She was about to get up when she remembered another question she wanted to ask. "Sir, could I knock off a little earlier than normal today? My car's in for its MOT, and Helen's already gone for her dental appointment, so I'm relying on public transport to get me home."

"Well, if you can wait thirty minutes, I'll give you a lift," said Brady. "You're on my way home, sort of."

"Thanks a lot," said Jenna. She smiled warmly at Brady, then got up and left the room. He turned his eyes back to the screen in front of him, unsurprised to find he was looking forward to the journey home a little more than he should have been.

\*

They'd chatted for some of the journey and had been quiet at other times. Jenna had hummed a tune through one of the silent periods. Not because she felt she needed to fill the space; she felt comfortable in Brady's presence. He was encouraging and laughed easily with her. She hummed precisely because she was at ease with him.

They sat in the car outside her flat. "You sound as if you've inherited a typically robust set of Welsh vocal cords," Brady commented, smiling.

"Well, I was born in Cardiff, and my father sang in choirs. Proud of his heritage, he was…" Jenna suddenly adopted a strong Welsh accent, "… down in the val-leys… that sort of thing." She dropped the accent. "Spoke nothing but Welsh till he was seven, actually. Had me singing "Land of my Fathers" – in Welsh – by the time I was three." She turned to make sure Brady was following.

He laughed. "You mean the anthem? Yeah, I've watched the rugby. It's one of the more stirring tunes, that's for sure! But you didn't stay in Wales. Why's that?"

"The work dried up for my dad, and he had to come to London."

"My father was the same," said Brady. "Had to leave Cork and come to London to get employment. So I have Irish roots, of which I'm proud, and a Catholic upbringing, but I'm a Londoner through and through." He paused." Oh, and my wife's Irish, of course."

Jenna looked more seriously at Brady now. The evening light had grown dim, but she could still make out his profile and could tell the mood had changed. "How is she now, by the way?" she asked softly.

Brady was silent for a few moments. "Kathleen suffers

from depression," he said at last. He felt relieved sharing what was becoming an increasing burden. "To be absolutely honest, it'll take a miracle to get her well again." Jenna's face was in shadow, but he could see that her eyes, usually bright, green and vibrant, were sad.

No words were spoken for several moments as they held each other's gaze. Then Jenna spoke. "I'm sorry. If there's anything I can do for you, please let me know." She suddenly had the urge to plant a kiss on his cheek, a sign that she was there for him if he needed her. But she stopped herself just in time. "Thanks for the lift. I'll see you tomorrow," she said, getting out of the car. She made her way down the shadowy path, past the giant cedar, towards her ground-floor flat. She stopped only once to look around. She could still make out Brady, sitting there in the dim light, looking at her.

\*

The long-bladed knife had been at work again, slicing tomatoes and chopping avocados as before, but this time, the flatmates were laying out the vegetable pieces on top of a large fillet of white fish, which had been oiled, salted and peppered.

"Did you realise that all the men in the room today were captivated by you?" Helen asked teasingly. As men weren't her thing, she was often able to set herself apart from the social dynamics surrounding Jenna and look on, bemused.

"Well, I hope they were captivated by my theories rather than me," said Jenna, and she meant it. Her professional pride was important to her. "Although I was only joining up some pretty obvious dots. Anyway," she added as she spooned basil pesto into the crevices between vegetables and fish, "most of those present today are married, and those who aren't…" she thought resentfully of Andy's put-down earlier on "… aren't worth considering. Which reminds me…"

"What's that?" asked Helen as she whisked milk and cream together. She poured the mixture over the dressed fish.

"Do you fancy going to The Oasis Club on Friday night? I've been meaning to go for the last two Fridays, but first, we had that late meeting, and then the following week, I had all that paperwork to catch up on. I'd ask Lucy as well, but she's on nights this week, isn't she? I've heard it's good there." Jenna smiled excitedly at her friend, who immediately picked up the non-verbal clues in her expression.

"Jen, you're hiding something from me, aren't you?" Helen chuckled and pointed the dripping whisk accusingly at Jenna.

"Put it this way," said Jenna coquettishly, "there might be a rather charming young man there on Friday. With Scandinavian good looks," she added, "and I'd rather like to bump into him accidentally!"

"Someone from the agency?" Helen asked. "I thought you said you'd had enough of internet dating."

"Er, no, actually. From Ace Haulage!"

"Blimey!" Helen replied, chuckling. "No wonder you were all ready to go back for some more questioning!" She picked up the fish dish, placed it in the middle of a very hot oven and set the timer to twenty-five minutes. "Of course, I'll come with you!" she said. "Providing we're not working late again, of course, which is always on the cards in our job. You go and look for your nice young man and…" she turned, tipped her head to one side and fluttered her eyelashes… "I'll go and look for a nice young lady!"

*

Brady had parked the car at Ham Common. He'd woken very early this morning after a fitful night and, unable to sleep any longer, he'd decided to take a stroll by the river before going to work. Dewar's body had been discovered on the north side of the river a few days before, but Brady reckoned he'd already worked hard enough this week: he would cut himself some slack, avoid the murder scene, which in any case was still being worked by forensics, and walk on the south side. He desperately needed to clear his head. He locked up and made his way down an old road lined with sturdy Victorian villas. This led to a tree-lined footpath, which, after fifty metres or so, joined the towpath. Recent rains had ceased, and the early morning sun lit up the water and made it glitter.

Brady ambled along, taking in the fresh air. The towpath was deserted, except for one cyclist who slowed to a halt to allow Brady safe passage on a narrow stretch of path. Brady nodded his thanks, observed without surprise that the cyclist was an elderly man (which explains the good manners, he thought cynically), and then proceeded on his way. He walked slowly and thoughtfully and, for fifteen minutes, barely noticed his surroundings. Then, he came to a wooden bench. He stopped, checked it for bird droppings, and sat. Sunbeams continued to dance across the water. He watched, mesmerised. He sat and stared for some time. And there, with his gaze held by the morning light show, his mind seemed to explode.

"Jesus!" he muttered to himself.

He shut his eyes and explored the darkness behind his lids: the darkness of the deeds he dealt with professionally and the darkness of the abyss, which was Kathleen's illness. Then his eyes opened, and he looked again at the light on the river surface. And this time, it was his heart which lurched. 'One of the best I've ever worked with.' The words he'd said to Delgado. And now *her* lovely face was etched on an almost tangible canvas in his imagination. His pulse quickened.

'Get a grip on yourself!' he said out loud, and, suddenly embarrassed, he quickly glanced over his shoulders to make sure no one had heard his outburst. Thankfully, he was alone.

He'd always been a loving and faithful husband to Kathleen and a good father to the two children, and he didn't intend to do anything that would jeopardise everything he held important. As if the opportunity would ever present itself, he thought and uttered a brief self-deprecating laugh. He gazed again at the river. He watched as a fallen branch repeatedly dipped and surfaced, helplessly carried along by the current. He watched the branch struggling to survive the flow. Surrender, he thought. That thing's bigger than you.

A parallel thought mushroomed in his mind as he pictured himself struggling against an emotional current. He breathed hard, tried to establish some control over the supernova brightness which had set his brain alight, waited for the starburst to recede, and picked his way through the fallout until he uncovered the white-hot core of the matter.

*I'm falling in love...*

Oh boy!

As if his life wasn't complicated enough already...

His eyes searched again for the branch in the river, but

it was gone. Pulled under by forces greater than itself, it had surrendered.

Well, I don't intend to, thought Brady, trying his utmost to pull himself together. He summoned his strength, got to his feet, turned and headed back the way he'd come.

\*

Maggie, the owner of the florist shop, called for Denise Ambrose to come out to the counter. The young trainee, busy assembling a bouquet of autumnal colours, reluctantly left her work and headed out to the front of the shop. She was surprised to see two uniformed policemen there, talking to the owner.

"And you say there's no CCTV here?" one of the officers was saying to Maggie.

"No. Too expensive to install," she replied. "Ah, Denise," her boss said as Denise came forward and joined them, "these officers would like to ask you a question."

Denise felt her heartbeat increase. She'd been at a party the previous Saturday night and had been persuaded to take some ketamine. Was that why the officers were here? She'd never taken drugs before. And she certainly didn't intend to make a habit of it. But she'd been carried away in the moment. She took a deep breath. "Yes?" she said meekly.

One of the officers smiled at her. "Just a quick question for you, miss," he said. "Have you recently sold a single rose to anyone?" The question was so unexpected that it caught Denise off guard, and she had to take a moment to focus again, her mind having already veered off down the path of finding excuses for experimenting with ketamine.

"Er, I…" She saw the officers look at one another and then back at her. Then she remembered. "Actually, yes, I have," she replied.

"And would you be able to describe the person?" said the other officer who hadn't yet spoken.

Denise remembered the purchaser well because he was such a good looker. "Nice face," she said. "Dark hair."

"I take it this person was male?" the first officer enquired with a slight smile. Denise nodded. He went on, "Age? Height? Black? White?"

"Twenties. Medium height," said Denise. "Oh, and white," she added.

"And approximately how long ago would this sale have taken place?" asked the second officer.

"About, er, two or three weeks ago," Denise said. She watched as the first officer hurriedly wrote down a few words on his notepad.

"Did this man indicate why he was buying a single rose rather than a bunch of roses?" the second officer asked.

Denise tried to recall the customer's actual words. "I think he said it was for an intimate moment," she said.

"Well, I think that's all we need to ask for now," said the second officer while the first finished making his notes. "But please get in touch with us immediately if the same customer returns. Thanks for your help," he said, and with that, the two of them nodded to her and Maggie and strode out of the shop.

"So I wonder what that was all about," Denise said to her boss.

Maggie Fowler shook her head. "Honestly, you never know what's going to happen next, do you? I read in the papers last week that a young man living just down the road here killed his girlfriend after a blazing row. And he'd just bought her a bouquet to make up for a previous argument. The police found the flowers strewn all over the place."

Denise smiled. "Well, these two didn't say anything about a murder, did they? And the man I sold the rose to didn't look anything like a murderer anyway," she said with assurance. "His eyes were too kind."

\*

The Oasis was dark and crowded. Dancers swayed and shimmied on a parquet floor in the centre of the room. Their hot faces sparkled brightly under flashing multi-coloured strobe lights as they endeavoured to talk to their dance partners above a noisy R'n'B thrum. Each light sequence would end in two seconds of darkness when the more daring would try and move in closer to a chosen target. Jenna and Helen made their way carefully past the dance floor to the nearer of the two bars, ordered a glass of wine each, then turned round to take in the scene. Jenna's eyes quickly scanned the dance floor and the more shadowy outskirts of the room, but she could not yet see the face she was looking for. For a few moments, she was disappointed. She'd been so looking forward to this evening. And she'd made a real effort to look her best tonight. She'd chosen a short, tight-fitting cream lace dress to wear and had put on her patent leather coffee-coloured heels to match, and she knew that the dress length and high heels showed her legs off well. Helen always said that Jenna's legs were her second best asset and they'd both laughed when Helen added in one of her funny voices that it was a shame that Jenna couldn't be 'turned'.

Helen was also busy scanning the room, Jenna noticed. Come on. I mustn't be disappointed, she thought. We're here to have some fun. Today was their first free Friday night in weeks, and while the two of them were here, they felt they ought to make the most of it. Besides, Jenna reflected, I might have misinterpreted someone's friendliness for something more than it was.

The barman returned with the drinks, and the girls paid and lifted their glasses to each other.

"Be lucky in love! Cheers!" Helen's voice was raised above the noise.

"Same to you! Chin-chin!" Jenna returned loudly, and they chinked their glasses together.

"Don't think we'll get much conversation in tonight!" Helen said, exaggerating her lip movements to improve communication. The beat of the music seemed to be getting louder by the minute.

Jenna raised her voice to reply. "Who's here for conversation?" They laughed, sipped their wine and watched the dancers.

Jenna's eyes were continuing to scan beyond the heaving mass in the middle of the room when her attention was caught by movement on the flight of stairs, which led down from street level to the venue itself. She caught her breath. "Oh no!" she muttered. She turned and frowned at Helen.

"What is it?" Helen was more or less shouting by now.

Jenna nodded her head towards the stairs at the back of the room, where a pair of sharply dressed men had just arrived at the bottom of the flight. "Is that who I think it is?" yelled Jenna. "Foot of the stairs." Helen caught sight of the pair, pushed her lips forward into an 'O' and dipped her head slightly. "What are Andy and Jamie doing here?" Jenna enquired.

Helen lifted her head again and mouthed sheepishly, "I told them."

"You did *what*?" Jenna was already hot in this overcrowded room, but her rising anger increased her body heat.

"Sorry," Helen mouthed over the din, but Jenna had already turned on her heels and was pushing her way through a mass of bodies towards the powder room. Helen followed, her heart beating fast. She found Jenna there, arms crossed, glaring furiously at her. "Jen," said Helen. It came out too loud. Normal volume was all that was needed. "Jen," she said a second time and much more quietly. "I'm sorry. They asked what I was doing over the weekend, and it just, you know, slipped out." Jenna didn't bat an eyelid. She continued glaring. "You know what?" Helen's voice changed, and the tone became a little harder. "I think my mind was on the case if you want the truth. So, okay, I was distracted. They caught me unawares." Jenna's stern expression relaxed ever so slightly. "Look," Helen continued a little more gently, "you don't have to spend the evening with them. Let's say hello, tell them we're expecting some friends to turn up, which we sort of are, aren't we, and hope they get the message. Come on, Jen. I'm sorry! Let me do the talking, and I'll make sure Andy can't annoy you all evening."

Jenna let her arms fall to her sides. She closed her eyes, took a breath and snapped them open again. "You know what? I'm going up to road level to get some air, and while

I'm out, please do exactly what you said so that by the time I come back, those two will know precisely what the score is. Okay?"

Jenna forced a smile. She knew her friend would never have deliberately set out to make her evening uncomfortable, but underlying the shock of seeing Andy was the disappointment of not seeing the security guard, and she could just envisage the evening ahead going from bad to worse. She touched Helen's hand in a small sign of reconciliation, then strode out into the club and, careful to avoid her two male colleagues who were, by now, at the bar where she and Helen had left their half-empty glasses, she took the circuitous route round the dancers to reach the exit staircase. Up fifteen stairs and past a burly-looking bouncer, Jenna hit the night air with relief. She wandered past two smooching couples and a group of smokers and finally stood a short distance from the club entrance. A full moon lit up the street. She gazed at it for a few moments, then closed her eyes and breathed deeply.

"Hello!" A voice behind her, which had come out of nowhere, made her start. She swung round to her left, and there he was: the security guard, complete with laughing eyes and that gorgeous smile under a halo of moon-silvered blond hair. "Running late tonight, but here I am!" Jenna felt her mood lift instantly as she purposefully peered into the young man's eyes.

"Well, what does a girl have to do to get a drink around here?" she asked playfully.

"Perhaps have a dance with me," he replied, still laughing. "I'm Ben, by the way." His hand touched her arm with a brief stroke.

"Jen," said Jenna with a suppressed giggle.

"Well, what d'ya know? We rhyme!" said Ben. "I'll take that as a good omen!" He escorted her back inside the club, down the staircase and straight onto the dance floor where – she couldn't believe how quickly her luck had changed – the DJ was now playing a slow soul number. Ben took Jenna in his arms and held her tight as they began to relax into the rhythm and sway gently together.

Over at the bar, Jenna's three colleagues each ordered another drink. "I thought you were making it up," said Andy to Helen. "You know, that stuff about waiting for friends. I thought it was your ploy to keep me away from," he put on an affected voice, "the lerve-ly Jenna Jones."

"Well, see for yourself," Helen replied. "She's taken!" A wave of genuine disappointment rippled across Andy's features, surprising her. She continued to watch him for several moments and noticed that his eyes remained fixed on one pair of dancers only: Jenna and her new friend.

But he always sets out to annoy her, she thought. And yet here he is now, brimming with jealousy…

She gave her head the slightest shake. Men, she thought. I'll never understand them!

\*

A ghostly noise spiralled up from the depths of the earth. It began as a murmur, which faintly vibrated on the stillness of the night, grew to a distant but piercing pitch, and then finally subsided, leaving a deafening silence in its wake. Samuel and Alfie snuggled down together under the covers and held each other tight.

"I told you there was a ghost in the cellar," whispered Alfie.

Samuel was speechless with fright. He wanted to go and pee, but he didn't want to step out into the darkness and leave the safety and warmth of the bed or Alfie's reassuring presence. He held on. There it was again. Distant but menacing, now louder, now fainter. Samuel finally found his tongue.

"Maybe it's an owl," he whispered into Alfie's ear, which was pressed up close against his lips.

"Doesn't sound like an owl to me!" Alfie whispered back.

They clung to each other: Siamese twins bound by fear with their eyes frozen open and their hearts thudding against their ribs. They remained like this for some time, not daring to put their heads above the covers. Gradually, the vice-like grip that each had on the other relaxed as they drifted off to sleep.

Two floors below, in a converted basement room uninhabited by owls, a man knelt carefully in the darkness to retrieve his shirt and trousers and put them on. He winced. His left hand was bleeding a little where the young woman had bitten him hard, and his left cheek smarted where she'd scratched him. Hellcat, he thought, but she so utterly quenched his sexual thirst that he always came back for more despite the battle wounds he endured. She lay there now, breathing heavily, and he was tempted to stay longer and ride the roller-coaster again. But he had an important meeting to attend in the morning, and he knew he must go. He went and stood over her. The lack of light hid all but the outline of her head, but he homed in on her mouth for a parting thrill, only to have her spit back in his face. He grabbed her roughly around the jaw. "Behave!" he whispered harshly. He knew he'd left his jacket on a chair near the door, and, leaving the woman on the bed and tethered to the wall, he crept across the room to get it. The darkness made him pick up his jacket at an odd angle, and he heard his wallet slip to the floor, where it landed with a soft thud, spilling some of its contents.

A few coins went spinning and rolling away over the cold concrete, but he ignored them and concentrated on finding something of far greater importance, which had also slipped out of his wallet. It wouldn't do for other punters to find this, he thought. You never knew who you could trust. The woman had started moaning again, and he really had to leave. But it was vital to locate this item above all else, so he knelt and sightlessly brushed his hands over the concrete until he found it. A wave of relief washed over him as he put his warrant card back in his wallet and left the room. Upstairs, he quietly let himself out of the building as he always did and walked off into the night.

\*

Mavis Brewer left the huge Edwardian kitchen with a breakfast tray in her hands and headed for the large oak door, which led to the basement. The tray had been neatly arranged for the 'patient' and contained a small portion of cereal with warm milk, a piece of buttered toast and a plastic beaker of water. Mavis Brewer looked over the food and salivated. It was a crying shame that the girl continued to refuse good food, even after all these years. If she would only eat a decent meal now and then, perhaps the girl wouldn't be so badly behaved. But she only ever picked at her food. What a waste. Lacking nourishment, no wonder she was skeletal… and wild. She placed the tray on the small mahogany table next to the door, as she always did at this time of day, retrieved a large bunch of keys from her belt and selected the long brass-coloured one, which permitted entry to the basement. She took great care of the keys. There were places in the home where the children were allowed to go, and there were areas that were out of bounds to them. And there were one or two locations which were even out of bounds to members of staff: the basement was one of them, except in the case of an illness of epidemic proportions when one of the downstairs rooms might be turned into a sanatorium. But Mavis Brewer was privileged. She was allowed entry to the basement because she'd been entrusted to look after the 'patient' and understood why the 'patient' had to be kept there at all times. Mr Hope, the manager of the children's home, and his predecessor, Mr Fox, who was now retired, had both placed their trust in her and because of that, she was proud.

The basement door was a large oak structure with giant metal hinges, which opened begrudgingly with a low groan, and Miss Brewer had to lean her considerable weight against it to allow her stout body and the tray to gain entry. She closed the door behind her and, in semi-darkness, made her way carefully down a flight of stone steps to the floor below. There were three further large oak doors down at this level. The one she wanted lay to her right. She switched on an overhead light, placed the tray on a hall table next to the door, picked up the bunch of keys, and, this time, chose a smaller pewter-coloured key with which to gain entry.

Anticipating the usual nonsense from the wild child, she braced herself and went in.

The 'patient' sat on the bed, staring straight ahead and humming tunelessly. In truth, she was not a girl any more; she was a young woman. But she was feral. She bit, kicked, hissed and spat. Miss Brewer had never seen anything like it in all her time here as the housekeeper. Her behaviour was worse than a wild child's: it was the behaviour of an animal. Small wonder then that Mr Fox had decided, many years ago, that it was best to keep her in solitary confinement, where she could not influence the other children. "Not fit for upstairs or indeed for society," Mr Fox had added. "Best for everyone that she's kept down here. Out of harm's way." Miss Brewer closed the door and cleared her throat to announce her arrival. The young woman turned her head, stared blankly at the housekeeper and then went back to staring ahead and humming. Miss Brewer placed the tray of food on an invalid table, which bridged the end of the bed and drew nearer to the 'patient'. What a sight she was! Her long, unkempt mane of hair half covered her sallow complexion but didn't quite hide her dark, menacing eyes. And frankly, she smelt. She often did.

"Dear me!" exclaimed Miss Brewer. She looked at the stains on the bed linen. "You've wet yourself again, haven't you? Goodness, girl, you have a chamber pot by your bedside. Are you just too lazy to use it?" She tutted and shook her head, reflecting on the countless times she'd seen stained bed linen down here. Lost cause, she thought. Hopeless. "Now eat up your food while it's still warm, and then I'll come back and give you a good wash. And then," she snapped, "you'll help me change your sheets." Miss Brewer was not afraid of handling the girl as her size and strength enabled her to overcome easily any adverse reaction from her emaciated charge. In fact, it was another point of pride that both her present and previous employers had told her that she was better able to handle the 'patient' than anyone else. Mr Hope had actually remarked to Miss Brewer how sweet and fresh Miss Brewer often managed to make the wild child look by the end of her shift at eight o'clock in the evening, but the truth was that Mr Fox had started that little custom. "Get her clean and looking pretty," Mr Fox had often said. "Give her some self-respect."

Self-respect, that's a joke, thought Miss Brewer as she walked out of the room and locked the door behind her. She climbed the staircase at a slow pace dictated by her size and headed back towards the dining room to oversee the breakfast behaviour of her other daily charges, continuing to reflect on the 'patient'. Self-respect. Had this girl ever had any? Miss Brewer didn't think so. Here was someone absolutely beyond redemption. She'd even messed around with some of the young boys during her teenage years and got herself with child. More than once. Why Mr Fox had ever seen fit to let her out of her room when he'd clearly said she wasn't fit to mix with others upstairs was beyond comprehension.

It would never have happened on my watch, thought Miss Brewer. I would have kept her secure.

The little whore!

# PART 3

# CLUBS

Midnight and all was quiet. Cameras indicated that the premises were secure. Not much doing tonight. Two tours of the buildings and one of the external area, currently being carried out by a colleague, confirmed that, thus far, all was as it should be. He sat at his station and nibbled his way through a bag of crisps. Two targets down and three to go. He reflected with satisfaction on his actions of the past month. Target number one he had stumbled on by luck. Fancy landing a job at a firm run by one of his quarries! Target number two he'd found easily on the internet. Too easily. But now there were the others. Tracking them down might not be as simple: two of them must be retired by now and possibly long gone (Costa del Sol? Please not. His heart sank a little.) And the last? Yes, the last… Arrogant bastard! He must have worked his way up professionally by now. Was probably a high-ranking officer. Untouchable. "We'll see," he muttered to himself. He finished the crisps, crumpled the bag and shoved it in his trouser pocket. Opening a can of caffeine drink, he took a swig and thought about his remaining targets. Another few swigs and he found he was beginning to concentrate a bit better as the liquid hit the spot. He opened up his laptop, logged on and then paused. What search engine could he use next? So far, nothing had helped him trace the 'Silver Fox'. The man had no website and didn't appear to be a tweeter or a blogger. He scanned the security screens again and then looked back at his own screen. Another swig. Come on, think! He shut his eyes, and his mind began to wander. Back through the years. Back to the bad times.

As he sat there at his station in the hushed stillness, lit only by eight black and white screens, he made himself visualise Stanley Fox, the manager of the children's home – now retired, according to the website – tall, silver-haired, even back then, with that sly smile. 'Never smile at a crocodile,' the children in the home used to sing to each other. They'd all understood which predator they were singing about. He saw him in his mind's eye, approaching his bedside, trousers already betraying a small bulge in the semi-darkness. He opened his eyes quickly as he could feel the old panic starting to rise in his chest, but he knew he had to go back and search again for something, anything that would put him on the Fox's trail. He reached for his drink and swigged, then closed his eyes and let his mind wander back in time again. Self-hypnosis. He conjured up the Fox's face, but this time, he steered clear of the dormitory scene and sought a different setting. He watched him in the dining hall, overseeing mealtimes. He watched him talking to Miss Brewer, that fat gargoyle with the stern face and grey hair drawn severely back from her ears into a bun. Did she even have a neck? He recalled trying to tell Miss Brewer once what Mr Fox had done to him, and she'd struck him hard around the jaw and told him never to tell such evil lies again. He watched him now in his office. He'd been summoned there for some ill deed, no doubt, as he had been on several occasions. The office: he panned around it in his mind's eye. Desk, chairs, bookcase, wall paintings, cheese plant, filing cabinet, trophy cabinet... Wait a moment! He opened his eyes, finished his drink, double-checked the eight security screens and then returned to his laptop. Trophy cabinet! Yes! How old would the Fox be now? Seventyish? And what would he most likely be up to in his retirement, given that he was good enough at this sport to have won several trophies over the years? Of course. He entered 'Golf Clubs: southwest London' and pressed 'search'.

*

The next two days were free. Having finished a week of day shifts and one emergency night shift to cover for a colleague, he now had Sunday and Monday off before resuming a night shift pattern on Monday night. It was just after midday. He'd slept for five hours after his emergency night shift and was now ready to trawl the net again. With coffee and toast at his side, he opened up his laptop and logged on.

On duty last night, he'd identified ten golf clubs in southwest London. Ten was not an insurmountable number, he thought, but now, as he entered each website in turn, it became clear that there were obstacles he had to get over in pursuit of Stanley Fox, the golfer. Data protection was one such obstacle. It meant that he was unlikely to find members' names on any website, although he did notice that one of the clubs had published the names of members who held an office, such as vice-captain or treasurer. But there was no sign of Stanley Fox on this particular list of names. Another website ran a series of slide photographs to illustrate its home page, and one of these images showed a large group of members enjoying a formal meal. He peered very closely at the faces in this slide but, once again, no sign of Fox. If websites didn't name their members, and he had never really believed they would, then what were his options? He carried on reading the information set out in front of him, but the more he read on, the more obstacles he saw looming before him – golfing costs, waiting lists, handicap requirements – all standing between him and his quarry. He could feel the frustration raising his heartbeat with each click of the mouse, and the words suddenly began to swim in front of his eyes. He slammed his laptop shut and pushed it away across the table, sending his toast flying over the carpet.

"Fuck it!"

He stood up and headed for the bathroom. Perhaps a wash-down would cool his brain and help him think. He slipped out of his T-shirt and tracksuit bottoms and stepped into the shower. The warm water cascaded over him, and he began to relax. The knots in his neck unravelled slowly as the water beat a steady, soothing rhythm upon them. He gelled up and then let the hot stream wash the foam away. At last, he breathed more easily. He stepped out of the shower, grabbed a large towel, rubbed himself down, put his clothes back on and headed for the kitchen to get a fresh coffee.

Ten golf clubs, he thought. He could be in any one of them. Or, he had to admit, he might not belong to any of them. He grimaced, and yet he felt more determined than he had been before his shower. He made the coffee, sat and sipped. In a more relaxed state now, his military training kicked in, as it always did when he was searching for a solution to a problem. 'Be systematic,' his trained mind told him. 'Go to each club in turn. Ask to have a look round with a view to joining.' He sipped more coffee. He was feeling much more alert now. Lie about your golfing credentials, he thought. He really was feeling a lot better now. 'Take a good look at the trophies in the clubhouse. Chances are his name will be somewhere. Let them know you're ex-army because most mature middle-aged golfers will consider you a hero, and if a hero asks awkward questions, he's more likely to get an answer. Drop Fox's name into the conversation: someone might just forget their confidentiality agreement and provide you with the breakthrough you've been waiting for.'

Pleased with his thoughts, he picked up his coffee mug and returned to the sitting room, where he retrieved his laptop, opened it up and pressed the refresh button. An itch in his scarred finger caught his attention for a moment. It was the only war wound he carried, and for that he was grateful when he thought of the many who'd served with him who'd come off much worse. He scratched at the old injury, considered if his brand of shower gel might be an irritant and held his hands out at arm's length for inspection. Yes, the golfers might think of him as a hero, and yes, they might just give away more than they should. It was worth a try. He entered the name of the first golf club on his list of ten and located a phone number which dealt with enquiries.

\*

Dominic Brady sat in his kitchen with the previous day's newspaper spread out on the breakfast bar in front of him. He looked over the photographs of Nate Compton and Colin Dewar on the front page of his broadsheet and considered what Jones had said about possible links between them. Two victims of strangulation. Were there going to be more? Did the two whose faces peered out at him from the newspaper have other connections who were potential targets of the killer? Did they belong to a group that shared a guilty secret? For now details of the rose and felt-tip signature had been withheld from the press. The last thing they needed was a copycat murder to complicate matters. Brady reminded himself to chase up Cartwright and Grant tomorrow to see if they'd made any headway with old paedophile rings.

He drummed his fingers on the granite surface of the breakfast bar. His mind simply wouldn't switch off, and he realised he needed some fresh air. Kathleen lay upstairs resting, and Kieran had already gone out to his basketball practice. That left Shona, whom he could hear rummaging around upstairs in her bedroom. He closed and folded the newspaper, got off his stool, and tiptoed up the stairs, thinking of surprising his daughter.

Her bedroom door was ajar, and he peeped around it. There she stood with her back to him, bent over a drawer and shuffling its contents around. "Okay, freeze!" he joked in a pseudo-American accent. "Now, stick your hands in the air... slowly!" He had hoped to see her jump, to hear her giggle, to recreate a little of the old magic they'd had between them when she was much younger and they'd played cops and robbers. Instead, he saw her shove something deeper into the drawer, slam the drawer shut and swing around to confront him.

"Dad, do you mind? This is my private space!" Her voice was raised.

"But your door was open," he said, dismayed to see her looking so angry.

"Even so, you should knock," she said accusingly. In the blink of an eye, he saw her glance at the drawer and then back at him. "What do you want?"

"Well," said Brady, feeling somewhat diminished, "I was going to ask you if you wanted to go for a cycle with me." They both enjoyed the freedom of two wheels. "But now you're upset with me, so I suppose I'll have to go on my own. Sorry." He stuck out his lower lip and bent his head, mimicking a naughty boy waiting for punishment, which was a routine she'd seen before. It did the trick. Her lips twitched into a half-smile.

"All right," she said, moving away from the chest of drawers. Her voice was calmer now. "Give me ten minutes to change, and we'll get the bikes out." Brady mouthed 'okay' to her. The anxious activity at the drawer had probably been nothing more than a teenager's need to hide a diary. He respected that need and dismissed the whole episode from his mind.

\*

They set off up the road and presently turned into Bushy Park. It was a beautiful golden October day, a marked contrast to the recent inclement weather, and Brady felt hot in his lycra and cycle helmet. But the faster they pedalled, the more breeze they created. By the time they reached the Diana Fountain, he was cool and comfortable. Brady signalled to Shona to stop, and they both set their bikes down, whipped off their helmets and took a breather.

"Are we taking the usual route?" Shona asked.

"I think we'd better," Brady replied. "Through the park to the river, along the towpath to Richmond, then back. Mustn't leave Mum on her own for too long, must we?"

A group of roe deer broke from a nearby wood and began to graze near them. One, the alpha male with a magnificent set of antlers, barked loudly, ensuring that no other male approached his harem. The sight of the animals cropping the grass, together with the uplifting sounds of trickling water and birdsong, was at odds with Brady's darkening mood. Shona's silence suggested to him that she was thinking similar thoughts.

"How bad is Mum?" she said in a small voice.

It was time to stop trying to conceal the truth from his daughter. She was old enough and wise enough to see for herself. "Bad," he said. He watched her nod wistfully. She played with her ponytail. "But I think you know that already, don't you?"

"Yeah," she murmured.

"You know everyone's doing everything they can for her?" he said. "And," he added, trying to sound as positive as he could, "if illness can be cured in the body, then the same is true of the mind." He had no idea how well statistics bore out his statement, but he thought it sounded reassuring. He patted his daughter on the knee. "Don't lose hope."

"You know my friend Gillie?" said Shona after a while. "Well, her mum had a nervous breakdown, and now she's better. So I suppose you're right."

"Course I am!" said Brady. They rested a little longer, deep in thought. At last, Brady stood up and nodded towards the bikes. "Come on," he said. He went and retrieved both helmets and passed Shona hers.

"By the way, you know those photos on the front of yesterday's newspaper?" Shona said matter-of-factly. Brady's ears pricked up immediately. "Well, Gillie's brother Jake said he knows one of them."

"Which one?" Brady asked. He could guess.

"The fatter one with the long, lanky hair."

Brady knew she meant Dewar.

"And how does he know him?" Brady's adrenalin was starting to flow.

"He had piano lessons with him two or three years ago." She suddenly swung her head downwards to flick her ponytail forward and trap it in the helmet. Raising her head again, she went on. "Jake said he didn't like him. Said he was weird. Always putting his hands on him, stroking him; creepy stuff like that. He got his mum to find another piano teacher. You ought to talk to Jake. He might be able to tell you more." She picked up her bike, mounted and rode off towards the path, which led to Church Grove Passage and the exterior gate.

Brady secured his helmet under his chin and set off after Shona, buoyed by the idea that you never knew where a breakthrough might come from. Perhaps Jake could give them a much-needed lead.

\*

"Sir?" Detective Constable Jamie Grant stuck his head around Brady's door.

"Yes, come in," said Brady. He'd enjoyed his cycle ride the previous day. When he and Shona had returned home, they'd even found Kathleen up, dressed, and cooking dinner. So today he felt upbeat, refreshed and ready to tackle the case again.

"You asked me after the case review last week to look up old paedophile networks, and as I've been on duty more or less ever since," he grimaced playfully, "I was able to do some research."

"Find anything?" Brady asked. He wasn't expecting miracles.

"Well, in the last fifteen years, the Met has uncovered several networks in the London area. I've followed up on eight nonces who were brought to trial. Two did time, got released, reoffended and are inside again." Brady tutted and shook his head. "Two have died."

"So there is some justice!" Brady exclaimed.

"One went to Australia."

"The old penal colony," Brady remarked. "That fits! Have you made sure he's still there?"

"Of course," said Jamie. "So that leaves three out in the community. I noticed that one of them was convicted at a trial twelve years ago when you were the reporting officer."

"Name?"

Jamie consulted an open file in his hands. "Oswald Dixon."

"Jesus! That old scrote Ozzie Dixon." Brady shook his head again. "Do we know where he is now?"

"I've got the addresses of all three I mentioned. The other two have moved away from the London area, but Dixon is still local. I'll email the info through to you."

"Well, well, well," said Brady, rubbing his hands together. "Good work. I think I'll go and pay Ozzie Dixon a visit. See if he's been following this case in the newspapers lately."

Jamie was about to leave the room when he hesitated. Brady looked at him. "What is it?" he said.

"Have you seen the *Thames Herald* today, sir?" His voice was pitched low as if to warn his boss to prepare himself.

"No," Brady replied. The *Thames Herald* was a red-top, and he preferred to read broadsheets. He'd always thought the news in a broadsheet might just contain something approaching the truth. "Why?"

"The article covering Dewar's death refers to a signature on the buttocks."

Brady swore under his breath.

"I thought we were keeping certain angles out of the public domain."

"That's what's supposed to happen," Brady returned angrily. "So has the journo described the signature?"

"No," said Jamie. "It just says there *is* one. At least there's no mention of the rose."

"Yet!" said Brady. "Who is the journo anyway?"

"I'll go and get the paper for you," said Jamie, who disappeared from the office for a few moments. When he returned, he placed a copy of the paper in front of Brady and pointed to the article in question.

Brady searched for the writer's name. "Brogan!" he said with a harsh laugh. "I might have bloody well guessed."

\*

Josh Brogan was a reporter for the *Thames Herald*. Twelve months previously, he'd been writing for a local rag, whose editors had required him to track down Z-list celebs and catch them doing their grocery shopping. Preferably without their make-up on. Petty stuff. It wasn't exactly the sort of journalism he'd dreamed of. He'd always had bigger ideas. National scoops! That was where the action was. That was where the money was.

Then, a few months later, he'd listened to his flatmate's girlfriend telling him and his mate about a murder victim's post-mortem. She'd witnessed the autopsy. It turned out that the deceased had gone to pick up an interesting delivery with astronomical street value but argued over the fee he was supposed to pay for the bundle, and some Mr Big or other had decided to make an example of him.

Since the dead man was also the son of a prosecution lawyer, the police had tried to keep as many of the sordid details out of the newspapers as possible. However, through his mate's girlfriend, Josh got hold of a few of those details and decided to approach the *Herald* with his article. Suddenly, he was some sort of journalistic hero, and his work was splashed across the front page of the paper. The police, including Brady, who was a member of that particular MIT, couldn't understand how Brogan knew so much. Meanwhile, Brogan landed a new and much more lucrative job at the newspaper.

Now, things were looking even better for Josh Brogan. Not only had he got a new job, but he'd also got a new squeeze. His flatmate's girlfriend had hit a bad patch in her relationship with Brogan's mate, and Brogan was doing what any good mate should do: listen to his mate's side of the story over a pint and listen to his girlfriend's version in her bed.

And in return for his listening ear, he asked her to help him out with his article. After some sensational sex, she'd come up with the snippet about the signatures on the buttocks of the two victims.

Life really was *so* good!

\*

Jenna Jones sat at her desk in the communal office, drawing up a set of questions to ask the teenager, Jake Lawrence. She'd phoned his mother earlier this morning and was due to talk to him later on. But she was distracted. She'd met up with Ben twice more over the weekend, and her heart was still a-flutter. They'd danced the night away on Friday, had met for a cappuccino and a walk along the towpath on Saturday morning and had taken a riverboat ride to Hampton Court late on Sunday afternoon. It was lucky their shift patterns had coincided, Jenna thought. The coming week didn't look quite so promising, however, with her on days, barring emergency gatherings and Ben on nights. Never mind, she thought, love would conquer all. Love? This was the first time in this very new relationship that she'd acknowledged her feelings. Was it love? No matter! Whatever it was, for now, it felt good.

She looked back at her notepad and determined to concentrate, but she simply couldn't get Ben out of her mind. Fiddling with her pen, she relived the feel of his arms wrapped tightly around her; she replayed his cheerful chatter; she conjured up his beautiful eyes again in her imagination. On parting company after the boat ride, he'd finally planted a light kiss on her lips and had left her standing there by the river, spellbound. She replayed the kiss now in her mind. Bliss! She'd stood for a while, as if in a dream, enjoying the sweet scent of a spray of freesias he'd brought to her. When she'd finally got back to the flat, she'd put some music on and re-enacted their Friday night slow dance with the flowers clutched to her breast, reliving the magic moments of the weekend all over again.

"Wow! You've got it bad," Helen had observed. Jenna, still enraptured, had said nothing. "So, what do you know about him?" Helen had asked. Jenna had stopped dancing. Mildly annoyed at this interruption, she'd bristled a little.

"What do you mean?" Jenna had asked abruptly.

"I mean," said Helen firmly and seemingly with her working hat on again, "who is he? What do you know about him?"

"Nothing." Jenna replied, and with an air of defiance, added, "Exciting, isn't it?"

The trouble with Helen, Jenna now thought, as she doodled around the questions intended for Jake, is that she worries too much.

\*

"Hello, Ozzie." Brady stood at the door of a dingy apartment on the fourth floor of an old tenement building in London's East End. He'd had to use the stairs to get up here: as usual, in this part of the world, there were no working lifts. The pungent smell of stale urine permeated the air in the stairwell. "Aren't you going to ask me in?"

The man who'd opened the door shuffled nervously in his ragged slippers. He was shorter than Brady and had to look up to speak to him. "Do I know you?" he asked in a voice that lacked confidence.

"I think you do, Ozzie," said Brady. "We had a date at the Bailey a few years back. Remember?" Ozzie Dixon went to close the door, but Brady had already put his boot over the threshold to act as a doorstop. "Now that's rather unfriendly, Ozzie. A few minutes of your time is all I ask. Then I'll go away and leave you in peace."

"And if I refuse to answer your questions?" Ozzie's voice wavered, and he fiddled with the frayed sleeves of his dirty green jumper.

Brady moved in a little further over the threshold. His face was only inches away from Ozzie's now, and the smell of the man's body odour was rank. Unable to maintain eye contact, the ex-con diverted his gaze and shuffled backwards a little. "Well, let me see," said Brady. His voice was even, slightly mocking. "You answer a few questions truthfully, and we leave you alone. You refuse, and we can make life a little more difficult for you."

"I do have rights, you know, Mr Brady. I could complain."

"Paedophiles don't have rights, Ozzie. Oh, you might do on paper, of course, but in the real world, everyone's against you. Surely you know that, Ozzie. Who would listen to the complaint of a nonce?"

Ozzie Dixon peered furtively out of the door, then nodded to Brady to come in. He led the way through a small room piled high with junk of every kind and into a kitchenette at the back. Without removing his trench coat, Brady took a seat at a small kitchen table. He observed the filthy sink and the plates and dishes stacked up on the draining board, probably several days' worth. The living conditions here were poor and cramped but good enough, Brady thought, for someone with Dixon's history.

"So, Ozzie," Brady spoke slowly, deliberately. After years of dealing with criminals, he was good at reading body language, and he wanted to be sure he didn't miss any subliminal signals in Dixon's stance or expression. "We've got two stiffs in the morgue. Their photographs have been all over the papers this week. What I want to know is, did you know either of them?"

Dixon wiped his bald head with tobacco-stained fingers. Subliminal signal number one. "No."

"Now you're going to have to try a little harder, Ozzie. Cos, I can see that that's not entirely true, is it?" Brady gambled.

"I'm not sure, Mr Brady." Dixon had remained standing in the kitchenette and was now shuffling uncomfortably in his ragged slippers. Subliminal signal number two.

"A little help is all I ask," said Brady softly. "Then I'll be gone, and if what you tell me turns out to be the truth and you keep your nose clean, you'll never see my officers or me again. Can't say fairer than that, can I, Ozzie?" Oswald Dixon's eyes were wide open. Subliminal signal number three.

It suddenly occurred to Brady that this particular nonce could be active again, and he had to suppress the sensation of rising bile in his throat. A clock ticked on the wall, but otherwise, there was silence as Ozzie collected his thoughts. Then:

"I knew *of* the piano teacher," said Ozzie quietly. "I didn't know him, but I knew *of* him..."

"There," said Brady. "Now that wasn't so difficult, was it? And in what context did you know *of* him?"

"I think our paths may have crossed once or twice," Ozzie replied.

"How? Where?"

Ozzie Dixon fiddled again with his frayed sleeves.

"People's houses. Parties. That sort of thing," he muttered. "I said all this at the trial."

"Ah, but you refused to name names, Ozzie," said Brady. "The fact you fraternised with Colin Dewar is new information to me."

"I hardly knew him, Mr Brady, but, like I said, our paths may have crossed now and again. But I didn't know the other one."

Brady took a long, hard look at Ozzie Dixon. He wondered how far he could push him. "Got any more names for me, Ozzie? Anyone else from the good old days?" He thought he'd stoke the fire even further. "What about the kids you…" he chose his words carefully. "Dallied with? Any of them stand out as being unusual?" He was fishing for a name from the past, someone who might fit the profile of their killer.

Ozzie looked puzzled as if wondering what Brady was driving at. "I don't remember the children really, Mr Brady and most of the adults I…" Ozzie shuffled again "… hung around with are either inside again or dead. I can't tell you any more, Mr Brady, honest I can't." For the first time, Dixon looked Brady straight in the eyes, and Brady thought he'd probably got as much from him as he was going to. At least his visit had confirmed that Dewar had moved in paedophile circles, and by association, that meant Compton might well have done too. "Well, at least you've given me something to be getting on with, Oswald," he said. "Thank you." He got up to go.

Ozzie Dixon trotted ahead of him, clearly pleased to be getting rid of this unwelcome visitor. He reached the apartment door and was just about to open it to let Brady out when he suddenly turned, having obviously remembered something. "'Course, I don't know what happened to the copper," he said.

"What do you mean, 'the copper'?" Brady didn't like the sound of this.

"You know what I mean, Mr Brady. One of ours was one of yours."

"Well, that wasn't in your statement, was it?" said Brady, ruffled. He wondered if Dixon might actually be winding him up.

"Oh, but it was, Mr Brady!" Ozzie replied. "Not the one that was brought to court, of course. No. That was a doctored version of what I'd said in my original statement."

Brady frowned at him. He still thought this could be a wind-up.

"So why didn't you say something at the time?" Brady asked disbelievingly.

"Well, as you said, Mr Brady, everyone's against us. I thought you lot would all close ranks and stick up for each other. Who would believe a nonce pointing a finger at the establishment? Waste of time. I let it go."

Brady's heart rate had increased. If what Dixon was saying was true and they got to the bottom of it and discovered a corrupt officer involved in paedophilia, the case could have huge repercussions for the Met. Now, he was on the back foot.

"Got a name for me, Ozzie?" Brady asked, annoyed that a note of humility had crept into his voice.

"Not exactly," said Ozzie. His confidence had grown over the last few minutes, and he had an inkling of what it felt like to be the cat playing with the mouse. "But I'm pretty sure it was a foreign name."

*

It was Saturday night, and the French restaurant, which had recently opened and came highly recommended, was very busy. Fortunately, Ben and Jenna had been given a table in a cosy nook. They sat across from one another and studied their menus. The atmosphere around them was buzzing. Waves of chatter and laughter ebbed and flowed. The smell of mussels in garlic, alternating with grilled steak, wafted beneath Jenna's nostrils and increased her already sizeable hunger. The waiter arrived with the drinks. Jenna took her lime and soda spritz and Ben his glass of Rioja. All was set for the perfect evening.

And yet, something wasn't right. Jenna looked across at Ben, who seemed distracted. He'd had the same page of the menu open in front of him since they'd first arrived fifteen minutes ago, and, she realised, he'd hardly spoken a word to her since they'd first met this evening.

"Are you all right?" she asked him.

"Yeah," he said and flashed a forced smile at her. The usual smile was gone. There were a few moments of silence.

"Tough week?" she persisted. This was definitely not the same Ben who'd charmed her last weekend.

"Oh, you know, night shifts. They're pretty tiring."

"Tell me about it," Jenna replied. She watched him wriggle in his seat and noticed him wince once or twice.

"Hey, if you just want to eat something and go home, you know, cut the evening short, I won't be offended," she said.

The waiter arrived again to take their orders. Ben asked for a small salmon salad from the starters list and made it clear to the waiter that was all he would be having. When the waiter had left, Jenna leant forward. She could see he wasn't right.

"When we've eaten, I'll take you back to your flat if you like."

Had he been his old self, Ben might have smiled at the perceived innuendo in this suggestion; he might have jokingly protested at her 'brazen' approach and secretly anticipated a delightful range of possible outcomes back at his place. But he did none of these. He merely nodded and mouthed 'thanks'.

Having had a frustrating week, Jenna had been looking forward to a lovely night out. Midweek, she'd gone with Helen and a detective from the Child Abuse Investigation Team to interview several children at two different children's homes, as well as a few others who'd had private piano tuition with Colin Dewar. The children had revealed nothing. Either they knew nothing, or they'd had no wish to talk about what they did know. Maybe, Jenna thought, they'd even been threatened. Whatever the truth of the matter, the detectives had drawn a blank.

Jenna had also gone to talk to Shona Brady's contact, Jake Lawrence. He'd said Dewar was a weirdo – he might even have said paedo – but that hadn't told Jenna anything new, and it certainly hadn't given the team any new leads. Another blank. So the thought of dinner out with Ben on Saturday night had kept her buoyed as the working week drew to a close. Yet now, as they sat and waited for their meals to arrive, Jenna felt her mood dipping. There would be no magic tonight; that was certain. Ben was still wriggling in his seat, fiddling with his cutlery and foregoing conversation. Either he's already had enough of me, Jenna thought in a resigned fashion, or he's going down with something.

\*

After a one-course meal, Ben was grateful for the lift back to his flat. He didn't live far away; his home was on the north side of town but close enough for him to walk to the restaurant. However, he clearly didn't feel up to walking back. This was the first time that Jenna had been to his place, and she quickly took in the man-pad: a ground-floor flat in a smart Edwardian terrace but, with clothes strewn everywhere, empty crisp packets abandoned on chairs and computer leads lying in a tangled mess on the floor, it was a typical lads-renting-together scenario.

"I'll let you get to bed," said Jenna.

"Yeah. Sorry if I've spoiled the evening," murmured Ben. He'd lost all colour in his face by now.

"Don't worry. It can't be helped," said Jenna. "You're obviously not well." She pecked him lightly on the cheek. "I'll text you tomorrow. See how you are." His lack of colour was really beginning to worry her. "Is your flatmate due in soon? To make sure you're all right?"

"Yeah, actually, there's two of them. They'll be here later," Ben muttered. He wasn't even making eye contact now.

"They will look after you, won't they?" Jenna asked,

concerned that his flatmates might not take his health seriously.

"They're good guys," Ben replied. "The three of us always look out for each other." He watched Jenna move towards the door. "Don't worry about me," he said. "I'll be fine."

Jenna turned to look at him again. "Take care," she whispered and left.

Ben Russell slumped on the settee and ran his hands over his face. He really didn't feel good and wished he'd had water to drink instead of that glass of Rioja. It was true; he was tired. Night shifts always did him in. But his mood was low as well. He'd spent the previous few days, before his shifts began, trying to track down someone from his past, but he'd got nowhere. And he needed to locate this brute because it was payback time. You destroyed her, he thought, and you nearly destroyed me. But I'll find you, you bastard.

He got to his feet, realised he was a little unsteady and decided that bed might be a good option after all. And then an acute pain in his abdomen bent him in two and made him curse again. He waited for the agony to subside, regretting that he'd eaten anything at all this evening.

"Don't let me be ill!" he uttered through gritted teeth. "I've got a fucking job to do."

He didn't mean security.

\*

Jenna didn't head home. It was still early in the evening, and there was someone she wanted to see. She drove northwards to Sheen. Traffic was flowing, and it took her no more than twenty minutes to arrive. She parked her car on the tree-lined road and found a familiar wrought-iron gate. She pushed it open, made her way up the paved footpath to a tiled doorstep and pressed the doorbell. She waited. Misgivings about turning up unannounced began to blossom in her conscience, but she had little time to examine them as the door opened. Jenna stepped forward and flung her arms around the man who stood in front of her.

"Jen!" he said and hugged her tightly. "What a nice surprise!" He kissed her forehead and then took a step back from her to look her up and down. "You're looking good, honey!"

"Thanks, Dad!" said Jenna, with a huge smile. "How are you?"

"Oh, not so bad. Come in! Come in!" Gareth Jones beckoned her in, closed the front door and stepped ahead of her to lead the way through. Jenna picked up the faint aroma of whisky on her father's breath. It immediately took her back in time to that dreadful period they'd endured in the wake of her mother's death from cancer twelve years earlier when her father was hardly ever sober. It had taken a lot of effort from Jenna, her brother Clive and one or two family friends to bring him back from the brink of despair and rein in his drinking. However, she was not here to check up on his old habits – or was she? Wasn't that why she'd come unannounced? To get the true picture? But, determined not to put a dampener on the visit, she quickly put negative thoughts aside and followed her father through to the sitting room. The TV was on, and Jack Bauer was jumping from the back of a truck and landing effortlessly in a ditch. Gareth put the TV on mute.

"Can I get you a drink?" he asked.

Jenna noticed her dad's whisky tumbler and a half-empty bottle of Scotch sitting on a small table next to his armchair. "I'll have a cup of tea," she said. "I'll get it. Do you want one?"

"No, I'm sorted," her father said.

Jenna went to the kitchen and made herself tea. She looked around, assessing how well her father was taking care of himself and was pleasantly surprised to find things fairly clean and tidy. She returned to the sitting room to join him.

"So, how's life in the force then?" he enquired.

"Oh, challenging… and exciting! Depends how you look at it," she replied.

"You're in the murder squad, aren't you? A bit stressful, isn't it?" Despite all these years in the London area, traces of his lilting Welsh accent remained.

"Well, someone's gotta do it!" She forced a laugh. He was right, of course, but she meant it: she and the team always figured they owed it to a victim to give it their all when tracking down a perpetrator. However, eager to stop him from worrying too much, she changed the subject. She'd noticed, on the way in, an open photograph album lying on the floor near her dad's feet. He'd obviously been reminiscing.

"Memory Lane?" She nodded at the album.

"I suppose so," he replied. He picked up the album and flicked back through the pages. "There are some lovely shots of your mother here, you know."

Jenna put down her mug and knelt at her father's feet so that she could get a better view of the photos he was looking at. And it was true. There were two or three shots of her mother looking gloriously happy and stunningly beautiful. He flicked the pages back again, and Jenna was relieved to see him smiling. "Look at you there!" he said. He pointed to a photo of Jenna, taken when she was five years old. The ice cream cornet in her hand was nearly finished, but most of the ice cream seemed to have ended up around her mouth rather than in it. Happy times… Jenna took the album from her father and continued to flick through the record of her childhood: Jenna alone at five years old; Jenna with Clive at seven and nine, respectively; Jenna at eight years old with her mum; Jenna at ten years old with her best friend, Lauren.

She stopped.

"Lauren Bristow!" she exclaimed. "What *did* happen to the Bristows? Did anyone ever find out?" A strong wave of emotion suddenly reared up inside Jenna. Lauren had been there one day and gone the next, but no one seemed able to say why.

"We never found out," said her dad. "But, you know, people up sticks and leave for all sorts of reasons, don't they? Maybe they were in debt, and the debtors caught up with them. Or maybe they were being blackmailed or something."

"Dad!" said Jenna. She could see he was smiling, enjoying his flight of fancy.

"Or maybe Bristow was a bigamist, and his first wife caught up with him!" He'd used his dramatic voice for this one.

"Dad! Really!" But Jenna was half smiling. Her father's imagination had always been fertile. It meant he'd been able to tell brilliant stories to her and Clive when they were young.

He became serious again. "Actually, rumour had it that Bristow was a contractor and that he'd moved on somewhere else. It happens, you know." Jenna smiled to herself, recognising her dad's tendency to speak to her as if to an infant. "People have got to go where the work is. And you two were only kids. Why would you keep in touch?" He paused thoughtfully. "You know, they never got involved down at the school. Course, your mother did so much there, so there probably wasn't anything left for anyone else to do!" Gareth Jones wore a tender expression as he recalled the qualities of his late wife, who was always willing to help others. "I remember your mother saying that it was usually the Korean children, with their high-flying executive fathers, who had the highest turnover at your school, but I dare say that others like Bristow also had good reason to move." He sat back in his chair, evidently satisfied that there was a perfectly reasonable explanation for why the Bristows had disappeared from the neighbourhood.

Jenna looked back at the photograph, and her smile quickly disappeared. "But," she said sadly, "she never even said goodbye." She ran a finger over the image of Lauren's face. A sense of grief had overcome her in the weeks and months which followed the Bristows' sudden departure, and she was feeling some of that emotion again. "Two little girls," she said dreamily as she gazed at the photograph. Her mind wandered…

*Two little girls in blue gingham dresses sit together on a sunlit lawn. Daisies and buttercups sparkle like jewels in the grass around them. The flaxen-haired girl plays with the raven-black tresses of her friend.*

*"I am Cleopatra," says the dark-haired girl. They have studied Ancient Egypt at school and are both enthralled by the power behind the name. "Dress my hair."*

*The fair one parts the dark hair into three long strands and makes a plait. She stops and stares at the hair which she holds in her hands. There is a copper sheen overlaying the ebony depths, which the bright summer sunshine has highlighted. The girl with the golden hair twists a band around the end of the plait and runs her hand admiringly over her work.*

*"Shall I put treasures in your hair, Your Majesty?"*

*"Of course," says the raven-haired one. Her tone is haughty.*

*The fair one selects several daisies and buttercups from the lawn and plants them at intervals in the plait. "Silver and gold," she whispers. The sharp contrast between the dark hair and the bright jewels planted there makes her catch her breath as she gazes in admiration. "You're so beautiful, Your Majesty," she says and slips her arms around the dark one's waist.*

*The girl with the ebony hair has slipped into a trance-like state. She rocks gently back and forth, and the movement rocks her friend, too. She hums in a minor key. The two little girls remain in this embrace while the sun reaches its zenith, and then the fair one gradually lets go.*

*Clouds are now gathering above them.*

*The Queen of the Nile picks up the skipping rope they've been playing with, holds it at arm's length and turns one of the handles towards her. It's a pretend asp. "Look at me," she whispers oddly. The sound that escapes from her lips sends a chill up the other one's spine. Cleopatra closes her eyes and imagines what it would be like to feel that sudden sharp pain in your chest, knowing that the next few breaths would be your last. She brings the wooden handle swiftly down and crashes it against her ribs.*

*Her scream of pain momentarily extinguishes the sun...*

Jenna snapped the album shut and looked up at her dad, who'd just spoken. "Sorry, what was that?"

"I said, why aren't you out on the town tonight?"

"Actually," said Jenna, "I've just had dinner out with my..." She hesitated a second "... boyfriend, earlier this evening, but he wasn't feeling well, so I took him home."

Her father seemed pleased that there was mention of a boyfriend. "So, how is your love life going?" he asked. His face was bright with anticipation.

Jenna sighed. "Ups and downs," she said. "But I've recently got myself a nice guy, so I'm happy for now. What about you?"

"Well, you'll be pleased to hear I've joined a gym."

"What?" Jenna was delighted but surprised. She looked straight at the whisky bottle and then back at her dad, trying to reconcile how one lifestyle could fit with the other. Her father followed her gaze.

"Oh, this is now my weekend-only treat." He waved his empty tumbler as if to emphasise he didn't need a refill. "No, I go three times a week. A bit of cross-training, a little swimming... and I'm feeling good!"

Jenna rose on her knees and gave her dad another hug. At last, at sixty-one, he was taking his health seriously. "And," he added, "I'm interested in the yoga class."

Jenna's jaw dropped. Her dad chuckled. "Oh, all right then! I'm interested in *someone in* the yoga class!" Jenna chuckled with him, and for the first time in years, she caught a sparkle in her dad's eye.

*

Stanley Fox stood in front of the mirror and observed his reflection. He'd aged well, he thought. Nearly seventy-two now, but – a smug flicker of a smile graced the corners of his lips – he still had *it*: sex appeal. His hair might be silver, but his skin was still smooth in appearance, his eyes were bright, and his teeth were all his own and in relatively good condition. Yes, he'd kept well; there was no doubt about it. As he ran a comb through his hair, he thought again with satisfaction about the previous night's activities. He'd had a new mistress now for a few weeks, a forty-something Polish divorcee called Mira, who'd been working behind the bar at the golf club for several months. She'd been charmed, in the first instance, by his slick conversation. She had then noticed his habit of buying champagne for everyone after a good round of golf, not to mention his brand new red Ferrari, parked in front of the clubhouse, so, he had to admit it, she'd probably also been attracted by his wealth. But when he'd finally got her into bed, he'd surprised her with his sexual prowess. She hadn't been expecting that. He'd actually shown her he could keep going longer than she could. And she loved it. She told him she found him irresistible, and when she whispered that word in his ear in her sexy Eastern European accent, it turned him on and kept him going even longer.

Luckily, his wife, Elvira, turned a blind eye to his sexual peccadilloes. She always had done. Even when he'd managed the children's home all those years ago and had begun to seek pleasure with various young conquests there, Elvira either hadn't realised the extent and nature of his night-time activities or had chosen not to acknowledge them, although they were right under her nose. Well, let's face it, he thought, she had a meal ticket for life with me. Why upset the apple cart? He placed the comb in the inside pocket of his jacket, took one last, long, approving look at his reflection in the mirror and left the bathroom.

\*

Mira enjoyed rough sex. The rougher it got, the better she liked it. Last night, they'd scratched and bitten each other until they'd drawn blood. Perversely, it had heightened their desire. Fox realised as he reversed his Ferrari out of one of his three garages, that he hadn't enjoyed sex so much since he'd been with his wild child back at the children's home. He'd made it very clear to his ring of 'brothers' at the time that he was the alpha male in the pecking order and should have priority access to her. He even came up with his own pet name for her, which reflected her animal behaviour and which he'd then used exclusively for the next seven years before his retirement.

He pondered now, as he drove down the long gravel drive and out into the lane, why he hadn't been back to the home for a while to seek pleasure with her. If he thought about it, she was, quite simply, the most thrilling fuck he'd ever had. He supposed Mira had only recently reminded him of his true preferences: he loved a bit of sadomasochism. And, of course, where the wild child was concerned, there was that added frisson of shared DNA… well, it was the cream on top of the milk. It had been a few years since he'd been back, but maybe he'd get in touch with Gerald soon and sort out a date for a visit.

He parked his Ferrari in front of the clubhouse but left the engine running as the radio was playing one of his favourite sonatas: the Moonlight. As he listened to his favourite pianist, Murray Pariah, play, he gave serious thought to going back to his old workplace to rediscover the thrills he'd had there. He had decided long ago that boys weren't really his thing. True, he'd had a bit of fun with some of them at the famous (or infamous, depending on how you looked at it) parties, usually after he'd had a bit to drink.

But on the whole, he preferred to leave the boys to the others. Girls were his thing and the wild child in particular. There was one exception to this preference, however, and as he continued to listen to the sonata, he could see, in his mind's eye, the dark-haired lad with the long lashes and the perfectly formed lips playing this very piece. Maybe it was because this boy had possessed such gloriously feminine facial features that he was so attracted to him – that and his musical gift. What a shock it was then to find he'd run away the day after they'd had the best party ever, which had included a spot of voyeurism while they'd all pleasured themselves. And then group sex with the two minors to follow. What a panic had set in when the young lad couldn't be found the next morning. Supposing he'd gone to the police and talked? Fox remembered how quickly he'd contacted the DCI who'd attended the party the night before and told him he was leaving any covert damage limitation in his hands, although as it turned out, the boy just seemed to vanish into thin air despite all efforts by the regular police force to discover his whereabouts.

Fox looked at his watch. The sonata had drawn to a close, and the news had come on. He realised he was already five minutes late for his round with a local dignitary. He was about to switch off the engine when a news item caught his attention. Police were asking for anyone to come forward who might have information linking the recent murders of a company CEO and a music teacher in the south-west London area. Fox recognised the names immediately and knew very well what linked the two of them. His heart jumped. These were two of the ring of 'brothers'. His ring of 'brothers'. Was someone hunting them down? He thought he'd better have a word with his police contact since more damage limitation might be required.

*

Stanley Fox played a very good round of golf and finished on seventy-nine. He was pleased with himself, especially as he'd beaten the local mayor by five shots. As they made their way back to the clubhouse, Fox thought that life couldn't get much better. Mira would be waiting at the bar to congratulate him on his win and serve them chilled champagne and salmon tartlets. He intended to sidle up to her when his golfing partner was looking the other way and whisper filthy suggestions in her ear, which he could put into practice at her place later on. The mayor had already entered the clubhouse, and Fox was about to follow when he noticed a male figure in a black leather jacket standing by his Ferrari. He often had people stop and admire his car, but as he didn't recognise this young man, he thought he'd better check him out to make certain that admiration was all it was. After all, some unlucky owners ended up with scratches scored all over their new cars. There were some sick, jealous bastards out there, for sure. He parked the trolley and headed over to the car.

"Nice set of wheels you've got here," said the young man.

Fox breathed a small sigh of relief and relaxed a little. This, after all, sounded like admiration.

"Thanks," he said.

"Gas guzzler? How much do you get to the gallon?"

"About eighteen, but those are eighteen glorious miles! Worth every damn penny! You like?"

"Do I!" said the young man. He continued to admire the bodywork.

Fox thought briefly about offering him a quick spin in his vehicle. He'd done so for a few previous admirers, always enjoying the chance to show off. But something about this stranger made him more wary than usual. He couldn't quite put his finger on it.

"You're not a member here, are you?" he asked.

"Er, no," replied the young man. "But I did come to have a look round with a view to joining. See what the membership terms were. Compare them to a few other clubs I've looked at."

"And how does our club compare?" Fox asked pleasantly. The man seemed genuine enough.

"Very favourably," said the young man. He suddenly looked him straight in the eyes and smiled oddly. "This club might just have everything I've been looking for." He turned to go but swung round again and said, "By the way, like the registration."

Stanley Fox watched the young man walk across the car park to the exit footpath, and then he looked back at his Ferrari with pride. 'FOX 1' was another reason why life couldn't get much better.

*

The smartphone buzzed.

"Moses?"

"Yes?"

"It's Saladin."

The ring members had long ago chosen to use code names in case their calls were ever monitored. The only link to their first names was the code name initial, which they'd agreed to keep in order to make identification easier during covert calls.

"Napoleon and Cortes are dead. What's going on?"

"I'm keeping an eye on it. I'll let you know when I know more."

"Who's investigating?"

"An MIT operating out of Kingston nick."

"We can't have them finding anything incriminating, can we?"

"Listen. One phone call, and I've got it covered. I've got to go."

"Do they already know how the two are linked?"

"They've already interviewed some kids, if that's what you mean."

"Does Geronimo know?"

"Some of the kiddy interviews actually took place at Geronimo's. Fortunately, he'd already taken precautionary measures: the prize was well hidden. Now I've really got to go."

He switched off his smartphone and shoved it into a pocket, annoyed that Fox didn't seem to trust him. Had he forgotten that he, 'Moses', was in a powerful position, enabling him to cover tracks with the utmost effect? The commander picked up the phone and proceeded to arrange for a Continuous Improvement Team to review Kingston MIT's findings to date under the guise of Child Protection.

He needed to see what the MIT team had already found out.

\*

He'd hit gold. After a frustrating last week, he finally had the Silver Fox in his sights. Greenacres was the fifth club he'd visited in twelve days and, frankly, he was getting utterly bored listening to golfing enthusiasts chunter on about the quality of their fairways and greens, the calibre of their members, and the joys of the 'nineteenth'. Bla-bla-bla. He'd feigned interest and had even bluffed a bit of knowledge, but as he began to hear the same old flannel churned out at each club, he really did think about giving up or, at least, moving the search on for now to number four.

It hadn't helped either that he hadn't been feeling so good last week. Maybe it was something he ate. But with traipsing around courses, pretending to give a damn about what they were saying when he had no intention of ever coming back and feeling a bit off on top of it all, things had begun to look pretty grim.

And then he arrived at Greenacres. He hadn't even got as far as the clubhouse door when he saw the Ferrari in the car park and found himself thinking that if Fox were going to treat himself to a car which would even *begin* to accommodate his ego, that would be the one. And then he spotted the registration. He nearly laughed out loud. Gotcha!

Now, as he secured his helmet and started up the Suzuki he'd hired, he began to make a mental list from which to select a site of execution.

\*

"Dom? Get in here fast!" Carlton Delgado released the button on his phone pad and scowled. Okay, so they weren't making much headway with the case, not through lack of trying, he thought, but now they were going to have their efforts impeded by an inspection team. Christ Almighty, they'd been working the case for less than two months. What did they expect? Miracles?

He went over again in his mind what had been done to date: house-to-house, sniffers, post-mortems, hard drive analyses, numerous interviews, and interim case reviews. Had he missed something?

A light tap on the door announced Brady's arrival. The DI had just been chatting with Andy Cartwright about the possibility of tailing the journalist, Brogan, to see if they could identify his sources when Delgado buzzed. Brady had picked up the urgency in his superior's voice. Now he could see him, the fact he was stressed was confirmed.

"Sir?"

"Brace yourself, Dom. We're getting a visit from high command."

"In relation to what?" asked Brady, rattled.

"The rose murders."

"Shit!"

"Precisely!" Delgado pushed himself forcefully away from his desk. His chair, which was on castors, rolled backwards several inches. "They say it's to do with Child Protection. I suppose they were alerted by the fact we teamed up with CAIT to do those child interviews. Not that they got us anywhere."

Brady hoped that that wasn't a comment on the proficiency or otherwise of his officers conducting the interviews, but he didn't interrupt. He could tell there was more to come.

"So CIT are now on their way."

"The Continuous Improvement Team?" Brady spelt it out. "Don't they conduct reviews on an annual basis?"

"Annually or as the need arises," replied Delgado, shaking his head. "My question is if we're not part of an annual review – and we're not; I checked it out with the powers that be-then what's made them think the need has arisen? Do you know," he said with a cynical laugh, "if I didn't know better, I'd say there was something fishy going on here."

Brady had thoughts of his own but kept them to himself. Always the pragmatist, he said, "There's no sense in fighting against it, is there? So what will it mean in practical terms?"

"That we will have to turn over everything we've discovered so far and let them ride roughshod over it." He was very heated now, and though his fury was hard to detect in his dark skin, his eyes were red and flaring. "That we will have to spend precious time answering their questions when we could be tracking down a serial killer."

"And when are they due?" asked Brady. The sooner his team knew what was coming, the better.

"Any fucking time now," snapped Delgado. Brady realised he'd hardly ever heard his boss use the f-word. Anger with a capital A. "So anything that needs putting in order, you'd better put in order right away!" He barked this at Brady without eye contact.

Brady remained silent but raised his eyebrows, waiting for his boss to look up again. When he did, he said with pointed phlegmatism, "I think you'll find that everything's already in order."

"Yeah, of course it is. Apologies. I'm just feeling hacked off with it all."

"Yeah." Brady knew the feeling. He tapped on the desk. "Leave it with us," he said. "We'll deal with them so efficiently that we'll have them out of here in no time." He got up to leave.

"Dom?"

"Sir?"

"Thanks. I know you've got a crack team, and you're doing everything you can."

Brady returned to his office. The phrase 'something fishy' loomed large in his mind. Supposing there did exist a corrupt officer, as Dixon had suggested? Maybe he'd be a senior officer by now. And suppose he was able to pull strings in any way he wanted? That could account for this unexpected turn of events, couldn't it? And what would he be hoping to find?

"And maybe you're letting your imagination run riot," Brady muttered to himself. He pressed a number on his keypad, which would alert Jenna to put out the call for everyone to assemble.

But as he sat and waited for the team to arrive in the

incident room, he couldn't help wondering if there was any piece of evidence that should be hidden from the CIT team in case it alerted a certain party further up the chain of command.

\*

The team members were briefed.

"Any questions?" Brady asked. Many serious faces looked back at him in stunned silence. "The bottom line is, we've played this by the book, so let them ask their questions, but try and proceed with your work as if they weren't there. End of the day, we've still got a killer to find." Brady waved his hand to signal they could go. To Jenna, though, he mouthed 'stay'.

When the door had shut, and it was just the two of them, Brady spoke in hushed tones. "You're my acting sergeant at the moment, and I need to share something with you. We've known each other less than a year, but I already know you're someone I trust completely and someone whose professional opinion I value." Jenna said nothing but nodded to show she was ready to listen. However, he shook his head. "Walls have ears," he said, even more quietly than before. "Let's get out of the building. Fancy a stroll by the river?"

"Sure," she said.

\*

It was a cold November afternoon, and they'd both wrapped up warmly, Brady in his trademark black trench coat and Jenna in a long, padded navy jacket. They both donned scarves and gloves before they left the station. Now, they crossed Kingston Bridge and headed along the towpath upriver. Despite the cool weather and a fresh wind, a watery sun glimmered in a pewter sky. There were plenty of people on the opposite bank, feeding swans, enjoying afternoon tea in fleeces and body-warmers or taking a breather during the matinee interval at the Rose Theatre. Fortunately, there was hardly a soul on their side of the river. Brady looked around to check they really were alone and then began to talk. He mentioned his visit to Ozzie Dixon's flat, he described Dixon's allegation that there might be a paedophile police officer at large, and he then let that sink in in the context of Delgado's remark that something fishy might be going on with the CIT visit.

"In other words," he said to Jenna, "are we being overhauled because some corrupt bastard, someone with the clout to order a review on some flimsy pretext, is really trying to find out if we know anything which could incriminate *him*?"

Jenna's reaction so far had been muted. She was not incredulous because the more experience she had gained in the job and life, the more she believed that anything could happen – and very often did. But she did wonder why this conversation was not being shared with a superior officer.

"Have you not said any of this to Delgado?" she asked.

"Well, here's a detail to make you think," said Brady. "Dixon said the corrupt copper had a foreign name."

Jenna stopped dead, and Brady had to turn round to catch her eyes widening and her mouth gaping. "No!" she said. "You don't think…?"

"Well, up until today, I didn't know what to think," said

Brady. They began walking again, side by side. "But now... no, I don't think... Because he wouldn't have called in the CIT team. It has to be someone of a much higher rank – if, of course, my imagination hasn't got the better of me. Let's face it, Dixon could still be winding me up, and the review could still be a perfectly legitimate activity, monitoring an investigation under the Child Protection umbrella." Now Brady stopped walking. "What do you think?" he said.

"Wow!" she said, slowing to allow him to catch up with her. "'Where to begin?' is my first thought." They continued to stroll. "Is there some way of checking the validity of Dixon's allegation? Can you retrieve his original statement?" Jenna asked.

"He didn't name names. That much I do remember," said Brady in a resigned tone.

"So, do you know of any foreign names amongst the ranks who have the authority to order a CIT review?" she said.

Brady shook his head. "Do you know how many officers we're talking about? There are well over a hundred Met officers above the rank of superintendent. And what constitutes a foreign name these days? For all I know, 'Brady' might be considered foreign by some! Honestly, it's a needle in a bloody haystack."

She grimaced, and they walked on. "Well, okay then, if there is such a person and he can't be rooted out – and that would be difficult even if we did know who he was..." She paused as Brady uttered an exasperated grunt. "... then we've got to decide what it is he might be looking for."

"I agree," said Brady. They carried on along the towpath for a while, both immersed in their thoughts. At last, Brady said, "So how's about being cagey with the CIT team?" Brady looked at Jenna with one eyebrow arched, to which Jenna replied with a nod and a wide-eyed smile. "Of course, if we play that little game," Brady went on, "Our lot need to know what's going on so that we can all be consistent in what we show and say to our visitors."

Brady stopped again. "Do you know what my gut is telling me? That Dixon's telling the truth; that Delgado's 'fishy' theory is right, and that someone up the food chain is looking to cover up incriminating evidence."

"And has your gut ever been wrong?" said Jenna.

"Hardly ever," Brady replied.

\*

The biker switched off the engine again and removed his helmet. Five minutes of sitting and thinking about executing Fox had convinced him that he really only had one choice, and that was to follow him home. Even then, he would have to think again about the how, where and when. He'd toyed with other ideas. Taking him out in the clubhouse gents was his first thought, but he decided it was not a remote enough site. Then he considered an execution on the golf course itself but knew there would be too many observers out there. He loved the idea of executing the man in his blessed Ferrari, but how would he gain entry? In the end, he opted to follow him home, and if it only turned out to be a reconnaissance exercise, at least he would know where he lived for future reference.

He'd parked the motorbike at a reasonable distance from the golf club gates to avoid being spotted. Now, he locked the vehicle and helmet together again, wandered back into Greenacres' grounds to check there was no activity around the red car, then retreated and walked across the road to a cafe for a bite to eat. His appetite had returned after his stomach upset last week, and he suddenly felt ravenous. A chicken and salad half-baguette did the trick. He washed it down with fruit juice and then sauntered back to the bike. He took his time. It was only 15.40, and it meant he still had over three hours before he needed to start his next shift. Plenty of time, he thought, for a little recce before getting back to the flat for a shower and another bite to eat before work.

He sat on the bike and waited. He thought about his mission. He had to admit that the second time was easier than the first, so the third time should present him with no problem at all. Compton gone, Dewar gone and now he had Fox in his sights. That would leave him the priest and the mystery man, although he had to admit that these two were going to be more difficult to track down when the only thing he knew about them was their faces. Still, he was determined to find a way; there was always a way, he thought. They were out there somewhere. And then it would all be over. He realised he was actually looking forward to settling back down to a normal civilian life. Maybe even a love life.

He glanced up as a young mother walked by, pushing twin toddlers in a large black buggy. This vision of contented parenthood made him visualise his own perfect mate: blonde, funny and pretty. Had he already met her at his place of work? He imagined walking her down the aisle; he saw them living together in a smart little semi; he dreamed up two cute children of his own and a puppy to complete the picture. He was recreating in his mind's eye an Arcadian dream, which sprang from a distant memory of his life, as he perceived it, until the age of seven.

The light before the darkness.

He needed to find inner peace after all of this was over, and he reckoned somebody special in his life might help him achieve it. He and she would make fine parents, he thought, just as his parents had been before their untimely deaths, and their children would never know the betrayal, the suffering and the shame that he and the other children in care had known… especially the girl in isolation.

*The girl in isolation*: a sudden vision of her facial features twisting and contorting as she struggled for breath under the pressure of his own body brought his adrenal gland to life, and he had to swallow hard and fight back the tears which were now pinpricking behind his eyelids. The anger that welled up in him once more was urgent and overwhelming. How could *they* have done *that* to him? How could *they* have made him do *that* to her? The pair of them had been so utterly betrayed. He suddenly felt fully justified all over again and realised he now had renewed vigour with which to continue his mission of vengeance.

The revving of a powerful engine and a flash of scarlet snapped him out of his reverie. It was the Ferrari. He pulled on his helmet, started up the bike and sped away in pursuit of an unsuspecting Stanley Fox.

It was late in the afternoon by now, and the traffic was heavy. It was school run time; the popular view that there were too many unsavoury characters around to let children walk home these days had obviously brought out dozens of protective mums in their four-by-fours. Well, don't you worry, ladies, the biker thought. I'm about to reduce that threat to your offspring. Give me a few days, maybe a week and the world will be a safer place for your children.

The traffic worked in his favour. Where the Ferrari got caught in queues, the Suzuki could weave its way through. So, despite the difference in horsepower, the biker was able to track the driver close enough to keep him in sight but at a sufficient distance to maintain cover. At last, after a few traffic-congested miles, the red car turned into a leafy lane lined with huge houses with sweeping driveways. The biker stopped at the corner of the road and observed his quarry from behind his dark visor. Three houses down, the car pulled up in front of electronic gates, and the driver was evidently operating a remote because, within seconds, the gates parted, allowing the vehicle to enter.

The biker continued to watch.

The car progressed slowly up the drive and stopped in front of a neo-Georgian entrance. Fox got out, locked up and walked to the front door.

The biker thought he had all he needed from this initial recce and was about to turn the Suzuki around and head back when the sound of a barking dog caught his attention. A large Afghan hound had come bounding out of the front door as Fox had opened it. The animal was clearly excited at its master's return, and Fox had to remonstrate loudly with the pooch before it would calm down and come to heel.

Behind the dark visor, the biker smiled with deep satisfaction. He had day shifts next week. That meant his evenings would be free. And dogs needed walking by their owners before bedtime, didn't they?

Finally, he knew how he would get Stanley Fox on his own.

\*

Shona and Gillie sat huddled together on a bench on the Thames towpath. They had both told their mothers they were staying behind for drama club but had actually left school promptly at three-fifteen and had made their way to the river crossing at Teddington Lock. Now, as the chill of late afternoon began to set in, they waited for the occupant of a shabby green and gold houseboat to return.

"What time did he say he'd be here?" asked Shona.

"Four," said Gillie, who was admiring the faded but pretty rose motif on the side of the vessel. Shona shifted uncomfortably on the bench. "Stop worrying!" Gillie assured her. "It'll be all right. I've talked to him a few times, and he's really nice."

Shona had seen that look in Gillie's eyes before, the one that meant she was getting a crush on someone. "So you walked your dog down here a couple of times and got talking to him, is that right?" Gillie nodded. "And how old is he?" Shona asked. The occupant of a houseboat obviously wasn't going to be a schoolboy, was he? She hoped her friend wasn't biting off more than she could chew here.

"Early twenties, I'd say," said Gillie with a giggle and there it was again: that sheepish look Gillie took on when she fancied someone.

Shona was worried for a number of reasons. Number one, supposing he was a rapist? Number two, their mums would expect them home by five, and they had at least a forty-minute walk to get back. Number three, her father was a police inspector. What if he found out they were keeping a clandestine appointment with an older man who lived on a shabby houseboat on the river after all his warnings to her about staying safe? And number four, there was that small matter of the tiny package which Gillie had asked Shona to look after for her because she'd said she couldn't trust her mum to keep out of her bedroom. In a weak moment, Shona had agreed to look after it. She'd guessed what it was and had nearly had the shock of her life when her father had come into her bedroom just as she'd been hiding it away in her top drawer. But what was Gillie doing with it in the first place? And yesterday, she'd had another weak moment, agreeing to come with Gillie after school today to meet this guy on the houseboat. At least the alarm Dad gave me is in my pocket, Shona thought. She touched it for reassurance.

Her thinking was interrupted by the approach of a tall, dark-haired young man.

"Hey!" he said and smiled. He was very good-looking.

"Hi!" said Gillie, smoothing down her long, blonde hair and fluttering her lashes, which she'd hurriedly coated with mascara in the toilet block, before leaving school. "Er... this is my friend, Shona."

"Blake," he said to Shona and smiled again. "Come aboard, girls. Be my guest!"

Gillie followed Blake aboard the boat, Shona walking reluctantly after her.

\*

"Want some coke?"

The girls had perched themselves on a faded banquette-style seat, which ran much of the length of the boat's living quarters. They both nodded. Blake walked ahead to a kitchenette area, pulled a small glass phial from his pocket and emptied a tiny heap of white powder on a stainless steel tray, which was sitting on a work surface. He opened a drawer, pulled out three straws and popped them on the tray; then, he made his way back to where the girls were sitting.

Shona raised her eyebrows. "Oh, sorry!" she said. "I thought you meant…"

"What, cola?" Blake laughed. "Come on! You'll get more of a buzz with this." He pointed to the powder on the tray, which was now balancing on his lap. He took hold of a straw and used it to manipulate the powder until it became a white line. Then, he snorted nearly half of it into his right nostril.

Gillie was bemused, Shona uncomfortable.

Blake dropped the straw, tapped his nostril with a fingertip, and breathed deeply. "Good stuff," he said and passed the tray to Gillie, who followed suit. To Shona's horror, the tray was then passed to her. Refuse and lose face? Accept and wave her principles goodbye? She felt cornered. Reluctantly, she took up a straw and snorted just a few grains of the powder, trying hard to keep her breathing shallow and hoping that the white dust would simply fall out of her nose if she didn't tap her nostril like the others had done. She returned the tray to Blake.

"So, did you try one of the sweets I gave you?" Blake said to Gillie.

Gillie glanced at Shona and then back at Blake. "Not yet," she said. "I thought I'd wait until the Christmas holidays in case they made me feel like funny or something like I might need to sleep it off."

"Okay, if it worries you, try your first one here. I can look after you, make sure nothing bad happens to you." Blake suddenly swapped seats, moving swiftly from his side of the boat to sit next to Gillie. He slipped his arm around her.

Oh my God, thought Shona. What next? The feeling of discomfort continued to grow inside her. "Do you mind if I get a drink of water?" she said to Blake.

"Help yourself," he whispered. His smile was already a bit silly, and his eyes a little glazed. Gillie also looked dreamy and had now put her head on Blake's shoulder. Shona closed her eyes for a moment to make sure she didn't feel dizzy. Then, she stood up, passed by the others, and entered the kitchenette. She looked around for a glass. She felt slightly euphoric, a sensation she'd never encountered before, but she still had control, unlike Gillie, who was now letting Blake snog her. God, they had to get out of here soon.

Still hunting for a glass, Shona went to open a cupboard door at head height but stopped short: two newspaper articles pinned to a noticeboard next to the cupboard had caught her eye. They were the news reports dealing with the two murders her dad was currently working on. She recognised the photos of the victims immediately. So why did this guy Blake have them pinned up here? And, more to the point, why were both faces crossed out in black felt-tip?

She spun round on her heels and strode purposefully back to her friend.

"Gillie, we've got to go NOW." Blake was busy putting his tongue inside Gillie's mouth: another first for Shona. Never mind being uncomfortable, Shona was now highly disturbed. "GILLIE!"

The raised voice did the trick. Blake and Gillie pulled out of their clinch. "Come on. We've gotta go now," Shona repeated. She grabbed her friend by the wrist and dragged her to her unsteady feet. Gillie giggled, but Shona kept hold of her and pulled her towards the exit. "Sorry," she yelled back at Blake, "we've got to leave now, but thanks for…" She let her sentence tail off. The images of the two murder victims rose again in her mind's eye, and she suddenly put on a spurt and raced out onto the small wooden gangway, yanking a stumbling Gillie behind her.

\*

The two men on the houseboat sat back and relaxed. They'd smoked a little weed and now felt chilled. One closed his eyes and thought about the blonde girl; the other was making a mental count of the profit they'd brought in during the current month. They both wore a smile.

"I think I've found another runner," said Blake. His eyes were still closed.

"Who?"

"A girl I've met. She's already interested in a bit of personal use. But, once she's hooked, just think of all those schoolkids she could sell to in return for a few mind-blowing treats. What a market."

"How young?" Ashley Brown had already done bird for illegal possession and hadn't forgotten that it was a thirteen-year-old who'd shopped him.

"Coming up sixteen, I'd say," said Blake. He opened his eyes. "Just about legal. Lovely." His smile broadened. "I might have to fly the flag again, you know." The flag was a mock-up of a skull-and-crossbones, which the guys ran up the boat's mini flagpole whenever one wished to warn the other, if he was returning to the boat, to stay away; sex in progress.

Ashley laughed but stopped abruptly at the sound of footsteps on the gangway. He peered out of a peephole they'd rigged up to cover the entrance to the houseboat. Both men had tensed, but as Blake saw Ashley relax, he, too, breathed normally again.

"It's only Ben," said Ashley.

\*

*Keep the past at bay; keep the nightmares away...*

He felt as if he was surfing the crest of a wave. A powerful surge carried him through a light blue haze, and when he breathed, his lungs seemed to expand beyond his body's limits. Was he flying? Was he floating? Air or water? Either way, his senses were cranked up to the heights. Brilliant. The mind-blowing journey continued for a while, right up into the dark blue ether, then, gradually, allowed him to descend to earth, fluttering like a feather. He landed gently somewhere on a silica beach where turquoise waters lapped quietly at his feet, and he slept.

When he woke, Ben felt more relaxed than he had been for some time. The coke he'd got from the guys on the boat was top dollar, the best he'd ever used. Add in the fact that his stomach pains seemed to have settled down and, best of all, that he'd made some progress this week in tracking HIM down, and he had to admit, things had ended up looking pretty good right now.

There was just one problem: Jenna. The night they'd met up at the restaurant when she'd had to bring him home early, she'd let slip what she did for a living. If he was going to carry on seeing her – and he wanted to – he'd have to be very, very careful.

The sound of a key in the door brought Ben back to the present moment. There was no need to hide the evidence of his little habit: both his flatmates knew he liked a little coke now and again. Ben heard one of them in the hallway shuffling around, stripping off his outer clothing, and then the sitting room door opened.

"Hi there, bud!" said Ben's flatmate. "Have you eaten yet?" Ben saw him whip out his phone to order some food, but after his trip, he wasn't really hungry. In truth, he was still enjoying the warm afterglow of the experience.

"No. You go ahead. I'll eat later," said Ben.

Rory looked at him, frowned slightly and then smiled. "Have you been at the white stuff again?" He tapped the side of his nose playfully. Ben looked at him blankly. Rory approached Ben and bent over him. "There's a bit of snowy residue under one of your nostrils," he whispered. He stood back and looked at Ben more seriously. "You'd better clean up if you're intending to see your police lady friend tonight, don't you think?"

\*

Rory headed for the kitchen. Strong coffee always helped Ben to stabilise after a trip. He switched on the machine and tapped his fingers rhythmically on the work surface while he waited for the coffee to brew. The opening of the front door made him look up: it was Greg, the other flatmate. Rory heard his footsteps as he made his way down the passageway and his hesitation at the open door of the sitting room where Ben was still reclined in a dreamlike state. There were tuts before Greg resumed his walk straight into the kitchen. Rory observed his concerned expression as he came to a halt in front of him.

"Is it what I think it is?" Greg said gravely.

Rory nodded. He pointed to the machine, which was noisily announcing that coffee was ready. "Thought he could do with sobering up."

"Jeez, no wonder he never has any money," Greg said, exasperated. "That stuff's damned expensive." He shook his head as if in disbelief. "I mean, we've spared him the rent on more than one occasion, haven't we?" He pulled a face. "But we can't do that forever. Guy's gotta take some responsibility."

"Come on, bud," Rory replied with a trace of indulgence in his voice. "He's under a lot of stress at the moment." He glanced at the coffee maker. "Want some?"

"Yeah." Greg drew up a breakfast bar stool and perched himself on it. He watched as Rory poured out three coffees. "So what are we gonna do with him?"

"Be patient," said Rory quietly, in case Ben's sense of hearing was awakening and returning to normal. "Be there for him, you know, like we were for each other when the going got really tough." He paused for thought and then added, "He's got stuff from the past he's trying to deal with."

\*

Shona checked the whereabouts of her mum and brother: both were in their bedrooms with the doors closed. Good.

More important still was to double-check there was no sign of her dad. She peeped out of her bedroom window at the empty driveway and then looked at her watch to try and gauge his time of return. She surely had another hour or two before he came home. Then she went to her top drawer and removed a tiny package from it. She felt slightly sick at the thought of how silly she'd been, both for agreeing to look after the package for Gillie and then for saying yes to that little trip to the houseboat. What was she thinking?

In truth, Gillie was eight months older than Shona – it sometimes seemed like eight years when you saw how mature and attractive Gillie could make herself look – and Shona had to admit her charismatic friend enthralled her. But this time, Shona felt that she herself had gone too far, even for the sake of friendship. She hated the fact she'd gone behind her parents' backs and that she'd abandoned her principles and taken cocaine, even though it was a minuscule amount. And at this very moment in time, she hated herself.

She slammed the drawer shut, immediately regretting that she'd made such a noise, in case it brought her mother rushing in, and she threw herself on her bed. The little package was in her hand, and she lay there staring at it. Gillie had entrusted this item to her for the time being, but as she turned it over in both hands now, she decided she wanted out. Enough. She sat up and ripped open the package, which had been wrapped in white tissue paper. Inside was a small transparent plastic wallet containing six pink pills. What were they then? Ecstasy? Something stronger? Dr Death? She groaned. No!

No way! These had to go back to Gillie. Shona would tell her she couldn't do this any more. ('You do know my dad's a police inspector, don't you?' she mentally rehearsed) and if Gillie protested, called her a wuss or threatened to call off their friendship, she would just have to get on with it. Perhaps the price of Gillie's friendship was too high. She thought about this for a while as she eyed the contents of the little wallet, then she lay back down on her bed and stared up at the ceiling. And just who was this Blake character Gillie was getting involved with? Laughing at them when they thought they'd been offered a fizzy drink, pressuring them to take drugs, doing that tongue thing to Gillie and giving her other drugs to try.

And then there were those newspaper cut-outs.

She closed her eyes and saw again the faces of the two victims with a black felt-tip cross through each one. Why would Blake have done that?

Shona's stomach lurched.

"Oh my God!" she whispered.

She drew herself into a foetal position and whimpered, realising that if she shared her suspicion with her dad, then he'd have to know the rest of the sordid story that went with it, and she wasn't ready to tell him that yet.

\*

They'd come to a nightclub in Richmond called The Blue Bayou and sat on bar stools, picking at olives and sipping drinks. Jenna would have liked a glass of wine to take the edge off the atmosphere between them – Ben seemed rather moody again – but as she was driving, she stuck to a lime and soda spritz. Her date had his usual Rioja. A jazz trio were playing tonight, and the singer was doing a lovely rendition of the old Peggy Lee number, "Fever". It had captured the audience. When it was over, there was loud applause and one or two cheers.

"They're good, aren't they?" Jenna said. "Is that why you suggested coming here?"

"Yeah," Ben replied. "One of my flatmates, Rory, he's into bluesy stuff and recommended this place. The trio sing here at least once a month." He smiled, and Jenna relaxed a little. Ben's smiles had been few and far between since they'd last eaten out together, and she couldn't help wondering if it was because she'd told him that night what her job was. After all, that news seemed to have scared off others. Why not Ben? She smiled back at him and sipped her drink. Decided to play it cool. See where that led.

"Shall we get some more tapas?" Jenna asked. She eyed the menu.

Ben said, "Sure. You order. I'll have whatever you have."

Jenna ordered some chicken on skewers for the two of them. The trio had struck up again and were now doing "Cry Me a River". The singer was only of slight build, but she could really penetrate the depths with her voice, technically and emotionally. The notes were pure velvet, a rich shade of indigo. The audience, once again, was spellbound. Jenna watched Ben out of the corner of her eye. Why did he look so sad? Haunted, even. By what? The music seemed to be reaching into his soul and baring it. He looked so troubled.

The chicken arrived, and they both took a piece, but just like the last time they ate out, Jenna seemed to be the one with the appetite, and so, for a second time, she found herself asking Ben if he felt all right.

"Yeah, I'm fine," he said with a forced smile. The trio took a break, and punters got busy catching up on conversation. Jenna observed a young couple nearby, chatting away animatedly and then roaring with laughter. She envied them and their obvious rapport; she certainly didn't have that with Ben at the moment.

"Do you want a walk by the river?" she asked him. "We could take a short stroll and then come back and catch some more of the performance. What do you think?"

"Sure," he replied. His eyes were everywhere but on her.

That was the moment when Jenna decided that she'd reached the point where questions had to be asked. She'd rather have no relationship than this strained apology of one.

"Eat up!" she said abruptly. She ate; he nibbled.

They wrapped up in heavy coats and put their gloves on. The weather forecast had threatened snow – unusual this side of Christmas – but it certainly felt cold enough outside. They made their way from the bar to the High Street without conversation and then cut down an alleyway to the water's edge. The wind was biting, and they had to keep up a brisk pace just to keep warm. No sitting on a bench tonight, then, romantically wrapped in each other's arms and gazing at the moonlit river, mused Jenna. The thought occurred to her that they wouldn't be doing that anyway, even if it were midsummer. She stopped, took a deep breath and turned to him.

"Do you want out?" she said.

"What?"

"Do you want to finish, you know, go your own way, and I go mine?" Ben looked stunned, and Jenna wondered if she'd jumped to conclusions about him far too hastily.

"Why do you say that?" he asked. He sounded genuinely hurt, and Jenna began to regret asking the question. However, there was no denying that he hadn't been happy in her presence for a couple of weeks.

She softened her voice. "You don't seem happy to be with me any more," she said, searching Ben's face.

He was quiet for a moment. Then he said, "I'm not very happy at the moment, but it has nothing to do with you. I promise." He touched her on the cheek, and she felt her heart melt a little. Then he took her hand in his and lifted it to his lips. She was just going to put her arms around him when he suddenly emitted a loud groan. His face contorted in front of hers, and he bent over.

"What is it?" she yelled.

He drew breath in sharply through his teeth, hissing now in obvious pain, and his features were thoroughly distorted. Then he screamed. "*Aaaaaagh!*"

"Oh, Ben!" Jenna reached into her bag, grabbed her mobile and snapped it open. "Ben, I'm getting help!" She tapped in 999. "Try to take shallow breaths," she said. "I'm calling an ambulance."

\*

Jenna followed the emergency vehicle to St. Joseph's Hospital. She drove at breakneck speed to keep up- not what she would have recommended others do, but with a good excuse and a warrant card in her possession, she thought, what the hell? The ambulance did cross one set of red lights, and she thought she'd better not push her luck too far by doing the same, but she soon had the flashing blue light ahead of her again and reached St. Joseph's A & E in time to see Ben being wheeled into the building.

After explaining to a triage nurse that she was a friend of Ben's, she was then shown to a visitors' room while his condition was assessed. The nurse left her for a short while but soon returned to tell her that Ben was being prepared for surgery. "We think it's appendicitis," said the nurse. "The surgeon's been called, and he's on his way."

So all those suspicions she'd had about Ben faking illness because, she thought, he'd had enough of her were absolutely unfounded. Jenna felt a strong pang of guilt. "I ought to stay," she said to the nurse. "But I do have to be up early in the morning." They both looked at the clock on the wall. Five past eleven.

"Well, he could be some time in surgery, and then he'll probably be out cold for a good while after." The nurse waited for Jenna to say something, but when she didn't, she continued. "So it might be as well to go home and get some sleep."

"I'm actually on an early shift tomorrow," said Jenna. "But I'll come back later in the day." An idea had occurred to her. "I'll see if I can get one of his flatmates to be at his side when he comes round," she said.

Jenna left the hospital, and this time, observing the speed limits with care, she drove to the north side of Kingston. She pulled up in front of Ben's flat and parked behind a motorbike. The clock on the dashboard showed 23.35. She hesitated a moment, wondering if it was right to disturb Ben's flatmates at such a late hour. But she still felt guilty over misjudging his body language, and this made her determined to have someone there when he woke up. She reached the doorstep and rang the bell. A light came on in the hallway, and the door opened. There stood a slim, dark-haired young man of athletic build, looking surprised.

"I'm sorry to get you out of bed…" Jenna began.

"I hadn't got that far, actually," said the young man. He waved an open book in front of her. "One of those 'unputdownables'!"

"… only something's happened to Ben. You're one of his flatmates, right?"

The man looked concerned. "Yeah. What's happened?"

"He's been taken into surgery," Jenna replied. "Looks like appendicitis."

"Are you the police?" Rory asked.

"Well, yes, I am, but I'm off duty at the moment. I'm Ben's girlfriend, actually. Jenna."

Rory half smiled. "Oh, the police lady. Yeah!" He stood back as if to invite her in.

"Er, no," said Jenna, "I won't because I'm on an early shift in the morning and really ought to get back. But I called to see if you or your other flatmate could go up to St. Joseph's so that Ben would see a familiar face when he came round."

"Greg's on night shift tonight," said Rory, "and won't be home till morning. But, yeah, I could go. I'll get my gear on." He indicated the motorbike, which Jenna had parked behind. "Had we better take each other's numbers?" he added.

Jenna was slightly embarrassed that she hadn't thought of it herself. She was clearly too emotional to think straight. "Yes, of course!" she said. They exchanged contact numbers. "Could you let me know first thing in the morning how things have gone during the night?"

"Sure," said Rory.

"Oh, and do you think we should let Ben's parents know that he's in hospital?" Jenna asked.

Rory frowned. "Ben hasn't got any parents," he said almost inaudibly. "Same as Greg and me."

\*

Stanley Fox played golf twice a week, as a rule. Tuesdays and Thursdays were his golfing days. On the other weekdays, he would visit his gym, meet up with his stocks and shares group or take Elvira out to lunch. Best to keep her sweet. And then there was the sultry Mira. They hadn't yet established a routine. In fact, quite the opposite. They liked to play it by ear and liaise as the fancy took them. Much more interesting. It meant he had a certain amount of freedom – he was sure Mira did too – to indulge himself as he pleased.

Tonight, he'd indulged himself back at the children's home. Gerald had left the back door key in its usual hiding place, and Fox had let himself in and made his way down to the girl's room in the basement. At first, he'd been somewhat taken aback by how thin she'd become. Weren't they feeding her properly? But luckily, her lack of flesh didn't seem to spoil the two hours of aggressive sex that followed. At midnight, he'd finally torn himself away from her, later than planned. After all, he still had the wretched dog to take out.

Thoroughly sated, he had reshackled the girl and had let himself out, replacing the key where he'd found it. He'd then climbed back into his car and driven home at some speed.

It was now nearly a quarter to one in the morning as he arrived home, grabbed the leash, summoned Flossie in a stage whisper so as not to disturb Elvira, and set off down the road towards the common. It was late, but he promised himself he would sleep in tomorrow. Maybe he would then have lunch at the golf club and finish up with a steamy session with Mira. She had lately begun to experiment with a bit of bondage and had asked him to restrict her throat. He'd never done the asphyxiation thing before, but he had to admit, it had been exciting. He'd asked her to try it on him. Same effect. He couldn't wait to try it out again.

The dog trotted on ahead of him, following a familiar route. He followed Flossie across a road and presently found the path over the common. The night was cold, and the grass already sparkled with frost under a bright moon. Fox enjoyed the peace and tranquillity around him. He could hear no sound save for the muffled rustlings of the dog in the undergrowth, the occasional click of a swooping bat and, yes, perhaps one other person taking a late stroll at some distance behind him.

The path across the common wound its way through a semi-wooded area. Man and dog walked on. Fox breathed in the night air and continued to reflect on his newly discovered pleasure. Maybe he would try the asphyxia thing with the wild child. But then, he thought, she would never cooperate. Whatever he'd wanted from her, he'd always had to take by force. Actually, he had to admit, that was part of the fun.

He realised he'd temporarily lost track of the dog. "Floss," he called out in the silence. He listened. He could hear two noises: her rooting around some way ahead of him… and the sound of those footsteps approaching behind him.

Asphyxiation, he thought again, as he carried on walking. What a revelation! He realised he was becoming aroused. He closed his eyes to relive the thrill…

… and, for just one nanosecond, wondered what sort of surreal experience he was undergoing as his throat suddenly seemed to be constricted for real. He thrust his hands upwards, only too aware in the next second that someone really *did* have a cord around his neck.

"I'm the one who got away," the assailant whispered harshly in his ear. Fox gasped for air, but he'd heard, and he'd registered what was said.

"You said I was *yours*," the biker continued through gritted teeth. His grip on the ligature was unrelenting. His prey now suspected he knew who this was but was powerless to act. He began to weaken at the knees and go limp.

"Well, now you're *mine*," the killer said.

The last sensation Stanley Fox felt was the gush of warm urine down his legs as his bladder released.

\*

"Shona Brady!" Shona sat up with a start.

"Yes, miss?"

"Shona, you're in detention for not paying attention in class on more than one occasion this week, and here you are still staring out of the window!"

"Sorry, Miss Oliver," said Shona. The apology was sincerely meant.

"What's going on? You're not normally like this. I don't think we've ever had you in detention before, have we?"

"No, miss."

"So, what is going on?"

Shona thought quickly. She did her best to make her voice sound pathetic. "Problems at home, miss," she said.

Shona knew that her mother's illness was well known to many of the school staff and that they were, on the whole, sympathetic to the disruption to family life that it could cause. The gamble worked.

"I'm sorry to hear that, Shona." The teacher looked at her watch. "Listen, you've been here long enough now anyway. Pack up, go home, and try to come back tomorrow with a better work ethic. Okay?"

"Yes, miss. Thanks, miss."

Shona packed up her things, put on her coat and scarf and headed out into the exit corridor. It wasn't quite four-fifteen, but the light outside had already grown dim. Luckily, she'd been able to leave a message on her mum's mobile, telling her she'd be late tonight. She'd given the reason that she was staying at another after-school club, but, God, how many more lies would she have to tell to cover her tracks?

Back in her bedroom, she rummaged through her drawer and put her hand on the little wallet with the six pills inside. She bit her lip. When was she going to find the courage to give this back to Gillie? She felt sick. Even more so when she asked herself the inevitable follow-up question: when was she going to tell her father about Blake?

She lay on her bed. Tears welled up in her eyes, and she rolled over, buried her face in the duvet and sobbed. She imagined herself telling her father what she'd been up to, how disappointed he'd be. But then something her dad had said to her a long time ago flashed up in her memory: 'Always consider the worst thing that could happen, then the problem itself won't usually seem so bad.'

The Brady family all knew the worst thing that could happen: that unspeakable act that could deprive them of their mother if depression ultimately got the better of her. Nothing could be worse than that, Shona thought. She wiped away her tears, rolled over again and sat up.

Resolve.

Immediately, she felt a bit stronger. She steeled herself, grabbed hold of her mobile and tapped in Gillie's number, and when Gillie answered, she told her, just like that, that she couldn't look after the little package any longer; that she was bringing it straight round to her; that she didn't want to be involved in the drugs scene, thanks. Shona hardly waited for her friend to reply before she cut her off and immediately tapped her dad's mobile number. Brady picked up at the other end.

"Dad?"

"Hey. What's wrong?" Brady wasn't used to getting calls from his daughter while he was on duty, and his mind naturally leapt to the conclusion that something was up with Kathleen.

"I've done something very silly, Dad, and I need to talk to you about it." She sounded distressed.

Brady's office door was open, so he headed towards it.

"Do you want to tell me about it now?" he said, closing the door.

"No." He heard Shona sob. "I'd rather not tell you on the phone. When are you coming home?"

Brady looked at his watch and then at his desk. His heart sank. It was covered in files. The CIT team had had a field day in here today. But he had an idea. "I'll be home within the hour." There was no reply. "Shona?"

"Yes?" came a small voice laden with tears.

"Darling, whatever it is, we'll get it sorted out. Hang on in there. I'm heading home now." He closed up his mobile and summoned Jenna on the office phone. When she arrived, he pointed at his desk.

"Would you do me a favour?" he asked. Jenna could tell by his voice that something was wrong. He sounded exhausted and deflated. She guessed that a problem had arisen at home.

"Of course," she said. "You need to go."

They stood and looked each other straight in the eyes.

"I'm very grateful," he said in little more than a whisper.

Jenna's heart went out to him. She touched him on the arm. "Go!" she said.

In a little over thirty minutes, he was back home with Shona, sitting on her bed, mouth agape at what he was hearing.

\*

Blake Drummond sat across the table from Detectives Cartwright and Grant in the interview room while Brady, Jones and Atherton looked on from behind a one-way glass. Brady hadn't wasted any time after Shona's confession; a phone call to the team had stopped anyone due to leave from going home and had precipitated a swift arrest of Drummond and Brown. Both were now in custody. Atherton had already run preliminary checks on the two young men, and it had turned out that one already had form for possession of a class A drug.

But possession of drugs was one thing; murder was quite another, thought Brady.

He studied Blake Drummond carefully. Did he fit the

profile they'd begun to build for their killer? Young, athletic and strong. That was a good start. Grant was now asking him why he had pictures of the two murder victims displayed in the houseboat. Brady focused hard on Drummond's face. After so many years in the force, he'd almost got it down to a fine art, detecting a lie in a facial expression. But Drummond was looking genuinely scared.

"Hey," he said, "the fact they're dead has nothing to do with me." Brady noticed he looked Jamie straight in the eyes when he answered him.

"Then why the display?" asked the detective.

"And why," asked his colleague, "have you scored out their faces in felt-tip?"

Drummond was silent for several moments, and then, to everyone's surprise, he put his fingers on his eyes to hold back tears. Cartwright and Grant exchanged glances. Behind the glass, Brady and the women did the same.

"Crocodile tears, do you think?" whispered Atherton to her boss.

"Not sure," said Brady thoughtfully. "Let's see what he says next."

The detectives waited for Drummond to compose himself. It took a few minutes, and then he dropped a bombshell.

"*They fucked me*," he said. His voice was high and shaky.

"Tell us more," said Jamie, adopting a quieter, more sympathetic tone.

Drummond heaved a sigh, wiped his face on his sleeve and then spoke haltingly. "I was taken into care in a children's home when I was eight." He paused and wiped his nose again. "There were some men who used to visit… They abused us…"

"How many men are we talking?" asked Cartwright.

"Four," Drummond replied, barely audibly. "Oh, and the manager. Five."

"And is there a connection between those five men and the faces displayed in the houseboat?" Grant asked, trying to avoid a leading question.

"Yeah," Drummond replied. "They were two of them. I was just glad someone had the balls to finish them off after what they did to us. That's why I saved the newspaper cutouts." His chest heaved – another dry sob. "You know, like displaying their scalps?" he intoned as if it was a question.

"Which children's home?" Cartwright asked.

"Merrydown."

Behind the glass, all three detectives looked at one another.

"And who were the other three men?" Grant continued in his sympathetic voice, which seemed to have calmed down the interviewee.

"Well, like I said, there was the manager, the one who ran the place, Mr Fox. Then there was a priest. Always came in one of those long black robes…"

"Catholic," whispered Brady behind the glass.

"… and there was one other man who came, and all the children were told to be on their best behaviour with him; otherwise, he might arrest us and lock us up. Well, anyway, that's what we were told. So we thought he must have been a copper."

"Shit," said Brady under his breath. He turned to look at Jenna, who raised her eyebrows to him.

"Did you ever learn these men's names?" asked Cartwright.

"No, apart from Stanley Fox, of course." Drummond paused again and pulled a quizzical face. "They used to call each other silly names, you know, fictional stuff, like Bluebeard or something. But other than that, I couldn't tell you any more."

"And how long did the abuse go on for?" asked Jamie.

"It was still going on when I left, as far as I know."

"And how old were you then?"

"Sixteen." Drummond wiped his nose again.

"Why didn't you report the abuse to the police when you left?" Andy asked.

Drummond shrugged his shoulders. They all waited for a reply. He shuffled a little in his seat.

"Because one of them *was* the police, so I thought you guys weren't to be trusted. Anyway, by then, I was on drugs, wasn't I?" He looked down at his hands, which he'd interlaced, and then up again at his interviewers. "I needed something to blot out the memories," he said defensively. He paused. "And you don't think I was going to come anywhere near you lot with that sort of habit, do you?"

\*

The five detectives sat in Brady's office.

"He could be genuine," said Brady.

"Or he could be a great performer," said Andy Cartwright.

"But if he's genuine," said Jenna, "we might need to know who else was at Merrydown with him."

"True," said Brady. He crossed his arms, deep in thought. The others waited. "Helen, I want you to run more substantial checks on Drummond and Brown. Has either had military training or anything approaching physical training – gym membership even? You know the sort of thing." He turned to Jamie, who pre-empted him.

"Do you want me to go back to Drummond and ask him for information about the kids who were with him at the home?" he asked.

"Yeah, see if he remembers anything unusual or significant about anyone who was there. Andy, start the interview with Brown. Was he a resident of the home, too? Ask the same questions you asked Drummond." Brady turned to Jenna. "Jenna, I want you to go to Merrydown."

"That's one of the children's homes we went to, isn't it?" said Helen to Jenna.

"Yes, I know," Brady cut in before Jenna could speak. He sounded a little exasperated. When he was delegating, it didn't go down well if his train of thought was interrupted, in case he lost track. "But in the light of new evidence, Jenna, I think it's time to look through their files: paper files, e-files, whatever, especially relating to the period Drummond was there. I'll arrange for a warrant for tomorrow morning. I'll also arrange one for the houseboat, so you two…" he indicated the two males "… can locate its owner and then do the boat over."

The phone on Brady's desk rang, and the younger detectives waited while their boss took the call.

"Shit and more shit!" Brady spat the words out. "They've just found another body."

\*

Unusually, Stanley Fox's body had not been discovered by a dog-walker. December had arrived, and a spell of very cold weather had prevented the corpse from rapidly decomposing. Scents that a dog may have picked up were, therefore, at a very low level. Instead, it was the misfortune of two thirteen-year-old boy cyclists on their way home from school who, needing to relieve themselves, had entered the thicket on the common and got a whole lot more than they'd bargained for.

Dr Keith Wilson guessed, before he and his forensic team had even arrived by the victim's side, what they might see. The victim lay on his side, and sure enough, the purple face, the swollen tongue, the bruised throat and the incongruously placed red rose were all there to greet him. So was the 'V' signature on the buttocks. Brady had sent Helen Atherton and three other DCs, including Pete Chambers, the dog handler, with an eager German shepherd by his side, to attend the pathologist, and they immediately set up police tape and began scouring the area around the body. The murderer seemed to operate like a shadow, without a trace on either the corpse or the site. No footprints. Of course not. The ground was rock hard. Helen suddenly found herself thinking of Jack the Ripper: that famously unsolved mystery. Would these murders also go unsolved? The killer always seemed to be at least one step ahead of them.

While her colleagues combed the thicket, Helen ducked her head into the forensic tent and watched Wilson turn the body a little more and push up clothing from the waist. He was looking at the livor mortis. "Allowing for freezing temperatures affecting the movement of blood," said Wilson, "I'd estimate time of death at approximately forty-eight hours ago."

"Then that at least eliminates one of our theories, doesn't it?" Helen said. Wilson looked at her and temporarily halted his examination, inviting her to explain. "After the case review, Inspector Brady memoed all of us about Sunday possibly being a significant day for the murderer. Can we now safely say that Sundays have no significance?"

Wilson nodded. "This act was definitely carried out later than Sunday. I'd say Tuesday night." He looked back at the body." When you're finished here, I'll get the deceased moved," he said.

Helen left the tent and stood and waited for the dog handler and his reliable sidekick, Mitzi, to complete their search. After a while, Pete shook his head as if to say 'nothing here'. Helen popped her head back inside the tent. "Yeah, time to move him," she said to Wilson. She would have loved to find something crucial to report back to everyone, but this time, at least, it wasn't to be. She left the pathologist instructing his forensic team to prepare the body for the journey back and nodded to the others who'd scoured the thicket to stop their search. The scene of the crime appeared to be spotless.

She turned to make her way back to her car, which she'd parked on the edge of the common when she was promptly approached by a young man who'd been skulking on the perimeter of the thicket. He was holding a notepad in one hand and a biro in the other. "So is it true that a body has been found on the common?" he said. His pen was poised to write, and she immediately realised he was a hack.

"There has been an incident," Helen replied, "but right now, it would be best to keep away from the area and let forensics do their work. A full report of the incident will be made public in due course," she said.

"I'm from the *Thames Herald*," he said as if that would persuade her to tell him more.

"So?" she said curtly.

"My readers need to know if they can safely walk this common or not."

"As I said, Mister…?"

"Brogan. Josh Brogan," he said.

"As I said, Mr Brogan, there has been an incident that the police are investigating. So let me just say: the sooner you let us get on with our work, the sooner we'll have information available for the public." And with that, she stepped to one side to indicate that, for her part, the conversation was over. She thought he would take the hint.

Instead, he said, "Has the killer used the same signature on the victim's butt?"

"No comment!" she replied. "And may I remind you that hampering an investigation is an arrestable offence, so please don't go beyond the tape and make a nuisance of yourself."

"Don't worry. I have other sources," Brogan said cockily and, winking at her, he turned and walked back to his car.

Helen decided that when she got back to the station, the encounter with Brogan would be the first thing she would report to Brady. She'd found Brogan's allusion to 'other sources' especially worrying.

*

Dominic Brady sat in his office, consulting the Missing Persons database. Andy and Jamie were currently looking over the houseboat at Teddington Lock while Jenna was revisiting Merrydown. So he was on his own at the moment.

On his own, that is, except for those nice people from the CIT team (or the Shit Team, as Andy called it.) Actually, Brady thought, as he scanned the most recent postings, they have at least been polite and methodical. It wasn't their fault they were called in. He continued to search, scrolled over something, which switched on a light bulb in his head and scrolled back to it. A Mrs Elvira Fox had called the police the previous day: her husband, Stanley, had not returned from walking the dog the night before.

Stanley Fox: the manager of Merrydown when Drummond had been a resident. If this new victim turned out to be Fox – and Helen had phoned in to confirm it *was* a rose murder – then the man was the third of the five men Drummond had mentioned. Of course, Drummond himself was still not in the clear. He did have an alibi for yesterday when he'd been helping the team with their enquiries, but he'd still been at large the night before that. So, in theory, he could have carried out this murder as well.

But Brady's gut told him otherwise.

He picked up the phone, dialled Mrs Fox's number and braced himself.

\*

"Other sources?" said Brady to Helen as she stood before him in his office. He was due to see Mrs Fox in the next few minutes, but this was important and needed his attention. "So, who's passing Brogan information, then?" The question was meant more for himself than Helen, but she answered anyway.

"Has to be someone on the inside, doesn't it?" she said.

"Listen, I've got someone coming in for a possible identification of the dead body from the common, and I've got to go," said Brady. "But leave it with me. When I've finished downstairs, I'll get Andy and Jamie to go and lean heavily on our nice neighbourhood reporter. See if he cracks under pressure."

\*

Elvira Fox couldn't help but remember what her father used to say: "It's an ill wind that blows nobody any good." Usually, he wouldn't even finish the line. He'd say, "Ah well! It's an ill wind..." As little girls, when she and her sisters heard him say it, they had no idea what he meant, but they nevertheless had fun mimicking that very phrase when their father was out of earshot. But the older Elvira had grown, the more she'd understood what her father had been driving at. It's not often that you can't find something good resulting from something bad. She hadn't been overly distraught when she'd identified her husband's body, although the sight of his swollen, bluish face did cause her to catch her breath. But Stanley had always put Stanley first. Sometimes, he'd hardly even give her the time of day, so hell-bent was he on pursuing his own pleasures. She also knew he was promiscuous and had been throughout their marriage. In the end, she'd stuck it out for the trappings: money was plentiful, and life was easy.

And now he was gone.

Not such a bad thing, although she wouldn't have wished the manner of his going on anybody. What had really worried her was that Flossie had also been missing. Living without her dog would be much more difficult to adjust to than living without her husband.

But then that nice inspector, the one who looked like the actor in *Schindler's List* with the Irish name, he'd been so kind, assuring her that if Flossie was micro-chipped, which she was, then there was every chance of getting her back. 'Why not contact Battersea?' he'd suggested. 'Chances are she's already there.' And Elvira did. And she was!

Once her mind had been put at rest over her dog's whereabouts, Elvira found that she was much more relaxed, which disposed her to answer the inspector's questions more fully. She was able to tell him about her husband's stocks and shares club and could even name all of its members for him. She gave him details of the golf club, where Stanley seemed to have spent an increasing amount of time recently, and she told the inspector that her husband regularly used a gym and gave him that address, too.

The inspector had then asked her to cast her mind back to the time Stanley had been in charge of the children's home. He enquired if Stanley had fallen out with anyone there, also wanting to know if she could remember any unusual or significant event that occurred there while her husband was in charge. She didn't really understand where he was coming from with this question and instinctively answered no. Not that she had much to do with the day-to-day running of the home. Dyslexia had prevented her from undertaking secretarial or administrative work there, and besides, she didn't like children anyway. But she would have liked to stay longer with the inspector. He really was so handsome and charming, though his furrowed brow betrayed the fact that he carried the weight of the world on his shoulders. So she thought she would go home (after collecting Flossie, of course) and give a lot more thought to his question about unusual or significant events at the children's home. See if she could come up with something. That would give her an excuse to see the inspector again.

Yes, it was an ill wind!

\*

Brady took Detective Helen Atherton with him to Greenacres Golf Club the next day. Jenna had called in early with a migraine, unusual for her. In fact, when Brady thought about it, he'd never known Jenna to have a single day off. As they drove through the rush-hour traffic, he asked Helen if Jenna had suffered from migraine before. Helen said that she'd known Jenna since the beginning of secondary school and only remembered two previous occasions: at fourteen, when her mother died, and at eighteen when she was involved in a car accident during post-A-level celebrations. "She wasn't the one driving, by the way!" Helen quickly added.

Brady was thoughtful. "So what might have shocked her?" He perceived a common link to the migraines and asked the question as much of himself as of Helen.

She, though, was irked by the question. It seemed intrusive. What was up with him? Didn't he trust Jenna? Did he think she was throwing a sickie? When Helen had left the flat earlier, Jenna was on her back, white as a sheet, complaining of blinding lights disturbing her field of vision. Such genuine suffering made Helen feel protective.

"She was quite ill when I left her this morning, sir," said Helen defensively. "So you don't need to doubt her word," she added sharply for good measure.

Brady immediately saw he'd been misunderstood. "I

don't doubt her, Helen." He gently braked as he approached a crossing. "I would never doubt her." A moment of silence followed this statement, which made Helen turn to observe her boss. She was startled to see something approaching tenderness in his expression. "You have to remember," he said, and Helen watched his expression quickly revert to normal, "that as a superior officer, I have a duty of care to her and all of you, so if I've exposed her to a situation which has affected her well-being…" he paused to turn into the gates of Greenacres "… then I need to help make it right. You know what I'm saying. Minimise risks to my staff; health and safety at work; all that."

"Sorry. Didn't quite see where you were coming from," Helen said, embarrassed. She wondered how much to tell Brady, but as he'd been open with her (more open than he realised, she thought), she decided to return the favour. "Actually, a couple of things have happened." She waited for him to park the car in front of the clubhouse and switch the engine off before going on. "Her boyfriend, Ben, is in Intensive Care with a burst appendix." Brady looked suitably concerned. "But, funnily enough," Helen continued, "I don't think that's what's got to her. I think it was something she discovered at Merrydown Children's Home yesterday." Now Brady looked very serious because this might really call his duty of care into question. "Her best friend from primary school days, a girl called Lauren, went missing when they were both ten," she told Brady. "And Jenna found out yesterday that Lauren was admitted around the age of ten…" She looked at Brady with a frown "… to Merrydown."

\*

Sebastian Clarke was a fit fifty-something who held the position of Club Captain at Greenacres. He showed Brady and Atherton into his office and shut the door.

"So Stanley Fox is dead?" he began, shaking his head in disbelief.

"I'm afraid so," said Brady. He'd already had a conversation with Clarke over the phone. "What we need to ask you for is any information about him that you think may be helpful to us."

Clarke shrugged. "Well, he was certainly here regularly. Played off a handicap of eight. Do you play?" He looked at Brady, who shook his head. "Fox wasn't everybody's cup of tea, though."

"What do you mean by that?" Helen asked. She was slightly annoyed that the golfing question had excluded her because she played off a handicap of twelve. But there, she thought, misogyny is alive and well, and I always knew it was, so why should I be surprised?

Clarke answered. "Bit of an ego, if I'm honest. Flashed his money around. It's not right, is it?" He stopped and thought. "Actually, you'll get more from Mira than you will from me. She knew him better."

"Mira?" Brady asked.

"Mira Dinetski. Works behind the bar here." He lowered his voice to a conspiratorial whisper. "I think they were having an affair, you know." Clarke let the information sink in, and then he said, "Treating your wife like that – it's not right, is it?" Helen observed Brady very carefully, but, as usual, his face remained inscrutable. The question was treated as rhetorical.

*

Sebastian Clarke had warned them that Mira had yet to be told of Fox's death, so Brady was left with only seconds to prepare to break the news to her. He looked up as a voluptuous woman in her forties with striking red hair was ushered into Clarke's office and introduced to them. Her warm smile soon evaporated, though, when Brady explained why they were there.

"So we'd be grateful if you could tell us anything at all which you think might be significant," he said. "Anything out of the ordinary…" He trailed off and silently appealed to Helen to do something as Mira's tears were starting to flow. Brady looked at Clarke for some unspoken male encouragement while Helen comforted Mira. It took a few minutes, but then, with tissues in hand and Helen's arm around her shoulders, Mira looked up at Brady and nodded to indicate that she was ready. "As I said," Brady continued, doing his best to keep his tone sympathetic and respectful, "if there's anything you can tell us…"

Mira dabbed at her face. Her make-up was obviously waterproof as it remained immaculate in spite of her tears. The officers waited for her to collect her thoughts. Initially, she looked off into the distance, expressionless. Gradually, her features became more animated and then she nodded again as if to signal that something had surfaced in her memory. She began slowly, in heavily accented speech. "Always same people here at club. So I notice new people if they come. New man come last week. He wear bike leather, but where is bike? No bike in car park." Brady listened attentively. "I see new man speak to Stanley by Stanley's car. Long time speaking. I watch them from clubhouse window. Stanley tell me later, new man have…er… family look…"

"Family look?" Brady turned to Helen.

"He think he knows him, but not sure," Mira said.

"Familiar look?" Helen offered.

"Yes. Familiar." Mira turned to the club captain. "Mr Clarke, you show him round, yes?"

"Well, yes, I believe I did," Clarke said. "Pleasant chap. Ex-army, I think."

Helen shot a glance at Brady, who wondered if they finally had a lead.

"We need to hear more about this individual from you, Mr Clarke," he said. "We'll also need a description of him from both of you, and I'm going to ask each of you to sit with one of our artists back at the station so that we can draw up a facial likeness."

"You asked us if we noticed anything out of the ordinary," Clarke said as he prepared to show them out. "Well, it's probably nothing, but I was surprised that the young man never took his gloves off, you know, not even to shake hands with me." He shook his head disapprovingly. "It's not right, is it?"

\*

The houseboat search was underway. Detectives Cartwright and Grant were not surprised to find a selection of cocaine pouches, ecstasy and ketamine tablets stashed away on board the *Rose Marie*, as Drummond had disclosed a drug habit during his interview, and Brown had already done time for possession. What did surprise them was the sheer volume of the stuff. Such quantities were clearly not just for personal use.

The two newspaper cuttings were still pinned to the noticeboard in the kitchenette. Andy looked closely at the manner in which the photographs had been scored out. Angrily, that was certain. But angry enough for murder? He knew his boss was unconvinced, but he wasn't so sure. He wandered back into the main body of the boat and perched himself on the banquette. "So what else did you get out of Drummond yesterday afternoon?" he called to Jamie, who was still rummaging through the boat's sleeping quarters. Initially, there was no reply, but then a partition curtain was drawn back, and Jamie emerged.

"What's that?"

Andy repeated the question.

"He told me what he could remember about being a resident at Merrydown," Jamie said as he approached the banquette and settled himself beside Andy. "Said they had 'parties' where the abuse took place. They called them 'parties'!" Jamie tutted with an ironic laugh. He closed his eyes and shook his head as if trying to imagine what life must be like for a child experiencing such abuse. "Anyway, he gave me half a dozen names of children he remembered being there with him at the home. We'll have to follow up on those when we're done here. He told me that one boy and one girl in particular were the favourites; of course, in that context, being a favourite meant getting abused more regularly."

"Did he remember their names? The favourites?" Andy asked.

"No. He was a few years younger than the two of them. But he did say that after he was eleven, he never saw them again. Apparently, one day, he asked the housekeeper where they were, and he was told to mind his own business." Jamie sighed. By nature, he was a glass-half-full person, but he had to admit that, some days, the nature of the job ensured that his glass was tipped over and completely emptied.

"Did he say anything else?"

"Well, there was a rumour that the older boy ran away. But Drummond never heard any more about the girl. What about you and Brown? How did you get on?"

"Brown was never in care," said Andy. "Lived with his mother and grandmother. Usual story: got in with a bad crowd and started using. Caught in possession. Did time." Andy shrugged his shoulders. "But at no time did I get the feeling that he was in any way involved with our murder enquiry." He looked at his colleague. "Not sure about Drummond's innocence, though."

"Brady doesn't think so, does he?" said Jamie.

"So he's never wrong?" Andy protested, his voice raised.

"You don't like him much, do you?" Jamie said.

Andy looked down at the floor. What did he really think of Inspector Brady? Actually, he admired him. He shrugged again. "He's always bloody right, though, isn't he?" he said in a calmer tone. "I'm sure Jenna thinks he's some sort of superhero."

Jamie raised his eyebrows in surprise. "What makes you say that?" he asked.

"Well, there's a way she looks at him." Andy mimicked crush behaviour, fluttering his eyelids and pursing his lips. It made Jamie half smile.

"So what's it to you how she looks at him?" Jamie asked jokingly, still smiling and anticipating a jocular return.

There was silence for a few seconds. Time for Andy to take a deep breath and for Jamie's smile to disappear.

Andy said, "Mate, I'm crazy about her."

# PART 4

# HEARTS

DCI Delgado had ordered another case review, and the team had now gathered in the incident room to exchange up-to-date information and ideas. This time, though, there were two extra personnel present: members of the CIT team. Before CIT had arrived at the station, Brady had decided, following his conversation with Jenna, that details of the rose should be removed from everyone's file until CIT had finished there. He knew he was stabbing in the dark. He'd actually played around with the idea of deleting the name of Merrydown from the files, but eventually, he thought this would hamper his team's discussions too much. After all, Merrydown now seemed to be at the centre of the entire investigation. So, the rose was his second choice. He'd been determined to hold back *something* from the visitors. He would have liked the 'V' signature to remain top secret, too, but thanks to Brogan and his 'source', the detail had already appeared in the papers. He was, therefore, forced to content himself with the enigmatic rose remaining undercover. Of course, he had to clear this action with Delgado. It took some persuading, but as soon as Drummond had mentioned that one of his abusers may well have been a police officer and Delgado saw that his 'fishy' theory might actually hold water, then he agreed to back Brady's idea.

"I'm putting my head above the parapet here, you know," he told Brady. "You'd better be right!"

Brady knew he was taking a risk by withholding information from CIT. He now stood in front of the incident board and prepared to recap. "So there's a killer out there somewhere who, we now have good reason to believe, may have been a resident at Merrydown Children's Home." He flipped the lid off a red marker pen, ready to assemble notes, which would present the team with their latest suspect profiles. They, in turn, were prepared to make their notes on paper or iPads.

"Suspect number one: Blake Drummond," said Brady. "What do we know about him?" Bullet points under his name soon accumulated on the board and included the fact that he'd been a Merrydown resident at the right time, had a motive and had two victims' faces displayed in his rented boat. "And suspect number two? What have we discovered about him?" he asked. A volley of responses ensured that the second profile rapidly grew. Brady wrote quickly, and then he stood back to allow everyone to assimilate the list. He read out each point in turn:

- Merrydown resident?/motive
- IC1 male Caucasian
- Mid/late 20s
- Biker?
- Tattoo?

Helen suggested the tattoo. She remembered the Greenacres Golf Club captain telling them that the mystery man who spoke to Stanley Fox sometime before his death had seemed not to want to take his gloves off. "Could be a distinguishing mark which he wishes to hide," she said.

They all had a copy in front of them of the artistic impression of this second suspect, which the two golf club employees had helped the police draw up. The young man in the illustration was dark-haired and had highly symmetrical features and strong lips. Brady asked them to look closely at the drawing and comment if they wished.

"He'd go down well with the ladies then?" Andy suggested, always keen to raise a smile in others.

"Not all ladies!" Helen quickly corrected him.

Brady looked at the CIT officers. They were busy making their notes. He hoped that his colleagues would remember not to mention the rose, although whether or not that made a blind bit of difference was anybody's guess.

He looked back at the list on the board. Surely there was something else – something that Clarke had said when he'd talked to Brady on his own and more fully. He fiddled with the marker for a moment while his gaze remained focused on the bullet points. Then it came to him.

"There's one more bullet to add for the second suspect," he said and proceeded to write 'Americanisms' at the foot of the list. He turned around and explained. "Sebastian Clarke said the young man was definitely English but used more than one Americanism."

"Such as?" asked Jamie. "Surely everyone uses Americanisms these days?"

"'Eatery,' replied Brady. "That one in particular jarred with Clarke." ('It's not right, is it?' echoed in Brady's mind.)

"Eatery?" said Andy, bemused. "What the hell's wrong with that? Everybody says 'eatery' these days!"

"Anyway, how might Americanisms be significant?" Delgado cut in, trying to move the discussion forward.

Helen remembered Clarke's confirmation that the young man he'd shown round the club was ex-army. "Sir, the use of Americanisms might show he's spent his military time in the company of Americans, in Afghanistan, say."

"And such a detail could help us narrow down our search," Brady added.

Delgado shook his head. "I'm tending to agree with Detectives Grant and Cartwright. People pick up all kinds of stuff off the TV these days. You don't need a tour of duty in Afghanistan to end up with a few American expressions in your vocabulary."

Brady shrugged his shoulders. "Fair enough," he said. "It was just a thought." He turned to Dinesh and asked if he had anything to add, following his thorough going-over of Fox's hard drive. Dinesh, who'd been especially busy recently, deleting rose details from e-files at Brady's request, shook his head. "Only to say that it contained the same kind of child porn as the other two, with plenty of adult porn thrown in for good measure. Oh, and I'll be looking into his mobile today."

"Good. Keep us updated." Brady looked anxiously at the pathologist. "Keith? Anything?"

"Same MO in all three cases," Keith Wilson replied guardedly.

Relief coursed through Brady's veins. The pathologist

had been careful to avoid detail, so at least one of the killer's signatures had successfully been kept from the CIT team – for now. "Well, let's get this guy's pretty face out in the public domain and see what the press release brings in," he said.

He noticed Delgado lifting his head to catch his attention. "Just to let everyone know," Delgado said, "that our commander, no less, intends to be present at the press release."

Brady nodded. "That'll raise the profile of our case in the public eye," he said. "And I hear the commander's got a reputation for crisis management. It's probably just what we need right now." Deciding it was time to conclude the proceedings, he added, "Does anyone have anything final to say?" He noticed Andy muttering something to Jamie and Jamie nodding.

"Yeah," said Jamie. "Andy just reminded me. When I spoke to Drummond earlier this week, he thought he remembered a rumour going around Merrydown that an older boy had run away from the home. He said this boy had been a favourite amongst the abusers. It's a bit of a long shot, I know, but if anyone should have a motive, you know what I mean? So you might want to add 'runaway' with a question mark to the second profile." Jamie stopped to let others take notes. "He said the boy was one of two favourites, actually," he continued. "The other one was a girl. And when the boy disappeared, *she* was never seen again either."

Jenna abruptly shut her eyes. In her line of vision, she could see flashing bright haloes.

*

She'd been taken to the station medical room and laid out on a bed there. Brady, still concerned about his duty of care, had stayed with Jenna for a while but, observing that her condition was not improving and realising she was unfit to drive, had insisted that he take her home. Horizontal, with eyes still firmly closed, she'd protested that she would soon be fine or, at the very least, that Helen could take her back later. But Brady had pointed out that Helen would be on duty for another six hours. He also had an ulterior motive: getting her to open up in private about this mysterious friend of hers at Merrydown might not only help Jenna to express bottled-up emotions, but it could also provide him with more information about Merrydown itself and its residents. After all, Jenna had spent the best part of a day there, and Brady hadn't really had time yet for a de-brief with her. In the end, his insistence had succeeded, and he'd driven her back to her flat.

He parked the car and hurried round to open the door for her. She was ghostly white. Without words, he helped her out, locked the car and fastened the two remaining buttons of her coat for her, as the wind was bitter. She stood, squinting through partially open eyelids, and when he put his arm around her for support, she offered no resistance and leant into him. Together, they slowly walked up the path, past the giant cedar, to her front door.

"Keys?" he said.

"In my handbag," she whispered.

He let go of her for a moment to fumble in her bag, located the keys and opened the door. Then he helped her inside. "My bedroom's down the passageway, on the right," she said. Finally, he helped her lie down on her bed and drew a duvet over her.

"Can I get you anything? Tea, for example?" said Brady.

In truth, she felt a little nauseous, but she thought tea might help. After all, she knew the root cause of her current problem was almost certainly shock, and sweet tea was supposed to be a well-known remedy.

"That would be nice," she said. He looked at her as she lay there, perfectly still, with her eyes closed. He thought she looked like an angel, and his breath caught slightly.

By the time Brady had found his way around Jenna's kitchen and brought her a mug of tea, the patient was beginning to rally. Brady moved her dressing-table stool to the bedside and sat himself down.

"So, do you feel up to telling me about your friend – the one who went missing – or am I asking too much?" Brady said softly.

Jenna squinted at him and laughed a little. "So that's why you insisted on bringing me home!" she said. "So you could give me the third degree!" She laid her head back on the pillow again and shut her eyes. Then she took a deep breath. "My friend who went missing? Her name was Lauren," Jenna began. "Lauren Bristow. When she disappeared from my life, it was like a bereavement because we'd been so close." Brady didn't interrupt. "I suppose Helen filled that space for me at secondary school…" Jenna opened her eyes, propped herself up on one elbow and sipped her tea. "But I never forgot Lauren. Then, the other day, I found her name in the files at Merrydown." She sipped more tea. He'd made it far too sweet for her, but it was going down well nevertheless. "And then I heard Jamie say… well, you know…"

"The girl Drummond said was a favourite," said Brady,

"that could have been someone else. Don't automatically assume the worst."

Jenna finished her drink and carefully sat up. "My vision's actually a bit better now," she said, "but I suppose I'd better see a GP, hadn't I?"

"If you hadn't mentioned it, I would have insisted, actually," Brady replied. "Do you want to phone up and see if they've got a free spot for you now?" He handed her handbag to her. "And if they have, I'll give you a lift there too. Then on the way, you can tell me more about your trip to Merrydown… and I can ask you how we might solve the problem of an annoying little journalistic turd called Brogan, who knows far more than he should but won't divulge his source of information, even when he's leant upon hard by Andy Cartwright."

\*

Jenna stood in her kitchen with all the ingredients for vegetable moussaka in front of her. She was feeling a lot better now. The GP had prescribed some medication for her, and she'd already taken two doses. It was working: vision normal and nausea gone. In fact, in place of nausea, there was hunger. How good that felt! She picked up her favourite chopping knife and began to slice through the aubergine, thinking about how the day had panned out. What a shame she hadn't been able to visit Ben this evening. She hadn't trusted herself to drive, even though she was feeling better. So she'd texted Rory and told him why she wouldn't be there, just in case Ben asked. With slices of aubergine sizzling in the frying pan, she began chopping onions and peppers. She'd also texted Lucy and asked her to pay a flying visit to Ben's bedside, on her behalf, after her shift in A&E, so at least she felt she'd done what she could for him today.

The lentils had been simmering for a while now, so she removed them from the heat, put them on one side, and did the same with the aubergine. Now, it was the turn of the onions and peppers. She scraped them into the pan with a little garlic, splashed on more oil and turned up the heat. She really did enjoy cooking, she decided. It was creative, gave her time for reflection, and, though she said it herself, it usually tasted pretty good. She pushed the vegetables around in the pan and thought now of her boss. He'd looked after her well today. But there had been that moment, leaning against him for support... Swiftly, she took hold of a can of Italian tomatoes and thrust it at the can opener on the wall. She wasn't going to let *that* thought surface. He was unavailable, and anyway, she was in love with Ben, wasn't she? Was she? A nagging doubt cast a shadow in her mind. Why did life have to get so complicated?

At that moment, the kitchen door opened, and Helen walked in. Jenna had been so wrapped up in her thoughts she hadn't even realised her friend had come in through the front door.

"Feeling any better?" Helen asked.

"Yes, thanks, and wow, am I hungry!" Jenna replied. "Here you are. Get mixing, then we can put this thing in the oven and relax." She indicated a jug on the side, which had tomato puree, cinnamon and a splash of cooking wine in it. Helen did as she was told, and soon, all the main vegetable ingredients were assembled in a casserole dish.

"Smells good!" said Helen. "So, did Brady bring you home today?" she asked.

"Yes," said Jenna. She'd made a ricotta cheese sauce earlier and was now beating an egg into it. She stirred energetically.

"He's very fond of you, you know," Helen said.

"Why do you think that?" Jenna replied. She wouldn't look at Helen.

"Oh, you know… the things he says… the way he looks…"

Jenna waited for Helen to turn it all into a joke, but she didn't. She quickly busied herself again, throwing chopped parsley over the vegetable mixture and pouring the sauce over it.

"He's married," Jenna said. She still wouldn't make eye contact.

"So?"

"So he's out of bounds!" She shaved Parmesan on the dish, the finishing touch, and placed the moussaka in a medium oven, setting the timer for an hour.

"Tell me," said Helen, "if he wasn't out of bounds, would you be interested?"

She shrugged her shoulders as if she didn't care. "Maybe and maybe not," she muttered under her breath and began wiping down all the work surfaces.

\*

Detectives Cartwright and Grant had gone out on the morning of the next day to interview two of the six people who'd been residents with Drummond at Merrydown.

Surely, at least one of the six would be able to shed a bit more light on either Drummond himself or other residents who might be likely candidates for their killer. The runaway, possibly?

The first interview, which the two detectives carried out as they followed up on Drummond's list, was with Sheila Mason, who worked at Heathrow Airport. Unfortunately for the investigation, she was reluctant to revisit her experience as a child at Merrydown Children's Home, believing that a bad past was best left buried, so, frustratingly, Andy and Jamie were unable to add to the information Drummond had already given them.

Their next interview, however, was far more productive. Andrew Lacey was a social worker in the London borough of Islington and seemed to be much more willing to talk about Merrydown to the detectives. "Yes, I remember Blake," he told them. "Cried a lot at night, but then most of the kids did…" His voice trailed off, and he cast his eyes downwards.

"Were you abused too?" Jamie asked. He used an appropriately respectful tone.

Lacey looked up again. "Once or twice." He forced a cough to clear his throat. "I was told I'd been a naughty boy, and it was to punish me. But you could say I was one of the lucky ones. When I think back, I can see that they really went for the lookers – you know…" He described a circle around his face with his forefinger, indicating gaunt, asymmetrical features. "… not like me, one of the ugly mugs!" He cackled bizarrely. "I suppose you could say that sometimes it pays to be unattractive!"

Andy and Jamie could hardly agree with the man, although they both saw where he was coming from.

"So if you were a nice-looking child," Andy confirmed, "you were more likely to be targeted; have I understood you correctly?"

"Yes," Lacey replied.

"Do you remember who the abusers were?" Jamie asked.

Lacey listed them in the same way as Drummond had done and added Mr Fox, the only one whose name the children officially knew, at the end.

"And amongst the, shall we say, nicest-looking children," Andy asked, "do you know if these men targeted any particular favourites?"

"Yes, there were," said Lacey. His brow furrowed oddly, making his gaunt features look even stranger than before. "The adults called them Valentine and Vixen," he said.

"Valentine and Vixen?" Jamie repeated, shooting a glance at Andy. "What were they then, nicknames?"

"Vixen definitely was, but I'm not sure about Valentine," said Lacey. "Valentine was a good-looking boy. Older than me and Blake. Very musical, if I remember rightly. Yeah, he was probably the best-looking boy there."

"And Vixen?" Andy enquired, making notes on his iPad.

"She was a pretty girl," said Lacey. "Long dark hair. When she first arrived, we were told her name, but I was only about seven at the time. I haven't got a clue what it was. I remember her making a fuss when she came into the dining hall one day; she threw something at the wall, and it smashed, and she was put in solitary."

"Solitary!" exclaimed Jamie.

"Yeah. We were all threatened with it from time to time, but I was never put down there, so I couldn't tell you what it was like."

"*Down* there? Do you mean below ground?" Andy asked in disbelief.

"Yes." Andy made a note, and Lacey continued. "Her outbursts got worse actually, and she seemed to be put down there more and more and then… she wasn't there any more."

"And do you know what happened to Valentine, or Vixen for that matter?" Jamie asked.

"Well, one rumour spread that both of them had been adopted, but another rumour went around that Valentine had run away," said Lacey. "At the time, I think I believed the adoption theory because they were both so sweet; I thought every family would want to take them in."

"And what do you think now?" asked Jamie.

"Hard to say," he said.

"When did you leave the home, Mr Lacey?" Andy said.

"At sixteen," he replied. "I was finally put with a foster family. They were really nice – saw me through sixth form and university. I kind of owe them my sanity, you know."

"Did you ever report the abuse that went on at the home?" Andy asked. Lacey shook his head. "Can I ask you why not?"

Lacey shrugged his shoulders. "I suppose I didn't realise at the time that you could tell the police about such things. I thought the police were there to catch burglars and stuff. And I suppose I didn't view what happened there as a crime. I saw it, at the time, more like us naughty kids getting a form of punishment." He looked at both detectives apologetically. "Of course, now I can see it for what it was."

Andy called up Drummond's list on his iPad. He and Jamie had drawn a blank earlier trying to locate the next two names on the list, so he wondered if Lacey could help them. Sheila Mason certainly couldn't… or wouldn't.

"I don't suppose, Mr Lacey, you have any idea where Gina Gardner or Matthew Briggs are now, do you?"

"I don't know about Gina," Lacey replied, "but I do know what happened to Matthew."

Andy prepared to make a note.

"He died before the age of twenty."

Jamie shook his head. "How?" he asked quietly, but he could guess what was coming.

"Overdose," said Lacey.

\*

Brady had ensured that the artist's impression of their second suspect was now with the media. He'd also restricted Jenna's duties during the day so that they were as light as possible following her migraine attack. So when she finally left work at the end of the shift and headed for St. Joseph's Hospital, she was actually feeling quite energetic and clear-minded.

This was the first chance she'd had since Ben's admittance to see him in hospital, and as she'd never set foot inside an Intensive Care Unit before, not even in the course of her work, she didn't know quite what to expect. Anxiously, she entered the ICU ante-room and asked the nurse on duty if she could go into the unit itself. The nurse peered through the door. The room beyond was only dimly lit, but she was able to see there was room for one more at Ben's bedside.

"You're in luck," she whispered to Jenna. "We stipulate no more than two visitors at any one time, within restricted hours, but there's only one other person by his bed at the moment so you can go in. But could you just…?" She indicated the hand-washing facilities in front of the door, and Jenna complied. Then she went in. Her eyes took moments to adjust to the low light levels. Then she saw Ben lying unconscious, surrounded by monitors and drips. She felt so sorry for him.

As the nurse had said, someone else was already sitting by his side, staring quietly at him. She made her way to the remaining chair and slipped in next to the other visitor.

"Hi, I'm Jenna," she whispered. She could see, even in the darkness, that this man's profile did not belong to Rory.

"Greg," he whispered back.

"How is he?" she asked.

"I think you could say he's had a close shave."

"And how's he doing now?" Jenna enquired.

Greg turned and looked at her. "He's stable, at least." He shook his head. "But they think this could take some time." He turned back and looked anxiously at his flatmate, and Jenna could tell, at that one glance, that Greg was fond of Ben.

"Are we allowed to touch him or talk to him, do you know?" she said.

"Actually, they encourage both," Greg replied.

She nodded, got out of her seat and approached the bedside. Ben's arms were both resting on top of the covers, but the arm nearest to her was fitted with a cannula and treble drip, which she didn't wish to disturb, so she went round the other side of the bed and touched his right arm. "Hi, Ben," she whispered. "I'm missing you." She felt a little self-conscious talking intimately in front of his flatmate and decided that "Hurry up and get better" was about the limit for now.

"Listen," Greg said, "I've been here a while. I'll wait for

you in the ante-room." He nodded at Ben. "Talk to him some more. Your soothing tone will do him a world of good." He got up and left the inner room.

She stood up and approached Ben again, searching for something to say. But nothing came to her, so she stood for some time in silence. She watched the lights flashing on the monitor; then she looked back at his face. She recalled the first time they'd met when the smile on that face had so attracted her. Had they really moved on from there and developed their relationship? She knew the answer was no. Things were still at a superficial level between them. More than that, she had to admit, they still hardly knew each other. And why was that, she wondered. Could it be that someone else was occupying a place in her heart? Her eyes searched the darkness; it made her think of that dark place within which hid an explosive emotion. She knew it wouldn't take much to light the touch paper. She looked again at Ben, but still, nothing came to her. No words. No emotions. Confused, she left Ben's bedside and went out to the ante-room.

Greg had waited for her. He was already gloved-up in preparation for the cold weather outdoors. Jenna noticed he had no coat, though. Instead, he was wearing a black tracksuit and seriously good Nikes on his feet.

"Are you off to the gym?" she asked him as they made their way back through the main hospital corridor to the exit.

"No, can't afford the membership," he said.

Outside, their breath spiralled away from them in little grey puffs as they spoke.

"Can I give you a lift home?" Jenna asked. She'd noticed

he had not turned with her in the direction of the car park. "It's pretty cold, and I notice you're coatless!"

"No thanks," said Greg. "I'm dressed up to run."

"You mean you're going to run home?" she asked. He nodded. "But it's miles away!" She thought of the guys' flat in north Kingston.

"Don't worry! I like a long run." He turned to her. Away from the dimly lit ICU, she could now see his face properly. "And the exercise makes me feel good." His eyes twinkled. "Especially as it's free!"

For the first time since they'd met, he smiled.

And his smile was as radiant as the sun.

And it blew her away.

\*

Back in her flat, Jenna sat in front of her dressing table mirror, her emotions in turmoil. She felt like a teenager again, falling for every male who happened to smile at her. You want to get a grip on yourself, she thought, peering critically at her reflection. What the hell's up with you? She knew what was up with her, actually. She'd had such a rough ride with Nick Bailey and one or two others before him, who hadn't been too honest with her either, that now she'd met Ben and his flatmate, not to mention Brady, their kindnesses stood out in such contrast to previous attachments that she must surely be mistaking their attentions for love.

"Well, it's not love, you idiot," she muttered to herself. "Brady was just being kind; Ben has never used the words 'I love you', and as for Greg." She tutted at her own lack of depth. "Having known him for less than an hour, he smiles, and I swoon! Aaaaaah!" she yelled in exasperation. The cry emerged at full volume and, within seconds, brought a knock at her bedroom door.

"Are you all right?" came Helen's voice.

Jenna wavered: she really wanted to share her anguish with Helen but didn't know quite what to say. That she was in love with Brady? No, she couldn't be. Helen had been right weeks ago asking her what she knew about Ben because – hey, well done, Helen! – the answer had been very little then and still was, wasn't it? And if all that wasn't enough, that she'd now got a crush on someone she'd met less than an hour ago?

"Jenna?"

She couldn't face the embarrassment of it all. "No, I'm fine," she called. "I just got my finger trapped in something," she lied. "Sorry about the noise!" She heard Helen retreat down the passageway. And sorry about the lie, she thought, looking back at herself in the mirror.

She sat quietly for a few minutes, turning the three faces over in her mind's eye: Brady, Ben, Greg. No, her finger wasn't trapped. But her heart? That was another matter.

\*

Shona was feeling much happier. She could concentrate again on her schoolwork. The Christmas holidays were just around the corner and even Gillie had, at least for now, come to her senses and realised what a dangerous game she'd been playing. It helped, of course, that Blake Drummond was still in custody, charged with possession and trafficking. So, as she made her way home from school in the grey December twilight, she was light of heart and hopeful about the future.

But no sooner had she got through the front door than she sensed something was wrong. There was an eerie stillness. She called out to her mum, but there was no reply. Yet her mum's coat, shoes and keys were all there in the hallway. She called again, even as she ran up the stairs.

Her mother lay on the bed, face buried in the covers, left arm dangling over the edge. Beneath her limp hand was the sight that Shona had always dreaded: an empty pill bottle. Swallowing hard and hands shaking, she grabbed the mobile from her pocket and tapped in the emergency number. Speaking at double-quick speed, she gave the operator the necessary details. Then, as she closed up her phone, she heard her brother's key in the front door.

"Kieran!" she shouted.

"What?" came a weary voice from downstairs.

"Get on your phone to Dad!" she yelled.

"Why?"

"It's Mum!" Shona was doing her best to stay calm. "I've called an ambulance, but I'm running out of credit. Tell him to meet us at St. Joseph's A&E."

The ambulance seemed to take forever to arrive. However, when Shona checked her watch on arrival at the hospital, she realised it had taken the paramedics less than twenty-five minutes to collect them, take them to casualty and prepare Kathleen for a stomach pump.

Brady took about the same time to join his family, borrowing a squad car and blue-lighting it through the busy streets.

The evening that followed was one of the bleakest of

their lives. Kathleen, still unconscious, was admitted to the ICU, and Brady was told, out of the children's earshot, that it was hard to make a prognosis.

His wife's life hung in the balance.

The clock on the wall ticked on, and staff came and went. And all the while, Brady held on tightly to his two children, one arm around each. No words were spoken.

At last, he thought he'd better arrange some childcare for the night. Mavis, his next-door neighbour, was always happy to help out, and when Brady phoned her, she told him to bring them home: she'd stay with them for the night and see them off in the morning.

Later, on his own at Kathleen's bedside, he felt he could be himself. No need for a brave face in front of the kids now they were taken care of; if he wanted to cry, he would cry. But he couldn't. He felt numb. He observed his wife and recalled how she'd once been the lovely girl with the twinkling eyes he'd fallen in love with. That seemed a very long time ago. It dawned on him that he knew even then, in the early days of their relationship, that the sword of Damocles was already suspended.

Brady stayed throughout the night, dozing once or twice, but at five-thirty, he decided that he'd had enough. There was nothing he could do except wait. What lay ahead, he didn't dare consider as he made his way back to the Kingston nick.

A phone call to Mavis at seven, with a white lie thrown in for Shona and Kieran about their mother's progress, reassured him that all was as well as it could be at home. Now he could think about the job again.

Fat chance.

He shuffled papers around. He switched on his laptop.

He wandered out of his office to get some coffee and walked back in again without shutting his door. The station was getting busier now, and he could hear the welcome sound of three or four recognisable voices belonging to members of his team. He drank the coffee and shuffled papers around again.

Suddenly, the enormity of what had happened last night hit him. Tears welled up in his eyes, and with one movement of his arm, he swept all the paperwork on the floor in anger. "Shit!" he cried. His fury was directed at Kathleen. How could she put them through this hell? Actually, how dare she? He rolled his chair backwards and stood up to survey the mess on the floor. Then, realising he was welling up again, he walked round to the other side of his desk, turning his back to the door in case any of the team came in and caught him crying.

Standing there hunched over his desk, resting on his two fists, with the back of his head turned towards her, was how Jenna found him when she came in minutes later. She abruptly stopped when she saw the paperwork all over the floor. Then she made her way around it. "Sir?" she said tentatively. "Are you all right?" She could see he was anything but. He remained quiet for a moment, and she could hear him swallowing hard. "Is it Kathleen?" she asked in hushed tones.

"We nearly lost her last night," he said. His voice cracked with emotion. Jenna walked up to him and put a hand on his back to comfort him. It seemed the natural thing to do. "If there's anything I can do," she began.

But he cut in. "Wish I'd never given up smoking," he said, his face still turned away.

She didn't know quite what to say next and found herself tamely uttering, "Well, try not to give in…"

He stood to his full height and turned to look at her. She'd come very close to comfort him, and now, as he turned his head to her, their faces were only inches apart. A single tear had rolled down his left cheek, and instinctively, she put up her hand to wipe it away. He lifted his hand, took hold of hers and clasped it to his upper chest. "Hard not to," he said.

There was a tap on the door, and Andy was suddenly there in front of them. "Sorry! Am I interrupting something?" he asked, his voice raised sarcastically. Jenna pulled away from Brady, mumbled something at Andy and left the office. Andy approached the desk and pointedly dumped the transcript of Lacey's interview on it. The action was not subtle, and Brady saw it. Andy then walked right up to him and, in a voice charged with emotion, said, "You wanna keep your hands off her. You're a married man!" He went to turn away and leave, but Brady wasn't having any of it. Lack of sleep, anxiety about Kathleen and overwhelming feelings for Jenna meant he was not in the mood for any further assault on his emotions.

"What's up with you?" he barked. "Jealous?"

Andy saw red. He reeled round and sent his right fist into Brady's jaw. Brady retaliated immediately with a swift left hook to Andy's mouth. It made Andy cry out and sink to his knees. Slowly, he sat back on his heels, dabbing at the blood which was trickling from his split lip. Brady, meanwhile, sat on his desk, nursing his cheek. It was still moist with tears, so the blow had glanced off, but he knew he'd probably end up with a bruise even so.

After a short while, Brady got up, went around to his desk

drawer and pulled out a bunch of tissues. He walked over to Andy and shoved the tissues at him. Andy took them and grunted. "We'll call it quits, shall we?" said Brady, looking down at the young DC. "I won't press charges if you don't."

Andy nodded his head slowly and uttered a muffled 'yeah' through the swelling. He gradually got to his feet, tissues held against his mouth, and he sheepishly made his way out of the office.

\*

Later that morning, when Brady was reading through the Lacey transcript, Elvira Fox turned up at reception and insisted on seeing him. He could have delegated the task of hearing what she had to say to someone else but decided that he could do with the comfort of human contact again, so he made his way to the room where she was waiting. She said she'd been trying her best to recall unusual or significant events in the old days at Merrydown and had actually remembered one of each kind.

"I was a florist when I first met Stanley," she said. She laughed with a touch of irony. "He was ordering flowers for someone else when he first asked me out. I should have known then he wasn't a one-woman man, shouldn't I?" She stopped to take a breath, looked back at Brady, relaxed a little and smiled. "So I was happy when we arrived at Merrydown to see that the gardens there were full of rose bushes." Brady frowned slightly; he couldn't see where this was leading and hoped that Mrs Fox wasn't going to waffle on endlessly. "As I had a bit of skill in flower arranging," she continued, "I always made sure, throughout the summer months when the roses were in bloom, that there were bunches of them in vases for everyone to enjoy indoors. It was one of the few things I was able to contribute to the running of the home. But sometimes, I'd look again at my arrangements and see that some of the roses had gone missing. I couldn't work it out. I asked Stanley about it, but he just said they'd probably wilted, and someone had removed them. But I knew how long flower arrangements should last; I'd had enough practice at it. I knew that if the stems sat in an oasis and the water had feed in it, the flowers should last and last. So what was going on there, I don't know." Brady made a note: roses going missing. "That was unusual," she went on, "but then I also remembered something you might call significant. I recall Stanley telling me that one of the boys had run away."

Brady's ears pricked up.

"When would this have been?" he asked.

Mrs Fox thought for a moment. "Oh, about ten years ago, no, maybe a little longer…"

"And do you know the name of the runaway boy?" Brady asked. It was a long shot, and he knew it.

"No," Mrs Fox replied. "But I do know that the police searched for him for a while, so I suppose you might have records of that search." Brady made a second note. When he looked up, she smiled at him again. "That's all I can give you at the moment, but I hope it's been of use," she said.

Brady did his best to smile. His jaw was now quite sore, and he realised he should have put something cold on it earlier to ease the inflammation. "You've been very helpful, Mrs Fox," he said. "Thank you for coming in."

She stood up to go. "And if there's anything else I can

help you with…" This time, she smiled rather strangely at Brady and adopted a come-hither tone. "Well, you know where you can contact me." She couldn't have made it more obvious.

Brady remained ice-cool but polite. "Thank you again, Mrs Fox. I'll ask one of my officers to see you out."

\*

The anger still simmered just below the surface as, once again, Brady sat in the dim light at Kathleen's bedside. He was angry with her; he was angry with himself for being angry with her; he was angry with himself for letting his emotions mushroom out of control: Jenna; Andy. He rubbed his jaw, moved his head from side to side to relieve tension in his neck, dropped his forehead onto his steepled hands and thought through the day's events.

Not a good start with that left hook to Andy's mouth. He should have risen above that. And then Elvira Fox. He welcomed the opportunity now, in the quietness of the dark room, to have a good think about what she'd said to him. Roses missing from her arrangements? Come on, he thought. Make some connections. His brain was exhausted. He'd missed a night's sleep, and his jaw throbbed, but he tried hard to join the dots. Roses go missing at the children's home… and roses turn up in the victims' anal passages. Coincidence? There was something else he'd seen today that also tied up with the rose information, but what was it? His eyes closed as he scrolled through his memory. Something to do with roses… Something Jenna had said to him in the early days of the investigation. He delved deep in his mind.

He suddenly opened his eyes as he located the name he'd read in the Lacey transcript today: Valentine.

Valentine, the runaway.

Valentine's Day – roses – killer's signature – 'V'. 'V' for Valentine?

He ought to share these thoughts in the morning with his acting sergeant.

Jenna.

Now, he'd really had enough of working his brain and let his thoughts veer once more towards the personal.

Jenna: herself, the perfect English rose.

What was he going to do? He looked now at his wife. If she got through this, what then? There was no easy answer. He knew what he'd seen in Jenna's eyes today. He wondered if he was occupying her thoughts just as she was occupying his. What do you do when your heart is bursting, but expressing it would hurt all the people you love, one of them possibly beyond repair?

He wondered if he did love Kathleen and felt guilty asking himself the question. But he thought it might clarify things if he was honest with himself, at least. He closed his eyes again and searched his soul. Yes, he did, he thought, but it was a love rooted in pity. It was certainly not the raging furnace that now burned within him for someone else. Jesus, even the touch of her hand on his back today had him, what? Aroused? He thought back through the weeks and months. So when was the last time he'd had sex? Obviously not once during this current phase of Kathleen's illness. She'd been unapproachable, of course she had, but he'd missed the intimacy; he couldn't deny it. And he just couldn't stop himself from imagining that intimacy with Jenna. He now knew every detail of her stunning face, the curves of her body, the beautifully cut legs, and he suddenly visualised her blonde head on a pillow, her body hot under his and…

He stood up abruptly. A nurse had entered the ICU and approached the patient's bedside to check her stats. "No need to get up," she said quietly.

"No, I thought I'd get myself some coffee," Brady replied in similar hushed tones. A cold shower wouldn't go amiss either, he thought guiltily.

"Machine's located outside the ante-room, just down the corridor," said the nurse.

Brady thanked her, left Kathleen in her care, went out into the corridor and approached the drinks machine. A young man was also approaching the machine from the other side. It looked like he'd just come out of the ICU male wing. He reached it before Brady and got himself a coffee. Brady nodded at him and then took his turn at the machine.

"Grim, isn't it?" said the younger man. Brady waited for him to elaborate. "Keeping a vigil at the bedside. Watching that goddamned machine and wondering if it will… you know…"

"Flat-line?" said Brady. The moment he'd said it, he wished he hadn't. How tactless! Supposing such a scenario actually happened to either of them when they returned to watch those dreaded monitors again? Ah, but he was so weary… "Sorry," he said hurriedly.

"No problem," said the younger man.

They both fell silent and drank their coffee, deep in their own thoughts. And then, a nurse came bustling down the corridor towards them from the male wing. She looked excited. "Ben's vital signs look to be improving," she said, urgently beckoning to the young man to indicate that he might want to come back immediately.

Ben? Brady thought. Jenna's guy?

The young man finished his drink, looked around for a litter bin, took aim and threw in his Styrofoam cup. The perfect aim. He turned back to Brady. "Good luck!" he said.

"And you!" said Brady.

\*

Asking after each other's patient the next morning, Brady and Jenna realised they'd only just missed each other at the hospital the night before. But now there was work to do.

"So you've looked through the Lacey transcript?" said Brady. He was determined to keep the tone professional, cool even, having decided that he'd wandered far too near the flame yesterday and that he needed to retreat for the moment. She'd felt it, too: there was no doubt about that. But she took her cue from him and maintained a cool exterior.

"Yes," she said.

"What do you think?"

"Sad," she replied.

"Tell me, when you looked through the Merrydown records, you didn't come across the name of Valentine, did you?"

"No," she said, "but then I wasn't really looking for any particular name so I may have missed it."

"And any idea if the basement is still in use and if so, what for?"

"Again," said Jenna, "I don't think I was even aware there was a basement there."

"Hmmm." Brady moved on to the next subject. "Stanley Fox's widow came to see me yesterday and spoke about roses going missing from her vase arrangements back in the old days. What do you make of that?"

Jenna clasped both hands around the back of her head and leant back into her own cradle as she gave the question some thought. Brady looked away to avoid watching her shift of posture. "All I can think," she said, "is that you give roses to your Valentine. But that's just too obvious, isn't it? Like we're trying to force a connection between the missing flowers and the name of Valentine?"

"Sometimes," Brady said, "what's staring you in the face can turn out to be all-important."

Jenna shut her eyes and thought again, still cradling her head in her hands. "Do you remember when we discussed the rose signature in the case of the first victim, and I said something to you about giving roses to people on Valentine's Day?"

Brady nodded. He remembered that discussion had followed a sleepless night spent up at St. Joseph's when Kathleen had cut her wrist. He was as exhausted then as he felt this week.

"Well," she said, "I'm certain I'd have spotted a name like Valentine if it had been in the Merrydown records, having already mentioned Valentine's Day to you. It would be an unusual name these days, don't you think?"

"A nickname, perhaps?" Brady asked. "That could explain why it's not recorded."

"Or a surname?"

"But a surname would be in the records, wouldn't it?" said Brady.

Jenna paused. "Not if it's been doctored... or removed," she said, with one eyebrow raised.

Brady closed his eyes to think. "When you interviewed Dewar's pupils at Merrydown," he began, opening his eyes again and looking at Jenna, "did you get the feeling you weren't getting the whole truth?"

"Absolutely!" she said without hesitation.

"So..." Brady pushed a pen around on his desk. "Do you think the culture of abuse died out with Fox, or could it still be going on?"

"It's possible," she replied.

"Who runs Merrydown now?" Brady asked. Jenna told him. "Right. You and I ought to pay a visit there. We'll have a chat with Gerald Hope, and then we'll go into the records again. We'll see what we can turn up, shall we?"

"Is it worth asking to take a look at the basement?" said Jenna.

"Well, remember we don't have a search warrant for the premises yet, but we can ask nicely, I suppose," Brady replied.

Jenna left her boss to make arrangements for the visit to Merrydown. She'd decided to take a fifteen-minute breather out by the river in lieu of a coffee break. Having spent hours the previous night at Ben's bedside, she had missed out on sleep. He seemed to be making some progress, although he was still unconscious, so she and Greg had had reason to feel in better spirits after their visit. Greg had actually accepted her offer of a lift home this time and had sat with her in the car outside the flat in north Kingston, enjoying easy conversation for a further hour or so. It was, therefore, gone midnight when she got home. Now, the late hour was catching up with her, and she needed to clear her head. As she trotted past the Rose Theatre, she could smell the river in her nostrils. That dank odour mixed with the cold air revived her somewhat, and she stood by the Thames, observing the swans and the river traffic.

Her mobile buzzed in her coat pocket. She took it out and flipped it open. It was a text from Greg. They had decided to swap numbers, just as she had done with the other flatmate, Rory, in case they needed to pass on information to each other about Ben.

The text said: 'Ben awake. G.'

She closed the mobile and replaced it in her pocket, deciding to reply when she had more time later on during her lunch break. As she turned back to watch the water flow on its never-ending journey, she sighed heavily, wondering, now that Ben was getting better, how she was going to end the relationship without hurting him.

\*

Much later that afternoon, Brady and Jenna sat opposite Gerald Hope in his office at Merrydown. Hope was polite but cold. Reptilian, even, thought Brady, with his large staring eyes, mouth slightly open and fleeting smiles betraying yellowish-brown tombstone teeth. Brady took an instant dislike to him but did his best to maintain the appearance of professional respect towards Merrydown's manager.

"I know you're aware, Mr Hope, that we are searching for a killer," Brady began, "and, as I explained on the phone, we have reason to believe that our perpetrator may have been a resident here at your home many years ago. Can I ask how long you've been in your current position?"

"Between seven and eight years now," Hope replied.

"The profile we have of our killer matches someone who would have been here before your time, Mr Hope. Nevertheless, I need to ask you if you ever heard of a boy named Valentine."

Brady watched Hope's features carefully. The face was almost inscrutable, but a tiny muscle near his eye twitched minutely. He shook his head. "Never heard of anyone with that name," he said and forced a laugh.

"Or a girl nicknamed 'The Vixen'?" chipped in Jenna.

The muscle near the eye twitched again. "Not as far as I know," said Hope.

"Are you aware that a boy ran away from this establishment some time before you arrived?" Brady asked.

"I don't believe we've ever had a runaway here," replied Hope, flashing a reptilian smile at them.

"Some former residents have told us otherwise," said Jenna.

Hope made a strange noise: part ironic laugh, part snarl. The yellowish-brown teeth were bared before them, momentarily mesmerising Brady by their freakish appearance. He swiftly regained his composure.

"Mr Hope?" prompted Jenna.

"Come on! You know what children are like," Hope replied. "They have inventive minds. Runaways, indeed! They fantasise. Why, we've had all sorts of tales here: ghosts, vampires, you name it. They're children, Mr Brady and Miss Jones. Vulnerable children. They dream up fiction and then spin it into fact as soon as dammit." He paused for effect. "They're emotionally damaged. They lie all the time, even when they've grown up."

Jenna tried a different tack. "Do your children have visitors?" she asked.

"Sometimes," said Hope. "Prospective adoptive or foster families may be directed here from time to time."

"Any others?"

"No, I don't think so," said Hope.

"Apart from music teachers?" Brady said.

A defensive look crept across Hope's features, and Brady caught it. "Well, yes, okay then, one or two others." Brady noticed that Gerald Hope's bald head had started to shine. So he was working up a little sweat, was he? Well, let's crank up the pressure, he thought.

"One or two others? The clergy, for example?"

"Actually, I stopped the clergy visiting when I first arrived. We started taking the children out to church instead and have done so ever since." He fired a 'so-get-out-of-that-one' look at Brady.

Touché, Brady thought. It was clear that they weren't going to wring too much more information out of Gerald Hope. Now, Brady looked to Jenna to indicate that the time had come for that awkward question when he might need her support.

"I understand there's a floor below ground level here," said Brady. Hope looked slightly unsettled but nodded. "To follow up on one or two statements we've already taken, may we have a look down there – just to apprise ourselves of the full layout of the premises?"

\*

Jenna inwardly applauded the DI for putting the request so innocently. She was learning a lot from Brady. And it worked. Hope seemed to have no problem in leading them down a flight of stairs to a basement corridor and confidently declaring that this was the below ground level consisting of four rooms. He pointed to the first on the right. "Storage and cleaning materials only," he said. "We keep it locked as it contains bio-hazardous chemicals, and if children are down here in our infirmary," he pointed to the rooms ahead of them, "then at least we know they would be safe if they did begin to wander." He walked on quickly. "And here," he said, "are the rooms which are used if our children fall sick." He let his visitors look into each room in turn. There were camp beds in every room. It all seemed completely innocuous.

"Well," said Brady to Hope, "This has been very helpful. A look at the Merrydown records, Mr Hope, and then I think we can be on our way."

"Of course," said Gerald Hope, leading them up the flight of stairs again and out into the ground floor corridor. "Our records office is this way." His smile was now wider and prolonged as if he was beginning to relax at last in their company. Almost as if he was relieved, Jenna thought.

On their own, in the records office, Jenna showed Brady some of the items she'd come across on her previous visit here, including that heartbreaking find: her missing friend's name. This time, she had come prepared, and the shock factor was no longer present. They looked at the records for some time, searching in particular for a Valentine or a Vixen amongst the names they knew from the era: Lacey, Drummond, Mason, etc., but there was no sign of them. They had to be nicknames.

Brady looked at the pages in front of him again. "Hang on," he said. "Go back to your friend's name. Remember, she was more of a contemporary to the alleged runaway than Lacey and Drummond, who said they were younger than him." Jenna flicked back from the Lacey era to find the name Lauren Bristow. Three pages back, Brady suddenly slapped his hand down to stop Jenna from turning any more. "There… Look! Are you seeing what I'm seeing?" he asked.

With his forefinger, he traced a line of Tipp-Ex, yellowed with age, painted across one of the entries. He looked at Jenna, and she nodded back solemnly. "Someone's had their name scrubbed out," she whispered.

\*

The hour was late when they emerged from the records office. "Did we lose track of time in there or what?" said Brady, checking his watch in surprise. They had each separately planned to visit St. Joseph's ICU during the evening, but as Jenna had left her car at the nick and it was already past seven and they hadn't even eaten, she wondered what to do. "And there was I planning on going up the hospital," said Jenna, wearily.

"Listen," Brady said. "Leave your car at the nick tonight. I'll take you up to St. Joe's – I've got to go there anyway. We'll get a take-away on the way, and I'll drop you at home later. Sound like a plan?"

"Definitely!" she said, and her spirits lifted.

Winter's first flurry of snowflakes touched down softly on the pavement around them, visible in the neon lights, which lit up the road where Brady had parked. Jenna watched them swirl delicately in the beam of the headlights as they pulled away. "Are you okay with curry?" he asked.

She told him it was her favourite take-away, so he drove to one of his preferred restaurants and picked up some chicken tikkas. Brady mentioned something about bringing in the record, which had been tampered with, for forensics to have a look at and then promised not to speak of work again that evening.

As Jenna sat by Ben's bedside in the ICU later on, it was that feel-good factor of the meal, which she'd shared with Brady, that kept her buoyant. Ben was conscious now but still heavily drugged, so there was little conversation.

Brady meanwhile sat at Kathleen's side, preoccupied with his thoughts. There was no change in her condition, so he could do little but sit and think. He closed his eyes. He was not a religious man, despite, or maybe because of, his Catholic upbringing, so praying was not something he did. But he believed in the value of positive thinking and sincerely hoped for Kathleen's improved mental health, although… although what? He couldn't stop himself from running future scenarios in his mind. The one in which Kathleen gets better, returns home, sinks into the abyss once more and promptly takes her own life. Or the one in which he asks Kathleen for a divorce so he can be with Jenna, which pushes his wife over the edge anyway. Whichever way Brady looked at it, the future was full of complications.

Jenna.

So he was taking her home. So what? His instinct told him it was an opportunity. His conscience told him to behave. At least he could talk with her over coffee later, maybe. There was no harm in that, was there? He pictured her face in his mind's eye. A moment later, he was out in the ante-room and on the phone with his neighbour, asking her to stay with the children because he might be very late that night. 'I just want to talk to her,' he told his conscience, 'just talk.'

Sometime after eleven, Brady parked his car beside the path that approached Jenna's flat. Before she could say anything, he got out and came round to her side to let her out. When she'd emerged, he crooked his arm in mock-chivalrous fashion for her to latch on to and said theatrically, "Fair lady, allow me to protect you from the dragons of the night."

She laughed. "It's all right," she said. "The only dragon in this neighbourhood is the local Chinese! You don't need to…"

"But it's dark," he cut in with a smile. "Anything could be hiding behind that tree." He nodded at the giant cedar.

"I have had combat training, you know," she said.

"But not against dragons!"

She laughed again and threaded her arm through his. They walked up the path together. The snow flurries, which had fallen earlier, had been too light to settle, and now the sky had cleared again, and the moon lit their way. But the shadows of the cedar soon encroached, and, despite her bravado, Jenna was actually glad of her escort.

They reached the doorstep, and she took off her gloves to find her keys. One of the gloves dropped on the flagstones between them, and they both bent down together to pick it up. Face to face again, they slowly rose. This time, there were no smiles but an urgent exchange of unspoken passion.

Against all her principles, she whispered, "Come in?"

And in that split second, he decided to smother the voice of conscience. He couldn't fight it any more. Fever pitch. He nodded. "What about Helen?" he whispered.

"Sleeps like a log," she replied.

"And the other one?"

"On night duty."

"I'll switch off my phone."

Her heart was pounding and making her hands shake, but somehow, she got the key into the lock. He, meanwhile, thrust his hand into his pocket and located the off switch on his mobile. They stepped over the threshold and into the darkness of the hallway. Jenna went to pull her scarf off but found it had lodged under her coat collar, just below her neck. She squealed softly, impatiently, quietly appealing to him for help. Brady's hand went round to the back of her neck, dislodged the scarf, tugged at it and let it drop. But his hand remained there and cupped the back of her head. He joined his other hand to the first and pulled her head gently towards his.

And he found her lips, and he kissed her.

Deeply, slowly, longingly.

But the magic was abruptly shattered: a mobile pinged somewhere on Brady's person. He pulled away as he grappled to find the source of the noise.

"I thought you switched it off," Jenna whispered harshly, frustrated in every sense.

"I switched off my work mobile," Brady replied quietly. "This one is personal: the children's emergency hotline." He opened the front door once more and stepped out into the porch light to read the text. Then, he looked back at Jenna. "It's Shona," he said. "The hospital called. My wife's had a stroke."

\*

Detective Chief Inspector Delgado buzzed Jenna the next morning and asked her to come into his office. "Inspector Brady's taking two days' compassionate leave," he told her. "His wife is seriously ill in hospital."

The surprise of being summoned by the DCI made Jenna forget whether she was supposed to know about Kathleen or not. She thought it best to react as if she was hearing the news for the first time and expressed her sympathy.

"Thing is," said Delgado, "You're his acting sergeant at the moment. How do you feel about stepping into his shoes for two days? Shake things up a bit?"

Jenna raised her eyebrows. "Wow!" she said.

"Can you keep the investigation going or not?" he said crisply.

"Of course I can, sir," she replied, conscious that she should sound more professional.

"Good. Set yourself up in Brady's office. The computer's already on. Then, I'll call the rest of the team together for a short briefing. At least you won't have to worry about the CIT team any more. They've gone."

She nodded and turned to leave.

"Jones?" he said.

"Sir?"

"I've heard you're good… but if you need advice, just ask!"

\*

Jenna sat at Brady's desk after the team briefing and attempted to put together a to-do list. Thinking now with a clear head, she realised that both she and her immediate boss had been distracted lately by hospital visits and, she had to admit, by each other. In one way, although she missed him, it was a relief not to have Brady around for a while. She could actually concentrate on work again.

Her list would encompass the loose ends, which she intended to do her best to address before Brady returned. First up was the entry in the Merrydown records, which had been scrubbed out with Tipp-Ex. She knew that if Brady were here this morning, his priority would be to get it in and have forensics take a look at it. If they were lucky, they might actually end up with a reasonable part of the mystery name revealed.

She stopped writing and thought back over other aspects of yesterday's visit to the children's home. Something was bugging her about the basement. She nibbled at a nail, searching her memory. It dawned on her that dangerous chemicals should be represented by a bio-hazard sign on the door. Was it merely an oversight on Gerald Hope's part that no such sign was visible? What else would explain its absence? She made a mental note to talk this one over with Brady on his return and then went back to her list.

She knew that Andy and Jamie had worked their way through Andrew Lacey's list of ex-Merrydown residents, but she now needed to find out where they were up to on that list and have them progress that particular line of enquiry. She also made a note to check if DC Rob Flynn had come up with anything in police archive records regarding the Merrydown runaway and to find out if IT had retrieved anything of interest from Fox's mobile analysis. And then there was still the problem of the newspaper reporter who bragged about his sources. But at least he'd been quiet for a while, and frankly, the team had enough on their plates right now. Sniff out an information leak or catch a murderer? Jenna knew which would be Brady's priority. Looking back over her writing, she felt satisfied with her first half hour of work in his shoes.

\*

Two detective constables were dispatched to Merrydown to collect the required records pages for the forensics team to scrutinise. When they were on their way, Jenna buzzed for Andy, Jamie and Helen to come to Brady's office. She asked the male detectives where they were up to interviewing Lacey's contemporaries.

"One's dead, as you probably know," said Jamie, "and we've drawn blanks on two others, but yesterday we managed to locate the sixth person on the list. Name of Hannah Bickford. Luckily for us," he indicated himself and Andy, "it's a south-west London address."

Jenna, however, was concerned that Andy and Jamie were becoming a bit too comfortable working together. They called each other 'mate'; they were always ribbing each other, even when there was serious work to be done. She had also heard them passing unprofessional comments to each other about women they'd interviewed. It was all a bit too 'boys-behaving-badly' for her liking. She decided she might just break up the cosiness.

"Jamie, when you've fixed up a meeting with this lady, I'd like you to take Helen with you this time," she said.

Andy's face dropped. "Are we allowed to ask why you don't want the usual formidable A and J team to go?" he asked.

"Delgado asked me to shake things up a bit," Jenna replied. "Besides, Andy," she said in a mock-seductive tone, "I want you here with me." She gave him a lovely smile, and even though he could see right through her, it did the trick and shut him up.

\*

Jamie was in luck. Hannah Bickford was a teacher in a private nursery school, which had already broken up for Christmas. So when he phoned, she was not only at home but available. He and Helen arrived at her rented flat in Strawberry Hill a little before three o'clock that afternoon.

"Come in," she said, opening the door wide for them and smiling warmly. "Please forgive the mess everywhere. I always intend to do the big tidy-up whenever the school hols start, but I'm afraid..." she let her knees give a little beneath her as she pretended to collapse "... I'm just too tired at the moment."

They followed her into a kitchen-diner and accepted her offer of refreshment. Helen watched her flick her dark shoulder-length hair away from her face and then bustle happily around the kitchen, making tea. She warmed to her immediately. When they each had a mug to hold in their hands, she said, "Now, how can I be of help?"

Jamie proceeded carefully, as he had done when interviewing Andrew Lacey. But as soon as he mentioned Merrydown, the smile left Hannah's face. In fact, she paled. Putting a hand out to her and touching her arm to reassure her, Helen asked if it was all right to carry on. Hannah took a few moments, sipped her tea and then nodded. Jamie paced the questioning slowly, and although Hannah's childhood was clearly painful for her to talk about, they began to make headway.

She recognised most of the children's names, which Lacey had identified. And like him, she only knew the one abuser, Stanley Fox, by name. But then Jamie asked if she remembered any child by the nickname of 'Valentine' or 'Vixen'.

"Yes. Actually, Valentine," she said, "wasn't a nickname: it was the boy's real name – his surname. I don't remember his first name." Jamie made a note on his iPad.

"And Vixen?" prompted Helen, staying very still.

Hannah drank again from her mug. She looked as if she was bracing herself before relating the next instalment. "Now, that was a nickname. When I was about ten or eleven, a new girl arrived, and we became friends. We played together. Slept in the same dormitory…" Here, she stopped and took a deep breath. Shadows of the past crept across her face, and Helen's heart went out to her. "What happened in that dormitory and elsewhere put me off men for life, I can tell you!" She shot a glance at them to see if they'd understood her meaning. "Actually, the very first day after arriving, she had a bit of a strop and threw a glass at the wall. Miss Brewer, the housekeeper, was outraged, and so was Mr Fox, who came when he heard the commotion. Brewer and another member of staff moved all the children away from the shattered glass on the floor and got them out of the room, but somehow, I escaped their notice. I don't know how, although I was small for my age. Anyway, I managed to dive under a table out of sight. So when Mr Fox came and grabbed her roughly and spoke to her, I heard every word he said."

"And what did he say?" asked Jamie.

"He said, 'You little vixen!' He said it harshly, as if he was spitting the word out. 'Now you've really asked for it,' he said. I remembered the word 'vixen' because I'd never heard it before. I thought it was a strange thing to call somebody, and it sort of stuck in my mind."

"Am I right in thinking that your friend was put in some sort of solitary confinement to punish her?" Jamie asked.

Helen gave him a strange look, surprised that he hadn't asked the more obvious question first. So she chipped in.

"Can you remember the real name of this friend of yours?"

Hannah took a few seconds to think. Helen desperately hoped she wouldn't hear Hannah utter the name of Jenna's missing friend. But her hopes were dashed.

"Lauren," she said.

\*

Back at the nick, Dinesh had just finished showing Jenna and Andy some of the images he'd retrieved from Stanley Fox's mobile. He had decided before the two detectives had come down to his department that some of the images involving children were so obscene, levels four and five, that it would be best to hide them for now and show them to Brady on his return since there were a few faces visible which might be of use to the investigation. He felt it just wasn't right to allow a young woman to view such filth, despite her rank, so Jenna was not made aware of the full extent of depraved behaviour on show, but what she did see sickened her.

"Talk about sinking to the depths of depravity," Andy

said to her afterwards as they sat in Brady's office. He shook his head slowly.

Jenna said nothing. Really, she thought, I shouldn't be surprised by anything I see in this job. Having just about got used to preparing herself to look at murder victims, she realised she was now witnessing horror of a different kind.

"Are you all right?" said Andy, worried by Jenna's pallor.

"Yeah," she said heavily. "Just sick at heart." She looked at Andy, appreciating his concern for her. "I don't know about you, but sometimes I feel I'm on the side of our killer. I mean, he's doing a good job, isn't he, ridding society of such scum?"

"I know what you mean," said Andy, "but we can't let vigilantes do as they please, or we'd have anarchy."

"No, I know. But our man isn't the usual sort of killer, is he? I mean, he's not a threat to anyone else in society, is he, except that particular group of paedophiles?"

"Not unless he's cornered," said Andy thoughtfully. "Then he could be dangerous."

The phone rang, and Jenna answered the call. It was the forensic department with notification of an email they were sending through to Brady's computer. Apparently, they'd retrieved something worth looking at from the doctored Merrydown page despite the Tipp-Ex and some underlying scratch damage. It only took a minute or two to bring up the email in question. Jenna nodded at Andy to move his chair closer so that they could both view the image, which she'd clicked on.

"'RY... VAL'," said Andy, reading off the image. "What do you make of that?"

"'VAL'?" said Jenna, beginning to feel the excitement of the hunt. "That has to be VALENTINE, doesn't it?"

"Could be," said Andy. "Notice that forensics said they pulled this from the middle of the scrawl, so that would suggest we're looking at the end of a first name and the beginning of a surname."

"What first names end in ry?" Jenna asked.

"Barry, Gary... er... Harry," replied Andy.

"Terry, Perry..." Jenna added. She stopped playing the guessing game as she could hear the voices of Jamie and Helen now in the larger office space outside Brady's room. They'd obviously just returned from their visit to Strawberry Hill. "Andy, would you go and catch up with Rob Flynn in Archives and see if he's got anything on the runaway boy from police records? I'm going to see how Jamie and Helen got on this afternoon."

Andy nodded and walked out of the room, leaving Jenna feeling much more positive towards him. She buzzed the other two and had them come into the office.

"So, how did it go with Hannah Bickford?" The pair looked at each other, and Jenna could see something was up.

"A wasted journey then or what?" said Jenna.

"No," said Helen. "Not wasted." She looked at Jamie.

"We picked up two new bits of information which could be helpful," he said but then went quiet again.

"Well. Come on then," said Jenna, beginning to get impatient with them.

"Valentine was someone's surname," said Jamie. Jenna nodded, thinking that his comment tallied with the emailed image she'd just seen.

But then they stayed silent.

"And the other bit of news?" What was the matter with them?

Jamie looked at Helen, who, to Jenna's surprise, suddenly got up, came over to her and put a hand on her shoulder.

"Jenna," Helen said softly. "We found out the identity of the girl they called 'The Vixen'."

Jenna needed no more clues. Their reticence to relay the news and now the tone of Helen's voice and the hand on her shoulder told her everything. "It's Lauren, isn't it?" she said.

\*

That evening in the lounge of their flat, Lucy, Jenna and Helen leant back in their faux-leather chairs again. With their differing shifts, they rarely seemed able to have a good old get-together, but it had looked to Lucy as if this evening would be different, and she'd anticipated a decent catch-up with her friends. However, Jenna and Helen had made other plans.

"But I've even made a shepherd's pie for us all. It's cooking now," she said, disappointed.

"That's really nice of you, Luce," Jenna reassured her. "I'll have some later, I promise, but I can't run on a full stomach." Greg had listened to Jenna recently, bemoaning the fact that she didn't get much exercise these days, and had urged her to try running. Tonight was her first time pounding the pavements, and she was track-suited up and ready to roll. She was also looking forward to getting out and being alone: an opportunity to reflect quietly on the day's events.

"And what about you, Helen?" Lucy turned to her other flatmate, who, at this time of the evening, was usually dressed down and cleared of make-up. Instead, she was dressed and made up as if for a date.

"Yeah, save some for me, too," she said. "Thanks, but I've got to go and see someone this evening."

"So, come on then," said Jenna "spill the beans!"

Helen tapped the side of her nose. "All in good time!" she said.

\*

The night was cold and the sky dark, although the neon lighting bathed everything in an eerie orange glow. Snow had been predicted again, and there was a severe chill in the air as Jenna began to jog. She started at a slow pace but gradually picked up speed as she established a rhythmic balance between her strides and her breathing. And an increased speed ensured that she soon felt warmer, too. So, feeling comfortable after half a mile or so, her thoughts were free to roam.

Lauren.

Actually, discovering she was The Vixen hadn't been quite the shock that her colleagues had anticipated since Jenna had made herself believe the worst for some time. So when the news finally hit, she was ready for it. And where was Lauren now? Living happily ever after? Hardly. What then? Mad? Dead? Jenna stepped up the speed again. It seemed the more her muscles ached, the less emotional she felt because her mind could only focus on the pain. That was good. She was now prepared to let her thoughts range across other emotionally challenging areas while temporarily anaesthetised.

Ben.

She hadn't visited the hospital tonight, having decided earlier that she was too tired after a busy day. Yet here she was running. She'd already covered more than a mile now. So she knew the real reason she hadn't gone to see him was not tiredness. The truth was she couldn't face telling him she was breaking up with him. And what was she going to say when she did pluck up the courage to visit him? That she was enjoying the company of one of his flatmates? That she nearly slept with her boss last night? Yeah, that would help his recovery, wouldn't it? And that moved her thoughts on to her number one problem.

Brady.

There was no doubt in her mind that she was in love with him. And everything she'd observed in him lately told her that he loved her in return. But he was married. And his wife was very ill. But did she feel guilty about what nearly happened yesterday? She explored her conscience. Yes? No? Whatever. It had just felt so right at that moment to follow her heart. And if that moment occurred again? She stopped suddenly as a car tooted its horn at her. So lost was she in thought she'd nearly run into the road. She waited at a pedestrian crossing for the lights to change, jogging on the spot to keep warm. The green man appeared, and she ran on, even faster now. Focus on the pain. Let it eclipse all other feelings. Breathe in. Breathe out. For a while, her mind was exclusively occupied with her breathing and stride pattern as she reached and maintained her top speed of the night. A mile or two like this, and her mind at last became clear enough to plan a personal to-do list without emotional interference.

Lauren: she would do her best within the team to find the serial killer and establish the truth about the abuse at Merrydown.

Ben: she would visit him tomorrow, no later, and let him down gently.

And Brady: she would love him... but she would love him from a distance. It was a solemn pledge to herself.

Jenna slowed to a gentle jogging pace again and gradually circled her way back to the flat. Checking her pedometer, she was pleased to find she'd covered nearly five miles. Not bad for the first time. And now she was ready for a shower... and Lucy's shepherd's pie.

\*

Ben had been moved from Intensive Care to Special Care. The peritonitis which had nearly killed him was now well under control, and he was expected to move to an ordinary ward within days. Fully alert now, he lay there thinking. Before he was taken ill, he'd made good progress with the search for his stepfather, Lenny Dawson, the man who'd beaten his mother black and blue until the only refuge she could find was in drink. Ben didn't want to kill him; that wasn't his way, even though things had got so bad that his mother had died of cirrhosis. No, for his part, he just wanted to see that Dawson got a thorough going-over so that he'd know what it was like to be on the receiving end for a change. And he was so close now: one or two more phone calls, and he should have him in his sights. Then he'd call in the help of either Rory or Greg, who both had a few useful connections. Either way, he'd make sure that Dawson got what was coming to him.

But Ben wasn't naïve. He knew what he was trying to arrange was illegal. He'd come to realise that he now had more than one reason to be wary of his police officer girlfriend. Rory had let him know that Jenna hadn't been able to visit the hospital the previous evening because she'd had a particularly busy day at work. Maybe her absence was a good thing: it meant he'd had time to decide what he was going to say to her when he did see her. He'd played around with excuses which would offer her a reasonable explanation for ending the relationship: I've got important family matters to attend to; I need more time to focus on them; I ought to go back and treat my former girlfriend with a bit more respect. He actually felt pleased that none of these excuses was a lie. Yes, it had to be done. Sweet as Jenna was, he knew he'd be better off calling it a day with her. Then, he'd be free to sort out his affairs properly, away from the intense gaze of the law.

\*

Nothing about a runaway in the archive records then, Jenna reflected as she drove into the hospital grounds that evening. Yet Mrs Fox had definitely told Brady there had been a police search for him. So, it must have been recorded. She puzzled over this one as she looked for a parking space in the hospital car park. As usual, nothing near the building. She eventually found a spot in a poorly lit corner of the park, as far from the main complex as it could be. She groaned. Her legs ached from yesterday's run, and she could have done without the long walk. She made her way to the entrance, considering the possible explanations for the missing record. Either Mrs Fox was lying – but why would she do that? Or the police themselves had been careless with the record, and it was lost. There was always the potential for human error, she supposed. Or someone had removed the record altogether. In light of the scrubbed-out name in the Merrydown log, that might be the most likely of the three options. The spectre of a corrupt senior officer was looming large again.

However, as she was now approaching the Special Care Unit, her thoughts turned to Ben and what she must do tonight. She realised her heartbeat was slightly raised, and her palms were damp. It was never easy telling someone that a relationship was over. She stopped in the ante-room, washed her hands, took a deep breath and entered the SCU. Ben was partially raised on several pillows, the first time Jenna hadn't found him lying on his back since he was admitted, and he gave her a welcoming half-smile. They exchanged pleasantries, each enquiring about the other's health. Then, there was a pause during which he appeared to Jenna to be a little nervous. She was just about to start with some opening sentences, which she'd been rehearsing, when he said, "Jen, I really appreciate all your visits while I've been in here. You've been a good friend to me." He'd put her off track for a moment, and she had to think hard about the sentence she'd intended to begin with. But her thinking was interrupted again. "The thing is, I'll be home soon…"

"That's good then, isn't it?" she said, trying to show some warmth while keeping her focus on her intended speech.

"But…" She noticed he was getting increasingly nervous. "When I get out, I've got some pressing family matters to see to…" She began to have an inkling of where this might be going. "And I kind of need to be on my own for a while to sort some things out."

"You mean you'd like to take a rain check on our friendship?" she asked, trying not to sound too relieved.

He nodded. "Don't get me wrong," he said. "It's been fun, but I need a bit of time and space. You know how it is."

She smiled. "That's fine with me," she said. "To be honest, things have been getting a bit complicated in my life too. So what you've just said… well, I was about to say something similar."

"I've also got a girlfriend," he said, "who I've treated pretty dishonestly, and I really ought to go back and give her the respect she deserves."

"You're a good man Ben," said Jenna. She went right up to his bedside and kissed him on the forehead. "Well done for having the courage to say what you said, and I hope things go well with your lady friend."

They held hands for a moment, a reassuring gesture to each other that their friendship had been worthwhile, albeit short. Then Jenna left the SCU and made her way downstairs and out of the main hospital building.

\*

Brady, who had been in to visit his wife, was also on his way out. Emerging from the main doors, he suddenly spotted Jenna's figure at some distance from him, making her way across the car park. He broke into a run to catch up with her and reached her in the dimly lit corner where she'd left her car.

"*Jenna!*"

She swung round, saw him and broke into a smile. He walked up to her slowly with his arms outstretched, inviting, so she took a couple of steps towards him. His black coat was open, and she was able to slip her arms around his waist and feel the warmth of his body. He held her in a tight embrace for a few seconds.

"How's Kathleen?" she asked, moving her head to look at him.

"She's very sick," he said. "How's Ben?"

"He's much better." She smiled fleetingly. "But it's over between us." He frowned slightly and she heaved a sigh. "I couldn't carry on pretending to be the loving girlfriend when… I'm in love with someone else." He held her closely and kissed her.

"I would have stayed the other night," he said.

"I wanted you to," she said.

"Listen…" It came out as a breathless whisper. "The children broke up for the Christmas holidays today. They're going to Kathleen's mum's tomorrow for three nights." He paused and looked her straight in the eyes, appealing to her. "Stay with me?"

She lifted her head and looked at the stars for inspiration while he kissed her exposed throat softly, waiting for his answer. The hardest decision of her life was now upon her, and she was sorely tempted. But she had made a pledge to herself only the night before. She lowered her head and let her forehead rest against his. They stood there silently for a few moments. Then she pulled back a little to look into his eyes.

"I love you," she whispered. He went to kiss her, but she pulled back again. "But I don't think we can do this to your wife. She needs you now more than ever." He knew she was right. But his heart ached. "So…" She kissed him lightly on the cheek. "I'm going to go and have some fun with my friends and let you go and be a good husband and father."

She stopped for breath. Her voice broke up as the emotion overtook her, and she realised that what she was saying was not what she wanted at all. It didn't help that she could see tears in his eyes. But she pressed on, knowing that she was doing the right thing. "And we'll just be good together, professionally… like we've always been." Now, her eyes had begun to sting.

"Jen," he said softly, and she nearly caved in: he'd never called her that before. "I love you." Her tears began to roll, but nothing more was said. What else was there to say?

Jenna brought his hands back from behind her waist, gave them one last squeeze and then turned and walked to her car. Pressing the key fob, she threw one final hesitant look his way, but he'd already turned to walk off. Then she got in, slammed the door, slumped over the wheel and cried her heart out.

\*

Back at work the next day, after his period of leave, Brady sat at his desk, deep in thought. Dinesh had called him down earlier in the morning to view some material retrieved from Fox's mobile: two images which Dinesh had said he'd kept hidden from Jenna and Andy. "For your eyes only, sir," he'd said. Brady was initially concerned that the IT whizz-kid had taken a bit of a liberty deciding who got to see what but soon understood the motive. The material was, as he'd expected, utterly sickening, but, as Dinesh had pointed out, the faces of the two adolescent children were discernible and, in Dinesh's words, could perhaps be of use to the investigation. Brady had studied them closely. Were these the two favourites the team had heard so much about? He'd had Dinesh enlarge the images to their maximum and looked again. The girl looked wild, as if she'd been brought up by wolves, as in some dark fairy tale. As for the boy... Brady thought there was something about him that was familiar. Hadn't he seen those features somewhere before? He'd decided they matched the e-fit of the biker, which had been put together with the help of Sebastian Clarke and Mira Dinetski. A person of increasing interest thought Brady.

He was just about to look over the suspect profiles again when a call came through from reception, telling him that someone had come in to see him. Brady groaned inwardly. He'd heard that Elvira Fox had tried to see him while he was on compassionate leave, and he thought she might have come back to make eyes at him again. For crying out loud, he thought, she's turning into a stalker. But the duty sergeant on reception assured him that this was not Mrs Fox. In fact, he said, it was a young man claiming to have some information relating to the current spate of murders. Brady, therefore, asked for the caller to be shown to one of the interview rooms.

When Brady arrived and opened the door, he saw a dark-haired man in a leather jacket, aged early to mid-twenties, sitting at the interview table. Brady extended his hand to shake the other's, but the young man kept both of his beneath the table, on his lap. It wasn't taken personally: many people felt uncomfortable around the police, particularly, of course, if they were ex-offenders. He looked straight at the man, trying to make out into which category he fell.

"So, the sergeant tells me you have some information for me," Brady began, taking a seat opposite the visitor.

"Yes, I do," the man replied.

Brady waited a few moments, watching the man shift about in his seat. He observed the eyes glancing here and there. "Information regarding what exactly?" he prompted.

"Your serial murderer," said the young man. He moved suddenly and sat on his hands.

"And what can you tell me?" Brady asked.

The man remained silent, his eyes now downcast.

"Sir?" Brady prompted again.

The young man made eye contact for the first time. "I'm the murderer," he said.

In his years of experience, Brady had come across many time-wasters. Some people liked getting themselves into the limelight; some were fantasists; some needed bed and board and, therefore, appreciated being locked up for the night. But his experience had also taught him that you just never knew. If ninety-nine out of a hundred were hoaxers, supposing this was the hundredth?

"Shall we start with your name?" said Brady.

"Liam Johnson," said the young man. His eyes were flitting again.

"And your occupation?"

"Currently unemployed," said Johnson. Brady sighed inwardly, anticipating that what came next would imply the need for somewhere to spend the night that wasn't a doorstep or a park bench – not that this young man appeared to be sleeping rough. But that didn't happen. Instead, Johnson said, "I've been in the army."

Brady's mind shifted gear. He suddenly had the killer's profile in his mind's eye and was already ticking boxes: 'ex-army' was a key box.

"Mr Johnson, are you here to make a confession?" he asked.

"Yes," said the visitor.

"Well, I'll have two of my officers come down and hear what you have to say. Then perhaps we can have another chat afterwards. Okay?" Liam Johnson nodded. Brady stood up and extended his hand again, but there was still no handshake. He left the interview room.

Returning to his office, Brady called for DCs Cartwright and Grant. When they appeared, he told them about the man downstairs, who was waiting to confess. Andy shook his head in disbelief.

"Oh, come on, boss!" he said. "When does a real murderer turn up to confess his crime? This guy's wasting our time!"

"Male, IC1, in his twenties, dressed in a biker jacket... and ex-army." Brady waited for the information to be processed. "So I don't think we can afford *not* to take his confession, do you?"

Ever the mediator, Jamie Grant, looked at his hot-headed colleague and then back at their superior officer. "Unlikely, but not impossible, I suppose," he said.

"Especially if our killer is now having a mental breakdown, for example," Brady added. "That could explain why someone suddenly acts out of character." He thought for a moment. "Perhaps the burden of what he's done has become too great to bear." He recalled the visitor's eyes flitting everywhere. Jamie nodded as he left Brady's office. Andy followed, still shaking his head. Alone again, Brady decided he agreed with Jamie. Unlikely, he thought. And yet... He glanced down at his hands and remembered the rejected handshake in the interview room. And all of a sudden, he could hear the golf club captain's words ringing in his ears. "… he never took his gloves off, not even to shake hands with me…"

A shiver raced down his spine.

\*

No sooner had Brady sat down at his desk again than Andy buzzed him from the interview room.

"Boss – he's gone!"

"What do you mean 'he's gone'?" said Brady. "Gone where?"

"He's gone. Walked out."

Brady swore under his breath. "Seal off the room and get the chair fingerprinted," he said. "And ask the duty sergeant to arrange for us to have the last hour's worth of CCTV covering reception so we can get a still of our Mr Johnson." When he got off the line, Brady buzzed through on another for Helen and Jenna to join him.

He quickly got them up to speed. "So," he concluded, "Helen, can you deal with the CCTV when it comes through? Also, can you check on Johnson's army credentials? Where's he living now? What's he been up to since he left the army? And do we know anything about his current state of mind? Make this a priority, will you?"

Helen was about to leave the office when Jenna added, "While you're running an armed forces check on Johnson, how's about doing one for the surname Valentine?" She looked at Brady for his approval.

"If Johnson or Valentine were in the army, there would be photos and fingerprints on record. Get hold of what you can, will you?" he told them.

"Gut reaction?" said Jenna when they were alone.

"My gut reaction," said Brady at length, "… he's not our man." Jenna frowned at him, inviting him to explain. "Dinesh got a bit more off Fox's mobile this morning," he said, white-lying to protect Dinesh's motive in having held material back from Jenna. "I saw the faces of an adolescent boy and girl. They could be the two favourites we've heard about from all those years ago, in which case I'd strongly advise you not to go and look at them in case the female face…"

"Don't worry. I've already seen enough, thanks," Jenna replied.

"But the male face, well, I'd say it's definitely not the face of Liam Johnson, even though it was the face of an adolescent rather than an adult," said Brady. He frowned. "I've seen that face somewhere," he said, puzzled. Then his expression lightened. "Must be the e-fit."

\*

Gerald Hope always carried two mobiles with him. Hearing the more unfamiliar ringtone, he hurriedly reached into his inside jacket pocket.

"Yes?"

"I've read the report on the investigation."

"And?"

"They know the home is a common factor."

"Hmm. What would you advise?"

"They're bound to be back again. Make sure the prize is securely locked away throughout the day, and make sure the other room is dressed again to look like the sick room."

"Supposing they insist on looking in the locked room?"

"They can't easily insist without a search warrant."

"And if they bring one with them?"

"Unlikely, they'll have got that far, but if they have, call me immediately. I'll find a pretext to block the search."

"Did the report mention anything else of significance?"

"It's likely the guy they're after was a resident."

"How long ago?"

"Probably more than a decade. Don't worry: you won't be in his sights."

"What about you?"

"I know how to take care of myself."

The caller ended the call and thought again about what he'd read in the CIT report. Then he cast his mind back: which child could have grown up to match those suspect profiles?

He'd spoken with bravado just now, but in reality, he knew that somewhere out there was a deadly assassin… and Moses was only too aware that he could be the next target.

\*

The killer woke, gasping for breath. He'd been drowning in a sea of roses. Small white roses, bunched ominously together in wreath formations, like the ones he'd seen arrive at his home in the days leading up to his parents' funeral. And large red roses with eerily flabby petals, which brushed his face softly and whispered to him, dripping blood onto his lips and thrusting their sickly, heady scent up his nostrils. He was surrounded, trapped, airless. And underneath the surface, where he tried to tread water to stay alive, thorns like bony daggers tore at his legs and buttocks, poking, prodding and scratching until his lower half stung and he yelled out in pain.

It took him a full few minutes to regain his perspective and shake off the dream. Minutes in which he couldn't help turning over in his mind the image of the priest holding a single red rose in his hands and then offering it to him as a love token.

"Don't hurt me, Father," he'd begged.

"Why would I hurt you?" the priest had replied softly. "I love you."

He'd hated roses ever since. Crimson beauty, like the blood of Christ. Savage defences, like the crown of thorns.

He knew the words of the Church, though he hadn't set foot inside a place of worship since he was a child. But now it was time to make amends. Looking through Catholic websites, he'd managed to locate his photograph at last. What was that silly pseudonym that he'd once heard him called? The Archangel.

Satan more like…

And now he knew his real name.

With Christmas fast approaching, he thought the time really had come to attend a seasonal mass.

\*

Five days before Christmas, Kingston nick held its Staff Christmas Party. The MIT members were also invited. Brady had already made it clear to Jenna that he wouldn't be staying for more than fifteen minutes: just enough time, he'd said, to wish his team Merry Christmas and join the

DCI in thanking Kingston colleagues for making them feel welcome in the last few months. Jenna had tried to persuade him otherwise, but he'd protested that he wouldn't be able to bear not holding her close to him, which he could hardly do in public. "And besides," he'd added, "you told me to go and be a good husband and father, so I'll be going off to join my family." He'd looked at her disappointed face and smiled. "Only following your instructions!" It was meant light-heartedly and was taken that way. But when Jenna got ready for the event, much later on, it was with a heavy heart that she put on her low-cut black dress, gold stilettos and oversized Christmas tree earrings. She and Helen hired a cab back to Kingston that evening, intending to enjoy a few glasses of wine, which Jenna thought might help to numb her heartache.

When they arrived, they made their way into a large room, usually used for conferences but now splendidly decked out with paper chains, fairy lights and assorted decorations that had the wow factor. Along the length of the room ran a series of trestle tables decorated and covered with seasonal fork buffet foods and drinks in abundance. In one corner stood a huge Christmas tree laden with purple and silver baubles; in the opposite corner, a disco had been set up and awaited its DJ. Everything promised a super party. If only I didn't feel so bleak, Jenna thought. She sighed. Christmas was the loneliest time when you were on your own.

A young female officer got started on the karaoke and sang a cheeky "Santa Baby" in the style of Monroe-sings-to-the-President, which had everybody whooping and cheering. Others took turns with varying degrees of success. "You should have a go," said Helen suddenly. "You'd out-sing the lot of them!" Jenna was hardly in the mood to push herself forward and take the limelight, but Jamie had overheard Helen's words and took it upon himself to approach the microphone and announce that the next singer would be Acting Sergeant Jenna Jones. There was a loud cheer from several of her colleagues. Not wanting to let them down, she slid off her seat and walked up to the mic. The intro to Wham's "Last Christmas" was beginning, and she dutifully took centre stage and began to sing its sad lyrics. The audience hushed: she really could sing. Andy was smitten all over again, and Brady, who'd just entered the room, stood and stared.

"I keep my distance, but you still catch my eye..." he heard her sing. It just about summed up their situation, he thought sadly.

At the end, there was enthusiastic applause. Jenna returned to her seat, a little embarrassed by the attention. Brady approached her. "Well done!" he said rather formally, aware that others were listening in. "You've really set the benchmark there. I pity anyone else following your performance!" She thanked him. It all felt a bit false, and she picked up her wine and took a gulp. But someone else had taken up the karaoke now, and all eyes were on her. Seeing that they were now unobserved, Brady squeezed Jenna's hand. Then he left and went to join the DCI on the other side of the room.

She accepted the offer of more wine from someone who was going around refilling glasses. It was doing the trick and lifting her spirits. Beginning to feel heady, she decided to step out of the room for a breather. Andy followed her. "You've got a beautiful voice," he said admiringly.

"Thanks!" she replied. The wine was really kicking in now, and she looked at Andy in a new light. "I'm glad I kept you with me the other day," she said, her speech slow. "You're all right, really."

Andy's heart leapt. "I'm glad you kept me with you," he replied. He moved in closer to her, thinking this might be his moment. But Brady suddenly emerged from the party room. He stood there in front of them, and all three of them had an instant sense of déjà vu. There was an awkward pause, and then he extended his hand to Andy and wished him a Merry Christmas. Andy shook his hand.

"Andy, would you mind if I had a word with my acting sergeant before I leave?" Brady asked. He'd already got his coat on.

"Sure," said Andy and gestured to him to go ahead. He went back in through the double doors. Brady cocked his head and looked down the dimly lit corridor, indicating to Jenna that they should walk that way. Several paces down, another corridor ran off to the left. Brady turned into this one, dimmer than the first, pulled her towards him and wrapped his arms around her.

"Make that two words – Merry Christmas," he whispered, and he kissed her. "Actually, make that three words: I love you." He kissed her again. He looked down at her exposed décolletage and then up into her eyes. "You look stunning tonight," he said, and he let the nail of his forefinger trace a V-shape from just below her right ear, down towards her cleavage and up again to just below her left ear. It was one of the most erotic things anyone had ever done to her, and if he'd asked her now to stay with him, she would have answered 'yes', pledge or no pledge. But tonight, it was he who was strong. He brought her hands round from the back of his neck, kissed each one in turn and then placed them back at her sides. "I've got to go," he said and began to make a move. "I'll walk you back to the party. But I'll have to leave you there." They wandered back quietly down the main corridor, and, true to his word, he left her at the party doors and wandered on a few steps. But she stopped him.

"Dom!" she said. She realised she'd never used his first name before. It felt beautifully intimate. He opened his arms again, which, considering where they now stood, was taking a risk, but right then, they only had eyes for each other. She ran to him for one last kiss. At that precise moment, the DCI happened to come through the doors. Their body language said it all. Jenna backed off quickly, muttered, "Goodnight, sir," to the senior officer and returned through the doors to the party.

The two men walked off down the corridor together. "Dom, your personal life is none of my business," said Delgado abruptly, "but... a word of advice." His steps slowed almost to a halt. "Don't let your affair get in the way of work, will you? We've still got a serial killer to catch."

Brady, slightly annoyed by this intrusion into his private life, bristled. "First of all, sir," he replied pointedly, "I'm not having an affair, despite how it looks, and that's the truth." Strictly speaking, it was. "And secondly, the net is closing in around the killer, I can assure you." Hopeful of a lead from the armed forces' records, he stuck his neck out even further. "We might even nail him by the New Year."

\*

Jenna had had enough of keeping her emotional burden to herself. What were friends for if you couldn't share your innermost secrets with them? In the cab on the way home from the party, she told Helen everything.

"You always said he was out of bounds," said Helen, shaking her head.

"I know," wailed Jenna. She was past the euphoric stage and had now hit the depths of despair. Tears welled in her eyes. "I can't have him," Jenna said, trying hard to rein in the volume of her voice. Her emotional turmoil, exacerbated by wine, made it very difficult. "But I love him," she sobbed.

Back in the flat and well past midnight, Jenna was beginning to think more clearly. A couple of glasses of water had helped. She lay in her bed in the darkness and began to realise that she needed to resolve to start afresh. When morning came, Helen suggested a similar solution over breakfast. "You've got to back off," she said. Despite her misery, Jenna was keen to hear what Helen had to say. "I'm not going to tell you what you want to hear, you know. But I am going to tell you what is best for you." Jenna gave her a weak smile. "Listen, Ben is now history, and Brady is unavailable. So go out there and make an effort with someone else. Stop thinking about love and just enjoy someone's friendship instead." Jenna knew she was right. She drank her coffee thoughtfully. "What about this Greg guy you've been telling us about?" said Helen. "You said he was nice, didn't you?" Jenna thought of Greg's smile. Her friend had a point.

"It's just that every time Brady touches me, I go weak inside," said Jenna.

"Well, don't let him touch you then!" said Helen, looking straight into Jenna's eyes. "Jenna, it's the only way."

*

On her way to work, an hour later, Jenna determined that there should be no more physical contact with Brady. In a short space of time, she mused, he'd become like an addiction; she had to wean herself off him. Therefore, she decided that all interaction from now on had to be strictly professional. Smile and call him 'sir' again – but avoid his touch! And that meant that she would be free to develop friendships with others. Helen had reminded her that Greg was nice. Actually, he was more than nice, so that was a good start.

Her mobile buzzed as she was parking her car. As if on cue, it was a text from Greg.

The text said: 'Run with me 2nite? G'

Helen was right: Greg might be the way out of her emotional maze. She immediately texted back 'Yes' and attached a happy face emoji. Between them, she and Greg arranged for him to run to her flat and to start out running together from there.

She arrived in the MIT section twenty minutes later, feeling a little more positive. But before she could settle herself at her workstation, Brady asked her to go ahead into his office while he spoke to Helen. The screen in front of her was taking time to warm up, so Helen told Brady she would be a few minutes.

He left her, wandered back into his office and shut the door. He saw Jenna waiting by his desk, reading something with her back turned towards him. He couldn't resist it. Walking up quietly behind her, he slipped his hands around her waist, but she swung around suddenly. "Sir, don't! Please!" she pleaded. His hands sprang off her as if he'd just touched something hot and had burned his fingers. In a sense, he had.

"Sir?" he said quietly, disappointed. "What happened to 'Dom'?" He watched her frown and then squeeze her eyes shut as if she was in pain. When she opened them, she looked him in the eye. "I can't move on if you don't let me go," she said. Reluctantly, he backed off and sat down at his desk. There was a long pause in which she waited for him to say something. He was replaying in his mind what they'd said to him at the hospital yesterday: that a scan had revealed the extent of his wife's brain damage and that he would be well advised to seek full-time care for her now. He'd realised that he would never love or be loved by his wife again, that he'd be in limbo. But should he tell Jenna that? He didn't want her to give herself to him out of pity. He looked up at her now.

"You're right," he said gravely. "I have to let you move on."

She went and stared out of the window while he buzzed Helen. The next few minutes were silent and awkward. And then Helen came into the room.

Brady got on with the job. What else was there to do? "I noticed the armed forces have been in touch with you," he said to Helen. "Any luck, first of all, with Johnson?"

"Yes," she said. "Photos, fingerprints – the lot. But…" She shook her head. "He's been diagnosed with PTSD." Jenna turned back from the window and looked at her enquiringly. "Post-traumatic stress disorder," said Helen. "He's under a psychiatrist. I got in touch with this guy, Professor Philip McBride, and he told me that Johnson couldn't accept that friends of his had died when he hadn't, and he was always going on about how he deserved to be punished in some way. The professor agreed with me that owning up to a string of murders might be his way of attracting punishment."

"So we can eliminate him?" said Brady.

"I think so," Helen replied.

"So, who does that leave in the frame?" said Jenna. "Valentine?"

"He's our best bet, isn't he?" said Brady. He turned again to Helen. "Any joy with that name in army records?"

Helen pulled a face. "There were two Valentines. One was a retired brigadier, and the other was a corporal currently serving in Afghanistan, and he's already been there for eight months." She shrugged her shoulders. "I don't know where that leaves this investigation," she said, sighing with frustration.

Brady had been so hopeful that the army's records would turn up a lead for them, but clearly, it wasn't to be. He sighed heavily. "We could really do with a lucky break," he said.

\*

He didn't buy roses; he chose lilies. Eight white lilies. Clean and simple. The florist asked if he required the flowers to be wrapped, but he said that wouldn't be necessary as they were destined for the graveyard, which was only a five-minute walk away.

Thinking, he strolled along the road, turned through a large wrought-iron gateway into the graveyard and made his way first down the main pathway, then down a second leading off to the left.

And there they were: his parents.

Today was the anniversary of their passing.

He squatted down and, resting on his haunches, placed the flowers carefully beside the cremation urns, which held their remains. His mind drifted back, as it always did when he came here, to his childhood days. The clatter of a helicopter flying overhead broke into his bittersweet memories of those early years. He turned his gaze upwards, watched the rotor action, listened to the thrum of the blades and found his mind being propelled forward in time.

More bittersweet memories.

He peered down again at the double urn, reached out his hands and rearranged the lilies so that instead of lying in a single bunch, they were made to lie four on each side of his parents' remains. "That's better," he mumbled. Then, a little louder, "Love you." He rose from his squatting position, turned and headed back towards the churchyard gates. His bike was parked only yards away from the entrance.

Straddling the vehicle, he prepared to put on his helmet but then stopped and held it in both hands while he examined the feeling, which had just bubbled up. It was empty, raw and bitter. He recognised it immediately: it always overcame him at some point on this anniversary day. And he felt as he always did on this date: robbed.

He started up the bike, sped back to the flat, stripped off his leathers and made a beeline for his electronic keyboard. A little dabble in the blues always seemed to do the trick.

"Is that you, Rory?" a voice called from one of the bedrooms.

Rory didn't reply. He was already lost in his music.

\*

That evening, wrapped up against the cold, Jenna and Greg took their first run together. Greg's easy breathing and chatter contrasted sharply with Jenna's more laboured inhalations, so she was grateful that he had slowed his own pace in order to stay by her side. They planned to jog along the pavements initially and then, after the first few miles when they'd picked up the Thames towpath, to increase their speed until they reached Hampton Court and then turn past Bushy Park and head back towards Kingston, by which time, Greg suggested, they'd be able to hit their top speed.

Jenna was glad she'd already put in some running practice on her own. She dreaded to think what she would have been like otherwise. As it was, she felt comfortable enough jogging along but made sure to let her companion know at the outset that she couldn't run and talk at the same time, as she needed all her breath to fuel the exercise. "Tell me how Ben's getting on," she said, hoping this one question would keep Greg talking for quite a while and allow her to establish her footfall and breathing pattern.

"He's doing okay," Greg replied. He was then quiet for a quarter of a mile or so. There were certain aspects of Ben's life that Greg thought he'd better circumnavigate in the presence of a police officer. One was the drug habit; the other was concerning his intentions regarding his stepfather. Greg sifted through Ben's news in his mind, identifying what he could tell Jenna without landing his flatmate in the mire. At last, he spoke again. "Actually, Ben came back to work yesterday, and he didn't feel too tired at the end of the day. Mind you," he continued, "I did make sure he didn't do too much on his first day back."

Jenna hadn't intended to talk yet, but her surprise

demanded a comment. "You work together, then?" she said. It came out in a puff of breath.

"Yeah," he said. "Didn't Ben ever say?" She shook her head. "Rory, Ben and I all work together. Actually, Rory and I have known each other for a long time and, when we became flatmates, we advertised for a third person and along came Ben. We hit it off immediately. Anyway," he went on, "Ben's back with Lottie, and he's even taking her out tonight." He saw her frown and tilt her head a little. "Lottie Fisher, his old girlfriend. To tell you the truth, we were sort of rivals over her for a bit." They were nearing the river by now, and although the darkness hid the swirling rapids from sight, the rush of the weir and the watery odour hit their other senses. Across the bridge, they set off again, side by side on the towpath, and Greg took up where he'd left off. "Yeah, Lottie and I made a little connection for a while. Nothing serious. And then I realised that Ben was smitten, so I backed off."

Jenna thought this odd and felt the need to speak again. "If you'd really been in love," she said somewhat breathlessly, "then I don't think you would have given her up so easily, not even for a best mate."

"She was cute," Greg replied. His voice dropped. "But I wasn't ready for commitment."

The towpath narrowed and forced Jenna to run behind Greg for a mile or two. She was still thankful to him for maintaining a slowish pace: he was probably capable, she thought, of doing at least twice or maybe even three times his current speed. The night air was cold and made the airways sore. Jenna was also vaguely aware that the burn of lactic acid was beginning to register in her leg muscles. But as her mind was elsewhere, she ran on, oblivious to her aches and pains. Lottie Fisher, she thought. She tried to picture what Lottie might look like and visualised a pretty girl who flirted coquettishly at work, possibly with all three flatmates. And then Greg had 'backed off', he'd said, to let Ben step in? It occurred to her that Ben might have repaid the compliment and 'backed off' to let Greg step in with her. She'd liked the word 'connection'. "Lottie and I made a little connection for a while," he'd said a couple of miles back. Was that what he was doing now? Making a little connection with her? She liked the idea. Nothing serious, just an easy-going friendship: exactly what she needed right now.

They left the towpath to cross Kingston Bridge and then picked it up again on the other side of the Thames, heading upriver towards Hampton Court. This was the stretch of pathway where she'd walked with Brady that time when he'd told her about his suspicions that they may be dealing with a paedophile police officer. Were they *ever* going to make any progress with that line of enquiry? Greg dropped back by her side as the path widened again. "You're doing real good," he said. "I would never have known you were a novice runner."

"I'm going to need a breather soon, though," she spluttered, her breath rasping.

"Hampton Court, and then I'll let you rest!" He laughed. "It's not far."

"You're a hard taskmaster," she puffed.

A couple of miles upstream, they reached the imposing buildings and grounds of Hampton Court. The Christmas ice rink had been set up in front of the palace, and hordes of people were skating round the rink. Jenna stopped on the towpath, bent herself in half to let her head hang down and gradually regained her normal breathing rate. She drew herself up slowly. Greg stood in front of her, looking so relaxed he might have just arrived there by riverboat. She couldn't even hear his breathing, and they must have covered several miles by now. A group of noisy revellers on the ice rink caught his attention. "Looks like fun!" he said. He pointed through the railings, which separated the riverside from the palace gardens. Jenna followed his gaze. "Hey, wanna go skating?" he said.

"Not tonight," said Jenna, flapping her hands in front of her face to show she'd nearly had enough for one night. And they still had the return run to consider. She was sure that Greg, on the other hand, would have had the stamina for plenty more physical challenge tonight. "I'll come out with you Thursday evening, though, if you like," she said.

"You're on!"

"On one condition." She adopted a mock-serious expression.

"What's that?" he asked.

"That we drive here!"

\*

"I haven't skated since I was a child," said Jenna as she drove them away from north Kingston two nights later and headed over the Thames towards Hampton Court. "I could be spending a lot of time tonight, you know, sitting on the ice instead of skating on it!" She laughed.

"Don't worry," said Greg. "I'll be by your side. If you need to, just hang on to me."

"Yeah! I probably will. For dear life!" She chuckled again. "You sound confident," she said, taking her eyes off the road for a second and catching his expression. He looked assured. She looked back at the road. "Have you skated a lot?"

"I learnt to ice skate at a very young age, and then," he paused, " I didn't get to skate again for a long time. But I've been to the Streatham rink once or twice in recent times, and, well, I suppose it's like riding a bike. It soon comes back to you."

"Well, let's hope that it soon comes back to me!" she said.

They passed the famous Lion Gate entrance to Bushy Park and cruised around the corner towards the main gates of Hampton Court. Once the car was parked, they made their way towards the open-air rink.

The night was bitterly cold, much colder than it had been two nights before when they'd come out for a run; minute snowflakes had even begun to flurry around them. Jenna was glad that they were both well wrapped in hats, fleeces, scarves and gloves. She had even taken the precaution, before coming out, of putting on an extra pair of leggings under her tracksuit bottoms to give her some added protection in case she fell on the ice, an event which she considered highly likely.

Floodlights now lit up the rink in front of the famous palace façade in a glorious azure blue. Promenade lights, which encircled it, twinkled as they bobbed back and forth in the wind, and Jenna caught sight of a small child gazing up at them in awe. For him, the magic of Christmas had already arrived. Perhaps it had for her as well.

She and Greg queued briefly, showed their tickets, hired their skates and then sat and fastened them up. When they were ready, Greg held his right hand out to her, and she took it. He then put his left arm around her waist, and they set off very slowly on the ice.

At first, Jenna was hesitant but glad for Greg's support. Many parents had brought little children skating for a Christmas treat, and that meant that there were lots of small bodies wobbling, darting and sliding unpredictably all over the place. Several youths were also tearing round the rink at top speed, which Jenna found disconcerting. Greg said he'd go and sort them out – he seemed fearless – but fortunately, someone from the company came on to have a word with them and that put an end to their exuberant behaviour. Gradually, Jenna's confidence grew and at last, she indicated to Greg that she was able to go it alone. She carried on in a forward motion and was impressed to see him turn and skate backwards in the same direction, all the while holding her gaze. She felt her spirits lift. Her heart had been so weighted down recently that it was a relief to be enjoying the company of this new friend without serious commitment.

But then he put both hands out, took hers and drew her to him, and, for a moment, she thought he was going to kiss her. Instead, he looked into her eyes and said, "You've got some tiny snowflakes caught in your eyelashes." He smiled, and his face lit up warmly. "It makes you look really cute!" And then he let go of her hands, turned again and skated away at an impressive rate, leaving Jenna feeling slightly bemused. She hadn't got very far when she felt his hands land on her waist from behind. He'd obviously completed a fast circuit and had caught her up again, and this time, his support at her back propelled her forward faster. And she loved the feeling of the wind whipping up off the river into her face, and her spirits rose again. At last, he guided her to the side, where they both caught hold of the rail and took a breather.

"You're doing really well," he said to her. He slipped off one of his gloves and gently wiped a snowflake away from her eye.

And then he did kiss her.

It was their first kiss. Jenna was glad it was light-hearted and brief, as she certainly wasn't ready for more than that at the moment. But, she had to admit, there was potential with Greg. And she'd enjoyed that moment of intimacy with him. It was like a seal on their friendship. He studied her face for a moment. "You're very pretty," he told her. She was about to thank him when he continued, "I'm beginning to miss your face when it's not around," and she wondered where this was leading. Surely he's not going to ask me to move in with him, she thought. What sort of signals have I been sending out? But he hadn't got that far. Instead, he asked, "Do the police have some sort of website where I could find your face among the ranks and gaze at it when I'm missing you the most?" He was beginning to sound overdramatic, and she was relieved to think he might be teasing her. She touched him lightly on the chest with both hands, pretending to push him away.

"You're taking the you-know-what, aren't you?" she said laughingly.

"I'm serious," he said, smiling.

"Our identities are protected," she said in a cloak-and-dagger voice, "but I can give you a photo for your wallet if that'll keep you happy!" She was surprised that his face didn't immediately register pleasure after his stated desire to see more of her face, but then the message seemed to hit home.

"I'd like that," he said. He turned and looked round the rink. "Right, ready for more?"

Her growing confidence on the ice now made her more forward than she'd intended to be, and before she could stop herself, she replied, "More skating or more kisses?" She laughed playfully.

"Both?" he suggested. He looked serious again.

But she really wasn't ready for involvement. Brady was going to take some getting over.

She smiled her best smile at him, placed a finger on his lips and then pushed away from the rail and skated off. Her heart felt lighter than it had done in weeks.

*

The skating session lasted an hour, and then they slipped across the road to the famous Mitre Inn and ordered some drinks. As Jenna was the driver, she went for her usual lime and soda spritz while Greg asked for a beer. Then, they settled themselves down at a table for two in the corner. The place was crowded, only to be expected two days before Christmas, so they were lucky to be able to slip in just as another couple were leaving.

Jenna sipped her drink and looked at Greg with admiration. "You keep yourself super-fit, don't you?" she said.

She thought back to how easily she'd seen him run, as well as how capable he'd been on the ice tonight.

"Well, once you've got the exercise bug," he said, "it's hard to ignore it."

"And when did you catch the exercise bug?" she asked nonchalantly, looking round at the many different punters enjoying the warm glow of the open fire, the smell of wood smoke and the exciting pre-Christmas atmosphere of the Mitre.

"Exercise became a way of life in the army," he said. She looked back at him with a questioning expression. "Afghanistan," he said. "Rory and me – we were there together." He drank his beer and turned his face away from her to bathe in the warmth of the fire. Then, looking back at her, he said, "That's where we met, Rory and me, a couple of London boys with loads in common. Got on like a house on fire from the start." A smile played across his lips, evidence that he was recalling good times with his best mate.

"Oh," she said. And the two of them work at Ace Haulage, she thought. The next question bubbled up in her mind and tumbled off her tongue before she could stop it. "Neither of you has the name of Valentine, do you?" It sounded absurd, and she laughed nervously.

He put his glass down carefully and looked her in the eye, his face inscrutable. "*My* name's Thomas," he said. "Greg Thomas."

Relief washed over her, and she suddenly felt an urgent need to explain herself as the atmosphere between them seemed to have cooled a little. "Sorry," she said quickly. "That old cliché, you know: the police are never off duty – it happens to be true." But despite her declaration, she consciously avoided checking Rory's surname, thinking that she'd already taken a step too far. "It's just a line of enquiry we've been following. But to be honest, we seem to have hit a dead end." She stopped herself from going any further and took another sip of her spritz. She was well aware that she should not be discussing details of the case with anyone outside MIT.

"No problem," Greg said, smiling again. "Actually, it's good to know that you officers are always alert. There are a lot of evil people out there."

"Tell me about it," she said, visualising a purple face and lolling, swollen tongue. She drank from her glass. "What are you doing for Christmas?" she asked, quickly changing the subject.

"Oh, this and that," he said. "Hang around the flat, probably."

"No family to go to?" He shook his head. No wonder the three flatmates got on well, she thought. All of them seemed to be alone in the world. "Well, listen," she said, "I'm going over to my dad's on Christmas morning to cook us dinner, and you're welcome to come."

"Thanks for the invitation," he replied. He put his drink down, placed his hands on the table, and smiled. She was pleased to see that any awkwardness that her questioning may have caused a moment ago was no longer there. "Can I text you early in the day and let you know?"

"Of course," she said and placed both of her hands on his.

In spite of the heat inside the pub, she realised that his hands were still gloved. She instantly dismissed the question emerging in her mind as ridiculous.

\*

Jenna couldn't sleep. She looked at the digital display at 3.43, dozed and then woke abruptly and looked at the display again: 6.37. Her mind was overloaded and over-excited as she realised it was Christmas Eve. She pushed back the duvet and got up. She was aware that the darkness in the room had receded and that the shady outlines of her bed and other pieces of furniture were now visible. The heating was just coming on, but the ambient temperature was still chilly, so she wrapped her fleecy dressing gown around her, drew back the curtains and took in the first light of day.

Two contrasting ribbons of blue and gold had forged parallel pathways across the grey dawn, and in between, bright patches of yellow-white light glinted in the puckered fabric of a cloudy morning sky. It made Jenna catch her breath, just as she'd caught her breath for a split second the night before when Greg had scanned her face admiringly and had commented how cute the snowflakes in her eyelashes made her look.

"Lovely," she whispered aloud. Maybe *he* would help her heart to heal after all.

\*

Christmas Eve. Midnight Mass had taken place, and the Church of Our Immaculate Lady had emptied quickly. The priest sat in the confessional and ran the petals of the poinsettia between his fingers, slowly stroking its stem while listening to his young visitor. Here was a teenage boy, so confused, so utterly lost. As he listened to the youth talking, the priest reflected that it was quite unusual these days for teenagers to seek refuge and forgiveness in the Church.

Unusual, yes, but *very* welcome.

The priest listened intently, stipulated the need to recite the rosary as penance and then granted forgiveness. It was clear that the boy's voice was still breaking. First, it was high-pitched; then it became husky; then parts of sentences would go missing altogether as the larynx struggled to decide whether they belonged to boy or man. The overall effect in the priest's mind was of a vulnerable youngster looking for guidance; he would dearly like to spend time with him in total privacy, give him the advice he was seeking… and offer him even more. As the boy began to rise from his seat, the priest quickly specified a date on which, he said, he would like to see the boy return. It was an evening in the week ahead when the priest knew he would have the boy entirely to himself. To his delight, the young lad agreed to return. The priest eagerly anticipated the thrills which the following Wednesday evening promised.

\*

While the confessional had been in use, one other person had remained sitting in the pew, silently gazing at the altar. He watched, intrigued, as the moonlight, refracted by the multiple panels of stained glass, dabbed the white altar cloth in red, yellow and blue flecks. He watched for a while as the colours merged, danced separately and then melted together as a swaying tree branch outside choreographed the moon's rays. The swirling colours reminded him of a kaleidoscope, which he'd found in his Christmas stocking when he was seven, the last Christmas before the car accident, when his parents were still alive, a time of happiness before the dark years encroached. His eyes came to rest on a figure of the Madonna, the centre-piece of a Nativity, set up on the altar, and he found himself whispering a Hail Mary. But he quickly checked himself. Thinking back to his childhood had obviously prompted a childhood habit and one he'd long ago consciously rejected when he'd realised that the Church was not only unable to come to his rescue but had actually sent the Beast to him.

Hennessy.

He felt sure that Father Hennessy wouldn't recognise him. After all, he'd been a skinny boy at Merrydown; now, he was adult, swarthy, muscular. He continued to wait, at peace with himself and his mission, as he watched the colours on the altar cloth once more. Then, he became aware of murmurings in the confessional. Even at this late hour, a young male voice was opening his heart to the priest. He wondered what sin was being confessed, which was so urgent that it couldn't wait until after Christmas. If the congregation only knew the sins of the Beast, he thought. He toyed with the idea of actually going into the confessional. He savoured the irony of confessing his recent acts, then following up his words with a repeat performance on Hennessy himself. His thoughts dissipated as a teenager stepped out of the confessional and headed towards the back of the church and the door. Father Hennessy had also stepped out and was walking in the opposite direction, up the aisle towards him.

"Good evening and Merry Christmas," said the priest.

"Good evening, Father."

Father Hennessy genuflected, made the sign of the cross, then turned right and headed for the vestry. There was no one else in the church right now, and it seemed safe to go ahead. He swiftly followed the priest into the vestry. Father Hennessy swung round, surprised.

"Can I help you, my son?" he asked. There was no evident recognition on the priest's face, but the younger man recognised only too well the gentle eyes and kindly smile of the older man. What a contrast with the inner monster.

"Sorry to startle you, Father." His hand slipped into his pocket. "I wondered, is it too late to use the confessional?"

"Of course not," replied the priest. Father Hennessy began to step past the killer but suddenly stopped, turned and looked him straight in the eyes.

"I know you," he whispered.

In an instant, the ligature was out and up to the priest's neck, but Father Hennessy had managed to raise his own hands just as quickly to his throat and was able to deflect the pressure of the ligature with four fingers already under it. They looked each other in the eyes: a frozen moment in which each saw the fear in the other. That moment took both by surprise, and the ligature gave slightly with a small release of pressure, which was all the priest needed to be able to shift minutely sideways and thrust the whole of one hand under the cable. To seize the advantage, the killer suddenly whipped the ligature away with his right hand so that it flew across the room while simultaneously grabbing the priest round the back of his neck with his left.

But the priest was just as quick to react with his own hands and thrust them both into the killer's face, scratching him. The younger man yelped, amazed at the old man's strength, lost his grip on the priest's neck and stumbled backwards. The priest whirled around to try and make a run for it out of the vestry door, but the killer was too quick for him. He lunged forward, grabbed the priest by the hair on the back of his head and in less than a second, had both hands round his throat, this time from behind, with good purchase. Father Hennessy uttered a stifled groan, a noise reminiscent of that heinous groan of pleasure which the Beast emitted whenever he raped him all those years ago. His fingers continued to tighten their grip.

"I... know... you..." the priest croaked under the increasing pressure on his throat. The killer waited... and waited. He tightened his grip still further and waited. Then he heard a final guttural roll. "Rrrrr..."

The fingers did not loosen their grip on the old man's throat for a further few minutes while the younger man's mind continued to replay the horrors of his abuse at the hands of this monster. Finally, slowly, he let the lifeless body slip to the floor. In a foil wrapping, in his left-hand pocket, was a rose. He unwrapped it, knelt by the priest, took one last look at the face, now hideously red and swollen, rolled the body over face down, lifted the cassock, pulled down the old man's shorts and placed the flower in its final resting place: a tribute to justice.

"*Your* love token," he whispered. Then he reached into his pocket for his felt-tip pen, flipped off the lid and scrawled his V signature on the priest's pale flesh. He stood up, walked across the room, retrieved the cable, then left the vestry and made his way back through the silent church.

\*

Jenna had arrived at her father's late on Christmas Eve. She'd brought a turkey crown and trimmings with her, which she thought would be a sufficient yet special enough dinner for them the next day. She'd also brought a bottle of champagne, which they'd shared in good spirits straight away. After a restless night, in which excitement prevented any decent sleep, Christmas Day finally arrived, and Jenna got up and went to sit beside her dad at the computer, in their pyjamas, to await an early Skype call from Australia.

"What time did Clive say?" Jenna asked.

"About eight o'clock our time." Gareth looked at his watch. "Which is now!"

It would be late afternoon in Perth, where, three years ago, Clive had chosen to take his firefighting skills. Knowing her brother, he would already have enjoyed the greater part of Christmas Day, much of it on the beach.

The seconds ticked by. "Come on," whispered Jenna. She clasped her dad's hand. "Are you sure you've got the time right?" But before he could answer, there was a ringtone, and at the same moment, the screen in front of them suddenly burst into life, and a rectangular black space lit up with colour. The pixels morphed into Clive's face while his voice, initially staccato, soon came through loud and clear.

"Hey, guys! Merry Christmas!" he said in a marked Australian accent. His long-term girlfriend, Colette, was sitting by his side. She repeated the greeting and waved. "How are you?"

"We're fine, son. Merry Christmas to you, too," said Gareth. Jenna noticed that he'd slipped back into his strongest Welsh accent, a reaction, perhaps, to Clive's Aussie lilt.

Jenna asked how they'd been spending their Christmas.

"Oh, we've had a very Australian Christmas," Colette replied. "You know: swim, surf and barbecue!"

"Yeah – shame we can't be with you under those grey skies in the freezing cold," Clive said, laughing. "So, what are you guys doing today?"

"Dad and I are going to have a nice quiet day together," Jenna told him, "with turkey, wine and board games…"

"Maybe not so quiet," Gareth chipped in. "We might be entertaining Jen's new boyfriend later." He winked at the screen.

"I can't keep up with all these boyfriends of yours!" said Clive.

Colette took a friendly swipe at him.

"You'll have to forgive him, Jenna," she said with a grin. "He's had a lot to drink today!"

"No, you've got a point, Clive," Gareth assured his son. "It would be nice to see our girl find that someone special." As her father continued with other news, Jenna found herself thinking that one day she'd explain to her brother that she *had* found that someone special, but she'd had to give him up.

They chatted on in seasonal high spirits, exchanging tales of recent events and making promises to one another about reuniting in person in the not-too-distant future. Such promises were hard to keep but, when spoken, were meant from the heart. Forty-five minutes passed by very quickly, and then it was time to say 'au revoir' and blow each other kisses.

Still excited from the Skype call, Jenna was about to enter the shower when she heard the sound of an incoming text on her mobile. It was Greg, and her excitement rose still further when she read that he was coming over for dinner after all, and could she please remind him of her father's address. She tore down the stairs, all smiles and relayed the message.

"Steady on, girl!" Gareth said. "It'll be just your luck, now you've got your hopes high, that you'll get a call from work!"

"Ssssssh!" said Jenna, placing a finger over her lips. "Don't tempt fate!" She laughed and went back upstairs to shower and dress.

But fate had indeed been tempted. Jenna was just putting the finishing touches to her make-up when her mobile rang. It was Brady. His voice was grave. "You're not going to like this," he said. Her spirits plummeted; she could guess what was coming. "I'm standing over the body of a dead priest."

\*

Having texted Greg with profuse apologies, Jenna kissed her dad goodbye and threw in a see-you-when-I-see-you resigned shoulder shrug. Then she drove to the Church of Our Immaculate Lady in Maida Vale.

At the entrance to the church, a police notice indicated that all services for the day were cancelled. Jenna ducked under the police tape and, without a great deal of effort, eased open the door. The old-style Catholic churches were now few and far between in the London area and had been replaced by new buildings such as these in the 1950s and 60s. However, here, the architect had successfully retained most of the usual Catholic trademarks, including floor-to-ceiling stained glass windows, which dominated in every direction. As Jenna stood and absorbed her surroundings, the faces of the saints shone down on her in a riot of vermillion, jade, bright cadmium and cobalt blue. The saints seemed like tortured souls trapped within the layers of coloured glass, and, briefly, she was mesmerised by them.

Stepping further into the foyer, Jenna dipped the middle and fourth finger of her right hand into the font and trailed droplets of holy water on her skin and clothing as she signed the cross. "In the name of the Father, the Son and the Holy Ghost," she whispered. Being raised to attend Sunday mass regularly with her mother meant there were certain rituals she could simply not forego. She walked on into the nave, where the atmosphere was still thick with incense from the night before. Jenna pictured the acrid smoke, which would have lingered heavily when the priest anointed the air.

At last, her wide-eyed gaze descended on the aisle, which stretched ahead of her. Red poinsettias and Christmas berries brightened the end of every pew, and the gold glint of bows created warmth in the cold nave. Carol service sheets were laid out in readiness for a mass, which wouldn't now take place. "Once in Royal David's City" could just be heard, coming faintly from a speaker buried somewhere behind the Nativity, near the altar. Someone had obviously switched it on before finding the body. Normally, Jenna found church music a comfort, but the joyous swell of this particular melody today was at odds with the brutality of the crime which had been committed there.

Ahead of her, several SOCOs in protective suits were busy scanning various parts of the nave and comparing notes in hushed voices, but at the altar itself stood one figure alone: Brady. Brady looked suitably sombre in his black trench coat, in sharp contrast to the reds and golds of his surroundings. It still took a huge effort, she discovered, to quell the feeling that was swelling again in her heart as she turned to head towards him. For a split second, she even imagined him waiting there as a bridegroom for her. And she'd been trying so hard to make Greg her heart's focus. She lifted her eyes to meet those of the Blessed Lord on the crucifix, somewhere above the altar, and her thoughts became a prayer: Help me get over this obsession. She had to steel herself to rein in all emotion and act the cool professional, especially as they were now meeting in such serious circumstances. Thankfully, by the time she'd spurred her feet into action and taken slow steps down the length of the aisle, she had regained her self-control.

"I won't say 'Merry Christmas'," Brady said as she reached the altar, "because what you're about to see isn't very merry at all, I'm afraid. Number four: Father Aidan Hennessy… "

"*Hennessy!*" Jenna exclaimed, interrupting Brady in mid-sentence. "*Father Hennessy?*"

"Yes. Same double signature as before: a withered rose and a felt-tip V. The sacristan found him this morning in the vestry. Keith and the team have just arrived, and Keith's with the body now." He frowned. "Why the surprise?"

Jenna took a moment to collect her thoughts. "But I knew him. When I was a little girl, it was his services that my mother took me to back in Strawberry Hill." She looked at Brady, puzzled. "So why's *he* been killed?" She shook her head. "He seemed a lovely man."

Brady cupped a hand around Jenna's elbow and drew her gently nearer. "Appearances can be deceptive, remember. But we don't know the whole story yet." He lowered his voice. "We need to join Keith at the victim's side. Are you going to be all right?"

She breathed deeply and then nodded before following Brady to the right of the altar, through an archway and into a small, square, windowless room. What a contrast there was between the vibrant colours of the main body of the church and this bleak, achromatic little room. It was airless, too. As she went in, Jenna struggled to suck in a deep enough breath to prepare herself, again, for the sight of a murder victim. However, Keith, already kneeling beside the head end of the priest's body, which was lying face down on the grey flagstones, held up a hand. "If I'm not mistaken," he said, "this is the work of the killer's actual hands." He indicated what was visible of the victim's throat, which was mottled with patches of grey and purple. "There's no sign of a ligature this time."

"Why do you think the modus operandi has changed, Keith?" Brady asked.

Wilson continued to lift the head and palpate the throat carefully with his gloved hands. "The guy's panicked. He's been distracted. You name it." He placed the head gently down again on the cold stone floor. "I'll be able to tell you more after the full post-mortem."

Having managed to suppress the initial shock of knowing the victim's identity, Jenna moved back into detective mode. "Can you lift a killer's prints from a victim's body?" she asked the forensic pathologist. There were still gaps in her knowledge, but she was not afraid to ask questions to address them.

"It's not totally impossible, but it's rare to be able to lift anything worthwhile," Wilson replied. "But what might help you narrow down your search is the possibility of an unusual finger pattern I'm seeing around the throat. It's only my first impression, of course. Bruising is only just emerging. I'll know more by the time I've done the full autopsy, but it looks to me like your killer might be carrying a hand injury."

"What sort of hand injury?" said Brady.

"He may not have all his fingers."

\*

Brady sat down in a pew, and Jenna joined him. "So would you agree that the biker at Greenacres Golf Club is now our number one suspect?" she said.

"I would," said Brady reflectively. "And now we have a possible reason why he wouldn't remove his gloves." His eyes were staring straight ahead at the group of Nativity figures placed on a table near the altar. The peaceful scene was complete with animals, shepherds and kings bearing gifts, but it was the Mary and Joseph figures that created the iconic centre-piece. Joseph had a protective arm around Our Lady, who cradled the new baby, and all three were illuminated by a light, which had been strategically positioned above them to represent the Star of David. It was an enchanting piece of art. Yet the promise of hope and salvation, which the Nativity stood for, seemed to contradict the grim reality of the scene inside the vestry, so much so that Brady immediately lost his sense of awe and tumbled back into the real world. "It's not a tattoo which he's hiding, but an injury."

"An incomplete hand?"

"Could be a war wound," Brady suggested.

"God... Father Hennessy," Jenna said in a hushed voice. She shook her head again. "He used to hold meetings for recovering drug addicts and alcoholics. Seemed like a pillar of the community, a saint, even. Whoever would have thought?"

They sat in silence for a while, taking in the awe-inspiring church interior once again. "Did I interrupt your Christmas celebrations very much?" Brady asked at length.

Jenna half smiled. "You know you did," she said. "But

at least I got to talk to my brother." Brady turned to her with an enquiring look. "He's in Australia. We Skyped," she explained.

"You see," said Brady. "My timing, as always, is perfect!"

"So where do we go from here?" Jenna asked. She kept her voice low, and for a second, Brady thought that the question was personal, but realising that her quiet tone was in keeping with their surroundings and the gravity of the situation, he quickly readjusted his thinking.

"The body will go into the freezer, and then the post-mortem will be done on Monday or Tuesday," he replied. "And then we'll know more about the fingers when Keith has taken a better look at the bruise pattern."

"There's only one of the ring of five left, isn't there?" Jenna said.

"And he's probably one of our colleagues," said Brady with a shrug.

"How's the killer going to close in on number five when even we don't know where to start?"

"What would you do if you were the killer?" Brady asked.

"Hmm, that's a tricky one," she said. "Off the top of my head, I'd try and infiltrate somehow."

"What, infiltrate the police force?" asked Brady incredulously. "You couldn't easily do that unless you joined."

"True," agreed Jenna, "so the next best thing would be to befriend someone who was in the police force and see if you could get some information out of them, which would lead you towards your target."

Brady was sceptical. "Be careful who you make friends with, Jen!" he said in a dramatic stage whisper. But he was half smiling. He couldn't take the infiltration idea seriously. "Now go back and enjoy what's left of Christmas Day. We'll be able to focus on our work more efficiently after the postmortem."

"Merry Christmas, Dom," she said. His name slipped out unintentionally, but it nevertheless felt right beside the seasonal sentiment. "I'll see you on Monday morning." She stood up and wrapped her winter coat tightly around her.

"See you Monday," he said.

# PART 5

# THE HAND IS REVEALED

Solomon Jacobs ran his small Discount Electricals business off the City Road. He had a number of suppliers of saleable merchandise, no questions asked, of course, but the best of these was Charlie Slade, who worked the affluent areas to the south-west of the city and regularly came up with high-end stuff for Solly to fence. If a computer or laptop were part of the haul, Solly would pass the item on to Freddie Miles, whose skills were so good he could have hacked into the American defence system if need be. When the memory was wiped, he'd pass the item back to Solly to sell and then collect his cut.

Today, Solly had been hard at work, ignoring the Christmas hype all around him. Well, he had Jewish roots anyway and no family to speak of, so for him, it was business as usual, Christmas weekend or not. He could see that Charlie had lifted a state-of-the-art laptop and immediately passed it on to Freddie, who wasted no time hacking in. It took a while: someone really knew how to keep things secure here.

If he hadn't known better, he would have said this piece of merchandise had belonged to a spook. But Freddie had been at this game for decades. He knew all the tricks. So, he finally got in – he always did – and began to work his way around.

Now, Freddie had a nice little sideline going of his own. Occasionally, in his work, he'd stumbled upon things which the owners of the merchandise would prefer to keep under wraps. He would record these items of interest on a memory stick, store that in a safe deposit box and then contact the owner directly – contact details either available on the computer, thank you, or via Charlie Slade – and ask the owner what he thought it would be worth to keep those little shenanigans secret. To increase his security, he'd roped in a lawyer by the name of Billy Dodge, aka 'The Dodger' to the underworld, who, for a percentage, had agreed to make public everything stored on the memory sticks, should anything happen to Freddie. Billy Dodge was, of course, the only other person who knew the location of the safe deposit box and its entry code. So tracing bank notes to Freddie and having him arrested or bumped off were simply not options: he'd always make it perfectly clear that the consequences of so doing could be most embarrassing.

As he peered at the images which were currently in front of him, he swore with disgust, but he also saw his next big money-making opportunity. This laptop obviously belonged to a nonce, but a well-heeled nonce, perhaps someone who had a reputation to protect. He opened up file after file, and it soon became evident that this could turn out to be his best find ever – maybe worth millions. He also noticed that the files containing images of children were all saved under the same label.

"Well, Merry Christmas, Moses!" said Freddie, gleefully unwrapping a new memory stick. "What price silence, me ol' mate?"

\*

The commander stood there horrified. It wasn't the fact that his alarm had been disabled when he'd thought it was invincible, or the tangled mess of clothing, ornaments and papers strewn everywhere, nor was it the anger from knowing that someone had trespassed on his property that had stopped him short. No, it wasn't what he could see before him in his luxury Wimbledon two-storey apartment that was making his heart beat so fast. It was what he couldn't see.

His laptop.

Jesus Christ Almighty, he thought, as he stood there dry-mouthed and sweaty-handed. All those fucking images. He stood for a few seconds, wondering how to go about this. Get the local bobbies down here to check the place for fingerprints? He decided he had to if he was to stand any chance of finding out who'd burgled him and, therefore, who might have his laptop.

Fuck!

He phoned the local nick, told them exactly who he was and ordered them to get some boys round to his place right away. They, of course, reacted quickly to his call. When a commander orders something, you do it, and you do it pronto! So the flat was soon abuzz, especially around the points of entry and exit and around the alarm itself.

When he got the OK from the finger printers, the commander went to the drinks cabinet and took out a bottle of Scotch. It was already 10.30 p.m., but he knew the local officers would be there for a while, so he took himself off to the kitchen. He poured himself a large one and sat and drank, regretting that he hadn't been more careful. He used to lock the laptop away, for heaven's sake. He had a super little hiding place under the floorboards. And then, as the years went by, he began to leave it out. He must have become complacent, believing he was untouchable.

He knew the stats; he knew how common burglary was, especially in the select area in which he lived; he also knew that property could be especially vulnerable over public holidays when people might go out partying, become euphoric, lose touch with reality… just as he'd obviously done. Why shouldn't he fall victim like so many others? Well, now he had! He finished his drink, poured himself another treble and downed it quickly. His jangling nerves began to settle, but he realised he could do with a different sort of comfort. He wandered back into the lounge to find the officer in charge and asked him how long he thought his team were likely to be. Returning to the kitchen, he opened his mobile and called a cab. It would be a couple of hours before the local lads would be finished in his flat, and he'd thought of the best way he knew to while away the time and take his mind off things.

\*

The deed was done, and he lay on his back, staring into the darkness. Physically satisfied, maybe, but his mind was racing. Did whoever have that laptop realise they were in possession of a ticking bomb? That it was nuclear? Imagine the fallout!

What the hell was he going to do? The Vixen lay next to him, whimpering. He touched her hair, and she flinched. He thought about taking her a second time but realised he was too ill at ease to enjoy it. The effect of the whisky he'd had earlier was wearing off, and his nerves were now electric. So much so that the horrifying thought suddenly occurred to him: the laptop thief had already seen the images, uploaded them, and sent them viral. Mentally, he scrolled back quickly. He knew his face wasn't in any of the pictures. He hadn't been that stupid. But supposing there was something there that someone could recognise? His ring? His watch? Why hadn't he removed them?

Holy Moses! Yeah, it would be funny if he'd been in the mood to laugh.

He leapt off the bed, stuffed himself into his trousers, grabbed his jacket and raced up the stairs and out into the night. Down the road and well away from Merrydown, he hailed another cab, totally focused on the biggest damage limitation exercise of his life.

Down in the cellar, The Vixen had stopped her whimpering. In fact, she was unusually quiet. She was trying to work out if she was dreaming or if she really had been left unshackled with her hands free. She sat up and checked the shackle. It dangled from the wall. She got off the bed and went to the door. It was marginally ajar. She opened it a little wider and peered down the passageway and up to the top of the flight of stairs: another door stood slightly ajar.

In a flash, she glimpsed freedom.

She wheeled round, raced back into the room, opened a cupboard door, yanked out an old tracksuit and sneakers, dressed herself in seconds and tore out into the passageway.

Within a minute, she was outside and tasting cold, fresh air for the first time in over fourteen years.

And then she ran, at last, away from the prison that was Merrydown.

*

It was the day after Boxing Day, and Gareth Jones woke suddenly. Startled, he threw off the duvet. Someone was pressing the doorbell. Urgently. He looked at the digital display clock by his bedside: 05.09 and still dark outside. Who on earth? A prankster, maybe? Someone still revelling, perhaps, although, strictly speaking, the Christmas period had finished at midnight. Whoever it was was persistent; that was certain. He tucked his feet into slippers, put on his dressing gown and made his way down the stairs to the hallway. At the last moment, he armed himself with a sturdy umbrella which he'd left propped up by the front door.

The doorbell hadn't stopped ringing since he'd woken.

He drew back the door bolts and unlocked the door with the umbrella ready. And there before him, to his utter surprise, stood the emaciated figure of a young woman.

"Mr Jones?" she said. "Is Jenna there?" She sounded breathless, as if the effort of speaking was, in itself, too much for her. In an instant, Gareth took in the thin tracksuit and light sneakers, which seemed totally inappropriate for the time of year. Who was this woman, and where had she come from?

"Jenna doesn't live here any more," he said quietly. He was worried about disturbing the neighbours at this unsocial hour. "Who are you?"

"Lauren." She began to shake. "I need to see Jenna." She'd also started to cry. The shaking was becoming convulsive, and Gareth thought he ought to bring her in out of the cold.

"Lauren who?" he asked as he helped her inside and sat her on the bottom stair. He grabbed an overcoat from the hook by the front door and draped it around her shoulders.

"Lauren Bristow," she said.

"*Lauren Bristow?*" His voice pitched upwards as he repeated the name slowly. He couldn't take it in. The Bristows had been gone for fourteen years or more. "But…" He wasn't sure what to say next. The convulsive shaking hadn't stopped, in spite of the overcoat, so he whipped up the stairs, two at a time, fetched his duvet, brought it back downstairs and tucked it around her. "I'll make you a hot drink," he said, realising that she might be in shock as well as frozen. "Don't move."

The girl sank into her coverings and closed her tired eyes. It dawned on Gareth that he might need to call an ambulance for her, but as he made her hot, sweet tea, he decided that it would be best to ring Jenna first. After all, this all looked very odd to him, and maybe the police should know about it. And as Jenna was the police, she'd know what to do and the right order to do it in.

He returned to the foot of the stairs, mug in hand and roused the poor wretch and got her to drink. Gradually, her shaking calmed down, and her breathing became steadier. "I need to see Jenna," she said again, in a voice that was little above a whisper. Gareth could think of a hundred questions to ask but thought he should leave that to his daughter. He nodded and found his mobile phone on the kitchen table. The display read 05.36. He closed it up again. You can't ring someone at that hour, he thought. And what would I say? Yes, Jen, I know it's half past five in the morning, but you'll never believe it. Your old friend has just turned up on the doorstep after fourteen years, looking like nothing on earth!

He decided he would drive the girl round to his daughter's flat so that Jenna could see for herself how things were. He knew that Jenna normally rose at six and calculated that by the time they'd arrived, Jenna would be up and could take over from him. He felt confident his daughter would make the right decisions. And she had another police officer living there, too, didn't she? She could help. And a nurse? Even better. Yes, the girl would definitely be in good hands at Jenna's flat.

He went back to Lauren on the bottom stair. She'd dozed off, and his heart went out to her. Where had she been all this time? And how had she ended up in such a terrible physical state? He tiptoed up the stairs and dressed quickly. Then he came down again, carefully bypassing the little waif and the multiple folds of duvet spread around her. He went outside to fetch the car, which was parked a little way down the road. When he'd moved the car up outside his front door, he went back in and lifted the little thing into his arms, complete with the duvet and overcoat and carried her to the back seat of the vehicle. He gently placed her inside, rearranging the covers to fit snugly around her body and tucking some folds in underneath her head. She slept all the way to Jenna's.

\*

It was 6.15 a.m. Pouring the rest of her morning coffee down the sink, Jenna was about to take a shower when she heard a desperate knocking at the front door. At this early hour, it could only mean one thing: trouble. Nick Bailey had done this to her once last year, coming round at a ridiculously early time to beg her to take him back after he'd played away again. Surely it wasn't him now after all this time? He would be the last person she'd ever want to see again. Alarmed and with a rising heartbeat, she hurried down the passageway.

When she opened the front door, she caught her breath. A cold breeze had blown in, whipping her cheeks and stinging her eyes, but it was not the freezing air that had momentarily stripped her of oxygen. It was the sight of the small female figure standing on the doorstep, huddled against her father's body and, if she wasn't mistaken, wrapped in his heavy overcoat.

"It's Lauren Bristow," said Gareth quietly. He looked as if he was in shock himself.

"*What?*" said Jenna, wondering if she had heard her father correctly.

"Lauren – your old friend," he said. "Let's get her inside. I think she might need an ambulance."

Utterly staggered, Jenna tried hard to fight back the sense of surrealism which was threatening to engulf her. She opened the door wide and let Gareth help Lauren into the warmth of the passageway. Then she shut out the cold and showed them through to the kitchen. The girl was helped on to a small chair positioned next to the cooker, and Jenna knelt before her and whispered her name. The wasted figure opened her eyes sufficiently for Jenna to recognise something of her old friend in those hollow features under a mane of matted hair.

"Lauren," said Jenna again.

"Jenna," her friend said softly. And she began to cry convulsively.

The noise had brought Helen and Lucy from their bedrooms, and they now stood, dumbfounded, at the kitchen door, trying to work out why Jenna's dad was there at such an early hour and who the strange girl was.

"Where have you been all these years?" Jenna asked gently as the sobbing began to subside.

Lauren only half met her gaze. "In hell," she said. Her eyes were squinting against the bright kitchen light, and it suddenly occurred to Jenna that she wasn't used to such brightness. She motioned to her dad to switch off the main light and put on the small light over the cooker. Gareth did so and then turned to the others in the doorway, nodding his head to indicate that they should step into the passageway with him. Jenna put her arms around her friend. It was clear that Lauren had been traumatised. It was also beginning to dawn on Jenna that her reaction to bright light and her mention of being in hell could suggest that she'd been in a dark place. Had she been *held* in a dark place?

"Are you able to tell me," said Jenna "where 'hell' is?" There was silence. "Lauren, I'm with the police," said Jenna gently. "If you can tell me that," she continued quietly, "then I won't need to ask you any more questions for a while."

Lauren's lip quivered. She looked away and then back again. Her eyes seemed to roll in an unfocused way, a look that Jenna had seen before in drug addicts.

"Merrydown," she whispered.

Helen had come back into the kitchen just in time to hear the name of the infamous children's home. Gareth had explained who the stranger was, and now Helen and Jenna exchanged glances, having switched into professional mode.

"I'll phone Brady," said Helen.

"And I'll take Lauren to the hospital. Lucy can travel with her in the back of the car." Jenna looked anxiously at Helen. "We'll need a DNA swab before anyone does anything else to her," she whispered.

\*

Brady took the call from Helen at seven, just as he'd arrived in Kingston ready for the working day. He sat now in the car park, listening to Helen summarise what had been happening for the last hour. Years of professional experience had taught him always to expect the unexpected; indeed, he'd almost reached the stage where his level of surprise was indirectly proportional to the enormity of any given event. So he remained very calm and very collected as Helen described the astonishing occurrences of the previous hour. But his brain was in overdrive. Even before Helen had finished the account, Brady had identified several necessary next moves: Jenna to stay with Lauren since anything she had to say might serve as evidence for them; Lauren to be swabbed before any other nursing procedure took place (Helen assured him that Jenna had already thought of this); he to take a team to search Merrydown; Gerald Hope to be arrested and the current residents to be moved out with immediate effect. Before the call was over, he asked Helen to come into work as soon as she could to coordinate communications between himself at the children's home, the DCI at the station and Jenna at St. Joseph's Hospital.

Once inside the station, he put out a call for several of his MIT members to convene – the signal was coded an emergency – and while he waited for them to arrive, he gave Delgado an even briefer summary of events than Helen had just given him, but one which covered all key points.

By half past seven, nine of the team members were blue-lighting their way to Merrydown. No warrant needed: Section 17 of the Police and Criminal Evidence Act would enable them to force entry if need be. By 7.50 a.m., the convoy of squad cars had arrived. The only team member still missing was DC Pete Chambers, the dog handler, but Brady was informed that he and a second dog handler were on their way and would join them imminently.

A heavy rapping on the front door knocker of the huge manor house produced no reply from inside. "Mr Hope?" Brady shouted. "Police! Open this door, please." There was still no reply, although the voices of several excitable children could be heard from deep inside the bowels of the building. Brady rapped on the knocker again. "MR HOPE!" he shouted. He looked at the officers standing by, one with the 'rabbit', which could prise a door out of its frame and the other with the 'enforcer', which acted as a battering ram. He nodded at them to get ready. "I'll give you ten seconds to open up, or we're coming in."

"Do you have a warrant?" Hope's anxious voice came at last from the other side of the door.

"No!" yelled Brady.

"Then you're not coming in," Hope shouted, evidently thinking he would have time to have this police raid aborted.

"If you don't open this door," Brady called to him, "then we'll have to break it down." There was no reply. Brady yelled, "Stand back!" and then stood aside and let the two officers behind him go to work on the door. The 'rabbit' was put into position, its hydraulic pressure was applied, and the mighty oak door popped out of its frame. Then the 'enforcer' was rammed against the door: the heavy, old, wooden panels soon splintered, and, within seconds, the door was in pieces, and nine officers stepped over the woodpile and strode purposefully inside.

Brady had travelled in one of the squad cars with Andy and Jamie and had already delegated to Andy the business of arresting and cautioning Gerald Hope. He thought Andy's in-yer-face manner was just what Hope deserved. Two other officers had been ordered to monitor staff members and children, who by now were assembled in the dining hall for breakfast while the team awaited the arrival of Social Services. The other four officers had the job of searching the entire premises, with the exception of the basement. That was Brady's.

The door to the basement was locked, but it didn't take long for Hope, now under arrest, to realise that the game was up and to release the appropriate key. Brady took Jamie downstairs with him. He'd already half-expected to find the door to the so-called chemicals cupboard open, and sure enough, it was. Angry with himself for not having acted upon Jenna's suspicions about this room, he nevertheless had to put his feelings to one side to concentrate on the job at hand. He entered the room, and Jamie followed.

The first thing that hit him was the stale odour, which lingered within. Again, it was what Brady would have expected of a room being used for long-term incarceration, as he now suspected. But that didn't make the assault on the nostrils any easier to bear. He stood and scanned the surroundings. The room was dingy, with evidence of damp on the walls and ceiling. It was clear that the prisoner would have seen very little light in here. Brady then noticed that the bed in the middle of the room was queen-sized. He grimaced. "Notice the size of the bed?" he said to Jamie. Jamie shook his head and looked at his boss despairingly. "Glad to see someone had thought about comfort," he said with bitter irony. Brady drew nearer the bed and caught sight of the soiled linen. He immediately pulled a pair of protective gloves out of his pocket and put them on, gesturing to Jamie to do the same. Together, they stripped the undersheet off the bed and carefully folded it in on itself to preserve any trace evidence present. That was going back to Wilson's lab for a thorough examination.

It was Jamie who spotted the shackle. "Boss?" Still gloved, Jamie lifted the metal chain and cuff away from its anchor point on the wall and showed his find to Brady. "What in God's name was this for?" he asked in disbelief.

"*Fucking hell*!" said Brady under his breath. In his professional capacity, he rarely swore, but right now, it was the most direct way he had to express his abomination at the manner in which this young woman must have been treated.

Jamie just nodded slowly. "Prints?" he said.

"We'll get it dusted later," Brady replied. His mobile buzzed, a harsh sound in the dismal room. It was Pete Chambers, the dog handler. "Yeah, Pete. Thorough search of the grounds, please." Brady paused, listened again and then looked straight at Jamie, distorting his face and shrugging his shoulders. "Who knows what's out there?"

\*

Lauren lay in a private room annexed to the psychiatric ward at St. Joseph's Hospital. Having had to undergo various tests, including blood count and bone density, as well as a vaginal swab – all admissible evidence in court – she was now comfortably tranquillised and drifted in and out of sleep.

It was clear from the swab that sexual activity had taken place, although whether this had been consensual or otherwise, Jenna had yet to find out. Suspecting 'otherwise', she decided to be pro-active and phoned Brady to acquire his authorisation to act in lieu of a Sexual Offences Investigating Team Officer if need be; after all, she already had the victim's trust, and that was half the battle in getting a rape victim to talk.

But Brady had already departed for the swoop on Merrydown. So Helen, who was acting as link officer at the station, put her directly in touch with Delgado. But the DCI told her to hold fire. He explained that he needed to contact the Liaison Psychiatry Service to alert them of Lauren's case. After all, he said, it appeared the victim had suffered repeated trauma over a number of years and might, therefore, require a coordinated approach from a number of specialist agencies as well as themselves. So Jenna had to sit and wait for twenty minutes while Delgado spoke with the LPS. When she finally got the go-ahead, she prepared her dictaphone just in case Lauren felt up to talking. But, thought Jenna, that moment might be a very long way off. She settled herself down in a chair and prepared for a long wait.

A masked nurse arrived in the room, approached the bed, and drew the curtain partially around the patient without obscuring Jenna's view. Lauren's stats were checked, and then she was fitted with a cannula and drip as she was too weak to feed orally. The nurse also lightly touched Lauren's surgical mask to ensure it was tight enough to protect her from germs, which her immune system would almost certainly have forgotten about over fourteen years. Even the common cold could have a serious effect after all this time. Jenna took the cue and raised her fingers to her own mask to check that it was skin-tight. The nurse saw the gesture and nodded. Her eyes gave away a smile. The curtain was then drawn back, and the nurse departed, leaving Jenna alone again with her old friend, who was now apparently in a deep slumber.

As the morning hours went by and the intravenous drip did its work, Lauren gradually became more alert. Having sat still for hours, Jenna went out to fetch a coffee, telling Lauren she'd be right back. While she waited for her friend to return, Lauren surveyed her surroundings with interest. What a contrast there was between the dim and dingy cell, which had been her home for so many years she'd lost count and the bright white walls and ceiling of the room in which she now lay. How different the starched crispness of the linen on this bed to the threadbare sheets, grey with age and often soiled by semen, which she'd grown used to. And there were curtains here, too: deep blue curtains at the windows and a pale blue curtain for pulling around her bed. She'd almost forgotten what a curtain was. And she'd nearly forgotten the colour blue.

Jenna soon returned with her coffee and saw that Lauren was awake. "Hi, honey!" she said quietly. The mask slightly muffled her voice. "How are you feeling?"

"Okay." The answer was a whisper. Jenna noticed that the part of Lauren's face which was on show, was etched with trauma and still framed by that shock of matted hair, which no one had yet attempted to touch. Looking more carefully at her head, Jenna realised that Lauren was prematurely grey at the temples and other grey hairs were scattered liberally over her crown. She put her coffee down on the bedside cabinet and took Lauren's right hand in her own two.

"I've got permission to stay with you for as long as you need me," she said. She watched Lauren's eyes crease as if trying to smile. "As I mentioned, I work for the police," she added. Lauren nodded slowly. "And we're going to find whoever did this to you." Jenna paced her sentences to let each bit of information sink in. But, of course, she was steering her way to the most important sentence of all. She thought it was time to try it. "Whatever you can tell us, Lauren, about Merrydown and all that's happened to you will help us to…" she wanted to say 'nail the bastards' "… bring your offenders to justice." Jenna tightly squeezed her friend's hand. It struck Jenna that Lauren may not have understood her as her upper face appeared puzzled, so she paraphrased: "We're going to get the bad guys, Lauren, but we need your help."

Lauren closed her eyes and seemed to drift off again into a doze. Jenna released her hand and went back to sit in the bedside chair with her coffee. Perhaps she'd tried to push her too quickly into telling her story. After all, to ask someone to recount what might turn out to have been fourteen years of trauma was asking a lot. But just when Jenna thought she'd overstepped the mark, she heard a small voice say, "Do you remember the last time we saw each other?" Jenna stood up and went to the dictaphone, which she'd set up on the bedside cabinet. With a subtle movement, she pressed 'record'. Then she nodded to her friend to show she was listening. "It was the day we broke up from school for the summer holidays…"

## July 1999

Two little girls sat high in a tree, tinkering with the daisy chain bracelets they'd made. There was a companionable silence between them. The warm July heat penetrated the canopy above them and dappled their blue checked dresses in bright flickering light. The breeze ruffled their hair. School had just finished for the summer, a time when most children would be eagerly anticipating the weeks of freedom and fun ahead. But one of these girls didn't want this afternoon to end. She was troubled. She carried a huge weight in her heart: a sense of doom. But she couldn't put a name to it and therefore bore the burden alone.

The other girl was blissfully unaware of how her friend was feeling. "I'm going to have to go home for tea in a minute. But I'll see you tomorrow, okay?" she said. She shook her blonde hair out of her eyes and carefully began the descent from the sturdy boughs on which they were balanced.

The dark-haired girl avoided the question. Instead, she replied, "We'll always be best friends, won't we?"

The blonde looked up at her companion's sad face. "Of course we will," she said. Reaching the base of the trunk, she giggled at such a silly question and skipped off in the direction of her house, leaving the other sitting alone, up in the branches.

As the temperature began to fall, Lauren watched the goose pimples appear on her pale flesh. Her blue gingham dress started to flap in the cool wind, which had sprung up, and she wished she'd brought a cardigan out with her that day. She reached out her hand and placed a palm on the bough where Jenna had been perched, absorbing the warmth of the spot where her friend had sat. Lauren didn't have any other friends except Jenna, but Jenna was all she needed: her best friend in the world. They would race round the neighbourhood together on their bikes, make daisy chains as they had done today, invented imaginary characters and role-played the everyday dramas of their lives, and when they were tired, they'd sit and listen to or even make music together. Jenna's mum, who always wore a warm smile on her face, called them 'two peas in a pod'.

Lauren admired the daisy chain. It was perfect. Today, the girls had made each other's bracelets and had bound them round each other's arms: a token of their friendship. Lauren now touched the tiny daisies and marvelled at their simple beauty. She wanted to wear this bracelet always. She wished she could whisper a charm to endow it with magic: a protective circle to ward off evil. And now her heart sank again. Why did she have such a strong sense of foreboding?

She couldn't have walked home any slower. With pigeon steps, she traced every crack in the pavement, pondering what might await her at home. Was there to be another deafening silence when she arrived? Or one of her parents' now frequent arguments behind closed doors? Lauren considered the silence to be worse. Silence gave her imagination the means to grow like a cancer and mushroom ominously into an overpowering fear. Just recently, she had come to realise that her family life was far from normal. Her parents were exceedingly quiet. Actually, it seemed like they had intentionally withdrawn. Her stepfather had nothing to do with anyone in the neighbourhood and forbade friends from coming round and playing with her in the house itself. Her mother was timid, never questioning her stepfather's word. Well, she was so much younger than him that she could have been his daughter. Whatever he said was final and was never questioned – not until recently, anyway. Lately, it had dawned on Lauren, who'd just turned eleven, that her parents' separate sleeping arrangements were unusual. She'd now seen plenty on the TV and heard enough from the kids at school to have worked that out. And where were the photos of her as a baby, as a toddler? Such treasures adorned Jenna's parents' home, whereas her own home was bare.

Something was wrong. Had her mother been packing a suitcase yesterday? She thought back to the noises which had reached her ears from behind her mother's bedroom door. Were those yelps of pain? Was he hitting her? What was that about a deadline and a delivery that she'd overheard?

Lauren so desperately wanted to confide in her friend, but she hadn't anything concrete to offer her by way of explanation. But that overwhelming fear in the pit of her stomach telling her that something bad was about to happen seemed to her to be very real. Besides, when she wasn't in the house, she didn't want to be reminded of the negative atmosphere at home. So, when she was playing with her best friend, she avoided even thinking about home, never mind talking about it.

At last, the inevitable moment came, and she arrived at her front door. She lifted the key to the lock, but just as she did so, the door swung open in front of her. Her stepfather was standing there. Was that anger that she registered in his eyes? Usually, he didn't seem to care what time she came home. Anyway, it was only about six o'clock, not even teatime. In fact, she'd made it home earlier than usual. Lauren stepped inside and glanced ahead at the kitchen doorway. Her mother was standing there, sniffling into a tissue. What was going on? Perhaps her parents were splitting up. She looked around: there were boxes everywhere. They must be moving house.

"W... what's happening?" she managed tentatively. There was no reply, but her stepfather suddenly started towards her. "Why won't anyone answer me?" Lauren now grew anxious; blood drained from her head, and she felt as if she was in a spin. Her stepfather began to usher her out of the front door and back on to the driveway, still maintaining his silence. She peered at him with pleading eyes, but it made no difference to him. "Mum!" she yelled and turned around to run back into the house, but her stepfather caught hold of her by the waist, lifted her under one arm, threw open the car door and tried to shove her inside. Just before her head disappeared beneath the car roof, she craned her neck to see her mother. Perhaps there would still be a simple explanation for all this. That final image of the partially silhouetted figure quivering in the hallway would remain with Lauren for the rest of her life.

In the passenger seat, Lauren picked at the upholstery while she studied her stepfather's profile. He looked nervous, and his cheeks were flushed red. He indicated right into Argyll Avenue and then brought the car to a halt. Lauren wondered if they were visiting someone. Maybe, she thought, it would all turn out to be a nice surprise: after all, she'd only just had her eleventh birthday, and perhaps this was to be her birthday present. But the twitch just below her stepfather's lip and the wide-eyed panic which beset his other features told Lauren that her dream was futile. Suddenly, he reached into his pocket and pulled out a handkerchief and a second piece of folded material. Before she'd had a chance to react, the handkerchief was forced over her nose and mouth, and the fight seeped out of her as she began to lose consciousness. She was only vaguely aware of her eyes being blindfolded before she sank into darkness.

Less than an hour later, a limp little body was carried inside a large and imposing manor house. Lauren was beginning to stir. The cool evening air had helped to rouse her, but as her eyes were still blindfolded, she had to ascertain her whereabouts by her sense of smell. She knew she was in the arms of her stepfather because she recognised the scent of stale tobacco, which always hung around his clothing. But she also became aware that they were in the presence of another man, who seemed to be wearing a very pungent aftershave. Her nose also picked up a background smell of overcooked cabbage combined with… furniture polish, as if the place where she'd been brought had very recently been cleaned.

"You've done well," said the authoritative voice that was not her stepfather's. "The final instalment for this one will be with you shortly."

"What about her mother?" said her stepfather.

"She knows too much," came the reply. Then, sotto voce, "Take her out…"

The helpless girl felt herself tilt backwards a little – she could only think she was being carried up a flight of stairs – and then she was placed on a comfortable surface, which she assumed was a bed. A sharp pinprick in her thigh made her wince, and she was suddenly plunged back into unconsciousness.

\*

Sometime later, Lauren awoke. She felt groggy. There was no blindfold now, so she could look about her and take in her surroundings. The natural light peeping in through a high window was just beginning to fade, telling her that the evening was well advanced. She scanned the room and saw that she'd been brought to a dormitory consisting of six beds, each with a small chest of drawers at the side. She slung her legs over to one side of her bed and tried to draw herself up to a sitting position. It took a few minutes to achieve the position she wanted, as her arms and legs initially refused to obey her, but finally, she sat on the edge. There she stayed for a while, totally confused and thinking back over what had happened to her since she'd said goodbye to Jenna.

Her thoughts were interrupted by the door opening: a man with an air of authority stepped into the room. He came and stood over her, and she could smell his strong aftershave again. He tilted his head to look down at her. "Now, Lauren, this is Merrydown, your new home," he said. Her lip started to quiver. "Now, now, don't cry. Your parents had no choice but to bring you here because…" Lauren's tears had begun to fall. "They couldn't put up with your bad behaviour any more. But you'll soon learn how to be a good girl here," he said.

"And then can I go home?" she wailed.

"Er, maybe," said the man. "We'll see how it goes, shall we? Now, your stepfather left your case here. I want you to unpack your things." He indicated the chest of drawers by her bedside. "And then I'll get our housekeeper to come and fetch you for supper. You must be hungry," he said, putting his hand on her head and stroking it. "There, that's better, isn't it?"

He left the room, and she busied herself, putting her few clothes away in her bedside drawers. Badly behaved? She couldn't believe it. She'd hardly ever been told off at school and was always as helpful as she could be at home, especially to her mother. She just couldn't get her head round the man's explanation.

She'd just finished unpacking when a stout woman entered the room. "I'm Miss Brewer," said the lady. Lauren looked at her. Her grey hair was tied back from her face in a little bun, making her stern expression even more severe. "There's a little supper for you downstairs. Normally, you will eat with the other children at six o'clock, but as you came in late tonight, you will eat alone, and then we'll put you to bed. You can meet the others tomorrow." She turned abruptly. "Now, follow me!" she said and strode out of the dormitory.

Downstairs, and under the steel gaze of Miss Brewer, Lauren picked at her meagre supper. When she'd finally pushed her plate away, the housekeeper led her back upstairs and bade her change into her nightdress. "Mr Fox will be in to see you shortly, and I shall see you next at breakfast," she said, and she left. The man with the strong aftershave who'd spoken to her earlier soon arrived. She was in bed by now.

"Where are the other children?" Lauren asked.

"They're in the lounge, doing their homework before they come to bed. It's something they do every evening, and you will do the same after tonight. You'll meet them tomorrow, but it's time for you to sleep now." And she saw him take a package out of his pocket, strip it open and point a cylindrical object at her arm. "There," he whispered, "sleep well." She felt a sudden sharp pain in her upper arm, but before she could protest, she began to feel drowsy. As the darkness coiled itself around her, she could just make out the whispered words, "Welcome back," before she sank into total oblivion.

Fox didn't leave straight away. He stood over her for a while, admiring the rich, dark hues of her hair. He put his hand on her crown again and stroked it. Then he moved her covers down a little way and ogled her small pre-pubescent curves. He'd actually been careful in his time to approach only the youngest girls, and he'd insisted that 'the others' did the same, ensuring minimal risk of unwanted conception. But then the girl who would be Lauren's mum arrived at the home. She was the most seductive thirteen-year-old he'd ever come across, and he hadn't been able to resist her. When it was clear she was pregnant, he'd farmed her out to a reliable contact and paid for her keep. But when a baby girl arrived, he began to toy with the idea of having the little one brought back to him, further down the line, for his personal, incestuous pleasure. And now here she was at last, days after her eleventh birthday. "Ripening," he muttered under his breath, "like a juicy plum!" There was a gleam in his eye.

\*

The next morning, Lauren woke to find a girl of her age standing over her. She looked friendly and smiled at her, and for the first time since her arrival, Lauren felt her anxiety diminish just a little.

"Hello," said the girl, "I'm Hannah. You can come to breakfast with me if you like."

Lauren thanked her and introduced herself. The two girls dressed, and then Hannah showed Lauren downstairs and led her to the dining hall. To Lauren, it sounded like the hyena enclosure at the zoo, although the number of children there could not have been more than twenty. The stern-looking housekeeper stood at one end of the hall.

"Ah, there you are, Lauren," Miss Brewer said in her abrupt manner. "Find a seat, and I'll bring you some porridge."

Lauren's anxiety levels began rising again. "I don't want porridge this morning, thank you," she replied. The noise around her began to hush as the children realised this new girl had just opposed Miss Brewer's instruction. They lifted their eyes from their cereal bowls and watched her eagerly to see if they could learn anything from her that might serve them well in their future dealings with Miss Brewer. "I would like to speak to the person in charge, please."

Miss Brewer looked aghast for a moment. She was not used to having her word either questioned or dismissed in such a brazen way. "Mr Fox is a very busy man," she said, giving the new resident the benefit of the doubt. After all, she'd only just arrived and clearly needed to learn how things worked at Merrydown. "There will be chances to speak with him, but now is not one of them. Find a seat!"

"I think someone's made a mistake bringing me here," said Lauren. Her pulse had risen, and her voice had consequently grown in strength and volume. "I need to go back to my mother." A vision of the pathetic figure, whom Lauren had last seen shaking in the hallway of their home yesterday evening, rose in her mind and made her start to shake as well.

"You *will* sit down when I tell you to, girl," said the housekeeper viciously.

Lauren's world had been altering by the second since she'd arrived home the previous evening, and now she felt she was losing the very last vestiges of control she still had. Her right hand found its way to a glass of milk on the table, and as her confusion and frustration mounted to a climax, she grabbed the glass and hurled it at the wall. "WHY ISN'T ANYONE LISTENING TO ME?" she yelled and started to sob.

Some of the children jumped in their seats; others looked petrified for themselves and Lauren, as they were only too aware of the consequences that could follow such an action. An eerie calm ensued as if the eye of the storm had just settled overhead, and then they all heard the creak of footsteps on the floorboards in the corridor outside.

"Well, well, well… what have we here?" said Stanley Fox, turning into the dining hall and taking in the situation instantly.

"This girl has no self-control, Mr Fox," said Miss Brewer. "Perhaps you would deal with her while I sort out everyone else."

Fox took Lauren by the shoulders and pulled her to one side while the housekeeper and one other female member of staff ushered the other children away from the broken glass and out of the dining hall. Fox was momentarily distracted when a boy who was on his way out of the room tried to crush a shard of glass underfoot. While he turned his head to admonish the individual, two things happened in quick succession: a dark-haired boy slipped a shred of paper napkin into Lauren's hand and closed her fingers around it, while her new friend, Hannah, dived under one of the tables, hiding herself from the view of the adults.

Fox turned back to Lauren, his face red with fury. "You little vixen!" he snapped. Lauren had no idea what a vixen was, but she could see that the man in charge was livid with her. "Now you've really asked for it." Without any further words, he led her out of the dining hall and down the corridor in the opposite direction to the staircase, which Hannah had led her down earlier. They came to an oak door in the passageway, which Fox opened with a large key. Lauren just had time to slip the scrap of napkin, which had been hidden in her clenched fist, inside her dress pocket before she was hauled downstairs to the basement. Fox then opened up another door further ahead. The room he took her into was dark and dank, lit only by a single light bulb hanging from the centre of a low ceiling. Then he spoke.

"Behaviour like that cannot be allowed," he said. "You will sit here for a while and consider what you have done wrong, and then you will make amends." He bound her arms to the chair where he'd placed her, and then he walked out of the room, locking the door behind him. Lauren immediately burst into tears. Her world had turned upside-down, and the life she'd known already seemed a distant memory. If only someone would tell her what was going on, perhaps she wouldn't have lost her temper like that.

When her captor finally reappeared after what must have been a good hour, she pleaded with him to answer her questions. He raised his eyebrows at her. "And still no apology?" he barked. Shaking his head, he told her that she had yet to see the error of her ways and jabbed a needle into her thigh again. She sank once more into a deep sleep.

\*

Lauren opened her heavy eyelids with difficulty and let her sight adjust to the light in the dormitory. So they'd brought her back here. The clock on the wall showed it was nearly noon, and that would be midday Sunday, she thought, as she worked out the chronology of events since her arrival. She could hear the sound of children's voices somewhere in the distance. Were they outside? Perhaps if she could get out there, too, she could run away from this place. But how would she know where to go? She had no idea where 'this place' was. She could definitely do with some advice. Then she remembered the dark-haired boy and the scrap of napkin he'd thrust at her. She eased her hand into her dress pocket, carefully withdrew it and tried to see what was written on it. Her eyes were swollen from crying, and her temples were throbbing, so it took her several seconds to focus properly, but at last, she was able to read the message. It said: 'Room 14'. Was that where she would find the boy?

Unsteady on her feet to start with, she gradually felt stronger as she began to move around the room, and eventually, she felt well enough to leave the dormitory. As she closed the door behind her, she glanced up to register the number of her dormitory: 12. Then she wandered slowly down the corridor and round a corner until she reached the door with '14' on it. She curled her small hand around the brass doorknob, twisted it and opened the door.

"You should have knocked!" protested the dark-haired boy who was sitting on his bed, almost as if he were waiting for her to arrive. "This is a boys' dorm. Girls can't just walk in, you know!" But he wore a cheeky grin on his friendly face.

"You gave me this," said Lauren, holding up the crumpled napkin. "I thought it was an invitation."

Closing the book he'd been reading, he replied, "It was. Come and sit on the bed." He patted a little area next to where he was sitting on his duvet. Lauren perched herself next to him.

"A word of advice," he said to her. His brow was furrowed with concern for her as if he were a full-grown adult instead of a pre-adolescent. "Don't step out of line any more, or you'll end up down there again."

"I think that man drugged me," she said.

"Of course, you were drugged," he said. "But be good and…" He was about to promise Lauren that if she were good, nothing bad would befall her, but he knew he could not protect her from the terrible goings-on at Merrydown, so he let his sentence trail off and cast his eyes downwards.

She carried on as if he hadn't spoken. "He told me I was badly behaved, and that was *before* I threw the glass at the wall. I just don't get it. All the things I love – my mum, my best friend, my school – they've been taken away from me, and I don't know why."

They sat silently for a little while, and then the boy said, "You'll have to block all those memories out for now. It's your best chance."

"Best chance of what?" she asked.

"Survival. We must do as we're told until I can come up with a plan," he announced bravely.

"I'm Lauren, by the way." She looked at him enquiringly, and he told her his name. "Thanks for helping me," she said. She stood up and turned to go. "Now I need to find my other friend, Hannah."

"You won't find her at the moment, Lauren," the boy told her. "She's been locked up."

"Why?"

"Because, like you, she stepped out of line." Lauren stared at him, puzzled. He continued, "She hid under the table when we were all supposed to leave the dining hall, so when they found her, they took her downstairs." As he finished speaking, Lauren noticed that the boy was digging his nails into his palms. His face was red with fury.

\*

## Present day

Dr Keith Wilson and his assistant, Dr Sally Pritchard, had been working in the laboratory during the morning. However, they were well aware that the raid on Merrydown was in progress and knew they were on standby. Sure enough, at 10.21 a.m., Inspector Brady put the call through that their expertise would be required in the grounds of the children's home.

The sniffer dogs had discovered bones underneath the rose bushes.

Wilson and Pritchard took two assistants with them, along with their equipment, and met Brady in front of the manor house an hour after Brady's call. They were shown to the bone site, where they immediately set up the protection of a forensic tent. Brady left them to don their suits and get on with the job of unearthing evidence. He re-entered the house and caught up with Jamie Grant.

"Have the prints team finished in the basement?" he asked.

"They're nearly done, sir," Jamie replied.

"And the rest of the building?"

"The search team have finished. They're waiting for you to debrief them."

Brady ran his hands through his hair. What a morning it had been. One grim discovery after another. "Okay. I'll wind things up inside the building, and then I'm going to join Wilson outside and see what's coming up in the rose garden." He heaved a huge sigh. "Could you get on to the usual team and then wait until they've got the place secured?"

Jamie nodded. "Sure," he said.

"Talk about *Bleak House*," Brady said, gazing over their surroundings and shaking his head in disbelief.

\*

He watched the two doctors scraping away the soil from a group of bones. No one said anything. But after a while, Brady realised he wasn't being of any use; in fact, he thought he might even hinder the forensic work if he started asking questions. He would save those questions for later. So he left Wilson and Pritchard in the rose bushes and began to head towards a waiting squad car. He hadn't got far when he was approached by a young man who seemed to have come out of nowhere.

"Inspector Brady?" the young man enquired. He was

wearing a broad smile: the sort of self-righteous smile that gets under your skin and rankles. And then Brady knew who he was looking at.

"What are you doing here, Brogan?" he said wearily.

"Exactly my question to you!" came the reply. "What's going on at the children's home?"

Brady wondered how the hack had got wind of the police raid so quickly. Someone had obviously alerted him again. The same someone who'd let on that the priest hadn't been strangled by a ligature. It had been in the *Thames Herald* the day before, and Brady had read it with utter frustration, as that particular detail had only been known to a select few. But who was the mole?

However, he wasn't going to waste time asking the journalist. He simply said, "Get out of my way, Brogan," and stepped aside in order to walk past him.

"The public has a right to know what's happening in their neighbourhood," Brogan shouted after him, but Brady carried on until he reached the squad car. Then he looked back.

"One day, I'll find an excuse to have you arrested," he called.

"That's a threat, Mr Brady. I could complain of harassment," Brogan shouted back.

Brady got in the car and sat quietly for a few moments, thinking through what he had to do next once they were back at the nick. Then he indicated to the driver to get going. As they pulled away, he noticed Brogan was now standing in the gardens, beside the forensic tent – and standing there with him was Sally Pritchard, who appeared to be laughing at something Brogan was saying. It was just a quick glimpse of the two of them, but enough to arouse Brady's suspicions.

\*

That evening in the lab, Brady joined the two forensic pathologists. Where the bones were concerned, they were waiting for the opinion of the forensic anthropologist, who would be able to tell them how long the bones had lain in the ground. She wasn't due to arrive until the next afternoon. But something about the bones had certainly not required an outside opinion: it had been immediately obvious that they were too tiny to be adult bones.

"Babies," said Wilson, heavily.

Brady wanted to swear but checked himself in front of Dr Pritchard. Instead, he asked, "How many bodies are there?"

"We think at least two," said Sally Pritchard. "We'll be able to tell you more when we've sorted through them thoroughly."

Seasoned professional as he was, it was a rare occasion when the job made him feel sick. But right now, a wave of nausea washed over him. So those monsters had committed infanticide as well as rape, unless they were stillbirths. And how likely was that? Even if they were stillbirths, the bodies should have been disposed of by licensed means. God, the world was a sick place. Brady looked at Wilson. "Let me know what the bones tell you as soon as you can," he said. Another thought occurred to him. "Have you made any progress with the priest?"

"I've only looked at the victim's throat area so far," Wilson said. "But yes, I do believe I've got some useful information for you." He left Pritchard with the baby bones and walked over to a desk at the far side of the lab. Brady followed him. He watched the chief pathologist refer to a notepad. Wilson slowly spoke as he read from his notes. "We picked up dye and fibres from the neck. That tells us that the killer was wearing gloves. The dye's black; the fibres are suede. Computer analysis matched both to a brand known as 'Oxford Gentleman', a rare and expensive make."

Brady made a mental note. "And can you tell me any more about the finger pattern? Didn't you say the guy might have been missing part of his hand?"

Wilson nodded. "When I first saw the victim's neck, I could tell the pressure had been unevenly applied. Now we're two days on from then. As you know, the body was preserved in the freezer, but now it has thawed, the bruising has developed, and it shows the unevenness of the finger pattern even more clearly."

"And you can see that, even though the killer was wearing gloves?" said Brady.

"You know, you have to apply a hell of a lot of pressure to strangle someone," replied Wilson, slightly annoyed at having his analysis questioned. "Either his two hands don't match, or he has a strange quirk where his grasp doesn't involve his forefinger."

"So are we talking right or left hand?" Brady continued.

"Left. Just to confirm, I'd say he's missing part of his left index."

Brady made another mental note. "Well, I'll leave you to it, Keith," he said. "You and Sally have got your work cut out, what with the priest, the bones and all the prints from the building." He paused thoughtfully. "I'm particularly interested in the prints from the basement, by the way, especially those sited on the metal shackle, as well as any trace evidence from the bed sheet."

\*

Soon after six-thirty the next morning, Wilson was back in the lab, sifting through the prints, which had come in from Merrydown. He paid special attention to all trace evidence found in the basement rooms, particularly from the room with the shackle, as Brady had requested. Since Gerald Hope had been brought in under arrest the previous day, Wilson already had his prints logged for comparison. He also had the prints of the young woman who was lying in a bed in St. Joseph's, which he would use for elimination purposes. Carefully studying the prints on the shackle, he concluded that he was looking at four different sets. One set belonged to the patient herself, while Gerald Hope, in the previous day's interview, had mentioned that Fox had visited the basement at least once recently, so that accounted for a second set of prints. His own fingerprints were absent. That left two sets to be identified. He buzzed Brady and let him know what he'd found.

\*

Brady had worked very late the previous night. If it hadn't been for an urgent need to connect with his own children, a strong emotion brought on by witnessing the pathetic collection of baby bones in the forensic laboratory, he would have unfolded the camp bed always ready in the office cupboard for emergencies and spent the night at the nick. Nevertheless, he'd stayed in the office until gone nine, going over the day's events in his mind and figuring out a schedule for the coming day. His instinct had told him even before

Wilson's phone call that the prints in the basement, especially those on the shackle, were not Gerald Hope's. Since their first meeting, he'd always felt *his* preference might be little boys. So, as he sat quietly in his office, Brady's thoughts began to wander once again in the direction of a paedophile police officer. One possibly holding a high rank. One with a foreign name. "Let's find you, you bastard," he whispered to his computer screen as he clicked into the PNC files and began trawling through possible candidates.

There were, of course, hundreds of officers holding high ranks. Luckily, those with the most obviously foreign names numbered less than two dozen. He decided he had to start somewhere, so he singled out seven above his rank who had the most 'un-English' names and made a note of them: di Angelo, Gomez, Soderbergh; Schaefer, Berisha; Pattullo and Sotiris. Tinkering with his biro and notepad, he studied the seven names and sighed. It wouldn't be easy, he thought, getting hold of their fingerprints, and these were only the first seven. Still, since all officers had to submit prints at the beginning of their careers for the purpose of eliminating them from crime scenes, it wasn't going to be impossible. The prints would only be held at the local level, but maybe with Delgado's help and the assistance of *his* superiors, a comparison between these 'untouchables' and the shackle could be made.

Having received the call from Wilson, Brady opened up his computer again and clicked on Wilson's email attachment, showing the two mystery sets of prints. He was due to phone Jenna later and touch base with her, but, in her absence right now, he decided to buzz Jamie and get him into the office to bounce ideas around, particularly with regard to today's schedule. A light tap on the door announced Jamie's arrival, and Brady soon had him up to date on the fingerprint data.

"Still two sets of unknowns?" Jamie said.

"Precisely," said Brady. "So, how do you think we should prioritise today?"

Jamie answered promptly. "All the staff that were at Merrydown must be fingerprinted. Any one of them might have been in collusion," he said. "And even if they weren't, the girl had to eat, didn't she? So whoever brought her food or bathed her or whatever must have touched that shackle."

"Precisely," said Brady.

"And we haven't yet tracked down the fifth member of the ring," Jamie said. He ran his fingers over his designer stubble. It seemed to help him think. "One of those sets of prints could be his." After a deep inhale, he said, "Difficult if that's a high-ranking Met officer."

"Difficult," agreed Brady, "but not impossible."

"Are you going to liaise with Delgado?" Jamie asked. "He'd be able to get his superiors to open doors for you, wouldn't he?"

Brady smiled at the younger detective. "Actually, I've already set up a meeting with him. You'll be studying for your sergeant's exams soon. Would you like to observe?"

*

Brady spent the next half-hour briefing Delgado while Jamie looked on. The DCI agreed that they now had sufficient evidence to warrant requesting a comparison of the prints on the shackle with those of any number of high-ranking police officers. When Brady and Grant left him, Delgado was already on the phone with his boss, Detective Superintendent Anna Scott, to ask if she could get *her* superiors' help in setting up this rather delicate line of enquiry.

When Brady arrived back in his office, Helen was waiting for him. Jenna had given her the first instalment of Lauren's story the previous evening and had asked her to submit it to Brady this morning.

"I know you're busy, sir," said Helen, "but Jenna thought you ought to have this."

"The girl's statement?" Brady asked.

"First instalment," Helen replied. She grimaced. "I listened to it last night. It's awful enough as it is, but I think there could be worse to come."

She walked out and shut the door, leaving Brady alone with the dictaphone. He sat down and was about to switch it on when he remembered that lowlife by the name of Brogan. He buzzed Andy and called him into the office. "I want you to put a tail on that reporter again," he told him when the door was firmly shut. "But this time, I want you to do it late. Tonight."

Andy frowned. "How will I know where to find him outside of his working hours?" he said.

Brady gestured with a finger over his lips. "Try waiting somewhere near Doctor Pritchard's flat," he said in a stage whisper. Andy's eyebrows shot up. "Top secret!" said Brady.

\*

Commander Max Schaefer sat on the floor of his Wimbledon apartment. Beside his left knee was a bottle of whisky. There were two other items in his possession right now. One was the letter he held in his hand, signed 'Freddie'. It had arrived this morning – though not via the postman – while Schaefer had been out, so he hadn't seen who'd put it through his letterbox. When he'd come home and read its contents, he'd sat and stewed for a long time over how he was going to get out of this one. Even if he could run a fingerprint check privately and discover who and where 'Freddie' was, hunting him down seemed to be out of the question. Because first of all, the blackmailer had obviously taken steps to insure himself against being arrested. Or being bumped off. Clever really. Secondly, if he did do as 'Freddie' demanded, how would he raise the sort of money he wanted? Half a million? He'd have to sell his flat. And that would only be for starters, anyway.

Schaefer put the letter down and picked up the bottle beside him. He screwed the cap off, shoved the bottleneck in his mouth and took a decent slug of Scotch to calm his nerves. Replacing the cap, he set the bottle down and took hold of the letter again. Reading it through once more, he searched for inspiration. But none came. How many times had he read it now? Seven? Eight? He could just about recite it without looking. He replaced the letter in its envelope and swigged again from the bottle.

Running his hand over the third object he'd brought with him to this place of contemplation on the floor, his thoughts turned now to that other matter: the one he'd heard about on the eight o'clock news this morning when he'd switched on the radio. Merrydown Children's Home had been shut down following a police raid. He knew only too well that the place would have been scoured for evidence by dogs as well as officers. It wouldn't have taken the animals too long to reach the rose garden. And it wouldn't have taken the officers much longer to get to the basement, either, where he knew only too well that he'd left his prints on the shackle and his bodily fluids all over the sheets.

On hearing the news, Schaefer had gone straight to the cabinet and opened his first whisky bottle of the day. Half of it had disappeared down his throat when he'd suddenly had a horrifying flashback: maybe they didn't find the prize in the basement... because he hadn't put the shackle back on her, had he? It came to him, clear as day, and his heart rate soared until he could feel pain in his chest. Not only had he not re-cuffed her, he'd gone tearing out of the building and had no recollection of locking up after himself. So maybe she'd fled. Was that how the police got wind of it? Did her escape precipitate the raid?

Hours later and here he was now, halfway through his second bottle of Scotch. He hadn't even eaten today. No need. He'd just stuck to the drink and searched for a miracle. In one direction, there was 'Freddie' with all those murky secrets in his possession; in another, there was the police – his colleagues – almost certainly waiting with the evidence he'd left in the basement room and in yet another direction, there was the killer. Still at large. Because those fucking amateurs hadn't managed to catch him yet. Schaefer realised there would be no miracle.

He drank for the last time, and then he stopped, the bottle unfinished. He needed to quell the fear and yet still be alert enough to carry out the final act. At last, he stood up, resigned to his fate. He picked up the length of rope and headed for the stairwell.

*

Brady switched off the dictaphone. His head was aching. Opening a drawer, he grabbed a pack of paracetamol. The stated adult dosage was two. He took four. His insides felt hollow. That poor girl! He decided there was only one voice that could soothe him. He picked up his mobile and phoned Jenna.

"How are you doing?" he asked.

"Well, to be truthful, I didn't get much sleep last night. You forget what noisy places hospitals are, even at night," Jenna replied.

"Especially at night," Brady returned. "How's the patient?"

"She slept very soundly, though I'm pretty sure they put some happy juice in her drip to help her on her way. Was tempted to ask for some myself!"

"Yeah, and if there's any spare…" Brady said. "I've listened to the recording," he said, more seriously.

But Jenna was further down the road than Brady. This morning, Lauren had been talking again, and Jenna had been hearing even more horrific news of her friend's captivity. She felt she ought to prepare Brady for what was to come. "You wait till you get the next instalment," she said.

"That bad?" he said.

"Bad doesn't even begin to describe what she's been through. Anyway," Jenna sounded brighter, "the good news is that the doctor is so pleased with how she has stabilised that her drip has been removed, and she'll be eating a semi-solid lunch today. They even said she could get up later and begin to move around. I believe her first consultation with a psychiatrist is also due to take place early this evening. Do you want me to stay with her for now?"

"Yes, stay with her, especially as she's still relating her story. But don't be surprised if the psychiatrist won't let you witness the consultation later. Best friend or not, the meeting with Lauren is bound to be confidential. Anyway, buzz me tomorrow and keep me up to speed," Brady replied.

"I heard about the raid from Helen," Jenna told him. The pitch of her voice fell. "She told me about the rose garden."

Brady closed his eyes and relived the horror of seeing the assembled baby bones in Wilson's laboratory. "They've called in a forensic anthropologist to tell us how long the…" he nearly said 'babies' "… bones have been in the ground. We should know later today."

"Has Wilson got any more from the priest's post-mortem?" asked Jenna.

"Yes, the killer was wearing gloves."

A vision of Greg's gloved hands sprang up in Jenna's mind's eye. She hastily cast it aside, telling herself that it was winter, for goodness' sake, and most men were in gloves by now. "And the hand injury?"

"Possibly a missing fingertip; left hand," Brady said. "Talking of fingers, we might at last be making a bit of progress in tracking down our corrupt colleague."

"How so?" asked Jenna.

"Delgado has submitted prints from the Merrydown basement to Detective Super Scott. She's currently working her way up the chain of command to get the authority of one of the deputy assistant commissioners to run comparisons with the filed prints of several high ranks."

"Those with exotic names," Jenna said.

"Yes," said Brady confidently. And then he remembered. "Well, a few of them anyway! Gotta start somewhere."

"Wow!" said Jenna, impressed with the speed at which things were progressing. "We might be able to bring the remaining one of those five bastards to justice before the killer gets to him."

"Even better," Brady replied, "we might be able to bring paedophile and killer to justice."

They were both quiet again for a moment. Jenna spoke first. "Lauren's had a nap, but she's just coming round again now, so I'd better go."

"Okay," said Brady. Another pause. "Jen?" he said.

"Yes?"

"I miss you."

\*

No sooner had Brady closed up his mobile than the office phone buzzed. Brady pressed a button. It was Wilson in the lab. "Yes, Keith?" he said.

"I'm halfway through the full post-mortem now. But thought you'd like to know: I've found something of interest under the priest's fingernails."

"Go on," said Brady.

"Skin. He must have scratched his killer as they tussled."

"So we now have a sample of the killer's DNA," said Brady. Things really were looking up.

"Yes," said Wilson. But his tone was more guarded. "Unfortunately, you also need something to compare it with."

\*

The day dragged by. Jenna quietly observed Lauren as she slept and spoke gently to her about nothing very much when she woke. Many times, she watched as Lauren's fearful eyes seemed to focus on some perceived threat on the far side of the room, or she saw her tense every time the door opened. But to Jenna's surprise, her friend ate her lunch quite heartily and was ready to rise from her bed, with the help of two nurses, later in the afternoon.

Towards the evening, the meeting with the consultant psychiatrist went ahead as scheduled in an adjacent room. In Lauren's absence, Jenna set up another dictaphone at the bedside in case she felt like talking the next morning. However, as soon as Lauren returned, it was clear she wanted to talk immediately.

## July 1999

Lauren paced the floorboards of the dormitory. The boy in Room 14 had told her to keep quiet and lie low until he could 'think of a plan'. Perhaps he thought this bold statement would help her feel better. But in truth, Lauren felt even more exasperated after talking to him. Her future was so indefinite. She felt like she was staring down a bottomless shaft. Angry and frustrated, she noticed a prickling sensation all over her body and dug her nails into her forearm so hard that she managed to pierce the skin. She watched as a minuscule drop of blood trickled down her arm and meandered its way towards her fingertips. She let the tiny bead of blood drip onto the floor and experienced an immediate sense of relief.

When Hannah was allowed to return from the basement, Lauren observed her enter the dormitory and lie down quietly on her bed. Two other girls followed her in, whispering to each other. One fetched a book, and the other went to her drawer for a length of wool, perhaps for playing cat's cradle. The first one smiled at Lauren, then the two of them held hands and walked out of the room, leaving Lauren and Hannah alone in the dormitory. Lauren approached Hannah's bed, but to her surprise, Hannah turned onto her side and faced the opposite direction.

"Hannah?" Lauren asked tentatively. "Have I upset you?"

"No," came the meek reply.

"Then what's wrong?"

There was no answer. Lauren noticed that Hannah had placed her hands between her legs. She also seemed to be shaking just a little. "Are you hurt?" she asked. Again, there was no answer, but this time, Lauren heard Hannah sob. The only conclusion that Lauren could draw was that Hannah had been smacked on her bottom for daring to hide under the table after breakfast. She put her hand on Hannah's back and patted it gently. But she felt her flinch and decided that she didn't want to be touched at the moment.

Lauren went back to her bed and sat down. Once again, she felt the anger rising in her. She could now hear Hannah crying into her pillow. And her hands hadn't moved from between her legs. She was obviously sore there. How severe a punishment must she have taken? Lauren decided that, despite the warning from the boy with the dark hair to lie low, she had to say something on her friend's behalf. Lauren had always had a strong sense of justice, and this wasn't right. She determined to say something when the moment was right… and soon.

\*

Two nights later, Lauren was awoken by a noise. She peeped above the covers. The moonlight was weak but afforded some dim light into the dormitory, enough to make out the figure of a man at the bedside of one of the girls. It didn't look like Mr Fox, and he was the only man she'd met in this home so far. So who was he? She pretended to sleep on peacefully but kept a watchful eye on what happened next. The man drew back the duvet and climbed into the bed. It was Sarah's bed. Lauren could hear Sarah's muffled squeal. Soon, she saw the shape of the silhouette change: the man now seemed to be lying on top of Sarah. Was this some sort of punishment? More muffled squeals and a long throaty sigh, which wasn't Sarah's. Then everything went quiet and still. Minutes later, Lauren watched through almost closed lids as the figure of the man got out of Sarah's bed and tiptoed out of the room. It took her a long time to fall asleep again as she lay puzzling over what she'd just witnessed. The sound of Sarah quietly sobbing also kept her awake.

\*

"I need to talk to Mr Fox," Lauren announced loudly to Miss Brewer the next morning at breakfast. The housekeeper scowled at her as if to say, 'Not you again!' But by now, Lauren's anger had worked itself up to a pitch. She didn't even think about punishment: justice mattered more. To her surprise, Miss Brewer left the dining hall and went to fetch the manager. Shortly afterwards, stealthy footsteps announced Mr Fox's arrival.

"Ah!" said Mr Fox. "The Vixen! I hear you need to talk to me. Would you like to come with me? I think we should go somewhere a little more private." He smiled oddly.

Many of the children who were eating in the dining hall caught sight of his expression. A few of them recognised what it meant: punishment with the rod. Fox had three levels of punishment: hand, strap and rod, depending on the severity of the offence. The rod was the worst because it didn't just land on your arm, leg or bottom; it went right up inside you, and it hurt badly. But only a few knew this. They were sure that Lauren was soon to be initiated into their group: those who'd known the rod.

Fox took Lauren downstairs to the basement. This time, he chose a different room, the one immediately to his right at the foot of the stairs. He led her inside and closed the door, locking it behind him. She noticed that there was a bed in this room. Maybe very naughty children had to spend nights down here – that's what it would be for. Fox went over to the bed, sat on it and patted the area next to him, inviting her to sit at his side. Keen to have it out with him, she did as she was bid.

"Lauren," he said softly. The tone made her skin crawl, but she had no idea why. "I fear we've got off on the wrong foot."

"The wrong foot?" she replied. "I'll say! You tied me up the day after I arrived here…"

"Because you broke a glass on purpose, remember! It was my way of calming you down." Fox's voice was barely above a whisper. It really was most disconcerting.

But Lauren decided to go for it now that she had his undivided attention. "And my friend Hannah was so hurt by your punishment the other day that she cried nearly all day." Fox said nothing. "And another girl, Sarah, was punished by somebody in the night, and she cried so much I couldn't get to sleep for ages."

"Listen to me," said Fox. His arm suddenly snaked around her waist. "Dear child!" The volume of his voice had dipped again. It was barely audible now. "I have something to tell you. Your mother, Vicki, gave birth to you in this very place. Merrydown is your true home." He let his words sink in. "Vicki was lucky that a friend of mine, John, your stepfather, agreed to have her live with him and bring you up as his own child, but he couldn't be expected to look after you forever, now, could he? So you're back where you should be."

"NO... NO... NOooo!" Lauren yelled so loudly that her voice could be heard in the dining hall upstairs. Several of the children looked at each other, and the ones who knew the rod thought it must have been administered. Downstairs, Lauren had leapt up from the bed and was stamping her feet on the concrete floor. "I WANT MY MUM!" she cried. Fox sprang up and went to put his arms around her, but she ducked his advances and ran round to the other side of the bed. He came after her again and extended his hand to her face, hoping to soothe her. But she bit it as hard as she could. His expression hardened, and without further words, he grabbed her and threw her small body onto the bed. Lowering himself on top of her until she struggled to breathe, he locked his hand around her jaw so that she had no choice but to gaze into his glaring eyes.

"You're a whore, just like your mother," he whispered harshly. She didn't understand the description, and her fearful, wide-eyed stare narrowed into a frown. "I've seen you wiggle your hips, toss your hair and thrust your breasts forward." To her utter amazement, he suddenly burrowed his hands underneath her bottom and yanked her knickers down. "And as you're no longer a child, Lauren…" She noticed his breathing was becoming laboured. "When you get punished now, you will no longer receive a child's punishment."

He fumbled to untie his trouser belt, and then she felt him unzip his trousers and push them a little way down his legs. Paralysed with fear now, she lay motionless. He used his hands again to part her legs, fumbling again to move her knickers further out of the way. And then she felt the worst pain she'd ever known as his 'rod' moved between her legs and seared its way into her like a branding iron, again and again. She wanted to scream, but he had his hand over her mouth, and the more she tried to wriggle, the more he tightened his grasp until she felt she was going to lose consciousness. And then, just when she thought she was going to die, Fox released his grip, let out a prolonged gasp and went very still.

A little while later, he withdrew and got up off the bed. Lauren was shaking. She turned her head and retched. Now she knew what had happened to Hannah and Sarah. And she, too, began to sob.

\*

Back in the dormitory, she scrubbed herself between the legs until she made the soreness even worse. She scrubbed manically. Her tears flowed down her cheeks as the warm water mingled with her blood and trickled down her thighs. She washed again and again, hoping to rid herself of him. At last, exhausted, she dried herself with a little towel, put clean knickers on, and went and climbed on her bed.

Escape. She had to find a way. And until she did find a means of actual escape, she would have to resort to a mental form of escape, something she'd done in the past when her stepfather had got angry and grounded her. She reached under her pillow and retrieved the biro and paper that she'd stashed there. The children had access to stationery in the drawing room so they could do their school homework. But she'd smuggled some paper into her pocket and now had it in her hands as if it were her lifeline. It was a blank canvas on which she could create her own world or explore her reactions to the real world. She decided to start right now and log the horror which had just befallen her…

'I didnt want to beleve what happened to Hannah and Sarah. But I think deep down I knew. My stepfather never let me watch anything on TV rated above PG, but sometimes Jenna and I used to sneek a '15' when I went round there. And we had sex education at school. But that was mainly about periods and giving birth. It wasnt really about making babies. I never had a period before. But now Fox has sexed me, I'm bleeding. Is this a period? Could He have made a baby inside me? It wasnt like in the films. He was vilent and heavy and He did it to hurt me. And whatever He did to me He said he did to my Mum. What kind of sick place is this?

Will He do it again? I know him or his friends have done it to Hannah and Sarah and now me. Probaly some of the other girls too. How can this be happening? Do we have a choice?

I like drawing blood. From my arms. I never did it before I arrived here. When the pain gets too much or I feel confused, it seems to be the only way to take my mind off things. It sounds kind of wierd but I sort of like watching the blood trickle over my skin and on to the floor.

Maybe because I'm bleeding down there He won't sex me again. Not for a while. Maybe that will give me time to make a plan. To get away. I'd feel bad leaving the other girls knowing what there going through but if I can get out of here I can tell someone. Like the police. It would be embrassing telling them that a man did THAT to me but I would have to say it to save the girls back here.

And now I just need to go to sleep. I want to block out what He did to me. The insides of my legs are burning and I have scracth marks on my body. I feel filthy and I just want to get rid of him off me.'

\*

The next morning, while the children were having breakfast, Miss Brewer went from bed to bed, ensuring that all were made to Mr Fox's standards. Unfortunately for Miss Brewer, there were many girls at Merrydown who were just entering puberty and blood spots on sheets were a regular occurrence. The housekeeper, therefore, frequently had the thankless task of removing soiled linen and replacing it with freshly laundered sheets. But at least she had the satisfaction of knowing that Mr Fox appreciated her hard work: he always demanded that beds be spick and span.

As she strode through the dormitory, carrying out her inspection, she wondered what it would be like to be Mrs

Fox. Poor Elvira, she thought, condescendingly. All surface and no substance. If I were Mrs Fox, at least I would provide Mr Fox with intelligent conversation. And shared values like discipline, cleanliness, punctuality and good manners. Her imagination was just beginning to stray into other less well-known areas of married life, of which Miss Brewer had no experience but which she thought might nevertheless be rather pleasant with Mr Fox when she approached the bed of the wild girl by the name of Lauren. She exhaled loudly in frustration.

The bed wasn't made at all. That girl had been nothing but trouble since she'd arrived. Pulling back the crumpled heap of a duvet to reveal the sheet beneath, Miss Brewer let out a small gasp. Dried spots of blood darkened the linen. Surely, this girl was too young for her period. She was only just eleven. Miss Brewer shook her head, puzzled. But then, she'd heard that girls these days were starting their monthlies earlier and earlier. Perhaps it wasn't such a surprise after all. She grabbed the sheet and pulled it away from the bed, but as she did so, something fell from beneath Lauren's pillow and landed with a light thud on the floor. Bending to retrieve it, the housekeeper realised it was a bunch of papers folded together into a home-made notebook. She picked it up and started to flick through the pages. Very quickly she arrived at Lauren's latest entry, and outrage bubbled within her veins. Not on Lauren's behalf but on behalf of the master. How dare this wretch insult him like that? Who did she think she was? And who else was she spreading this poison to?

Without further ado, she headed straight for Mr Fox's study, next door to his office. Tapping lightly on the door, Miss Brewer waited for his summons.

"Enter," said Fox.

"Mr Fox," said Miss Brewer, "please forgive me for interrupting you. I know how much you value your quiet time."

"Not at all," replied Fox, with a polite smile. It always paid to keep the housekeeper on side. She already saw more than any other member of staff, and any betrayal from her would be far-reaching. It was unthinkable. "What can I do for you?"

"Well, actually, it was something I found in the girls' dormitory that I thought you should see." Miss Brewer handed the 'notebook' to Mr Fox and then watched as his eyes scanned the pages. "She needs to be stopped, doesn't she?" she said in a conspiratorial tone.

An enigmatic smile curled the edge of Fox's lips. "I couldn't agree with you more, Miss Brewer," he said. "In fact, before you came to see me, I had already made a decision. It's been a while since we've had to go to such lengths with a minor, but this little brat needs the ultimate controls." He'd been drawing up a plan for some time now to get his daughter isolated for the purposes of his sexual needs, but he had just been missing an appropriate excuse to put that plan into action. Now he had that excuse. "I will be removing her from the normal living quarters to somewhere where I can give her more attention," he said, "and bring her back into line, perhaps. Yes, I think she will benefit from a prolonged stay in solitary. After breakfast, bring her to me. She's going downstairs. Today, and for the foreseeable future."

\*

Six weeks later, still in solitary, she was staring into a darkness so intense that it was solid. Something had brought her out of her slumber. Something was shuffling softly in the corner of the room. She moved her right arm, causing the chain, which bound her to the wall, to rattle. She thought the noise might at least show she was awake and alert. Ready for a fight.

Always ready for a fight.

She cocked her ear and listened. The noise had altered: no longer a shuffling sound, it was now the soft pad of feet on the concrete floor. Approaching. She rattled the chain again, spelling it out: 'Come and get me, and I'll hurt you…' An injured animal in a trap.

The footsteps stopped.

This time when she cocked her ear, she could just make out quiet breathing. She waited. The only sound for a while was her own galloping heartbeat, echoing underground and surfacing madly in her head. Then, the soft footfall began again. She strained her eyes to see. Imagined shapes. Imagined monsters. She flared her nostrils. Fox had his own scent, but the faint smell that reached her now was different.

Stale. Earthy.

Someone new was coming for her.

She let out a high-pitched squeal from her throat and listened as it bounced off the walls around her.

She waited again.

All at once, out of the void emerged a figure. It towered over her right-hand side, and again she strained to see detail, but in total pitch black, there was none. A key had been inserted into the cuff, and her right arm was instantly freed. But only for a moment, for the figure had replaced the cuff with his own strong grip, which tightened by the second. She swung her left arm over, clubbing the assailant on the shoulders. She heard him cry out, but her victory was brief, as he swiftly grabbed her left wrist in his right hand and then pinned both of her arms to the pillow under her head.

Despite the lack of light, she could tell he was naked.

She started to moan, and the moaning grew into a wailing. She projected the sound as loud as she could to catch someone's attention upstairs.

Futile. Always futile.

Then she heard him softly snigger as his shadowy face descended towards hers, and she was horrified to feel a mouth closing over her own.

She bit hard into the top lip, and he recoiled in pain, releasing her left arm for a moment while he explored with his fingers the small injury she'd caused. She quickly thrust her left hand where she thought his eyes would be, but his head was turned to the side, and she only managed to scratch his right ear once more before his hands were back, gripping hers.

"Bitch!" he whispered, and, pinning her arms behind her head, he slid in on top of her.

He raped her until she was barely conscious.

\*

Two months after she'd first been placed in solitary confinement, Lauren was finally allowed upstairs. Fox had been approached by Miss Brewer, who, concerned about the girl's education, had asked him when she was to resume her studies and, in order to convince his housekeeper he was playing fair, he'd brought her back to her dormitory and told her she could mix with the other children again, provided that she behaved.

But the experience below ground had altered Lauren. She had become morose and unwilling to cooperate, taciturn and sullen. She'd sit for long periods, rocking back and forth, humming tunelessly. She didn't wish to mix with the other children, not even Hannah, who knew only too well what she'd been through and tried hard to maintain their friendship. But to no avail: Lauren increasingly withdrew. She ate little, cut into her arms with breakfast knives, which she regularly smuggled up to the dormitory and cried herself to sleep at night.

And then, one day, she snapped. In the drawing room, scissors were regularly made available to the children to cut out shapes for their geometry homework and other mathematical assignments. She selected a pair with the sharpest blades she could find and hid them down the side of one of her long socks. At dinner that evening, when Fox came to the dining hall on one of his tours of inspection, Lauren waited for him to approach and then reached beneath the table, withdrew the weapon and leapt up and sprang at him, stabbing the scissor blades into his face. There was a collective intake of breath from the assembled children and staff, followed by a silence in which the proverbial pin would have clattered to the floor.

Luckily for Fox, the small beard, which he'd recently grown, saved him from serious injury. The metal blades were somewhat deflected by the stubble growth and only just nicked the skin. Even so, Fox still bled from the scratch, and Miss Brewer, who'd been looking on in utter horror, grabbed a table napkin and raced to his side to dab the wound.

Not so luckily for Lauren, that episode put the seal on

her future. She was disarmed and marched straight back down to the basement.

She would not see the light of day again for more than fourteen years.

*

## Present day

Brady had spent another night tossing and turning in his bed. Brochures dealing with full-time care were scattered over the lounge carpet, and he'd finally abandoned them just before midnight. He had then found his mind too busy to sleep.

He knew he had no choice. His wife needed full-time care. Simple as that. Unless he stopped work and became her full-time carer, then what would they live on? Who would support the children? What about the mortgage? Later in his bed, these questions would recede in his mind as he dozed and then surface again urgently, forcing him to wake and confront them. And so it went on through the night.

By half past five, he was wide awake, his mind busier than ever. He got himself ready for work and then woke Shona at six, apologising for such an early wake-up call and checking that she would be okay looking after herself and her brother. Of course, they'd be alright, she whispered in her only-just-awake voice, and Brady felt a stab of pride as he kissed his daughter on the forehead. "Don't forget to lock up when you go out," he said quietly.

"Duh!" she said, her eyes still closed. "Never would have thought of it!"

As if to make up for a wakeful night, good news was waiting for him in the office. Wilson was also in early and told

Brady that one of the remaining sets of prints on the metal shackle had been identified. As soon as Helen and Andy were in, Brady dispatched them to arrest Mavis Brewer, who looked as if she'd colluded in at least one crime. Her prints on the shackle surely meant she was involved. Certainly involved in holding a person against their will. Whether or not she'd also conspired in the sexual abuse remained to be seen, but Brady couldn't see how anyone in their right mind who'd visited the basement room could *not* have known what was going on in there. He was confident that Helen's and Andy's assertive interview techniques would establish the truth.

A little later, he was busy helping himself to his first coffee of the morning when Delgado called him to his office. He went in, mug in hand.

"Bingo!" Delgado exclaimed.

"What?" Brady could see the excitement on the DCI's face. He thought it could only mean one thing. "Don't tell me we've found him?"

Delgado's nodding head, huge eyes and beaming smile were affirmation enough.

"Apparently, he hasn't even bothered turning up to work this morning," Delgado said.

Brady took a long sip of his coffee and savoured it. The world was suddenly looking a much better place. "Are you going to tell me who this individual is?" Brady asked.

"Max Schaefer!"

Brady's eyebrows shot up. *"Commander Schaefer?"*

"The very same," replied Delgado. "He lives in Wimbledon, and that's where you and I are going this morning."

"To *arrest* the commander?" Brady was still stunned.

"Don't worry. The super told me that someone very senior would be present. Schaefer certainly won't be able to pull rank on us." Delgado looked thoughtful. "You know, it's taken a while to find him, but you've done it, Dom. You never gave up on the idea that there was a rotten egg in the force's basket, did you? Well done!"

With a half-smile, Brady nodded his appreciation. But the smile evaporated just as quickly as it had appeared. "Now we just need to find our killer," he said.

\*

Brady's heartbeat was raised. He'd never had to arrest a colleague in the police force before, never mind one of such high rank. Luckily, he had a minor part to play in this particular sortie. He'd been called along to brief his superiors as necessary with details relevant to the charges, which were to be put to the alleged offender. The arrest speech itself was due to be delivered by Detective Chief Superintendent Carl Metcalfe.

Metcalfe now knocked at the door of the commander's Wimbledon apartment. Five officers, two uniformed and the rest in plain clothes, stood and waited for a reply. One of the uniforms held an enforcer in his hands. All was still. Metcalfe rapped at the door again. "Commander Schaefer. It's DCS Metcalfe here. I have a warrant for your arrest." Brady watched him breathe deeply and then peer downwards at his Ferragamo shoes. Silence. "Commander Schaefer? Are you there? Open the door, please," he cried. They all waited. Nothing. Metcalfe turned to the officer with the enforcer in his hands. "Please enforce," he said. The officer nodded. Metcalfe shouted, "Stand back!" The enforcer was rammed against the door. Two swipes, and it gave way. The officer who had broken it thrust his arm inside the gaping hole he'd just made, lifted a latch and opened it fully. The five officers, led by Carl Metcalfe, then tumbled inside.

They hadn't got far when Metcalfe stopped abruptly, and the others who were following so closely behind him hurtled into each other like a motorway pile-up. They quickly found their feet and followed Metcalfe's gaze upwards.

Max Schaefer was hanging in the stairwell.

The rope around his neck had been secured around three robust oak spindles on the upstairs landing. The rope had held fast. It looked like job done: life extinct.

Metcalfe whipped out his phone and made a call. The two uniforms meanwhile stood and gaped at the lifeless body. Delgado and Brady looked at each other. Brady saw the DCI mouth the word 'Fuck!' to him. Brady said nothing but gazed up at Max Schaefer's body. So this was the one he'd been after for so long. This was the 'foreign name' he'd first heard about when he went and leant hard on Ozzie Dixon. This was one of the monsters who, for so many years, had abused Lauren and perhaps others, including Valentine. May you rot in hell, he thought.

The DCS finished his call. "The local boys are on their way," he said. "They'll deal with things here. You two..." he indicated Delgado and Brady "... might as well get back. I'll make sure that any evidence, computer or otherwise, retrieved from this apartment is forwarded to you and..." He paused and looked up again at Schaefer's purple face and black tongue. "I'll see you get post-mortem results too."

\*

"Suicide?" said Jenna incredulously.

"He must have got wind of us closing in on him," said Brady.

Jenna tutted in disgust. "And couldn't face the consequences?" Her voice was hushed as she looked at a sleeping Lauren. She walked out of the room, gently pulling the door closed. "Lousy coward!" she said, making her way to the coffee machine.

"How's Lauren?" asked Brady.

"Asleep," she said.

"When I got back from Schaefer's place today, I listened to the next instalment of her story." Brady was silent for a moment. Jenna waited. "Sometimes I really can sympathise with the vigilante mindset," he said.

"You know what I'm going to say next, don't you?" said Jenna.

"That you've heard more, and it's even worse?"

"She had two babies, you know." Jenna's voice was quiet, resigned. "Not at eleven. Not that young. But later." Brady could hear her over the phone, swallowing hard. "She said each time they took them away. She doesn't know where to. She was crying, Dom. Convulsed in tears. You'll hear it on the next recording."

"Jesus," said Brady. It was tempting to let the emotion dictate the conversation, but he needed to resume a professional approach now and get back to the facts. "The forensic anthropologist examined the bone collection yesterday afternoon." He couldn't hold back on the truth any longer. "Babies," he said. " Two different sets. She said they were interred within months of each other, around ten years ago."

Jenna inhaled deeply. "So one of those babies could have been Lauren's," said Jenna.

"Wilson was due to receive the results of DNA profiling this morning," said Brady. "But as I was out, I haven't yet heard the outcome."

"And why," Jenna asked, sitting herself down on a chair in an empty corridor, "were there only two babies in the grounds? Could they have been stillbirths?" Her mind raced on. "Do you think any of the abusers ever used precautions?"

"*Precautions?*" Brady nearly smiled. Jenna was still quite naïve about the depths of depravity people could sink to. Refreshingly naïve. "Jen!" he said firmly. He trod carefully, not wishing to appear unkind. "Remember, these were men without scruples. It's far more likely," he said, "that they lost precious little time in finding someone to perform abortions for them or else gave the children away." He heard Jenna groan. "Let's leave that one there, shall we? I can hear I'm upsetting you." She was silent now. "Jen? Let's agree something," he said.

"What's that?" she said. Her voice was shaky, reflecting her shock.

"If one of the babies is Lauren's, let's agree not to tell her yet. Right now, it will do more harm than good. She can know later when she's stronger."

"She might want to have the bones re-interred in consecrated ground," said Jenna. She sounded exhausted, and Brady realised she'd been on duty as Lauren's SOIT officer for nearly three whole days and nights.

"You sound like you need a break, Jen," he said. "Leave

the patient in the nurses' care this evening. Take yourself off somewhere. Maybe there's a movie you've been waiting to see?"

"Actually, I might go for a run tonight. Only for an hour or so. I don't think Lauren's story is finished yet, so I'd like to be back to record whatever she has to say."

"Are you going to run alone?" asked Brady. For a moment, he wasn't sure why he was asking. Immediately, he wished he hadn't.

"No," said Jenna. "I think I'll ask Greg to join me. He's good at pacing my run for me."

"Oh?" said Brady with an edge to his voice. He wondered what else Greg was good at in her eyes. "Well, have fun," he said. It came out abruptly.

She caught the change in his tone. "He's nice, Dom," she said, "but don't worry – he's not in your league."

He so wanted to remind her that he loved her, but he simply said, "I'll talk to you again tomorrow."

He was closing up his mobile when someone tapped at his door. It was Andy, who looked as if he might have some interesting information for him. "Close the door," Brady said. He looked at the young DC hopefully. "Well?"

"You were right on the money, boss! Brogan arrived at Doctor Pritchard's flat at ten and was still there at 12.30 a.m. No sign of him emerging after that, so I decided to go off and get some sleep."

"Photos?"

"Of course," Andy replied.

"Yes!" said Brady, punching the air. "I'll go and have a word with the DCI. Pritchard could find herself suspended before the end of the day."

\*

Jenna was disappointed that Greg couldn't make it that evening, but she still managed to leave her SOIT duties behind for an hour or two. She enjoyed the freedom of calling in at the flat and then running once again. If nothing else, it was a relief just to get the surgical mask off for a while. On her return, she was pleased to hear she could actually leave the wretched thing off altogether: a nurse told her that the patient was ready to be re-introduced to the atmosphere so that her immune system would be called upon to work again. She also heard that, while she'd been out, Lauren had had another meeting, this time with a psychotherapist, and, according to the nurse, she'd come back from that 'with something of a smile on her face'.

But by the time Jenna reached Lauren's bedside, her friend was sound asleep, so she wasn't able to hear the patient's assessment of her psychotherapy session. Looking down now at Lauren, Jenna took the opportunity of studying her face closely. Without a surgical mask, the deep facial lines were plain to see. Jenna looked away. Her professional self bade her to keep her mind over matter, but her personal self felt the prickle of tears behind her eyelids.

Brady had indicated that tonight was to be the last night that Jenna should stay by Lauren's side. The patient had related a significant part of her story, seemed relatively happy in the company of her nurses and was now under the auspices of a psychiatric team, so, he said, it was time to leave.

"I've got to go back home," Jenna explained to Lauren the next morning.

"I want to come with you," said Lauren out of the blue. "But that's not poss…"

"I WANT TO COME WITH YOU!" Lauren yelled.

The volume of her voice brought a nurse running through the door. "Is there a problem?" she asked, looking from Jenna to Lauren and back again.

"I want to go home with my friend," said Lauren quietly but assertively.

"Well, it would be better if…"

"I WANT TO GO," Lauren shouted. The others looked at her, concerned. Almost under her breath, she added, "You can't keep me prisoner here." The two listeners felt the full weight of her allusion.

The nurse quickly glanced at Jenna. "I'll fetch the doctor," she said.

\*

The LPS agreed to release Lauren for one night as a first step towards rehabilitation in the outside world. As soon as she heard the decision, Jenna got on her mobile to ask her dad first of all if he could fetch down the old camp bed he kept in the loft and bring it round to the flat and then to ask Lucy, who had the afternoon off, to bring some of Jenna's warm clothes up to St. Joe's for Lauren. She also mentioned that a few more groceries might be needed at home if Lucy wouldn't mind calling in at the local store.

Jenna had intended to change the linen on her bed as soon as she got back to the flat, but when she and Lauren finally arrived there much later in the day, she discovered it had already been taken care of. Dear Lucy! She'd also set up the camp bed with a duvet and pillow beside Jenna's proper bed. I owe you, Jenna thought.

Lauren was shown her bed, and though it was only late afternoon, she stripped off her clothes and climbed under the duvet. Still heavily medicated, Jenna thought. She left her resting and joined her flatmates in the lounge. The atmosphere was quiet and tense.

"So, how long's she staying?" Helen asked. There was a slight note of resentment in her voice.

"Just tonight, I think," Jenna replied, reaching for her mobile, which had just pinged, alerting her to an incoming text. She read it. "Her care coordinator wants to see how she handles a night out in the big wide world. By the way, are you both in tonight?"

Helen looked at Lucy, who nodded back. "Yeah. Why?" she said.

"Greg's just messaged me. Wants to know if he can see me tonight to make up for not running with me last night."

Helen glanced at Lucy, who was shrugging her shoulders. She looked back at Jenna. "Supposing Lauren has a funny turn while you're out? She seems very dependent on your company at the moment."

This time, Jenna appealed directly to Lucy. "Oh, come on, Luce. Please!" She was realising just how much she needed another break from Lauren. "They gave me a pack of meds at the hospital, didn't they? Surely you can tranquillise her if necessary?" She knew that Lucy's kind nature would ultimately let her have her way. "Anyway, I'll only be gone about an hour," she added and thought she might try and make that two. "Tell you what, I'll prepare the dinner before I go out. How does that sound?"

The other two conceded. "You know how to drive a bargain, don't you?" said Helen, arching one eyebrow.

\*

Greg came round promptly at six. Jenna was dressed and ready in her tracksuit but was in the middle of chopping vegetables when the doorbell rang, so she asked him in, telling him she just wanted to finish preparing a casserole, which could cook slowly in the oven while they were out. Greg sat at the breakfast bar and watched as Jenna sliced through mushrooms and carrots and scooped them into the oven dish.

"Chicken?" he asked.

"Yes. Needs an hour and forty." She sprinkled salt and pepper over the food and placed the dish in the oven. "That'll give us time for a decent run." She saw his eyes still on the casserole dish, which was visible through the oven door, and she smiled. "I'd ask you to stay and have some later, but we have a guest staying tonight who is… er… just out of hospital. Perhaps another night?"

He returned her smile. "No worries," he said brightly.

Jenna cleared the worktop, picked up her long-bladed chopping knife, and gave that a wipe. "Do you know my dad bought this for me years ago in a French hypermarket?" Greg watched as she rolled the knife around in her right hand, using the forefinger of her left hand to caress the blade. "And it always stays sharp. It's unbelievable. The French certainly know how to make a knife." She turned to him and was surprised to see a look of terror on his face. She put the knife down immediately. "Sorry! Didn't mean to flash the knife around like that." She wondered whether his expression betrayed some kind of haunting memory and quickly put the offending object away in a drawer. "There!" she said, wiping her hands together briskly, "I'm ready to run!"

The two of them had been so focused on the chicken casserole and then on the chopping knife that they hadn't noticed Lauren peeping through the gap left by the partially open kitchen door. She kept quiet and watched, almost mesmerised, as Jenna deployed the knife and then stroked its blade. She watched as Jenna put the knife back in the drawer. She also observed the guest at the breakfast bar with interest. When she heard Jenna say, 'Ready to run', she stole away stealthily and headed back to the bedroom. Closing the door softly behind her, she stood still for a few moments. Then she smiled to herself, a plan beginning to take shape in her mind. She knew the weapon she would use. She just needed to find a number on Jenna's mobile. But her smile faded fast: she didn't know how to use a mobile. Fourteen years of technological advancement had passed her by. She needed to learn, and soon.

*

The next morning, Jenna woke unrefreshed, with her limbs aching. She had managed to grab only a few hours' sleep as the camp bed, which her dad had lent her, was rickety and uncomfortable. But at least Lauren had slept fairly well, although Jenna could often hear her murmuring or keening softly in her sleep. Once, she'd sat bolt upright and uttered something unintelligible, and Jenna had sprung out of the camp bed to comfort her, but by the time she'd reached

Lauren's side, she had put her head back down on the pillow and was fast asleep again.

Jenna stood now at the cooker, yawning and waiting for four poached eggs to firm up. Two of these were intended for Lauren, whose appetite seemed to be steadily growing. She cut two chunky slices of wholemeal bread and placed them under the grill. While she waited for these to brown, she considered how best to spend the free afternoon, which Brady insisted she took after returning Lauren to the care of the hospital. She decided she needed to do something restful, something fun, even. It occurred to her that when she and Greg had sat in the kitchen the previous evening, discussing the coming New Year's festivities, he'd let slip that his New Year break had already started and would last until January 3rd. So wouldn't it be a laugh, she thought, to drive over to his flat this afternoon and surprise him? And if he weren't there, fair enough, she'd turn around and head back to Sheen and see her dad. Tell him the news. Like it was time he bought a new camp bed, for example.

She served up breakfast and took Lauren's to her on a tray. When she'd finished hers, she checked on Lauren, who was still heartily tucking into her eggs. Then, she returned to the kitchen and sent a text to Mandy, her hairdresser. Mandy worked from home and had cut Jenna's hair for her since her teens. The bob she did was stunning. Jenna now wondered if she could come and do something with the nightmare that was Lauren's hair before she went back to St. Joe's.

Waiting for the return message, she sipped her coffee and found herself thinking back over Lauren's account of her time at Merrydown. She wasn't sure which had shocked her most: the years of sex slavery or the initial betrayal by her parents, though it did sound as though her mother may have been more sinned against than sinning. When she really thought about it, Jenna remembered noticing as a child that Lauren's mum was so much younger than the other mums at the school gate. Had she had Lauren in her teens? Possibly.

So perhaps it was Lauren's stepfather who'd ruled the roost. But who was he exactly? Jenna had only met him once. She recalled his stern face. To a ten-year-old Jenna, he'd been scary. And neither Jenna nor any other school friend had been allowed in their house. Now, an adult perspective allowed Jenna to see just how strange Lauren's background had been. As a police officer, Jenna couldn't help but suspect that the peculiar set up at Lauren's home had a criminal backdrop.

Perhaps the stepfather had been a paedophile, too, and had maintained links with the Merrydown ring. But he'd never sexually abused Lauren, Jenna was sure. Why not? It seemed as if he had surrendered Lauren, pure and virginal, to be used by others. In return for money, perhaps? Jenna shuddered. She was about to set her mind to figuring out how the police might track down Lauren's stepfather after all these years when her mobile sprang into life. It was Mandy, the hairdresser, telling Jenna that she could come over shortly and cut her friend's hair. Jenna drank the rest of her coffee and then went to tell Lauren that she was going to be 'made beautiful' again later that morning. Lauren stared at her blankly. Jenna might as well have been speaking Swahili.

*

At two in the afternoon, Jenna drove over to Kingston and parked outside Greg's flat. She'd left Lauren in the care of Isabel, her favourite nurse in the psychiatric ward who, as soon as she had spotted Lauren's new feathered bob, told her how pretty it looked though, out of earshot, she and Jenna had privately agreed that, unfortunately, the cut now revealed more grey hair than ever and emphasised Lauren's gauntness. "But don't worry!" Nurse Isabel had said. "The nutritionist is visiting today, and she's brilliant. She'll soon have her filling out nicely!"

Knowing that Lauren was in safe, professional hands again was a relief to Jenna. Now, her thoughts turned to Greg. She cut the engine and sat for a moment, wondering if springing a surprise visit on him was such a good idea. But having come all this way, she thought she might as well ring the doorbell. It had just started sleeting so she took her umbrella with her and climbed the three steps from the street to the front door with her brolly up. She was struck again by just how tired she was. I won't be running with you today, Greg, that's for sure, she thought as she pressed the bell. I'm too exhausted, and, in any case, she mused, peeping out from under her umbrella, we'll both get soaking wet.

Rory opened the door and gave her a big smile. "Hey! Come in!" he said warmly.

"Is it okay?" Jenna asked. "I wondered if Greg was in, but I haven't texted him or anything." She paused and collapsed her umbrella. "I was just kind of passing by," she said innocently.

"Greg's with our next-door neighbour, Amy," Rory said, showing her in. She dropped her umbrella on the mat. "Can I get you tea or anything?"

"No, no, that's fine," said Jenna and found herself scanning her emotions for jealousy. Happily she didn't find it, and why should she? She and Greg were just good friends, weren't they? All the same, she was eager to know more about his relationship with the neighbour. "Does Greg spend a lot of time with Amy?" she asked.

Rory saw her face had lost its smile and laughed apologetically. "Oh, sorry! I can see what you're thinking. I should have said: Amy is our elderly neighbour; she's eighty-something. Come on, I'll take you round there. We're always welcome at any time, and so are our friends." Rory cut past Jenna and led the way out of the door. They raced down the steps and up the next ones to Amy's front door, shielding their faces against the weather. Rory rang the bell. "Our house is split into flats, as you probably know," he pointed out. "But Amy owns the entire property here. Impressive, huh?" Jenna nodded. She was about to ask Rory if visits to Amy were a regular thing when the door opened.

A kindly-looking old lady stood before them. Jenna noticed that she was stylishly dressed; her white hair was neatly coiffed, and she had brightly painted nails. Even better, her eyes twinkled as she smiled. "Oh, Rory! Do come in. And bring your friend too," she said.

"Mrs Bracknell, this is Jenna. She's a friend of Greg's, actually," said Rory.

Jenna put out her hand, but Amy chuckled and opened her arms wide. "In my day, dear, we left handshakes to the men. Come and give me a hug." Jenna stepped inside to embrace the old lady. As she did so, she was suddenly aware she could hear a piano being played. She stepped back from Amy and turned her head towards the source of the sound. Amy ushered Rory inside, shut the front door and then walked back to Jenna and looked up at her. "He's so gifted, isn't he? He and Rory both play for me, you know. But," Jenna saw the old lady glance at Rory, "I think we both know, don't we, Rory, where the talent lies?" Rory nodded, laughing. Jenna also smiled, but her smile was wistful. She'd had no idea Greg was a pianist and, by the sound of it, a highly accomplished one. "Come and hear him play, my dear," she said to Jenna and proceeded to the top of a flight of stairs leading down to a basement. Jenna looked back at Rory and raised her eyebrows. He nodded his head at her, and then all three went downstairs.

Amy Bracknell opened a door on her left, and immediately, the sound of the keyboard was louder and richer. She turned back to Jenna, who was standing just behind her and said in a stage whisper, "It's one of Chopin's nocturnes, you know." Jenna didn't know but thought it was beautiful. They then stepped inside the room, and Mrs Bracknell quietly shut the door.

Greg hardly seemed to notice his audience; his music so enraptured him. Sometimes, he swayed and closed his eyes as he played; other times, he looked intensely at the keys, especially if he was introducing a strong accent into the melody. At this point, he would depress the keys, and his body would spring away in the opposite direction as if he were receiving an electric shock. Jenna smiled to herself: it was as captivating to watch his antics as it was to listen to his playing. At last, he brought the nocturne to an end. No one said a word. The atmosphere was hushed and magical. Rory was the first to applaud, and then Jenna and Mrs Bracknell joined in. Greg turned round, mouthed a surprised 'Hi' to Jenna and then broke into a beaming smile, the one that had so affected her on their first meeting. Her heart performed the tiniest somersault.

And then the spell was shattered.

"My very own virtuoso!" Amy Bracknell suddenly exclaimed. She turned to Jenna. "And you wouldn't even know he'd lost a fingertip, would you?"

\*

Jenna used the excuse that she'd only been 'kind of passing by' to leave. Her mind was spinning, and she had to get away to be able to think calmly and, like it or not, to feed this new evidence into everything the MIT team already had on their killer. Halfway up the stairs to the hallway, Jenna suddenly remembered she'd left her umbrella next door. Had Rory shut the front door? She didn't remember hearing it click. Perhaps it was on a latch. She hurtled out of the old lady's house and, tiredness forgotten, leapt up the three steps to the lads' front door and gave it a push. It *was* on a latch. She stepped inside, grabbed her umbrella, which she'd left on the mat – and then stopped. Just beside her now was a small hall table. And on the table was a pair of black suede gloves. Greg's gloves. The pair he always wore for running. The pair he'd worn when he went skating. The pair he didn't completely remove, even when he'd gone to the Mitre Inn for a drink. What if they matched the forensic evidence found on the priest's neck?

Oh. My. God.

Her hand reached out and curled around the gloves warily as if they were tarantulas. She quickly stuffed them into her pocket. Then she fled the house, leapt into the car and sped away fast.

\*

A few miles north of Kingston, she pulled into a side road, parked the car and switched off the engine. Her heart was hammering against her chest wall, and she did her best to breathe deeply and calm herself down. What now? She ought to phone Brady and tell him what she'd just heard. She ought to get the gloves straight over to Wilson's lab. She ought… She ought… Oh, but it couldn't be him, surely? She gripped the steering wheel until her knuckles were white. Surely this was a coincidence? How many ex-soldiers were there with body parts missing? There must be hundreds, maybe thousands. He wasn't the killing type, *surely:* he was too sweet and kind. And yet…

Her shoulders slumped. He'd already killed in the military, presumably. That must make killing easier. Slowly, she released her grip, took another deep breath and looked at herself in the rear-view mirror. "It can't be him," she said quietly to herself. Her eyes were now focused on the eyes in the mirror as if her reflection would provide the real Jenna with an answer. "Please don't let it be him," she whispered. She shut her eyes and looked away. When she opened them again, she felt the pinprick of tears under her lids. She swallowed hard. There was no getting away from it: she was facing a dilemma. Her head reminded her that she was a police officer and had a duty to report all relevant information to her superior officer and submit evidence gathered to the forensics department. But her heart told her she'd found a good friend. Someone who might have helped her get over her entanglement with Brady. Someone with whom she might have built a future.

Someone whom she wasn't ready to let go of yet. It was as simple as that.

And then she remembered his name: Greg Thomas. Immediately, her heartbeat slowed, and the world looked brighter, even though the skies above were leaden grey. Of course! They were after a guy called Valentine, weren't they? Not Thomas. She breathed a little easier now, though still in a mild state of shock. She just needed someone to put their arms around her and comfort her. And she could murder a strong cup of tea. She started up the engine, pulled away and headed for her dad's.

\*

Lauren sat in a chair in her hospital room and studied her new mobile phone. While Jenna had been out running the previous evening, Lucy had received a text from a friend and Lauren, increasingly alert, had asked how the mobile worked. Of course, she'd lost out on over fourteen years of technological advancement but was now ready to begin the process of catching up. So Lucy had spent the best part of an hour teaching Lauren how to use a mobile and, in particular, how to text. This morning, Lucy had come up to see Lauren before going on duty and had brought her a gift: a new mobile of her own. It was not state-of-the-art, not one of those smartphones with all the apps that the three flatmates all carried around with them. Just a simple call-or-text mobile phone so that she could communicate with any one of them whenever she felt the need.

Lauren eyed it now with awe and wonder. She flipped it open and shut it again. Put it in the pocket of the jeans she'd borrowed from Jenna. Withdrew it and flipped it open again. It was a lifeline, and she knew it. Earlier, Lucy had entered all three numbers into the phone under their respective names. Lauren thought she'd try one out. She texted: Thanks for my present, Lucy. Lauren. She pressed 'send'. A minute later, Lauren heard the mobile buzz. She opened it up, pressed 'Read messages', clicked again and then read: My pleasure. Love Lucy x. Lauren felt very excited. As with any new skill, each little success bred confidence. So she decided to continue practising and tried another text, this time to Jenna: Thanks for looking after me this week. Lauren. The fact that there was no immediate reply didn't worry Lauren since Lucy had explained that if someone didn't reply straight away, it usually just meant they were too busy at the moment and would return the message later on.

Lauren closed the mobile and put it back in her jeans pocket. It was a new toy, and her fingers curled around it and refused to let it go. Her hand stayed in her pocket. She shut her eyes now and thought back to the previous evening when she'd seen Jenna and her guest in the kitchen. She frowned and snapped her eyes open again.

Her gaunt face set hard as her mind began to formulate a plan, a plan in which her new mobile was going to play a key part…

\*

A short while later, Jenna appeared in Lauren's hospital room. Tea with her dad had done little to relieve the shock she felt after Amy Bracknell's revelation, and she couldn't face seeing her colleagues yet with all their probing questions and possible 'I told you so's. A final session as a SOIT officer seemed about all she felt up to for now. Then, she would phone Brady later and tell him that she needed to talk to him first thing in the morning.

It didn't take much encouragement to get Lauren talking again. Her psychiatrist and psychotherapist had evidently done a good job in persuading her to relate her story, even, and especially, the most difficult episodes regarding her babies. She wasn't sure which of the abusers had fathered which of her children, although, to complicate matters, Lauren did say that on one occasion, she'd also been raped by one of the residents: a teenage boy. To Jenna's horror, this reference put Lauren into a sudden frenzy, so much so that Jenna had to switch off the recorder and hold her friend tightly in her arms until she was calm again. Jenna let her talk on for several minutes, but when she tried to question her in more detail about this latest disclosure, Lauren froze and remained tight-lipped. It was almost as if this rape had upset her more than the others. Perhaps she felt an even greater sense of betrayal since this boy, up until then, seemed to have been her friend. She wouldn't name him.

"I think we need a tea break," said Jenna, exhausted. She surveyed Lauren's face, expecting to see her looking as weary as she herself was feeling. But surprisingly, Lauren was smiling oddly.

"Let's have tea at the flat," she said in a low voice. Her expression was strange.

"Well, I'll have to ask…"

"No, you don't have to ask anyone. Nobody has the right to keep me here. Anyway, I can continue receiving help as an out-patient…" She stopped to frown, widened her eyes and then smiled oddly again. "If I need it," she added somewhat cryptically.

*

The following day was New Year's Eve, and Jenna was in two minds about returning to Kingston nick. She'd phoned Brady the previous afternoon to let him know that Lauren was being released from full-time hospital care, and he, in turn, had given her the news that forensics had found a match between Lauren's DNA and some of the baby bones. Hearing Jenna sigh heavily, he gave her the option of returning to work the next day or taking a day or two of annual leave. How much she would have liked a break. But she remembered with a heavy heart that she had something to tell him and, therefore, said she would return to work.

Now, she wasn't so sure. On the one hand, she wanted to resume normal duties, see her colleagues, and, if she was honest, get away from Lauren, whose company was, to say the least, challenging. Jenna knew that was an understandable consequence of her ill-treatment, but that didn't make it any the less wearing. On the other hand, going to work meant she had to decide if she was going to tell Brady about Greg's fingertip. Or whether she was going to have his gloves examined.

She poured out some cereal and grabbed a banana from the fruit bowl. Actually, she knew what she had to do when she got to work. She opened the cutlery drawer. Greg or not, she had a responsibility to pass on the information about his injured hand and get his gloves looked at, though she was well aware she shouldn't have helped herself to them as she did. She searched through the drawer for her long-bladed knife. She'd known right from the day she joined the police force that good police officers must be prepared to shop their own grandmothers if the evidence was strong enough. Or their sweethearts. Now, where was that knife? She could have sworn she put it back in the drawer when she'd last used it. She lifted out a plain dinner knife and cut her banana with that instead.

As she ate breakfast, Jenna thought about the evening ahead: New Year's Eve… party night. A tingle of excitement rippled through her body. She and Greg had been invited to Lottie Fisher's party. Jenna thought it would be interesting to see Ben again and began to work out which outfit she would wear. But she suddenly stopped, her cereal spoon suspended in mid-air, as the reality of what stood in the way began to hit home.

The gloves. The fingertip.

She laughed ironically to herself. Guess what, folks? I could be going out with a serial killer. She put down the spoon and pushed her bowl aside. Closed her eyes; breathed deeply. And then she remembered just as she'd done yesterday when she'd sat alone in her car getting herself all worked up: his name is Greg *Thomas*. The gloves won't match, and the fingertip will be a coincidence.

"Which reminds me," she said, opening her eyes, "I must find out Rory's surname."

She looked up at the kitchen clock. Half past seven. She'd already made sure that Lauren was feeling okay and was up to amusing herself until Lucy arrived back from her morning shift, so she thought she really ought to be heading off to work. She glanced around the kitchen one more time to see if she'd left her sharp knife on one of the worktops, but there was still no sign of it. She'd have to ask the others later if they'd seen it. She picked up her shoulder bag with Greg's gloves inside and walked out of the flat to her car.

\*

"*You took his gloves?*" said Brady. "You do know that could compromise a court case, don't you?" His voice was loud and his face stern.

"I suppose I panicked," said Jenna. "If you really want to know, I'd just got hold of some information that shocked me."

"Go on," said Brady. His tone was severe, and Jenna found it upsetting.

"One of Greg's fingertips is missing," she said.

"Jesus! Is there anything else about him you haven't told me?" he asked, his voice raised. Professionally, he was concerned that Jenna may have concealed information from him and potentially hindered the investigation. Personally, he was just downright jealous that Greg had caught Jenna's attention like he had.

"He works at Ace Haulage," said Jenna. Each time she revealed something else about Greg, her voice dipped lower.

"Brilliant!" snapped Brady. "This just gets better! Any more?"

"He served in the army," she said. She was now on the verge of tears, and her hands were shaking.

"I don't believe it," Brady muttered under his breath. He went to his desk and buzzed the forensic lab. Jenna wanted to run out of his office. Had she made such an almighty mistake, keeping her private life, with Greg in it, just that:

private? She knew the answer was 'yes'. "Keith?" said Brady. He gazed out of the window as he spoke. "Detective Sergeant Jones will be bringing down an item of men's clothing. Could you run a comparison with the data you already have in your files? Also, run a DNA match if you find anything useful. Fast track. Thanks."

Jenna watched Brady carefully, but he wouldn't make eye contact with her. He pressed a button to end the call, and she saw him look at the plastic bag she'd placed on his desk earlier: the one with the gloves in it. Finally, he did look at her. "Take these down to forensics," he said. It was a long time since she'd heard his voice so lacking in warmth. "We might as well find out if it's him, even if we can't use the evidence in court."

"You'll find it won't turn out to be Greg anyway," she said defensively. She grabbed the plastic bag off Brady's desk.

"Because?" he said. He was still annoyed with her and for more than one reason.

"Because his name's Greg Thomas and, correct me if I'm wrong," she said, her voice rising with emotion, "but we're searching for a killer called Valentine, aren't we?" Her eyes met his in anger. "We should be looking into his flatmate, Rory, if you ask me. He's also been in the army, you know, and he works at Ace Haulage... *and he's a biker*." She turned and swept out of his office. He saw her toss her hair aside as she left the room. And he wanted her badly.

\*

"Brady wants you to go home, Jen," Helen said quietly to her later.

"Why? Because I cocked up?" said Jenna, voice raised.

Brady had taken Helen into his confidence while Jenna was down in the lab. She knew they'd had words. "No," she said gently. "He says you're exhausted from looking after Lauren all week, and you should take a proper break now and come back to work fresh on Monday."

"So that means I go home now and, let's see, oh yes, I get to be with Lauren again," said Jenna, still peeved.

"Lauren doesn't need you by her side so much now," said Helen. "She's on the mend. Well, physically on the mend anyway. You know that. Didn't you say your father offered to take her in as a lodger for a while?"

"Yes, he did," said Jenna, her temper subsiding. "But only when she feels confident enough to leave our flat." She heaved a sigh. Brady was right: she was extremely tired. Maybe that had affected her ability to make cool, professional decisions: ones that wouldn't compromise court cases, for example. She looked at Helen. "Do you think I ought to go?" she said.

"Yes," said Helen. "Go and rest. Take a nap. Have a bath. Get yourself ready for your party tonight."

Jenna frowned. "Should I still be going out partying with Greg, now he's under suspicion?"

"Innocent till proven guilty," said Helen. "Anyway, if you're with him, you'll be able to keep an eye on him!" She laughed, but then she saw Jenna's frown increase. "Joke!" she said.

"I'd better go and apologise to Brady for…" Jenna paused and then said, "… letting him down."

Helen patted her on the arm. "Go and clear the air with him," she said. "Then you'll be able to rest more easily at home."

"You will keep me updated on today's findings, won't you?" Jenna asked. "It wouldn't do to be going to parties with a multiple murderer, would it?" She forced a small ironic laugh.

"You'll be first to know," said Helen.

\*

Jenna knocked at Brady's office door. A brusque 'Yes!' was her invitation to go in.

"I just wanted to say…" she began.

"Shut the door," he said, sounding calmer now.

"I'm sorry I made a mistake. It won't happen again, sir."

"Don't!" he snapped. Her eyes widened, and he immediately regretted his tone. More quietly, he said, "Please, don't 'sir' me, Jen… Not when we're on our own." He stood up. "It puts a distance between us, and you know that's the last thing I want." He began to open his arms slowly, inviting her into his embrace.

She wavered, confused and vulnerable.

And so tired.

Tired of being at Lauren's side.

Tired of seeing the depraved acts that humanity was capable of.

And tired of pretending to herself that she was not in love with the man standing in front of her right now.

He saw the tears in her eyes and walked towards her. Wrapping his arms around her, he held her tightly. "I shouldn't have raised my voice to you," he whispered. "I'm sorry," and in spite of that plea she'd made to him the previous week to let her move on emotionally, he found her lips and kissed her.

And she opened her mouth to him. It was bliss. Even sweeter after their spat. If they could have frozen that moment in time… He slowly peeled his lips away from hers and planted kisses on her wet eyelashes. He held her close, and she stayed put.

"I still want you to be with me, Jen," he whispered into her right ear. "If you ever change your mind…"

Helen had told her how bad Brady's wife was. It had made her begin to reconsider her position. She pulled her head back a little so she could look him directly in the eyes: those fabulous, dark blue, come-to-bed eyes. "I'll think about it," she whispered back.

And it seemed like a bright shaft of light pierced the gloom in his heart. Hope, at last.

Letting her go, Brady wandered back to his desk, and Jenna walked towards the door. "We'll keep you up to date on…" He didn't want to say Greg's name because he didn't want him to come between them, not even in the form of a word: "… the evidence from the lab."

She opened the door. Despite Brady's apology and their embrace, her ego was still a little bruised. "It won't be him," she said as a parting shot. She left the room and went to shut down her computer before leaving the building.

\*

At half past two, a call came through from the forensic laboratory. "You might like to come and see what I've got here," said Wilson. Brady left his office immediately and made his way down to the lab. He found Wilson in front of a computer screen. "There!" he said to Brady. "See that?"

Brady looked at the screen. It appeared to be divided vertically into half, with a cylindrical shape in each half showing a similar spectrum of dark colours. Brady needed guidance. "What am I looking at, Keith?" he asked. He felt distracted, his head still full of Jenna.

"Glove fibres. The one on the left was taken from the priest's neck; the one on the right was taken from the gloves Sergeant Jones brought in."

Brady suddenly felt more focused. "They look very similar," he said.

"Similar?" said Wilson. He clicked on an icon and moved the right image until it was superimposed on the one on the left. "See that? They're identical." Brady's heart leapt. "And that's not all," Wilson added. "There's a minute shred of fingernail inside one of the gloves. If the DNA matches what was found under the priest's fingernail…"

"… then we've got him!" said Brady with gusto. Then his face fell. "Except we haven't because the evidence will be inadmissible. Shit!"

\*

Brady thanked the pathologist for his speed and thoroughness, especially as he was now working without the aid of his assistant, who'd been suspended the previous night on suspicion of breaking the confidentiality clause in her contract. He headed quickly back to the office pool. His first instinct was to share the news with Helen since Jenna was involved with the suspect. He knew Helen would be able to suggest how best to manage her friend's feelings in all of this. He invited her to join him in his office.

"Looks like we may have our man," said Brady, shutting the door. He indicated that she took a seat.

"Greg?" Helen knew all about the gloves.

Brady nodded. "But there are a few problems," he said. "One is Jenna. I'm hoping you'll help me handle any emotional fallout on her part – if we're right about him, that is."

"Why wouldn't we be right," Helen asked, "if forensic evidence points to him?"

"Because…" Brady thought quickly. "Because he may be guilty of one murder, but not the others. Because he could have been set up… and while I think of it, we ought to check out the flatmate who's been in the army with him." He paused. "And because…" he paused again, "… his name is Thomas, not Valentine."

Helen looked at Brady admiringly. He really did consider every possibility. "Any other obstacles?" she asked as if the ones mentioned weren't enough already.

"Yes," said Brady, pulling a face. "The evidence we have is almost certainly inadmissible in court." He explained what he meant.

He looked at Helen. "Any ideas?"

"I'll get Andy to check out the flatmate's details when he comes back from his tea break," Helen replied. "And as for me…" she stared into the middle distance "… I need to check something else back at my station."

"Okay!" Brady said, surprised.

"May I?" She stood up, looking eager to pursue her idea.

"Go ahead," said Brady. "But keep me in the loop."

She'd already said it to Jenna, but her chat with Brady had diverted the direction of her loyalty.

"You'll be first to know," she said and strode out of his office.

\*

Helen felt her enthusiasm draining away. She read, "There is no central register for name changes in the United Kingdom." Her shoulders slumped. She thought she might just have solved it: that Greg Thomas might once have been Greg Valentine; that maybe the rose emblem was an association with his name; that his abusers may have played on the idea; that in the end, it was such a yoke around his neck, always there to revive horrific memories of the past, that he simply had to abandon it in favour of something more innocuous, like Thomas. She swore quietly under her breath.

"Tea?" Jamie had noticed her look of dejection as he passed by her work station.

"Er, please," she said.

She looked back at the screen and was about to close down the site when another sentence caught her eye: something about optional enrolment of deed polls at the Royal Courts of Justice '… to make a safe (and public) record of your name change.' So, some name changes *were* put on record. She made a note of the telephone number of the Royal Courts.

\*

Searches for name change documents at the Royal Courts of Justice normally took five to ten working days following a written application, she was told. As soon as Helen heard the length of the waiting time, she put the phone down and sought Brady's authority to order a priority search, which would take hours instead of days.

He was annoyed with himself that Helen's idea about a change of name hadn't even occurred to him. But he was thankful he had her in his team. Helen has always been a good lateral thinker. Could she just have identified the final piece in the jigsaw?

He lost no time now. He directed Jamie to go fully into Greg's background, right back to his childhood, if possible, and he pointed out to him that if the trail went cold on 'Greg Thomas,' he should try 'Greg Valentine' or 'Gregory Valentine'. He hoped that the outcome of Jamie's search would coincide with the return call from the Royal Courts.

Meanwhile, he called Helen back into his office. "I think you should phone Jenna and let her know what's going on," he said. Helen nodded. "Start with the lab findings and progress from there. You can use this room, if you like, while I go and brief the DCI on today's developments." He walked to the door, opened it and then looked back at Helen. "Go gently on her," he said.

Helen phoned Jenna's mobile number. There was a muttering at the other end, and Helen immediately thought it was a bad line. "Hello?" she said loudly. "Jen? Is that you?" There was silence, and Helen was about to call off and try again, but to her surprise, she heard Lauren's voice. "Hello? Lauren?"

"Yes?" came the tentative reply.

"Lauren, it's Helen. Is Jenna there?"

Another few moments of silence followed, during which Helen wondered why Jenna's phone was not in Jenna's possession. The two were normally inseparable. "No," said Lauren. Helen waited for an explanation, but none was forthcoming. She tapped her foot impatiently. It really was impossible to have a normal conversation with Lauren, she thought, and then she felt guilty when she remembered the years of trauma the poor girl had been through.

"Lauren, where is Jenna?" Helen asked, emphasising each word.

Another silence, and Helen's anxiety increased. Something didn't seem right here. But Lauren answered, "She's gone to her father's house," she said.

"Without her phone?" Helen asked. The rarity of such an occurrence was now at the forefront of her mind.

"She forgot to take it with her," Lauren said.

"Could you do me a favour then, Lauren? Go into the 'Contacts' menu – Lucy showed you how, didn't she? – and get Gareth Jones's number for me, will you? I'll ring off and let you do that, then I'll call back in five minutes. Okay?"

"Yes," said Lauren and instantly shut the phone down.

Helen thought the whole conversation very odd.

\*

Back at the flat, Lauren sat at the breakfast bar and looked up the 'Contacts' menu on Jenna's phone. She picked up a pen and noted down Gareth Jones's number on the back of an envelope. Then she toggled further down the menu and found the name and number she was looking for. This was the reason she'd hidden Jenna's phone from her before she'd left for her dad's, and when Jenna had fussed that she couldn't find her phone, Lauren had reassured her that her handbag was so full of stuff, the phone was bound to be hidden somewhere at the bottom of it all. And Jenna had fallen for it and had left for Sheen without her mobile.

Lauren now had everything she needed to carry out her plan. Tonight, she meant to avenge the greatest wrong ever done to her.

\*

When Helen got hold of Gareth's number, she phoned Jenna immediately. She'd already decided that a conversation in which you have to manage someone else's feelings is best done face to face, so she asked Jenna to stop by the office as a matter of urgency.

Meanwhile, Jamie was making headway with his search. He'd discovered that Greg Thomas had joined Ace Haulage six months previously and that, prior to that, he'd been in the army for four years. When the trail went cold, before the army years, Jamie tried searching for 'Gregory Valentine' and found that someone of that name had been at Feltham Young Offenders' Institution for the previous three years. He told Brady of his progress. But the team was still not sure if these two people were the same.

It was now gone four. Andy had returned from his break and was settling himself back down at his work station when he spotted the note that Helen had left on his desk, asking him to check out the surname of the flatmate known as Rory. He instantly remembered the 'RY VAL' detail, that part of the runaway boy's name, which forensics had uncovered and which he had seen on the screen in Brady's office. 'RY VAL'. He recalled that he had suggested to Jenna at the time that these could be the last two letters of a first name and the first two letters of a surname. So that fitted very well with the name 'Gregory Valentine'. But the first two letters also fit the name 'Rory'. What if his surname was Valentine? Andy took hold of the computer mouse and drew up the Ace Haulage list of personnel.

He found Rory under the surname Chamberlain. He buzzed the information through to Helen.

\*

"Did you say Jenna was coming in?" Brady asked Helen impatiently. He looked at his watch. It was now nearly five.

"She said she would call in," said Helen.

"How long ago did you talk to her?"

"Getting on for two hours ago," she said. She thought Brady really could have worked it out for himself, seeing that he told her to make the call in the first place and then left her in his office to do so. But she buttoned her lip. He was looking stressed at the moment. Best left alone, she thought. She hoped that the Royal Courts would provide them with their missing link soon. That would calm the boss down. If she were right about Greg, that would mean they could go and arrest him tonight and charge him with *all* the murders and have a reasonable amount of evidence besides the gloves to put to the Crown Prosecution Service. And if she were wrong about Greg, then she would get the Royal Courts to run the same name-change check on Rory Chamberlain. Either way, they would surely have their murderer. They were so close now…

\*

At half past five, there was still no sign of Jenna. Brady began to wonder if, in her exhausted state of mind, she'd misunderstood Helen's words. "Get her on her phone again," he told Helen.

"I can't," Helen replied. "Lauren's got her phone, and Jenna's at her dad's. I'll have to call him again." She phoned Gareth Jones, only to be told that Jenna had left his house nearly an hour previously. Helen frowned as she closed up her phone. What was going on? She was now quite anxious. Was Jenna all right?

But Jenna was sitting in her car outside Kingston Police Station. She hadn't yet gone in because she was stalling, having guessed why she'd been summoned. If Greg was in the clear, they'd have put her mind at rest over the phone, wouldn't they? She sat desperately trying to search for an option that would clear Greg of all culpability. That he'd been set up was the only viable one she could think of. Someone must have taken his gloves and murdered the priest. But who? Ben? Rory? They all seemed too nice, but then wolves in sheep's clothing always did present themselves well.

Like Father Hennessy.

She quickly brought herself back to the present conundrum. The killer had to be one of the two remaining flatmates. They were the only ones who had free access to Greg's gloves. And wasn't the killer a biker? And didn't Rory ride a motorbike? And hadn't he been in the army? And, she cast her mind back to the Merrydown files. Didn't his first name end in 'ry'? (Yeah, so what are the chances, said a nagging voice deep inside her skull, which she was trying hard to ignore… what are the chances of them *both* missing a fingertip? *Pretty frigging slim, don't you think?)* Nevertheless, in her desperation, she decided to go to her work station, open up her computer and find Rory's surname on the Ace Haulage files. It had to be him. *Please!*

She thrust the car door open, launched herself out of the vehicle and slammed the door with all the force she could muster. The sleety conditions of the previous day had given way to a dry, cold spell, and a layer of rime had already coated the tarmac underfoot. Fighting back the tears again, she made her way carefully across the frosty ground and into the building. She walked straight past reception and up the stairs to the MIT section.

Helen saw Jenna first. "Where have you been?" she said, sounding like a relieved but nevertheless annoyed mother questioning her adolescent offspring.

"At Dad's," said Jenna, with a hint of defiance. "What's all this about?"

The beginnings of an explanation were on the tip of Helen's tongue when her desk phone rang.

It was the Royal Courts of Justice.

"I see," said Helen in a neutral tone. "Thank you. That's very helpful." She replaced the handset in its cradle and looked at Jenna. "Take a seat for a moment, Jen," she said. "I just need to tell Brady something."

\*

Brady nodded solemnly. "So the Probation Service entered Gregory Valentine's change of name at the Royal Courts just over four years ago, and the ex-offender has a new ID ready for a career in the army."

"Correct," said Helen. "He must have convinced them

that a name change would help him put the past behind him because there is a fee required, and I presume the Probation Service paid it."

"We need to arrest him," said Brady. "Now we've got evidence of the name change, we no longer need to worry about the CPS refusing the glove evidence. I'll buzz for the whole team to assemble. They all need to know. While they're coming together, use my office and tell Jenna, will you?"

"Thanks," said Helen. She was not at all looking forward to the next ten minutes.

\*

The MIT was briefed in the communal area. Delgado had joined them. Jenna meanwhile heard the news privately. Stunned, she left Brady's office silently. As Brady spoke to his team members, he saw Jenna and Helen, out of the corner of his eye, joining the group. Even with only a glance, he noticed how pale Jenna looked. But he had no time for emotion at the moment: his mind was fully focused on a swift and successful arrest. "So I'll go with Helen. And Andy and Jamie will be on standby as backup," he said.

"No!" said Jenna. She stood up slowly, and all heads turned to look at her. She took a deep breath and said, "Please let me go instead of Helen. I need to be there. I need to hear what he has to say. I thought I knew him, and I didn't. Please let me go." She could see Brady wasn't convinced. She looked at Delgado appealingly. He slightly raised his eyebrows but looked back at Brady as if to say, 'It's his call.' She tried again. "Please let me see if I can learn something from this."

Brady looked at Helen to see if she had any objection.

She turned her hands upwards and nodded to give him the go-ahead. "All right," said Brady. "I'll go with Jenna. Andy and Jamie will stand by as backup, and Helen, you can coordinate things here."

At around 6.20 p.m., Brady and Jenna set off for Greg's flat.

\*

The traffic was already at a standstill in the Kingston area. "Why do people start New Year's Eve celebrations so early?" said Brady, annoyed at their lack of progress. "Jesus! Look! They're out in their droves already, and it's only half past six."

Jenna, not in the mood for chatter, kept her silence. She felt silly, belittled even. There was she thinking that Greg might be the answer to her prayers, and all the while, he was a bloody serial killer. She bet he felt like he'd had the last laugh, going out with a copper. Oh, and 'please could she tell him if there was a website where he'd be able to see her pretty face?' And she'd been so flattered she'd fallen for it? Now she realised who he was really looking for: *the last of his targets*. Be careful who you make friends with, Jen, Brady had told her in church. God, she could scream. Well, now, the boot would be on the other foot: she'd make her feelings known to him.

Give him what for. Tell him that he hadn't played her along; she'd played him along because she was really in love with… Well, yes. She'd tell him. Here he is, actually. Your other arresting officer. This is the man I love. So you see, Greg, you never really did have that 'little connection' with me. I was using you while I was sorting out my mind. And guess what, Greg? My mind's all sorted out now. Soon, I shall be his lover. And yes, he does have a wife, but she's no longer capable of loving him, and he deserves better.

Such thoughts raced around her mind and were only interrupted when Brady switched the siren on. The traffic soon parted for them, and they swiftly arrived at the flat in north Kingston.

It was Rory who opened the door. "Greg?" he said. He looked at Jenna bewildered. "But you texted him a short while ago. You told him to come over early, didn't you? He's already left for your place."

Jenna, puzzled, shook her head. "I haven't texted anyone today," she said. "As a matter of fact, my phone's gone missing, so how could I text him?"

Then Brady remembered what Helen had told him earlier: that Lauren had Jenna's phone. A bad feeling formed in the pit of his stomach as his mind quickly wove together all the information it had gathered on Lauren and Greg into one terrifyingly dark picture. "If he was the boy who raped her when they were young," he said, "and she's now recognised him at your flat…" He stopped in mid-sentence. There was a moment of silence as all three stood and stared at each other. Then Brady turned and leapt down the front steps. "Come on!" he called urgently over his shoulder. "Let's hope we're not too late."

\*

"Gregory Valentine," came a slow, small voice from the shadows of the cedar tree near Jenna's flat.

Greg stepped off the path and moved cautiously towards the voice. "Jen? Is that you?" It didn't sound like Jenna. A glance at the windows of her flat told him there were no lights on. No one in? What the hell was going on? "Jenna?" The darkness pressed in on him, but since the voice that had addressed him was female, he was not in a state of high alert despite being unable to see clearly. "Who's there?" he said in a loud whisper.

There was no reply. Greg moved again towards the cedar. Someone was hiding behind it. The frosty grass crunched beneath his feet as he made his way slowly towards the giant tree. He really didn't have the time or inclination to be playing such games. Jen's text had asked him to come over at seven; his luminous dial showed 18.55. Then it dawned on him: this person had just used his old name. Who knew that? He could think of no one in his adult life who knew such an intimate detail about him. What was going on here? His mind began to revert to survival mode, military-style, and his limbs tensed in preparation for a fight.

"Listen, I've gotta meet somebody, so I can't hang around," he said to the darkness. "Either reveal yourself, or I'm going."

The moon suddenly broke from behind a cloud and bathed the scene in silver monochrome. Frost sparkled on the ground and shimmered overhead in the branches of the cedar. Greg watched his breath form small silver-grey swirls on the cold night air. He was starting to feel the bite of the plummeting temperature and, deciding he'd had enough, he turned to go but stopped abruptly when, a moment later, a small waif-like figure slid out from the shadows and stood before him.

"Don't you recognise me?" she whispered harshly. Her breath also swirled like a spectral mist in the freezing air.

"Should I?" he asked. The moon was still bright, and it lit up her face as she looked into his. He studied her carefully. He registered her furrowed brow and her sad, deep-set eyes. She looked careworn. He scanned her other features. It was true: there was something familiar there.

"I'm Lauren," she said.

"Lauren?" he repeated. He looked at her more closely. And then it hit him like a thunderbolt.

In his years of military service, he'd witnessed mayhem on a grand scale. In the thick of the action, almost on a daily basis, he'd felt the earth shake as bombs exploded; he'd heard the crunch of breaking bones, seen blood spurt and smelt the stench of burning flesh. With each assault on his senses, he'd gradually become anaesthetised to the scenes of Armageddon, which played out around him. Maintaining his sang-froid had been necessary to preserve his sanity. Thus, he thought, nothing more could shock him.

Now, as the adrenalin began to course through his veins and he looked deeper into the girl's eyes, he felt a tsunami on the move. Could this really be *that* Lauren? *The* Lauren. The one the adults had called 'The Vixen'?

"Merrydown?" he asked. His voice hadn't shaken since he was a teenager on the London streets. It was shaking now.

"Merrydown," she answered quietly.

"Oh my God," was all he managed to utter in reply. He moved towards her to touch her, but she stepped backwards.

"You raped me," she said, still in a slow, small voice. He closed his eyes momentarily and saw himself, at fourteen, lying on top of her. They'd been little more than children then, the pair of them. And both had been powerless victims of the worst kind of conspiracy. He opened his eyes and swallowed hard, trying to find the right words to say.

"They made me do it," he said quietly. "They stripped me and pinned me down and got me, you know, into a state, and they made me do it. They dragged me on top of you and held me there. I ran away after that."

"You abandoned me," she said, her tone still hushed and eerie and her face luminescent in the chilled moonlit air. "You left me to the wolves."

*"They told me you were dead!"* His voice was rising now with emotion. *"They told me you were dead and that I'd done it."* He was welling up now. "They did. That's why I ran away. I thought I'd killed you." He wiped his eyes with his sleeve. "Doing that to you after they'd all had a go. You weren't even breathing properly by then, so when they said I'd killed you, I believed them. I was terrified. I ran. The next day, I ran."

She continued to stare blankly at him. "You abandoned me," she whispered.

"No, I didn't," he said. "Because I vowed I'd get them one day. On your behalf. All of them. All five of them." He wiped his tears again. He was way out of his comfort zone now, not quite sure how to assume control.

Then it came to him. She needed proof.

"I've dealt with four of them… and the fifth topped himself," he said. He'd recognised the photo in yesterday's papers. He looked into those deep-set eyes again. It was like looking into the eyes of a zombie. "Did you hear me? I've killed for you. For us." He didn't know what else to say. He suddenly realised his plans were coming unstuck. The secret mission was no longer a secret. He'd just blurted it all out. Before he could begin to think of how to put this right, she spoke.

"You were as bad as *them*," she said. She spoke monotonously, peering at him with a glazed expression. "You raped me; then you abandoned me."

He had a bad feeling now in his gut. He needed to think. He went to turn away from her. He meant to look for somewhere to sit with her so they could think this through together. Could she keep his identity secret? Could she keep his mission secret? These thoughts blitzed his mind in the second he took to turn away from her.

But then she came at him. The move was so sudden, so completely unexpected, that he was caught totally off guard. Absolutely at odds with my usual capability, he found himself thinking fleetingly as the pain in his side began to register, and he realised a blade had been thrust between his ribs. He staggered, grasping the knife in his side with his incomplete hand, but he struggled to get a grip on the handle, which by now was wet with his own blood. His fingers slid off the metal as he fell to his knees and collapsed.

His last conscious thought was of his parents wishing him a happy seventh birthday.

The waif knelt beside him on the frosty ground and, emotionless, watched him die. She waited a few moments while a cloud covered the moon; then, as the light returned, she was able to distinguish the dark knife handle. She grabbed it and was about to remove the blade from his body when the sound of a police siren grew loud in her ears. She yanked the kitchen knife from her victim's body, oblivious to the blood which flowed copiously from the gaping wound. The sound of car doors slamming told her she needed to get away.

"Stop! Police!" A male voice shouted from a distance.

She turned, skirted the lifeless body on the ground and

tried to run, but the frost had thickened in the time she'd been there, and the thin soles of her sneakers slid in all directions. She stumbled and fell.

"Lauren!" A woman's voice, which she recognised, was close by.

"DON'T COME NEAR ME!" she screamed.

She got to her feet again as Brady and Jones caught up with her, coming to a halt a few metres away from her, more cautious in their approach as they realised she was holding a knife at arm's length and there was already a body lying face down on the ground.

"Lauren!" said Jenna as gently as she could, despite the fact that her heart was drilling through her chest. "Don't do this."

"He betrayed me!" she cried.

Jenna was suddenly aware of Brady's hand on her arm, stopping her from moving any further forward. A flash of the steel blade in the moonlight reminded her why he had hold of her.

"We can help you work things out," said Brady calmly. He pulled Jenna behind him and inched forward. "But you need to hand over the knife."

Lauren stood like a ghostly statue in the silvered darkness, still holding the knife at arm's length and staring blankly at the two officers. Jenna couldn't stand it any longer, and wanting to hold and comfort her old friend, she lunged in front of Brady.

And in one quick stroke, the knife curved downwards…

The scream was prolonged, high-pitched and shrill. The knife had been thrust under the ribs and upwards towards the heart, piercing its target. Lauren staggered in front of them, fell on all fours, still clutching the knife handle, which now protruded from her chest and groaned. As Jenna rushed to catch hold of her, Lauren keeled over on the hard ground. Her hands flopped down by her sides, her eyes closed, and, a moment later, she emitted one long last baleful moan. It sounded eerily tuneful.

Jenna draped herself over Lauren's body and wept. Brady hurriedly radioed for an ambulance, then moved forward and gently pulled Jenna away from the dying girl. Having covered Lauren's body with his coat, he stood up again and took Jenna back into his arms to comfort her. He could feel her shaking and dry sobbing against his chest. A second police car had arrived on the scene, and Andy and Jamie were already examining the first of the two bodies on the ground. The moonlight had dimmed again, and in the dark shade of the cedar tree, Jamie had to use a torch.

"Sir?" he said. "I think this is our man." He felt for a pulse. There was nothing. "He's gone."

Jenna lifted her head. "What?" she said. She'd been so focused on Lauren wielding the knife that she hadn't fully registered the body which was already on the ground. Brady, however, wanting to protect her from any further pain, tried to pull her towards him again. She wriggled away from him and walked, slowly at first and then, increasing her pace, finally ran towards where her colleagues were standing over Lauren's victim.

"The missing fingertip," said Andy. "It's Gregory Valentine."

"Greg!" Jenna wailed. "NOooooooo…" She'd been angry with him, it was true. But she'd neither wished nor expected to find him dead. She knelt beside his body, her own convulsed in sobs.

Brady nodded to the two male officers to indicate that they should go and wait by the female body. He paused a few moments and then walked over to Jenna, stooped and pulled her up again into his arms. This time, there was no resistance. She nestled her face, wet with tears, into his warm neck, and he held her even tighter.

"I'm here for you," he said.

"*Always.*"

# EPILOGUE

It was a bleak and bitter January day. The only sound that could be heard in the otherwise silent grounds of the cemetery was the wind, which moaned as it rushed in from the east. It had brought with it the snow, arriving overnight and settling gently on the multiple mounds where the bones of the dead lay in their permanent, uninterrupted slumber. All was still under a gun-metal sky. The soft counterpane, white as an angel's wing, was unbroken, save for seven pairs of footsteps which tracked back from the graveside to the chapel whence they came.

The four pall-bearers manoeuvred the wicker coffin, overlaid with a single spray of white lilies, into the hole in the ground, dug out the previous day and then hastily dug again during the morning to remove the fresh layer of snow at the bottom of the hole. Two on one side and two on the other, they used high-tensile straps to lower their load into the earth, and when the coffin met the batons on the floor of the hole, the men swiftly withdrew the straps, took a step backwards and lowered their heads in unison. Slowly and respectfully, they turned away from the graveside and headed back towards the chapel, leaving the three mourners in privacy.

Jenna stood with her shoulders hunched and her head hung low. To her right, her father, Gareth, followed suit. They were both chilled to the bone. A funeral is never a warming occasion, but when it follows a suicide, it makes the blood run cold, and Jenna was feeling the ice in her veins. She crooked her right arm through her father's left. Simultaneously, she felt the light pressure of Brady's hand on her back. He had made the decision also to attend Lauren's funeral for two reasons: firstly, because he wasn't convinced that he couldn't have done more to prevent the tragic events of New Year's Eve, and secondly, because he was only too sure that Jenna would appreciate him being by her side for emotional support. He had said he would always be there for her, and he had meant it.

It had been two weeks since New Year's Eve. The knot which had lodged itself in Jenna's gut on that traumatic night had yet to uncoil. There had been so many truths to stomach since she had discovered that Greg had been their serial killer. He had been dubbed 'The Rose Murderer' by the press. Still, as more and more articles were written about the case and further information spilt out about the villainous characters he had hunted down, he was painted less of a monster and more of a hero with each passing day.

But today was not about Greg.

Today, Jenna had come to lay her friend to rest. When she had walked away from Lauren's scarred and skeletal body lying on the cold slab of the mortuary, she had promised herself that there would be no more negative thoughts; that memories of summer sunshine, blue gingham dresses and daisy chains would now be the order of the day. But right here and now, as she stood over her friend's grave, she couldn't prevent a tear from escaping. It trickled down her cheek, spilling onto her woollen coat. Brady cupped Jenna's left elbow with his free hand and squeezed it gently.

Gareth Jones broke the silence. "Shame this little girl had no one but us to see her off," he said quietly. His words hung in the air for a few seconds until the wind carried them away.

Brady removed his hand from Jenna's elbow and slipped her arm into the crook of his. The three of them then walked slowly back in the direction of Brady's car. Having opened the rear door, Brady helped Jenna inside. Gareth sat himself in the back with his daughter and placed his arm around her to comfort her. "Come on," said Brady gently. "Sometimes we have to let go." He turned himself round in the driving seat so that he could look Jenna square in the face. "It's time to close this chapter," he said softly.

Jenna shut her eyes. Brady was right. Of course, he was. She had to let go. But she would always have the memories of two little girls in their school summer dresses, sitting on the bough of a tree making daisy chains together. She swallowed back the lump in her throat as she allowed Lauren's voice to emerge in her mind one last time. "We'll always be best friends, won't we?"

As the image faded, a lone tear dripped down Jenna's cheek.

Lauren was finally free.

In memory of Michelle

This book is printed on paper from sustainable sources managed under the Forest Stewardship Council (FSC) scheme.

It has been printed in the UK to reduce transportation miles and their impact upon the environment.

For every new title that Troubador publishes, we plant a tree to offset $CO_2$, partnering with the More Trees scheme.

**MORE TREES**
LET'S PLANT A BILLION TREES

For more about how Troubador offsets its environmental impact, see www.troubador.co.uk/sustainability-and-community